PRAISE FOR 1998
HOLT MEDALLION WINNER
EUGENIA RILEY!

"Ms. Riley's . . . characters are delightful, as are the various subplots that make this a wonderful romance."
—*Romantic Times* on *Bushwhacked Bride*

"An uproarious adventure from start to finish. This book has it all, humor, passion, and a cast of endearing characters that the reader won't soon forget. Ms. Riley has crafted an amazing tale that leaps right off the pages."
—*Rendezvous* on *Bushwhacked Bride*

"Eugenia Riley will sweep you away!"
—*The Literary Times*

"Eugenia Riley spins a brilliantly woven web, ensnaring readers with her ingenious plot twists, endearing characters and an unforgettable love story."
—*Romantic Times* on *Tempest in Time*

"A unique time-travel novel interlaced with mysterious secrets and intense emotions. Ms. Riley focuses on the magical potency of love, as it transcends the web of time to meld bleeding hearts together."
—*Romantic Times* on *A Tryst in Time*

"A captivating emotional tale with lush descriptions and engaging characters, charged with pure heart and smoldering sexual tension. Ms. Riley delivers another outstanding love story."
—*Rendezvous* on *Waltz in Time*

DANGEROUS LIAISONS

"You know, Charles, the truth is, something very strange and dangerous has been going on from the moment I met you. What do you have to say about that?"

Surprisingly, he flashed her an ironic though tender smile, reaching out to brush an errant strand of hair from her brow. "Strange? Dangerous? I agree, love. Completely."

And he lowered his face to hers and tenderly touched her lips with his own. It was a kiss of heady seduction, his mouth exploring, tantalizing her own. At first Teresa stiffened slightly in surprise, but soon she moaned in pleasure. That moan became a thrill of desire when Charles crushed her closer and claimed her mouth more passionately, his tongue flitting at her lips in teasing caresses until she parted them and granted him entry.

She eagerly moved her own mouth against his, stunned at the intensity of her own response, and her apparent inability to resist him. He'd spoken the truth right before their kiss, she realized poignantly. The fact that he was dangerous made him all the more irresistible to her.

Lovers and Other Lunatics

Eugenia Riley

LOVE SPELL BOOKS   ◆   NEW YORK CITY

LOVE SPELL®

April 2000

Published by

Dorchester Publishing Co., Inc.
276 Fifth Avenue
New York, NY 10001

Cover Art by John Ennis
www.ennisart.com

ISBN 0-505-52371-X

Printed in the United States of America.

*This book is dedicated to my editor,
Alicia Condon, with thanks for
her enthusiasm, her wonderful
sense of humor, and her
support of my career.*

Chapter One

The sign blocking the entrance to the escalator on the third floor of the posh west Houston department store read, ESCALATOR OUT OF ORDER. PLEASE USE ELEVATOR. This the summer shoppers noted, tucking packages beneath their arms and marching with brisk boredom from housewares and linens to the elevator located near Customer Service. The breaking down of the escalator represented no major crisis in anyone's life—

Except for one young woman, who stood holding her bundle of towels for dear life, her feet seemingly riveted to the floor. She was the only one among the throng of shoppers who looked ready to vomit; indeed, she appeared immobilized by fear.

Teresa Phelps was scared to death of elevators.

11

Escalators she didn't consider a barrel of laughs either, but at least while she was on one, she could see where she was going. Elevators, with their claustrophobic confines, scared the living hell out of her. They had ever since she and her mother had been trapped in one for almost three hours when she was a child. Since then, every ride in an elevator became an instant, guaranteed anxiety attack for Teresa. To make matters worse, she'd already been forced to endure one elevator ride this morning.

She mopped a wisp of limp brown hair from her moist brow and looked about warily. There was no help for it, she thought uneasily, no other way to get down to the parking garage and to the relative safety of her car. From head to toe, she could feel her skin breaking out with an unpleasant, needlelike tingling. She cursed herself for ever leaving home in the first place this morning. She cursed herself for ever returning from Louisiana, where she had spent the past few weeks with her parents.

There was no help for that, either—no further excuse to avoid clearing up the final details of Frank Phelps's life. Her older brother's accident had occurred over three weeks ago. Her parents were too elderly to settle his estate, which meant Teresa had been forced to stand on her own two feet—wobbly though they were.

The first step had been the unpleasant, dreaded visit to Frank's attorney in west Houston earlier this morning. She shuddered at the memory, thinking of the contents of Frank's safety deposit box, which even now she carried in her bag—a few pieces of antique jewelry which were family heirlooms, legal documents, a minuscule life insurance policy, and a rather large manuscript, one Frank was translating from French. A French professor without tenure, Frank had not been a wealthy man. The articles in her bag were all Teresa really had left of him, except for the tourist trash bracelet he'd sent her for her twenty-eighth birthday in May—a cheap collection of fake doubloons, a skull and crossbones, a treasure chest key, all smeared with a tawdry mixture of gold and black paint. Teresa wore the garish bracelet now strictly for sentimental reasons. She supposed Frank's heart had been in the right place, even though his wallet had always been tucked away where the sun never shone.

"Miss, the escalator is broken."

The sound of a deep male voice with a clipped British accent snatched Teresa away from her fretful thoughts. She turned to see an arresting stranger, who seemed to be in his early thirties, standing nearby, intently regarding her. Her heart thudded. He was tall, lean, black-haired, blue-eyed, and handsome enough to win the next contest for The New James Bond hands down. He was studying her with an unabashed curiosity she found unsettling; yet a glint of humor also lurked in the depths of his striking eyes.

"Yes—yes, I'm quite aware the escalator is broken," Teresa stammered back, clutching her bundle and her bag tightly. "Are—are you an employee here?"

He smiled agreeably. "No, miss. But I saw you squinting at the sign and rather wondered if you'd left your reading specs at home."

"No—no such problem," Teresa replied with a dry little laugh that did nothing to disguise how uncomfortable she felt.

"I'm bound for the elevator now myself, as a matter of fact, and I'd be delighted to escort you."

"I—well—how kind of you," she mumbled.

"May I carry your bundle?" he offered.

"I—uh, no thanks."

He started off with a grin, motioning for her to come along. Ah, yes, there was no help for it, she thought grimly, nothing to do but to fall into step beside the stranger and head for the elevator. She studied him from the corner of her eye. The man had surprised her, indeed, had flattered her with his kind concern. Teresa knew she wasn't bad to look at, but she was also one of those women with a mania for inconspicuousness. Her hair was short, wavy brown and nondescript, her dark green printed sundress and low-heeled sandals the height of understatement. She knew she had a pleasing, tall figure, slim and willowy, as well as nice legs, but she simply wasn't the type to stop traffic—particularly not stunningly handsome, sophisticated male traffic.

Which this man clearly was. His bearing and movements were lithe and assured, his light-weight tropical wool suit superbly cut, emphasizing his broad shoulders, the trimness of his torso, the leanness of his hips. He even smelled marvelous, wearing a spicy cologne with an underlying, sensual pungency.

They had now reached the forbidding doors of the elevator, and as they waited with the others, he punched a button and offered, "Are you certain I can't take that package for you?"

Teresa shook her head vigorously, continuing to clutch the bundle for dear life. Her gaze fixed fearfully on the gray elevator doors. Bizarre as it seemed, the package had become her rock, her security in a world going haywire. Besides, she somehow *had* to get these towels home in time for Aunt Hatch's visit; otherwise, her stormtrooper of an aunt would never shut up regarding the "rags" now hanging in Teresa's bathroom. "Thanks anyway," she muttered rather breathlessly.

The stranger shook his head as the gray doors opened.

The shoppers ambled into the car, then the man gestured for Teresa to precede him inside. When she remained transfixed, staring dazedly at the yawning cavern, he stepped inside and held open the doors. Again he motioned for her to join him, a slight frown marring his handsome brow. "Is something wrong, miss?"

"No, not at all," Teresa spouted with bravado.

Catching a ragged breath, she literally bounded into the car and dashed for the back, as far away from the stranger as possible. She hoped the other passengers would take little note of her private purgatory. She well knew a phobic's greatest fear was that others would discover the fear and think the phobic crazy. . . .

Which she clearly was. Teresa clutched her package and purse with one hand and held on to the railing with the shaky fingers of the other. The car was crowded and hot; the walls seemed to close in on her. And that was before the car started moving! When it did lurch into motion, she felt she would retch every time it started; she felt she would retch every time it stopped. There were four floors in all to the parking garage, and they dribbled by in unending torture, inch by agonizing inch. . . .

Were they—at last—reaching the ground floor? Only one more floor after that to the garage? It didn't seem possible—nor did it seem possible that the doors would ever open on the first floor, where they had now stopped! As the passengers murmured to one another and punched buttons to nudge the recalcitrant doors, Teresa's anxiety attack took full rein—her skin crawled, her heart palpitated. These conditions she managed to conceal from most of the other passengers, although the man in his sixties at her side could not have helped but wonder at the cause of her hyperventilation.

Finally, the doors grumbled open. Shaking their heads and muttering, the passengers left, except for Teresa and the stranger. She would have bolted out of the car, but it was difficult to move when one could no longer breathe.

Meanwhile, the man turned to her with a smile. "Parking garage, right?"

She nodded, catching her breath but still feeling nauseous. "B-but," she stammered, "didn't it take an awfully long time for the doors to open? I mean, perhaps we should take the stairs."

"There are no stairs. Don't fret—we'll make it."

Teresa at last gathered the momentum to step forward, but by now, the doors began to close, preventing her exit. The man regarded her quizzically, and, with a crooked grin, she fell back. The car lurched downward; staggering slightly, she again gripped the railing for support.

The man turned, lounging against the wall flanking Teresa and studying her with wry amusement. "Do elevators frighten you, miss?"

"Certainly not," Teresa replied stoutly. "Whatever gives you that idea?"

The car stopped and her hand flew to her mouth.

He chuckled, and they both waited in silence for the doors to open.

They didn't. By now, Teresa's blood pressure was near stroke level. In the tense silence, the stranger merely stared at her; yet there was now

16

something calculating in his expression that unnerved her. "Aren't—aren't you going to push the button to open the doors?" she finally managed.

"No, I'm not," he replied.

Teresa gasped, immediately noticing the change in his tone of voice—from bantering to deadly. And his eyes! What was it about his eyes? Yes, they had changed, too, changed most dreadfully. The laughter was gone, replaced by a frightening intensity, a ruthless determination.

"You're—you're not going to open the doors?" she asked, an edge of hysteria in her voice.

"No." He shook his head slowly, then abruptly pulled out a gun. "Teresa Phelps, I presume?"

Chapter Two

Teresa couldn't believe what she was seeing. Her eyes grew like saucers, and her heart seemed to lodge in her throat. "My God, that's a gun!"

"Correct."

"You're—you're carrying a gun!" Teresa's pulse was now pounding so fiercely, she could barely stand on her feet.

"You're right again."

"You—you could hurt someone with that!"

"That's rather the idea, love."

Teresa blinked at the stranger in horror. He was so levelheadedly maniacal about it all, so fiendishly polite, pointing the deadly steel-gray automatic at her as if she were a duck in a shooting gallery. "If—if you're aiming to rob me, I've nothing of value," she managed.

He smiled slightly. "That's not quite what I hear, love. But I'm not aiming to rob you."

"If—if you're aiming to rape me, I've always been told that I'm—I'm lousy in the sack."

He lifted an eyebrow. "That's not what I hear, either. But I don't intend to ravish you." Dryly, he added, "I'll keep the subject under advisement, though."

"If—if you're not aiming to rob or r-rape me, why the hell are you pointing that gun at me?"

"You left out mayhem," he reminded.

"What?" she shrieked.

"Isn't it 'rob, rape, and pillage,' or something like that?" he supplied politely.

"You're going to maim me?"

He laughed. "No, nothing that diabolical. I simply want you to come with me, and frankly, I can't afford to take no for an answer."

With these words, he punched the DOOR OPEN button. Within seconds, Teresa found herself looking out at a deserted parking garage. Oh, hell, there was absolutely no one around, and she was at the mercy of a lunatic with a loaded gun!

"Come with me now, Ms. Phelps," the stranger said with that same ludicrous courtesy. He even added with a nasty smile, "Please."

Trembling, Teresa left the elevator car, the stranger falling into step beside her. She gasped as he gripped her arm, her heart lurching at the feel of his strong warm fingers clenching about her flesh. As they walked he held the gun by his other side—not pointed at her now, but still ominously evident.

"Where are you taking me?" she demanded.

"To my car."

"Are you one of those serial murderers?"

"Heavens, no," he replied, laughing.

19

"Then what do you want with me?"

"Very little actually. Let's call it the pleasure of your company."

"I knew it! You do want my body!"

He fought a smile. "Don't get your hopes up, love."

She shot him a chilling look.

Undaunted, he tugged her on to a car, a late-model black sedan. Opening the door, he took her package and purse and tossed them inside. He glanced around warily for an instant, then turned her, pinning her against the fender with both hands behind her.

Feeling cold steel touch her wrists, she demanded, "What are you doing?"

"Putting on your handcuffs."

"Bondage?" she screamed.

"Hardly. And keep your voice down, damn it. I simply don't want you bolting out of my car before we reach our destination."

"Can't I at least have my hands in front of me?" she pleaded, turning back around.

He smiled with forbearance. "Sorry, love, but you could use the cuffs like brass knuckles on my delicate skull."

"Would I do that?"

"Most assuredly." He opened her door, pushed her head down and helped her in, as she had seen policemen do in movies.

"Are you a cop?" she asked with a suspicious glower as he strapped her in.

"For someone in a tenuous position, you ask a damn lot of questions, my dear," he replied curtly.

"Are you?"

"Well, let's just say I'll be your policeman for the next few weeks, dear Tess."

"Hey—how do you know my name?"

The door slammed and he strode around to the driver's side, getting in.

Watching him settle in his seat and shut the door, she continued, "Please—will you *please* tell me what is going on here? You've got me scared to death, you know."

"Good," he replied, turning on the engine. "It's about time you had a healthy scare, Tess."

"But why? Why are you doing this? I'm an academic, for heaven's sake. I live the typical, Emersonian life of quiet desperation—"

"Thoreau," he cut in.

"What?"

His expression grew almost expansive. "It was Thoreau who said, 'The mass of men lead lives of quiet desperation.'" He flashed her a smile. "Though of course we'd have to change that to 'women' in your case."

Teresa was regarding him, wild-eyed. "I can't believe I'm hearing this! Will you *please* stop with the inane quips and tell me why you're abducting me?"

"Why?" He backed up the car, then abruptly braked to a halt. Turning to her, he replied harshly, "Because, you little tart, I'll be damned if I'll let you break up my parents' thirty-five-year marriage."

The car shot forward like a bullet.

"What? What the hell?" Teresa shrieked at the maniac who held her captive. The car was now out of the parking garage, and they were turning onto Westheimer, the stranger expertly maneuvering them through the heavy traffic.

"You heard me—you're through leading my father down the primrose path."

21

Eugenia Riley

"Your—your father? You're insane! What on earth are you talking about?"

His laugh was biting and cynical, his gaze cold. "You think I haven't had the two of you followed? All those cozy little lunches at the harbor—the midnight rendezvous on the Bolivar ferry. Totally indiscreet, brazen. The two of you could have exercised a little restraint, Tess. As it is, the only reason you're alive at the moment is that Mother never found out."

"Mother?" The word came out strangled. Teresa felt as if she had lost her mind. She knew her captor had.

"Yes, Mother. That's why I'm keeping you on ice, darling girl, until my parents return to England next month. I've no intention of letting the likes of you break my mother's heart."

"Oh my God, this can't be happening," Teresa muttered, shaking her head in bewilderment. She was in the clutches of a totally insane stranger, who was babbling the most blatant idiocy as if it were eminently reasonable. It would help enormously if she could put her hands to her now throbbing head, but, unfortunately, they were painfully imprisoned behind her. Somehow, she realized, she must make some sense of this madness, find some way to reason with the wacko who held her captive. Otherwise, she would never make it out of this situation alive.

They were on the loop now, heading south. "Well," he demanded, "what do you have to say for yourself, you little homewrecker?"

"You've made a mistake," she said, with all the vehemence she could muster.

"Hah!"

"No, it's true," she insisted. Carefully, she went on, "Now, I take it from what you say that you're

22

kidnapping me to keep me from—from seeing your father?"

"Nail on the head, love."

"And he's planning to return to England with your mother next month?"

"Right again."

"But that's absurd!" she declared. "I don't even know your father—or any Englishman, for that matter."

"Lying will get you nowhere."

"I'm not lying, damn it. Tell me, what is his name?"

"His name?"

"Your father."

"Oh. Kingsley Everett."

"Kingsley Everett? For heaven's sake, of course I don't know him. If I did—who could forget a name like that?"

"Good try. But pictures don't lie, do they, dear?"

"P-pictures?"

"Yes, the pictures of you and my father having a little luncheon tête-à-tête."

Teresa was rendered speechless. Oh, merciful heavens, this nut was really off his rocker. And God only knew what he had in store for her.

"There—I see I've shut you up," he said smugly. "The truth will do it every time."

They were speeding south, and Teresa's heart was pounding so hard, she could hardly breathe. Since the moment when the stranger had pulled the gun on her, she had been too terrified to really be anxious, if that made sense; but now, she was suffering the horrors of another full-fledged anxiety attack.

"There, love, you don't have to hyperventilate," he reassured her. "I'm not going to shoot you."

Abruptly, he grinned. "Unless it's to put you out of your misery."

"Cute," she panted back. "Where are you taking me?"

"To my condo in Galveston."

"But—but I'll be missed. My Aunt Hatch is coming for a visit today. When she finds I'm gone, I'm sure she'll call the police."

"No matter," he replied. "You have a reputation as something of an eccentric, don't you, Tess? Living out there on the Bolivar mud flats by yourself, with your rather peculiar interest in waterfowl."

Her face flamed. "Just what are you implying?"

"Only that people might assume you were hot on the trail of some bird and fell in."

"That's ridiculous. And how did you come to know so much about me, anyway?"

"The private detectives, love. For an egghead, you're a bit slow on the uptake, aren't you?"

She bit her lip in furious silence. Her arms were aching like the very devil from the restraint, her nose itched and she couldn't scratch it. "Look, do you have a name?"

"Yes. Charles Everett."

"Well, Mr. Charles Everett, I've got to go to the bathroom."

"Hah! That's the oldest trick in the book!"

"Care to bet your upholstery on it?"

Her words left him scowling, and he studied her quizzically from the corner of his eye. "Are you telling me the truth?"

"Please—I'm dying," she pleaded. "I always have to pee when I'm being kidnapped," she added plaintively, hoping to strengthen her case.

He chuckled. "Well, I don't doubt I've made you a trifle tense." As she threw him a desperate look, he added, "Right. Hold it for a moment, will you?" He pulled off the freeway onto the feeder road and headed for the nearest gas station. "You won't be trying anything foolish, will you? Like endangering the life of the gas station attendant?"

She was stunned. "You're really serious about this, aren't you?"

"Deadly serious. Not a word to anyone, Tess." He pulled into the gas station.

"You'll have to—um—unshackle my wrists," she stammered. "I mean, I can't—"

"Right. A clinical explanation won't be necessary." He removed the key from his pocket and leaned over, unlocking the cuffs. "All right, let's go."

"You're coming *with* me?"

"I'll be outside every second, love."

She swallowed hard, flexing her aching wrists as he got out of the car and came around to her side. He helped her out and held her arm firmly as they moved toward the ladies room. The July heat hit them like a blast furnace, no help for Teresa's weak knees. She studied the station as they walked. Several people were milling about, but she realized ruefully that she couldn't risk trying to catch someone's attention; she could feel her abductor's gun, nudging her through the cloth of his coat.

At the door to the ladies room, he eyed her sternly. "Behave yourself."

Teresa didn't reply, ducking inside and flipping the bolt on the door as quietly as possible. Frantically she looked around for an escape route. Damn, there was only one tiny window above the sink. She knew she must try it, nonetheless. She clambered onto the vanity and stood on the counter, reaching above her and raising the small frosted pane. Pushing the screen out, she tried to squeeze her body through the small hole, and managed to get halfway out—

"May I be of assistance, love?"

Hanging out of the opening like a hunting trophy, Teresa cursed as she looked down at her smiling captor. Damn, he thought of everything! "I'm stuck," she informed him tersely.

"Are you, now? I must say, Tess, that you were raised with some rather peculiar bathroom habits. Whatever are you doing dangling out of the window?"

"You know damn well what I'm doing! Will you please come help me? I can't move either way."

His brow wrinkled suspiciously. "How do I know you're telling the truth this time?"

"Look at me! Any idiot could tell I'm stuck!"

"Well, you do look rather snugly wedged." He stroked his chin thoughtfully. "Actually, love, nothing would please me more at the moment than to come around there and give you a rather vigorous nudge."

Teresa fought a smirk. He'd have one hell of a time getting in through the locked door, she thought. Outwardly, though, she maintained her desperate expression. "Will you hurry? I'm really in a jam here."

"I've noticed."

No sooner had he disappeared around the corner than Teresa ducked back inside. With lightning speed she raised one long leg, then the other, shimmying through the window feet first, ripping the front of her skirt on the windowframe before she dropped to the ground.

"I also lie a lot, you bastard," she hissed under her breath as she took off at a run.

Chapter Three

Teresa tore around the back of the station, dodging old tire rims and discarded auto parts. At the front of the building, she spotted her abductor's car. "Oh, damn, Aunt Hatch's towels," she fretted. She made a dive for the car, flung open the door, grabbed the towels and her purse, cursed again when she spotted no key in the ignition, then sprinted out of the station.

Cars were gathered on the access road, waiting at a red light. Bolting along, Teresa heard, "Hey, stop! Stop!" from behind her.

Turning her head as she continued running, she spotted her abductor sprinting after her while talking on a cell phone. Oh, damn—he was hot on her trail already, and likely summoning the rest

Eugenia Riley

of the mob to come help shovel her under. She
lunged onward toward the corner, glancing
around desperately for some means of escape. As
she reached the intersection, she spotted a dilapidated camper truck with the word *Shrimp* emblazoned on its side and a small immigrant family
inside the cab. Good, they were probably from
Galveston.

She rushed up to the cab and peered inside.
"Can you take me to the police?" she panted,
wild-eyed. Oh, they'd never understand that. "Are
you going to Galveston?" she tried. "May I have a
ride, please?"

The mother, father, and three children, all with
enormous brown eyes and wearing baseball caps,
stared at her blankly.

"Oh, damn, they don't understand me," she
muttered to herself. *"Necesito un paseo en coche a
Galveston, por favor,"* she attempted desperately.

Oh, heavens—what was she saying? They were
Vietnamese!

"Sure, lady, you can have a ride," replied one of
the children, a boy who looked about seven.

"Thanks!"

Not about to look a gift horse in the mouth,
Teresa sprinted for the back of the camper. She
spotted her dark-haired English captor only a few
cars away from her, heading toward her at a dead
run and closing fast. "Damn," she muttered,
yanking open the door.

Mercifully, she had no sooner climbed inside
than the camper lurched forward. The light must
have changed, she realized.

The interior of the camper was filled with ice
chests and reeked of spoiled shrimp. Teresa collapsed onto an ice chest and struggled to catch
her breath. Her mind raced. He'd have to go back

28

to the station, get his car, wait for the light . . . Thank God for this wretched Houston traffic! Perhaps if she were lucky, she might make good her escape. Oh, she hoped so. It would be unforgivable to endanger this dear little family who had so trustingly come to her rescue—

Suddenly, Teresa screamed as she felt a clammy tentacle close about her ankle. She glanced down at the floor and did a double take.

"What's wrong, ma'am?" came a voice from the front of the camper.

Teresa gazed flabbergasted at the little boy who had turned to stare at her through the truck's open rear window. "Do you realize there's a baby back here?" she demanded, glancing from the boy to a toddler in a diaper who was gurgling up at her from the floor, clawing at her leg.

The boy in the front seat grinned. "Oh, never mind Adolph, ma'am. Mom lets him loose because he doesn't like to be closed in up here."

"Adolph?" she repeated, struggling to contain a hysterical giggle.

"Yes, ma'am, Adolph Loung. Mom decided when we became American citizens we should have American names."

"I see. So who are you?"

"Juan Loung."

"Juan Loung," she repeated with a hiccup. "That makes sense, I suppose."

The boy named Juan now climbed through the rear window to join Teresa at the back of the camper. She noted he was a cute, bright-eyed little urchin. His red baseball cap practically swallowed up his face, emphasizing his impishness.

He sat down on an ice chest next to hers and grinned shyly. "You sure are pretty, ma'am."

"Why, thank you, Juan," she said, charmed.

"And you know, I do like your name. As a matter of fact, I have a cat named Doris Juan."

"Cool, ma'am," he acknowledged solemnly.

Uneasily Teresa cleared her throat. "But—er—do you think your father can go any faster?"

Juan shook his head, grinning up at her engagingly. "With this crate, ma'am, we're lucky to move at all."

"I was afraid of that." Preoccupied, Teresa picked up the baby. He cooed at her, then warmth trickled down the side of her leg. "Oh, dear."

"I'll help you change Adolph, ma'am." Juan's dark eyes widened as they took note of Teresa's torn—and now damp—skirt. "Say, ma'am, are you in trouble?"

"You might say that," Teresa replied dryly.

"Thank you—thank you so much!" Teresa called, waving to the departing camper truck.

She was now at the entrance to the Bolivar Ferry on the east end of Galveston Island. The dear little Vietnamese family had taken her all the way to the access point. Luckily, the ferry was loading cars even as Teresa trotted up to the pedestrian boarding lane. She waited with the other walkers, holding her split skirt together as best she could as a couple of men waiting in line with her studied her, leering. Oh, dear. The two seemed to be seasonal workers or transients—rough-looking characters with bearded, weather-beaten faces, backpacks, and soiled, ragged clothing. From the brazen looks they cast her way, she appeared to be just the type of female companionship they were looking for.

At last the walkers were given the signal to board. Bounding ahead of the others, Teresa found an isolated position at the bow of the boat, in front of the cars. As the ferry rumbled forward, she drew her first deep breath in two hours. This was a nightmare! A nightmare!

Bizarre as it was, nothing mattered to her now but getting home and hanging up her new towels before Aunt Hatch arrived. Never mind that her insane British abductor likely knew where she lived—she would phone the police the instant she arrived at her beach house. Surely she would beat the man back there, and besides, he wouldn't automatically assume she would be foolish enough to go straight home.

She shuddered as she remembered him abducting her at the department store—the cold deadliness of his gun, his chillingly droll sense of humor. She'd been having an affair with his father—Kingsley Everett, indeed! What loony bin had Charles Everett crawled out of?

Teresa struggled to collect herself as the ferry chugged on with a groan of its engines. It was just after noon; the slight salty breeze did little to stir the oppressive heat as they plodded through the gray waters of the channel and headed for the Bolivar Peninsula ahead. Teresa's eyes, scanning the heavens, automatically spotted laughing gulls, ring-billed gulls, black terns, Caspian terns . . . It was strange how even at the most harrowing moments, the mind sought the sameness of familiar rituals.

The instant the boat docked, Teresa exited briskly, her plan of action firmly in mind. She left the ferry station and tore off down Highway 87, heading for her beach house.

The peninsula was only sparsely populated, with scattered bungalows and the small town of Port Bolivar up ahead; mud flats and prairie grass

31

stretched on either side of her, with only the splendor of an ancient lighthouse in the distance to relieve the monotonous landscape. It was a three-mile run to her cottage, but that was no obstacle. Teresa jogged religiously every morning—two miles up the beach, two miles back. The feat was a bit more difficult in the noonday heat, with sandals on instead of running shoes, she acknowledged to herself grimly.

The gray ribbon of road seemed endless as she continued, her shoes flip-flopping on the hot pavement. Every time a car passed, she cringed. Then all at once she heard the sickening shriek of wheels grinding to a halt behind her. "Hey, little lady, want a ride?" drawled a friendly voice.

She would have panicked, but she immediately recognized that it wasn't *his* voice. No, the man who had spoken definitely had a Texas drawl. She paused, panting to catch her breath, and turned to view a battered pickup truck stopped near her, with a huge, brightly painted ladybug perched on top of the cab. *This* was rescue? She swallowed a crazed laugh at the thought. Then she glanced inside the cab, where a pockmarked kid in a khaki uniform sat grinning at her, his carroty-blond hair protruding from a worn bill cap. He had an honest face, and looked about twenty-one.

"Are you going down the Peninsula?" she asked him, moving closer and wiping strands of damp hair from her brow.

He politely adjusted his cap. "Sure am, ma'am. I got a job down there. I ain't supposed to take riders, but you don't look like you'd do me no harm." He grinned at her tattered garb.

"Heavens, no. And thanks." Teresa swung open the door and clambered inside. The kid's eyes grew huge as her action made her skirt split even farther up toward her crotch. Pulling the edges together, she gasped as her bottom contacted something crunchy on the seat. Changing positions, she noted that the rear bed of the truck was filled with shards of glass! She picked up the fragment she had sat on and stared at it, mystified.

"Sorry, ma'am, I thought I got all them pieces of glass up off the seat," the boy said, stepping on the gas.

Teresa glanced around again as the truck rattled onto the road, then stared flabbergasted at the boy. "Your rear window has been blown out!"

"Yes'm," he replied matter-of-factly, shifting gears with an earsplitting screech. "A bunch of thugs with shotguns blowed out my rear winder this morning."

"My God—are you serious?" Teresa cried. "You mean they were trying to kill you?"

"Yes'm." He grinned, displaying tobacco-stained, uneven teeth. "Either that or they don't take kindly to big bugs." He guffawed loudly.

"My God, if this isn't the day to beat all," Teresa muttered, shaking her head in stupefaction as she ineffectually fanned herself with one hand. "Where on earth did this happen to you?"

"Well, like I said, ma'am, I got this here job down the Peninsula, and when I come there this morning, them fellars was waitin' fer me and started farring away."

"Farring?"

"Right. Farring. You know, ma'am, *ker-pow, ker-pow*. Blew the winder out of this here truck and even busted up my cell phone. It's a wonder they didn't take off my head. So you'd better believe I hightailed it, ma'am. Anyhow, I'm sure hoping them dudes is gone by now."

Eugenia Riley

"You mean . . . My God, you can't mean you're going *back* there?"

"Oh, yes, ma'am," he replied soberly. "Like I told you, I got a job to do down there and I don't want to get farred over this."

"Farred?"

"Yes, ma'am. My Uncle Clovis farred me off'n his oil rig last year, just 'cause I spent one itty bitty night in jail, and I can't afford to get sacked again."

"My gracious, how far did he send you?"

He frowned confusedly. "*Farred*, ma'am. I got farred. You know, furloughed. Laid off."

"Oh, fired! Fired," she laughed. Incredulously she added, "You mean you're going back to that house and facing those men with shotguns because you don't want to lose your job?"

He nodded vigorously. "You got that right, lady. I ain't sneezing away no steady employment. Good jobs ain't easy to come by these days."

"I can't believe I'm hearing this," Teresa muttered. She could only stare dumbfounded at the boy. How many lunatics would she meet today?

"Say, lady, whereabouts is this house of yours, anyhow?" the kid asked as they continued down the sun-baked highway.

"Oh, a couple more miles down the beach."

"You live there alone?"

She thought of the stranger and shuddered. "I sincerely hope so."

"What you doing livin' out there all by yourself?"

"I'm doing research for my doctoral dissertation."

"Say what, lady?"

"My doctoral dissertation. I'm a doctoral candidate in recent sedimentology. My dissertation is

34

on the effect of backwaters on mud flat formation."

He glanced at her in amazement. "No shit, lady."

"Well, actually, that's just the title I use with laymen," she elucidated. "The technical term wouldn't mean much to you unless you know a great deal about the cyclical nature of estuaries."

"Right."

"Look," Teresa went on, "I don't mean to be minding your business, but I do think it is quite unwise of you to be planning to go back to that house if there are a bunch of thugs there waiting to kill you. I mean, why risk your life for the sake of zapping a few cockroaches? Why don't you just stop off at my beach house and call the police? As a matter of fact, I might have a word or two with them myself," she added with a shrill little laugh.

"Oh, no, lady, I got to go back and do my job. How would that look—the Bug Brigade giving up?"

"The *Bug Brigade*?" All at once Teresa gave a shriek, her eyes huge, her mind splintering. "Oh, my God, the Bug Brigade! Don't tell me it's Tuesday?"

He pondered that a moment. "Yep."

"Oh, my God!" She reached out and clutched his sleeve. "Where are you going?"

He scratched his head. "Well, I don't rightly know what the lady's name is. I'm new on this here route, you see. Guess it's on my clipboard somewheres. Anyhow, my boss said she's some crazy lady living out there on the mud flats, counting birds or something. She keeps thinking she got riots under her house, but we ain't never seen none."

"Riots?" Teresa repeated, her voice rising in hysteria.

"Riots. You know, ma'am, them gray furry critters."

"Riots! Rats! Oh, my God!" Teresa had been so preoccupied, she had forgotten all about the rats and her Tuesday appointment with the Bug Brigade. She turned wildly to her rescuer. "Holy cow! You're talking about *my* house!"

Chapter Four

"My cottage is just beyond this neighborhood of houses," Teresa directed the exterminator. "It's easy enough to spot—rather battered and weather-beaten, standing alone on the mud flats."

The young man chuckled. "Begging your pardon, ma'am, but it may be a tad more battered now, I reckon."

"Oh, dear." Grimacing, Teresa pointed to a dirt access road to her right.

As the exterminator turned down the bumpy road, Teresa felt like a basket case; ever since she'd realized that her rescuer had encountered men with shotguns at *her* house, she'd been quietly going insane. Who on earth were the mysterious marauders he'd run into, and why had they targeted her home? Had her mysterious abductor in Houston possibly been one of them?

As they arrived on her property, Teresa cringed at the sight of her beach house at the edge of the billowing Gulf. The place was no feast for the eyes to begin with, old and gray as driftwood, beaten by the elements, seeming to sag slightly on its reedy stilts. It strained credulity to think the bungalow could appear any worse. But it did. She noted that the screen door hung open and askew, screens had been ripped off some of the windows, and several glass panes had been broken. She dreaded the thought of what she would see inside.

The exterminator threw her a sympathetic glance. "Looks pretty tore up, don't it, ma'am?"

"Does it ever." She gasped. "Oh, heavens, I hope Doris Juan is okay."

"Doris who?"

"Doris Juan. My cat."

The young man pulled a face but didn't comment. With an earsplitting crunch, he brought his truck to a halt and switched off the engine. He peered at the beach house—now more of a shack—and shook his head. "Sorry, ma'am, but it looks like them fellars with shotguns really did a job on your place after I hightailed it."

She gulped. "Might they still be around?"

"Nope. Their jalopy is gone."

"Well, thank heaven for small favors."

"You ready for a gander inside?"

She shuddered. "I doubt I'll ever be ready, but what choice do we have?"

"Right." He reached for his door handle.

Feeling a twinge of anxiety, she touched his sleeve. "However, before we attempt such a daunting feat, I would like to know the name of my—er—companion in this misadventure."

"Yes, ma'am," he replied with pride. "Billy Bob Crumpett at your service."

She solemnly shook his rough, bony hand. "Mr. Crumpett."

He grinned shyly. "Call me Billy Bob."

"Very well. Call me Teresa."

"Yes, ma'am."

Gathering her bag and bundle of towels, Teresa caught sight of Billy Bob grabbing his clipboard and adjusting his cap. "Armed and ready, eh?" she quipped dryly.

"Yes, ma'am," he soberly agreed, creaking open his door.

Teresa pushed open her own door and gingerly stepped outside, sand oozing over her toes as the warm ocean breeze tugged at the shreds of her skirt. With a cursory glance at the Gulf, where shorebirds swooped about the green, surging waves, she muttered, "Well, here goes nothing."

Billy Bob jogged ahead. "Hold on just a minute, ma'am."

Assuming he wanted to check on the house first, Teresa was only too happy to wait at the bottom of the steps. Then she became bemused when, instead of going up, he ducked under the house. "What are you doing now?" she called.

Billy Bob was peering about, eyeing her foundation from various angles. "Ma'am, I don't see no place for riots under here."

She groaned. "How can you think of rats at a time like this?"

"Ma'am, I don't want to get farred—"

"Right," Teresa cut in dryly. "If you must know,

39

I've heard them scratching at the floorboards, evidently gnawing to get in."

"Is that all?" He squinted up at her floorboards, then pulled a pencil from his pocket and began scribbling notes on his clipboard. "Matter of fact, ma'am, I do see signs of gnawing—"

Teresa glanced anxiously toward the road. "Terrific. Now may we please go inside before you get us killed? I feel like a sitting duck out here."

"Sure, ma'am." Sprinting out to join her, Billy Bob made a few more notes on his clipboard. "I'll put out some riot bait anyhow before I leave."

"You do that."

They climbed the creaky steps together and crossed the porch, exchanging a meaningful glance when both saw that the door stood ajar. Billy Bob gestured for Teresa to remain behind, then he strode in first. Hearing his low, amazed whistle, she quickly followed him inside and shut the door, only to gasp at the sight of her living room. Totally trashed. Her couch and chairs were overturned, bookcases dumped out, knickknacks broken. The room was also stifling hot; her window unit air conditioner at the back of the room was turned off just as she'd left it. At least the unit appeared undamaged, unlike her television and stereo, which had been horribly smashed on the floor. Video tapes had also been ripped from their plastic housings and scattered about in heaps of snarls.

"Looks like them fellars had quite a party," muttered Billy Bob, shaking his head.

"What a disaster," Teresa agreed. "I'll never hear the end of this from Aunt Hatch." She gaped about, then a sigh burst from her and she began prowling the room. "And where is my cat? Doris Juan? Oh, Doris?"

Billy Bob followed, eyeing her askance. "Begging your pardon, ma'am, but any cat that ain't hightailed it to the swamp grass by now is a pretty dumb critter."

"Oh, I suppose you're right," Teresa fretted, chewing her bottom lip. "I just hope she wasn't harmed."

Billy Bob pulled off his cap and ran his fingers through his mussed carroty hair. "S'pose we should call the cops?"

"Of course." Shifting her bundle and purse beneath one arm, Teresa crossed over and retrieved her phone from the floor. Lifting the receiver and punching buttons, she heard nothing. "It's dead."

"Yep, and my cell phone's busted."

"Great. Guess I'd best have a look at the other rooms."

Teresa started gingerly across the room, stepping over haphazard piles of papers and books and avoiding tangles of tapes. She stepped into the hallway, looked to her right, and grimaced at the sight of her bedroom—drawers yanked out with their contents scattered, the mirror on her dresser shattered, the mattress and bedding pulled off her bed. Then she turned to her right and winced at the sight of her office—files rifled, her computer monitor and power unit ripped off her desk and savagely broken on the floor.

"My God, the place is wrecked!" she cried. "My papers, my books . . . and Lord, they even smashed my computer."

"Sure did, ma'am," said Billy Bob from behind her.

41

"Oh, well, it was a dinosaur anyway."

"Huh? Never heard of that there brand, ma'am."

Teresa rolled her eyes and stepped into the bathroom. Although the medicine and towel cabinets were open, and towels scattered on the floor, nothing was broken. "Well, they showed a little mercy here." She set her bundle down on the toilet, ripped off the paper, and, in a touch of absurd whimsy, hung up her new green towels. "There. At least Aunt Hatch won't be able to complain about the linen service here."

"Whatever you say, ma'am. Well, guess I'd best go see about them critters under your house—"

"Will you stop already with the rats?" Teresa cut in. "My whole life has been trashed, thank you very much, and you're fixated on rodents. Show a little compassion for a damsel in distress."

He snapped to attention. "Yes, ma'am. What do you want me to do?"

"Oh, I don't know." Realizing her nerves were totally fried, Teresa flung a hand outward in frustration. "Hell, how 'bout a drink?"

A wide grin split his face. "Now you're talking."

"How 'bout *several* drinks?"

"Now you're *really* talking."

She chuckled. "You stand watch and set up some sort of civilized seating arrangement in the living room. I'll mix."

He saluted her. "Yes, ma'am."

While Billy Bob began righting the furniture, Teresa ventured out to the kitchen—which was in similar shape, with drawers rifled, silverware and gadgets scattered, but no real damage done. Although the cabinet doors had been opened, the contents—glasses, plates, and cups—had evidently been dismissed with a cursory glance.

What had the thugs been searching for? And why had they come here at all? Was their appearance linked to the bizarre Englishman who had abducted her in Houston? Again, she wondered if he might have been one of them.

Opening her refrigerator and absorbing a blast of frosty air, she shuddered as she remembered Charles Everett—the cold determination in his eyes, the gleaming steel of his automatic. For brief moments he'd held her life in his hands, moments which should have been the most terrifying of her entire life. Then why, through it all, had she felt strangely drawn to him, even finding him sexy and compelling?

She grabbed a bottle of daiquiri mix and slammed it down on the countertop. What was her problem, anyway? Was she some sort of masochist? Did she long for the kiss of death?

Shaking off these disquieting thoughts, she threw some ice into the blender, added the mixer along with plenty of rum, and flipped it on, letting its loud *whirr* blot out all other thought as she anticipated the dulling potence of the rum.

Moments later, carrying two champagne goblets filled with frozen daiquiris, she ambled back into the living room, where she found Billy Bob parked on the uprighted couch, an expression of bewilderment on his young face.

He brightened at the sight of the drinks. "Them daiquiris, ma'am?"

"Yes, sir." She handed him one.

"My favorite."

"Good." She sat down and raised her glass to his. "To us?"

Billy Bob glanced appreciatively at Teresa's shapely thighs, generously bared by her split skirt. "Yeah, ma'am. To us." He clicked his glass

43

against hers, and took a hearty sip. "Ah, that's tasty. You know, lady, this has been one bitch of a day."

Teresa harrumphed and slurped her own drink. "If you think you've had a bad day, just wait till you hear about mine."

Feeling emboldened by the alcohol, Teresa launched into a long discourse, telling Billy Bob all about the lunatic in Houston who had accosted her at gunpoint and kidnapped her. He listened with an expression of mystification, occasionally interrupting with a "No shit, lady!" or to ask a question or two.

"I'm lucky to be alive," Teresa vehemently concluded.

"Yes, ma'am, you sure are," he agreed soberly. "Can't believe that fellar just shanghaied you that way."

She took a gulp. "Well, he did."

"And you got no idear why he done it?"

"None whatsoever."

Billy Bob gestured at the wrecked room. "Do you s'pose he was one of the folks that done all this?"

"Who knows?"

Billy Bob chuckled. "Well, don't that beat all. Guess we're both just snakebit, lady."

Astounded, she replied, "We're *what*?"

"Snakebit."

"My God, are you saying a *snake* bit you?"

He laughed. "Oh, no, ma'am. I mean we're *snakebit*. You know, jinxed, hexed. Down on our luck."

"Ah, snakebit," she murmured, savoring the word. "Yes, I must agree. We're most definitely snakebit, the two of us. What a charming colloquialism."

Billy Bob was scowling. "If you say so, ma'am." He held up his empty glass. "How 'bout another?"

"You betcha." She grabbed his glass. "Wait right here."

She wobbled off to the kitchen.

The two had almost finished their second round, and Teresa was feeling blessedly light-headed, when there came a knock at the front door. Tensing, she grabbed Billy Bob's arm. "Do you suppose it's the thugs again?"

He shook his head. "Begging your pardon, ma'am, but them there fellars don't knock."

"Right." Courage fortified by the alcohol, Teresa got up, wobbled to the door, and flung it open. She cringed. Her captor, Charles Everett, stood on the porch, fixing her with his flinty stare and once again pointing his deadly automatic at her. Teresa should have been terrified, but she just felt too crazed and exhausted to really care.

"You again," she greeted him scornfully.

"Did you enjoy your little escape attempt?" he quietly mocked.

"Immensely," she shot back.

A muscle jerked in his jaw. "Then will you kindly come with me, Ms. Phelps, so we may avoid further . . . unpleasantries?"

His words made Teresa's blood boil. "Hell, why don't you just shoot me?" she retorted.

And she hiccuped, turned around, and staggered back into the living room. Wearing an expression of mystification, Charles Everett holstered his gun, closed the door, and followed her.

He gaped at the chaos. "Great Scot, what has happened here?"

Teresa collapsed on the couch and picked up her drink. Noting that Charles's gaze quickly became riveted to her bare, exposed thighs, she tried to tug together the shreds of her skirt. Feeling a perverse thrill at his perusal, she shot back, "What has happened? Why, some friendly neighborhood deranged maniacs decided to rearrange my home." She accented her pronouncement with another hiccup.

"What?" he cried.

"We had a visit from a certain unsavory element," she elucidated. "Being a member of that rather disreputable clan yourself, I'm certain you must know all about this, right?"

"Me?" he replied with a look of affronted pride. "How dare you intimate I could have anything to do with this sort of wholesale vandalism."

Teresa took a heedless gulp. "That's right—you only want to abduct and kill me. You're much too classy a fellow to stoop to trashing the furniture."

Charles regarded her in consternation.

Billy Bob spoke up. "Begging your pardon, ma'am, but this here fellar ain't one of the thugs that was here earlier. Nossir. They appeared Hispanic, from the look of 'em."

Teresa smiled sweetly at Charles. "Well, aren't we blessed? So now I'll only be murdered rather than serially pillaged."

Throwing her a chiding glance, Charles spoke to Billy Bob. "Who, might I ask, are you, sir, and what are you doing here?"

"Billy Bob Crumpett, the exterminator," he drawled back. "I come here earlier to kill the riots under the house—"

"Riots?" Charles repeated, his curious gaze shifting to Teresa.

"Don't ask," she advised with a reckless swig.

"—but I got chased away by them folks with shotguns that done all of this." Billy Bob emphasized his words with an expansive gesture at the damage. "Then later, I picked up Miss Phelps here, and give her a ride home. She was on foot on account of some fellar in Houston shanghaied her and . . ." He grinned at Teresa. "I don't rightly recollect the rest, ma'am."

Teresa smiled sweetly at Charles. "Oh, but a certain party here does."

"Huh?" Billy Bob asked.

Looking extremely uncomfortable, Charles cleared his throat. "So you saw the people who caused this destruction, Mr. Crumpett?"

"Yep. Bunch of Hispanic thugs with shotguns."

"Did they say what they wanted?"

"Nossir, they did their talking with a twelve-gauge, if you know what I mean. And I wasn't about to stick around long enough to shoot the breeze with 'em."

Charles appeared stunned.

Downing the last of her daiquiri, Teresa stood. "Care for a drink?" she asked Charles.

An incredulous smile lit his features. "You're actually offering your abductor a libation?"

"Why not?" she carelessly replied. "Billy Bob and I were just drowning our sorrows because . . ." With an eloquent gesture, she deferred to Billy Bob.

"On account of we're snakebit," he finished.

"*Snakebit?*" responded a clearly perplexed Charles.

"You know, jinxed, down on our luck," Teresa explained. "And come to think of it, you must be snakebit, too. After all, you can't even pull off a decent kidnapping."

"Cute," he mocked.

Billy Bob seemed to come to attention then, frowning at Teresa and jerking a thumb toward Charles. "Ma'am, are you sayin'—are you sure

'nuff tellin' me this here's the fellar that shanghaied you?"

"Yep."

Billy Bob scowled massively at Charles. "You
want I should box his ears?"

Teresa sneered. "Frankly, I don't give a rat's
behind if you box all of him, but perhaps he'd be
more harmless drunk. So which will it be, Mr.
Everett? A drink or an ear-boxing?"

Refusing to be baited, Charles smoothly
replied, "Actually, a libation sounds divine at the
moment." He fanned his face and grimaced. "I've
never quite become accustomed to the heat here
in the Colonies."

Teresa groaned at his droll humor, then turned
to Billy Bob. "Ready for another round, partner?"

He handed her his empty glass. "Yep."

Teresa got up and wobbled into the kitchen,
only to have Charles follow her. Flinging open the
refrigerator, she could feel his hard gaze boring
into her. "Look, if you're expecting me to apologize for escaping, don't hold your breath."

"No, I don't expect you to apologize," he replied
with surprising humility. "In fact, I can't say as I
blame you for giving me the slip."

She turned, astonished.

He offered her a lame smile. "You might say
you and I got off on the wrong foot in Houston."

"No shit, Sherlock," she muttered, slamming
shut the fridge with her hip and dumping ingredi-
ents on the counter. "You mind explaining to me
why you abducted me in the first place? Does it
have anything to do with my house being
trashed?"

"I thought I explained that I'm detaining you in
order to keep you away from my fath—"

"Spare me that claptrap about my being your

father's mistress," she cut in. "I'm in a pretty pissy mood at the moment."

To demonstrate, Teresa snapped on the blender, drowning out Charles's reply. A moment later, she shoved a drink into his hand. "Enjoy," she mocked, summarily heading off for the living room with two more.

Frowning, Charles followed her.

"Here ya go," Teresa said, thrusting a drink in Billy Bob's hand and sloshing some on his shirt-sleeve.

"Thanks, ma'am," he said with a grin, licking his sleeve, then taking a hearty gulp.

Charles, who had reentered the room, was frowning as he examined the damage from various angles. "I say, what a calamity."

"Looking for something?" Teresa asked sweetly.

"Obviously your visitors were. Do you know if anything was stolen?"

"How can I tell amid all the destruction?"

"Good point." His gaze narrowed with a certain tension. "You've called the authorities, I presume?"

"Can't," Teresa responded. "The hooligans cut my phone lines."

"And busted up my cell phone when they fired at me," added Billy Bob.

"Ah," murmured Charles.

"But if my phone *had* been working, I certainly would have summoned the authorities to arrest you," Teresa sarcastically informed him.

"I commend your restraint," he rejoined.

Suddenly, she snapped her fingers. "Hey, back when you were chasing me on the access road, didn't you have a . . . ?"

The rest of Teresa's sentence was curtailed as

another rap sounded at her door, and a shrill female voice called out, "Teresa? Oh, Teresa?"

Slamming down her drink, Teresa buried her face in her hands. "Oh, hell. What next? Aunt Hatch has arrived."

"Aunt Hatch?" queried Charles.

"Lillian Hatch, my mother's sister," she explained. "Alias stormtrooper from hell. And dean of the Fullenfelder School for Delinquent Girls. The very one who's now banging on my door."

Charles grinned. "By all means, let her in. The more the merrier."

"Yeah, sure." Teresa got up and staggered toward the door, then flung it open. "Hello, Aunt H-H-atch," she slurred.

"My heavens!" gasped a deep, commanding feminine voice.

In the doorway loomed Lillian Hatch, a statuesque woman of fifty, with sharp features and graying hair pulled back into a severe bun. A nononsense green linen suit ensconced her well-honed, athletic body, while sensible brown pumps sheathed her large feet. A leather bag was slung from one straight shoulder, a vintage '60s brown alligator suitcase held in her hand. Her mouth was hanging agape as she stared horrified at the scene.

"Won't you come in?" Teresa managed.

"You're joking, of course!" Lillian retorted. "What on earth has been going on here, Teresa? Why, your screen door is hanging by a thread and . . ." She glanced downward, then went wild-eyed. "Whatever has happened to your skirt? Why, it's ripped practically to your . . . Oh, my!"

"Shocking, eh?" Teresa quipped.

Striding inside the room and setting down her

suitcase, Lillian crossed her arms over her bosom and glowered at her niece. "Teresa, I demand an explanation!"

"S-search me," Teresa cockily replied, shutting the front door, then weaving back toward the couch. She plopped herself down and propped her feet on the coffee table, causing both men to gape again at her naked thighs. "Aunt Hatch, I'd like to introduce you to my exterminator and . . ." She paused to hiccup, then grinned almost fondly at Charles. "My abductor."

Gasping, raising a hand to her throat, Lillian continued to stare scandalized at the chaotic room, and at the two male guests—Charles seated near the tipped-over bookcases, Billy Bob lounging next to Teresa. "Teresa! For heaven's sake, pull down your skirt!"

Teresa dutifully tugged at the shreds, which quickly parted even further to reveal more of her charms. "Can't. Won't work. So I guess these two charming gents can just leer away."

Lillian drew herself up to her full height. "Why, Teresa Phelps! I never knew you were into kink! Who are these two shady characters and what has been going on here?"

Now Charles spoke up with a scowl. "Madam, I'll have you know I'm not the least bit shady. Though I can't attest for Billy Bob here—"

Taking his cue, Billy Bob solemnly put in, "Well, sir, I've always wanted to have it 'made in the shade' like my Uncle Clovis in the oil business."

Charles snapped his fingers and grinned at Lillian. "He's your shady one, madam."

"Why, I never! Teresa, explain this appalling situation!"

Teresa was again on the verge of replying, only to go wide-eyed when an earsplitting blast

51

sounded out, and suddenly and violently, half the living room window came flying in onto the floor. For a moment everyone froze, too stunned to respond. Staring flabbergasted at the shards of glass spewed everywhere, Teresa had just realized that the noise was gunfire when a new shot rang out and more of the window blew in!

"My God, shotgun fire!" Charles Everett cried frantically, waving his arms. "Get down, everyone—now!"

As a third retort split the air, everyone took Charles seriously; amid screams from the women, all four went diving for the rug, Charles grabbing Teresa's arm and tugging her down with him. Sprawled with Charles on top of scattered books and magazines, Teresa caught a glimpse of Billy Bob's body sailing over them, then heard him crash-land with a painful grunt.

"Ma'am, them there fellars sure have taken a shine to you," he gritted out from a few feet away.

"No kidding!" Teresa retorted. Then she flinched as Charles violently shook her; she gazed up into his fiercely gleaming eyes.

"Shut up and stay put!" he ordered hoarsely.

Teresa was in no frame of mind to protest. She watched Charles crawl off to the shattered window, take out his gun, and attempt to return fire. But nothing happened. Bemused, she observed him snapping his fingers, then pulling a bullet clip from the breast pocket of his coat.

The sight of the bullet clip sent Teresa into an unthinking fury. This nutcase had kidnapped her without having any bullets in his gun? Talk about adding insult to injury!

A cry of rage sputtered up in her. Heedless of her own safety, Teresa sprang up and tore across the room, flinging herself down on Charles, attacking him with fists flailing. "You jerk! You mean you abducted me using a gun with no bullets?"

As another volley of gunfire erupted, Charles dropped his gun, grabbed Teresa's flailing wrists, then quickly, forcefully, rolled, pinning her body beneath his own on the rug. She bucked violently, only to feel his hard body respond in a shockingly sensual way. With his rigid maleness pressing into her, his blue eyes sparkling with anger and boring down into hers, Teresa found Charles daunting in the extreme—not to mention sexy as hell.

"Oh, my," she muttered, face hot.

If he noted her discomfiture at his own state of arousal, he seemed too furious to take note. "Of course I didn't have bullets in my gun, silly girl. I didn't want to hurt you. Now if you don't want your bloody head blown off, Tess, I suggest you keep it down!"

Rolling off her with all the skill of a commando, Charles quickly retrieved his gun, peered over the window ledge, and began rapidly returning fire. Wincing at the loud retorts of his deadly automatic, Teresa grimaced and covered her ears.

For excruciating seconds, the firing continued. Then, just as quickly, it was all over. The guns fell silent outside; in the distance an engine throbbed to life, then growled and heaved.

Teresa raised her head slightly to see Charles kneeling at the window, peering anxiously outside. "Is it safe now?"

He held up a hand in caution. "Yes, it should be soon. I see several Hispanic youths with shotguns climbing into a low-rider . . . and driving off."

Taking a deep breath of relief, he turned and winked at her. "It seems Billy Bob was right. You are quite popular with the unsavory element, love."

Teresa flashed him her nastiest smile. "Present company included," she quipped.

Chapter Five

As Teresa cautiously peered about the room, she caught sight of Aunt Hatch, her bony rear end thrust in the air, draped over an overturned telephone table, the rest of her body buried beneath a tipped-over easy chair. Then her gaze swung to Billy Bob, who was now crouched in a corner, holding his ears, with eyes tightly closed and a grimace of horror fixed on his face. At least both appeared alive, and she spotted no obvious signs of injury.

Gingerly, she got up, brushing off her tattered skirt. "Hey, everyone, the coast is clear."

Hearing a groan from Aunt Hatch, she crossed the room and lifted the chair off the middle-aged woman. "You okay?"

Coiffure askew, face hot with exertion, Lillian

twisted about to hurl Teresa a scathing look. "Absolutely not!"

"I don't see any holes in you."

"Well, I never!"

Teresa offered a hand. "Here, let me help you up."

Lillian rolled her eyes but accepted Teresa's assistance. Pulling her aunt to her feet, Teresa winced at the sight of her clothing. "Oh, dear."

In horror, Lillian gazed down at her own suit skirt, which was now ripped halfway to her waist, her old-fashioned garters and hose exposed. Though her face was bright red, her voice came charged with fury. "Well, my dear, you no longer need explain how your clothing came to be in such a disgraceful state. Tell me, are you doing your dissertation on the social habits of gangsters and psychopaths?"

Teresa winced. "I'm sorry. And that is such a nice suit."

"*Was*. Indeed, it's the one I always wear for assembly—or used to."

"Assembly?" queried Charles, who had walked up to join them.

"Don't you remember, Charles?" Teresa mocked, turning to him. "Aunt Hatch is the head-mistress of the Fullenfelder School for Delinquent Girls. So you'd best watch your step."

He smiled nastily. "Ah. Not a worry in my case, as I'm a man. But a pity she couldn't have given *you* some training."

Teresa was all set to issue a blistering retort when Lillian concurred frostily, "Yes, a pity." She drew herself up to her formidable height and addressed Charles. "Young man, what on earth is going on here?"

Charles gave a shrug. "Ask your niece."

"Teresa?"

She groaned. "Actually, I have no idea."

"A bald-faced lie if I've ever heard one."

"Aunt Hatch!"

Before Teresa could protest more, Billy Bob ambled up, pulling a face and rubbing his back. "Damn, them fellars must have somethin' barbed stuck in their craws."

"You okay?" Teresa asked, touching his arm.

"Fair to middlin', ma'am. Almost busted my back as I sailed onto your chifforobe."

Teresa glanced at her pine armoire, overturned on the floor. "You mean my entertainment center."

"Weren't very entertaining when my back crash-landed on it." He grunted. "Well, folks, reckon I'll be moseying along."

"You're leaving me?" Teresa demanded shrilly.

"Begging your pardon, ma'am, but I doubt there's any more riots hanging around here after all that blasting. 'Sides, I got three more stops to make today, and I don't want to get farred over this."

"Right," Teresa muttered.

"But don't worry, ma'am, I'll stop off and tell the sheriff what happened here."

"Yes, please do."

"Young man, may I have a ride with you?" inquired Lillian, gathering up her purse and suitcase. "You see, a cab dropped me off."

Billy Bob grinned and took the woman's suitcase. "Why, shore, ma'am. Billy Bob Crumpett at your service."

Realizing her aunt intended to leave her alone with Charles, Teresa swung around to face Lillian. "What? You're leaving? But you're staying here with me."

"Here? In this disaster area?" Lillian inquired

with a scornful laugh. "That's totally out of the question, Teresa. Why, I'd sooner reside at the city dump."

"But—I bought you new towels," Teresa attempted desperately. "Don't you want to see them? They're hanging in the bathroom!"

Lillian rolled her eyes. "You've clearly lost your mind, child. At any rate, I'll be staying with Aunt Maizie over on Galveston Island until you pull yourself together."

Even as Teresa was about to protest again, Billy Bob chimed in. "Hey, ma'am, you s'pose Aunt Maizie has any riots or termites running around loose at her place?"

"I should hope not," Lillian responded coolly. Then, evidently fearing Billy Bob's offer of a ride would be withdrawn, she relented slightly. "But we can ask."

He grinned. "Yes, ma'am. Now you're talkin'."

Throwing a haughty glance at Charles, Lillian adjusted her collar and sniffed in distaste. "Well, goodbye, Teresa. I must say I'm appalled that you've fallen in with such a rough crowd." She offered her arm to the exterminator. "Shall we, young man?"

"Yes, ma'am." Billy Bob proudly escorted Lillian toward the door.

Glancing at Charles and absorbing his smug smile, Teresa felt panic encroaching. She tore after the departing couple, grabbing Billy Bob's arm. "Wait!" she cried, pointing at Charles. "You can't leave me alone with him! He's trying to kill me!"

"Me?" Charles inquired piously.

"Kill you?" Billy Bob repeated, snorting a laugh. "Heck, ma'am, seems to me that there fellar just saved your bacon."

And without further ado, he led Lillian out the

door, her ramrod-straight spine issuing a frosty farewell.

Silence fell in the wake of their departure. Teresa turned to stare at Charles, at her ruined home . . . and then burst into tears.

Charles Everett stared with compassion at the woman sobbing across from him. How vulnerable Teresa Phelps looked, and how lost. He was filled with a helpless desire to somehow comfort her. And guilt gnawed at him that he was at least partially responsible for her being in such a distraught state. So were the thugs who had just visited. They were an unwelcome complication, though not totally unexpected.

As for his target, Charles hadn't expected Teresa Phelps to be so appealing, or so sexy. Nor had he expected the softer emotion this woman stirred in him, much less the hotter desire that had spiked within him when he'd pinned her to the floor and had felt her feminine body bucking and trembling beneath his own. He'd come dangerously close to losing control. It was truly ironic that in so many ways, this woman posed more of a danger to him than he did to her. He knew it would be unwise to reveal any weaknesses to her.

Nonetheless, her helpless anguish wrenched his gut, and he found himself crossing the room, pulling her into his arms. His senses swam with the womanly scent of her, at the way her soft curves were nestled against him. Her shudders and whimpers stirred an unexpected tenderness in him.

"There, there," he murmured, stroking her back.

Teresa felt utterly disarmed to find herself held

in Charles Everett's strong arms. She reeled at his provocative proximity, the heat of his body, his male scent. Poignant emotion inundated her when he tenderly caressed her spine.

"Don't cry, love," he soothed in his deep voice. "You've had a bad scare, but you'll be fine."

She drew back slightly to regard him in bewilderment. "But you're the one who scared me—at least initially."

He smiled sheepishly. "I didn't mean to."

"You pointed a gun at me, damn it!"

"Without any bullets," he pointed out.

"But I didn't know that then!"

He held up a hand. "Very well, I won't belabor the point."

"And what about those thugs who just fired at us?"

"I know nothing about them."

"Really?" she mocked. "Seems to me you both have something in common. You both want to kill me."

He soberly caught her eye. "They may, my dear, but I assure you, I do not. I never did."

Teresa felt mystified, vulnerable, and didn't know whether to believe this bizarre stranger or not. "You mean you're really not going to shoot me now?" she sniffed.

He drew her close again, brushing tears from her cheeks with his fingers. "Of course not, love. Shooting you was never on the agenda, not at all. I just want to keep you away from my father."

She shoved him away. "That again!"

"Don't worry, love," he teased back, his gaze flicking over her. "I can tell you're in no condition to steal off for a lover's tryst. I think we'd best attend to the business at hand." He looked around, shaking his head. "You're going to need a lot of help putting this to rights."

Teresa was stunned and suspicious. "But why would you want to help me?"

He regarded her sternly. "You're forgetting—I'm along for the ride until my parents return to England next month."

She balled her hands on her hips. "Like hell you are. I'm not riding with you anywhere else, mister."

Harshness tightened his features. "Let me put it this way, then: I'm staying, whether you like it or not."

Teresa bit her lip in exasperation. She felt highly skeptical of Charles Everett's motives, even more so of his wanting to remain here. The vivid image of a grim-faced Charles drawing out his gun and kidnapping her was all too fresh in her mind, as was the memory of her own shocking response to his nearness. Both seemed warning signs that she must keep this dangerous stranger at bay. But now that she had calmed down a bit, she also had to admit that his using a gun with no bullets had demonstrated at least some concern for her safety. And as Billy Bob had pointed out, Charles Everett *had* just saved her life . . .

Just as earlier, he'd threatened it. Damn, she was so confused! But what could she do if he refused to leave? She could hardly throw him out bodily!

She drew herself up to her full height. "Look, as much as I appreciate your help just now, I want you to leave."

But he only shook his head. "Sorry, love, I'm not leaving, so why don't we call a truce for now—especially considering the danger you're in?"

"May I once again be so blunt as to point out that much of the danger I've faced today has been caused by you?" she half shouted.

"Teresa, I'm not leaving," he maintained stubbornly.

"Damn it, you are."

He flashed her a conciliatory look. "Look, I promise to behave myself."

"Yeah, right. Just like you did in Houston."

He opened his coat and retrieved his gun from his shoulder holster. "I'll even give you my bullet clip if it'll make you feel better."

"You will?" she asked, taken aback.

He snapped out the clip and solemnly handed it to her. "Here."

Teresa took the clip and grimaced at the feel of cold steel in her hand, bit her lip as she studied a bullet. "You mean I can hide this?"

"Be my guest," he offered magnanimously. "Just don't forget where you've stashed it in case we should have any more . . . well, unwelcome visitors."

Teresa hesitated for a long moment. Having Charles's bullet clip would give her a fair measure of control in the situation. Still, watching him replace his automatic in its shoulder holster, she was given pause. This man was no amateur, and his motives were clearly suspect. Was he with organized crime? Or perhaps even in law enforcement?

But people in law enforcement did not kidnap women at gunpoint! Which meant . . . Oh, hell, she didn't know what anything meant!

"Well, Teresa?" he prodded.

"I guess I can't budge you, can I?" she inquired grimly.

"No."

Though intensely frustrated, she conceded, "Very well. Excuse me a moment."

Teresa ducked out into the kitchen, glancing around for a hiding place, then smiling as she chose one. Peering back out at the living room to make sure Charles couldn't see her, she grabbed a chair, climbed up on it, then hid the clip in an opaque vase perched high on top of one of her cabinets.

Getting down and replacing the chair, she found she actually felt somewhat relieved that Charles would be hanging around for a while. To be honest, she was frightened at the prospect of being alone right now—especially if the Hispanic thugs returned again—and she didn't put a lot of faith in the Peninsula's deputy sheriff.

Charles sauntered into the room. "All done?"

Teresa glanced at the messy floor, where the goons had carelessly dumped the contents of drawers and canisters. "Hardly. Want to help with KP?"

"Sure."

She handed him a broom. "Be my guest. You clean the floor, and I'll wash up all the silverware and gadgets scattered everywhere."

He frowned. "Shouldn't we wait until the authorities come and evaluate the crime scene?"

Teresa chortled. "Now you're being lazy."

"Am not!" he protested with a scowl. "I like a tidy kitchen as much as the next chap. I'm merely trying to preserve the integrity of the evidence."

"Oh, give me a break. Besides, do you really think Bolivar Peninsula has a forensics examiner? We're lucky to have a resident deputy here. So quit trying to rest on your laurels and start sweeping, Sherlock."

He grinned and began to sweep.

Working together, they managed to restore some order in the kitchen. Moving to the living room next, they began clearing a path. Teresa felt a hard twinge of anguish as she spotted her brother's photo, smashed, on the floor. She carefully picked it up, emotion knotting her throat as she viewed his familiar, beloved visage. Frank had been an average-looking man in his early thirties, with brown hair and a sensitive, gentle expression; his thick-lensed glasses had obscured his fine hazel eyes. Now his smiling image was a maze of shattered shards, as was his life. At least the photo itself appeared unharmed, and the frame could be replaced. She carefully disposed of the glass fragments, and was laying the frame and picture inside a desk drawer when she felt Charles staring at her. She glanced up and closed the drawer.

"Something wrong?" he asked solicitously. "You just looked so sad there for a moment."

The tender look in his eyes almost made Teresa burst out crying again. But she was spared the necessity to respond when she heard a plaintive meow coming from outside her back patio doors. "Doris Juan!" she cried in delight, racing for the doors.

"Doris Juan?" Charles repeated confusedly.

Teresa popped open the doors to see her large orange and white, shaggy Maine coon cat sitting there, regarding her with wary gold eyes. Her anguish over Frank receded in her overwhelming joy at knowing her pet was safe.

"Doris Juan!" she cried, scooping up the furball. "I'm so glad you're okay! Did those bad men scare you away, sweetie?"

Doris purred in response and nuzzled her head beneath Teresa's chin.

Teresa turned back to Charles to see him regarding her with mingled perplexity and compassion. "My cat," she explained. "She's safe."

"So I've surmised. Mind explaining the oddball name?" He winked. "Or are you just an oddball yourself?"

Feeling a rush of good spirits, she wrinkled her nose at him. "Cute. You're not exactly charming me, Charles."

He chuckled. "And I want to so badly. Very well, then. Explain the name."

Teresa could see no harm in telling him. "Well, as a teenager I had a Maine coon cat named Don Juan."

"Ah. You needn't explain why he was so dubbed. I have a bit of knowledge about tomcatting."

"You would," Teresa rejoined drolly. "Anyway, eventually Don Juan passed away, but not before siring a final litter with our neighbor's female cat. Knowing how devastated I was over losing him, Mrs. Fisher let me have my pick of the litter . . . and 'Doris Juan' was the result."

"A touching tale," Charles agreed, moving over and petting the cat himself.

Teresa stared down at Doris, who in turn was gazing raptly up at Charles and purring even louder—the shameless creature. "Hey, she likes you. And she doesn't take to too many people."

Charles leaned toward her. "All females like me, love."

Highly discomfited, Teresa moved away, starting back toward the kitchen. "I—er—I think Doris Juan must be hungry. I'll feed her."

"Do that. Assuming the thugs left her anything."

"Right."

Teresa was in the kitchen and had just finished giving the cat food and water, when she heard two warning bleeps of a police siren. She reentered the living room to see Charles standing at the front windows. "Well, looks as if your county mountie has arrived."

Teresa walked over to join him. "Right."

A potbellied man in sheriff's uniform emerged from the cruiser. Hitching up his pants and spitting tobacco juice into the swamp grass, he sauntered toward the porch and lumbered up the steps. Catching sight of Charles and Teresa framed in the ruined window, with its few clinging shards of glass and splintered wood, he did a double take, then tipped his beige western hat.

"Afternoon, folks," he drawled. "Fella by the name of Billy Bob Crumpett stopped by to tell me you folks had yourselves a disturbance here."

"We were fired upon by three thugs with shotguns!" Teresa declared.

By now the man had plodded onto the porch. "Guess that qualifies as a disturbance, ma'am. May I come in?"

"Of course, Sheriff, I'll get the door," Charles offered.

He admitted the man, who trudged inside, glanced around the room, and whistled, then colored at the sight of Teresa's split skirt. "Looks like someone around these parts don't cotton to you, ma'am."

She again tried unsuccessfully to tug together the shreds of her skirt. "So it appears."

"Deputy Sheriff Bobby Mack Dilbreck at your service, ma'am." He took out a pen and began scribbling on his clipboard. "And you're—"

"Teresa Phelps."

"Spell it."

She complied.

"You the owner of this here property?"

"I'm the tenant."

He motioned at Charles. "Who's he?"

"My kid—"

"Her kid brother's good friend, Charles Everett," Charles interrupted smoothly, hurling Teresa a cautioning glance and offering his hand to the sheriff.

"Whatever." Shaking Charles's hand, Bobby Mack cleared his throat. "Ma'am, mind telling me what went on here and why them folks was shooting at you?"

"Why, we have no idea—that's why we called you."

He glanced around suspiciously. "Generally when I see this kind of mischief, there's something fishy going on, if you know what I mean."

"Oh!" Outraged, Teresa declared, "No, I *don't* know what you mean."

The deputy wiggled his eyebrows meaningfully and lowered his voice. "Well, ma'am, generally, there's been some kind of hanky-panky. You know, illegal activity. That ring a bell?"

Teresa laid a finger alongside her jaw. "Well, let me see. There's always my bird-watching for the Audubon Society. Most unsavory, indeed. As well as my research for my dissertation—you know, analysis of tidal cycles and barrier island erosion."

He squinted. "Say what, ma'am?"

Teresa's voice rose in outrage. "So, what do you want to do—impound my dissertation drafts, or my binoculars?"

The man colored and uneasily shifted his weight. "Now ma'am, it won't help at all you going huffy on me. What I mean is, generally when gang-banger types trash a house like this, it's either 'cause they're looking for drugs, or aimin' to steal valuables so's they can buy them."

"There are no drugs or valuables here," Teresa declared. "I'm poor as a church mouse."

"Yes, ma'am." He began scribbling again. "Okay, then. Can you describe the fellars that trashed this house and fired at you?"

Teresa and Charles provided what few sketchy details they could, while the deputy stopped them several times to ask questions.

Afterward, he shook his head. "Well, I tell you—I'll file a report, and notify the boys at Galveston and the mainland. But I'd advise you not to expect much."

"Considering the source, we won't," Teresa told him sweetly.

He eyed her reproachfully. "Ma'am, I'm just trying to say there must have been a reason."

Teresa was growing exasperated, clenching her fists at her sides. "Yes, there must have been. That's why we called you, Deputy—to *investigate*!"

"Yes, ma'am." With a shrug, he tipped his hat. "Well, so long, folks."

"So long, Deputy," she replied wearily.

Shutting the door behind him, Teresa waved a hand at Charles. "What an idiot."

"He wasn't exactly a rocket scientist."

"And how."

Charles was regarding her curiously. "You know, you didn't even mention my abducting you, after that one initial slip. You could have had me arrested for kidnapping then and there."

Teresa shrugged. "As Billy Bob pointed out, you saved my life—and his, and Aunt Hatch's. Not a very convincing capital case, I'd say." She studied him intently. "Besides, something tells me your presence here has nothing to do with my supposed affair with your lecher of a father."

He grinned slyly.

She snapped her fingers. "By the way, where *are* those photos of him and me together?"

Charles blanched. "They're er—at my condo."

"Sure they are."

He coughed and changed the subject. "You know the deputy was right about one thing. There must have been a reason for those thugs to attack. Think a minute, Tess. Who would want to ransack your house and possibly kill you?"

She smiled brightly. "That's easy. You're the only person I know who wants to kill me."

"Cute, Tess," he snapped back. "Now think hard. Do you have any enemies? Do you own anything valuable that someone might want to steal?"

For a long moment Teresa frowned and scoured her mind. Then she sighed in frustration as she reached a dead end. "Damn it, no. There's nothing I can think of. I mean, who would want to steal from an impoverished student?"

He nodded sympathetically. "Very well, Tess. Never mind for now. Perhaps a thought will come to you later on. Let's get back to work."

"Right," she muttered, then glanced down at herself. "But first, before we're graced by another visitor, I think I'll go change."

He sighed dramatically. "Must you? I rather favor your current costume. Most disreputable."

"Like you?" she echoed sweetly.

The rascal only laughed.

As Teresa left the room, she could feel Charles's bold, appreciative gaze following her.

Chapter Six

The one thing the thugs hadn't chosen to rifle was Teresa's refrigerator, and thank heaven, she had stocked it the day before. After spending several more hours righting furniture, sweeping up debris, and restoring a modicum of order at the beach house, both Teresa and Charles were starving. So she volunteered to cook some catfish while he nailed sheets over the blown-out front windows.

In the Louisiana tradition taught her by her mother, Teresa dipped the fillets in a mixture of cornmeal, flour, cayenne, and other spices, then began frying them in oil. She also started up a pot of rice and prepared a salad. The enticing smells of the food, and the comforting ritual of performing routine tasks, comforted her somewhat.

Smelling the fish, Doris Juan soon vaulted into the room, meowed plaintively, and jumped up onto the counter. Usually the cat was better behaved, but, under the circumstances, Teresa didn't have the heart to scold her. Scooping up the cat and setting her down on the floor, Teresa fed her some leftover scraps of raw fish, then washed her hands and continued cooking.

She still couldn't believe what had happened to her today. Why had Charles Everett kidnapped her, only later to become her defender? Why had the thugs shot up and ransacked her home? Surely they wanted something from her—and so did Charles. As appealing as he was, she mustn't forget that she couldn't trust him. He'd demonstrated that by abducting her at gunpoint. But she should try to find out what he really wanted.

Her thoughts scattered as she heard her large window unit air conditioner whir on in the living room. A moment later Charles sauntered into the kitchen, fanning his flushed face with a hand.

"Now that I've battened down the hatches, I've turned on your AC so the place will cool down."

"Thanks."

He moved toward the stove. "That smells divine, Tess."

She flipped a fillet. "You must be as hungry as I am."

"I'm always hungry, love."

Her heart fluttering at the sexy undercurrent in his voice, Teresa studied him from the corner of her eye. He had removed his jacket, rolled up his shirtsleeves, and unbuttoned several buttons on his fine white oxfordcloth shirt. His hair was wind-ruffled, his skin glossy with sweat, and he appeared very sexy, especially as she noted his own gaze appreciatively roving her body, making her wish she'd changed into something more substantial than cutoffs and a tank top, even in this heat. She knew she had pretty legs, long and curvy, and Charles's perusal certainly confirmed this. His gaze even lingered for a heartstopping moment on her finely shaped bare feet in their thongs, and her brightly painted toenails.

"Well, you're certainly looking domestic," he teased.

She forced a smile. "And I'll bet you're thirsty—there's beer in the refrigerator."

"Ah, manna from heaven." He opened the refrigerator, pulled out a beer, and popped the top. "Want one?"

She shook her head and saluted him with the glass of white wine she was drinking.

"Well, I covered the windows as best I could," Charles remarked. "But you'll need to call a carpenter tomorrow."

Teresa groaned. "I know. I'll have to call my landlord, and I'm dreading it."

"He's not insured?"

"He is, but he's quite a skinflint. On something like this"—using her spatula, she gestured vaguely in the direction of the front windows—"he'll surely blame me and want me to pay his deductible. Plus, I have no renter's insurance to cover the damage to my own property. And my computer is ruined."

"Ah, yes. That dinosaur. Looks to me like it needed to be put out of its misery."

Teresa felt her hackles rising. "That's easy enough for you to say, but I don't have money for a new one. I'm still a struggling student. But at least I had my dissertation backed up, and the floppy disks appear to be undamaged."

He frowned. "Dissertation?"

72

"I'm a doctoral candidate in recent sedimentology." She smiled nastily. "But then, you already know about that, don't you?"

"Do I?"

She stepped closer to him and raised her chin. "You know I'm here counting birds on a grant from the Audubon Society—seems like you mentioned something to that effect while you had me in handcuffs and were hauling me away from the store." She stared him in the eye. "Well, Charles? How do you know so much about me? And don't you dare say your father told you!"

For a moment he regarded her sheepishly, then he abruptly gestured at the frying pan. "Hey, your fish is starting to smoke."

With a gasp, Teresa turned and began flipping the sizzling catfish. "Good stall," she muttered over her shoulder, and heard Charles laugh.

"So tell me all about your dissertation—and recent sedimentology," Charles suggested.

His wry remark made Teresa burst out laughing. They now sat at the kitchen table, eating catfish, rice pilaf, salad, and drinking white wine. The atmosphere was treacherously cozy.

"Such scintillating dinner conversation," she teased back. "You don't want to know about all that."

"Oh, but I do," he insisted. "I can't remember when a woman's vocation has so intrigued me."

Teresa was still laughing, and feeling too charmed by him. "Very well. Sedimentology is a science focusing on sediments and sedimentary rock, the formation of barrier islands, the study of hydrologic cycles, and so forth."

He sipped his wine. "How fascinating. What did you do, live on a beach as a child?"

"In a manner of speaking, I did. My home is in Morgan City, Louisiana, and I did spend a lot of time along the Gulf shore while growing up. Shorebirds always fascinated me, as did the beach itself—the cycles of the tide, erosion, even the whole question of how it all began. Eventually this led to my interest in sedimentology, which I later studied when I went to college in Baton Rouge."

"And your dissertation?"

"I'm studying the effects of backwaters on mud flat formation here on the Gulf Coast."

He whistled. "How impressive. Do you also plot geographical changes in the region?"

She gave a shrug. "It plays a part in my research."

"How close are you to finishing up?"

She sighed. "I was hoping to turn in my dissertation by late winter or early spring. But then . . ." She hesitated as she thought of the trauma of losing her brother, and automatically touched Frank's bracelet on her left wrist. She realized she didn't want to broach that painful subject with Charles right now. "Well, lately I've suffered some personal setbacks, and now this. I'm not sure how much my computer disaster will affect my work."

He winked at her. "Well, I'm honored to know a woman of your intellect."

"Really?" she laughed. "Most men find my intelligence threatening."

"I'm not most men."

"Indeed you're not." She frowned. "If I may ask, just what are you doing living in the U.S. anyway? I mean, you are British, aren't you? Unless you're just faking that accent for the proper secret agent effect."

He frowned over her question. "Yes, I am British. But I have an aunt and uncle who live in Austin, Texas. As a lad I visited there several times with my folks, and I fell in love with the States. Later, I attended the University of Texas and eventually became a U.S. citizen."

"Hey, U.T. was my brother's alma mater, too." After blurting out the words, Teresa bit her lip.

"How interesting," he commented with a frown. "Is something wrong?"

Still unwilling to share such a sensitive subject with him, she shook her head. "I don't suppose you knew . . . ?"

"U.T. is quite a large school," he replied tactfully.

She forced herself to change the subject. "So it is. And what are you doing now?"

"Oh, handling my investments."

She raised an eyebrow. "A likely sounding story."

A sly smile pulled at his lips. "They do take a lot of managing."

"Not to mention all the time you're now spending managing *me*," she couldn't resist adding.

"Touché," he concurred with a laugh.

She propped her chin in her hand and regarded him sternly. "Look, Charles, why don't you just quit stalling and tell me the truth about why you abducted me today?"

"I told you. I'm keeping you under lock and key until my parents return to England next month." Though the words were filled with bravado, he avoided her eye.

"Don't give me that claptrap again! Look, this is nuts. And you can't expect to stay here—"

"Oh, but I do," he put in firmly. "For your protection if nothing else. Have you forgotten that

75

mere hours ago, your house—indeed, your person—was threatened by goons with shotguns?"

"No, I haven't forgotten."

"Well, you're a lunatic if you think I'll let you remain here alone tonight."

"Excuse me, but it seems to me *you're* the lunatic, Charles."

"Whatever." He gave her a mock salute. "One lunatic, armed—if without bullet clip—and at your service, miss."

Teresa couldn't help but laugh again. He seemed so absurdly pompous.

"And don't worry," he added with a dry cough. "I'll sleep on the couch."

She snapped to attention at that. Was there no way to convince this man to leave? "Sleep on the couch? Look, surely it must be—well, inconvenient for you to stay here. I mean, you have no clothes, no—"

"I've a bag in my car."

Her gaze narrowed suspiciously. "Well, aren't you Johnny-on-the-spot?"

"Always."

She ground her jaw. "Charles, you've been very helpful, and I do appreciate your pitching in to put this place to rights. But I want you to go after dinner."

"Teresa, be reasonable," he cajoled. "As you're well aware, we've already had this argument— and you lost. And have you really thought of how defenseless you'd be if I did leave? Why, you have no phone, not even a car."

She gestured in exasperation. "That's right— my car is still sitting in Houston, thanks to you."

"I'll take you there tomorrow."

"You could do it tonight."

"Tomorrow, Tess. No more arguing." He smiled,

savoring a bite of catfish. "Now, have I mentioned how wonderful this dinner is? Tell me—where did you learn to fry fish so well?"

Teresa gritted her teeth. "You're changing the subject, Charles."

"Indulge me anyway."

She relented with a groan. "I already told you I'm from Louisiana."

"Ah, yes." He devoured another bite with an expression of ecstasy. "That explains the wonderful crust. Old family recipe, eh?"

She nodded. "My mother's. My folks still live in Morgan City."

"And your brother?" he prompted.

She glanced away, eyes suddenly burning.

"Tess, what is it?" he demanded, appearing anxious. "You went pale before when we briefly discussed your brother. Is something wrong?"

She didn't answer.

"Tess?"

Losing ground rapidly, Teresa glanced up at Charles and melted at the look of tender concern in his eyes. Again she felt hot tears welling.

A second later, he crossed around to her side of the table and pulled her up into his arms, inundating her senses with his warm, protective embrace. Warring emotions twisted in Teresa's gut. For her, it was humiliating to have Charles comforting her again, so soon after her first outburst. But his strong arms holding her close also felt so soothing, so right.

He led her to the couch in the living room, then went off to the kitchen, returning momentarily with a snifter of brandy. Handing it to her, he waited patiently while she took several sips.

"All right, Tess," he said at last. "What happened to your brother?"

She eyed him helplessly.

"Tell me, Tess."

She sniffed. "He's dead, I'm afraid."

"Dead?"

"Frank was a French professor who lived in Houston," she explained hoarsely. "In fact, he was the one who helped me get the grant from the Audubon Society, so I could live here while I completed my dissertation."

"Ah."

She steadied her voice with an effort. "During these past months while I've lived relatively close to Houston, Frank and I have had a closer relationship than we've had in years. Then a few weeks ago—well, there was a terrible accident. Frank took out his sailboat at Clear Lake at night . . . and never returned. The next morning, a fisherman found his body along the shoreline, and called the police."

Charles appeared shocked and gravely concerned. "How awful. I take it he must have drowned?"

"Yes."

"But why?"

"I'm not completely sure. Frank was an excellent swimmer and sailor. But he did have an injury from some blunt object across his forehead. The coroner concluded that he must have been hit by the boom and knocked overboard. Of course, he likely would have been unconscious by then. . . ."

Charles squeezed her hand. "How tragic. Teresa, I'm so damn sorry."

"Thanks," she managed, taking another sip, then setting down her snifter. "We buried him in Morgan City several weeks ago, and I've only been back here three days myself." She shuddered. "My folks took it very hard."

"Of course they did. And no wonder you said you've had some setbacks in your life. But now I'm more worried about your safety than ever."

Teresa regarded him in perplexity. "Why?"

He was silent, frowning, for a long moment. "What if your brother's death wasn't an accident? What if it had something to do with those thugs who fired on us today?"

Teresa was stunned. "What? But that's absurd! Why would anyone want to kill Frank? He was a French professor, for heaven's sake!"

Charles shook his head. "I'm not sure, but something very strange and dangerous is going on here, and it worries the hell out of me."

"Me too." Though Teresa sniffed at new tears, she couldn't help eyeing him in doubt. "But you know, Charles, the truth is, something very strange and dangerous has been going on from the moment I met *you*. What do you have to say about that?"

Surprisingly, he flashed her an ironic though tender smile, reaching out to brush an errant strand of hair from her brow. "Strange? Dangerous? I agree, love. Completely."

And he lowered his face to hers and tenderly touched her lips with his own. It was a kiss of heady seduction, his mouth exploring, tantalizing her own. At first Teresa stiffened slightly in surprise, but soon she moaned in pleasure. That moan became a thrill of desire when Charles crushed her closer and claimed her mouth more passionately, his tongue flitting at her lips in teasing caresses until she parted them and granted him entry.

79

He took full advantage, slowly sliding his tongue inside her mouth, then thrusting, possessing. The intimacy was shattering for Teresa. She felt herself spinning out of control, clinging to him, and wanting to take off in flight all at the same time. Never had she experienced such a jolting first kiss. Charles tasted divine, and his hard body pressing into hers felt marvelous. She could feel the passion flaring between them as her tender breasts were crushed against his hard, warm chest. When he slid his hand beneath her tank top, boldly stroking her bare midriff, then ran his fingers teasingly down her naked thigh, heat seared her deeply. She eagerly moved her own mouth against his, stunned at the intensity of her own response, and her apparent inability to resist him. He'd spoken the truth right before their kiss, she realized poignantly. The fact that he was dangerous made him all the more irresistible to her.

At last the incredible kiss ended, and Charles pulled back, breathing heavily. The ardent look in his beautiful eyes made her go weak inside. He touched the tip of her nose and spoke in a voice roughened by desire. "I think you'd best go on to bed, Tess. All you need right now is one more complication in your life."

Teresa nodded, wondering what on earth had just come over her, over *them*. "Right," she muttered.

She got up and went wobbling toward her bedroom. She reeled as she realized how very attracted she felt to Charles Everett . . . a man she didn't trust!

With a frown, Charles watched Teresa leave the room, his gaze riveted to the enticing sway of her hips, the gorgeous length of her legs.

He hadn't intended to kiss her just now, but her tears over her brother's death had touched him greatly. Frowning abstractedly, he strode over to the desk where he'd earlier spied Teresa secreting Frank's picture. Opening the drawer and turning over the frame, he stared at the photo and sighed. A shame about poor Frank, especially his dying in a tragic manner that had caused his parents and Teresa such pain.

With a groan, he shut the drawer. There was nothing he could do for Frank now.

But Frank's sister was another matter. Charles really wanted to help Teresa Phelps, to protect her if he could. But he knew his runaway emotions were already getting in the way of his objectivity. She had felt so sweet, so vulnerable in his arms just now. And so soft, warm, womanly, sexy. Even now he yearned to follow her, take her in his arms again and pursue this glorious attraction between them, feel those exquisite long legs twisting sensuously about his body as he joined them intimately.

He smiled. A bit of an oddball she was, an obvious loner who mixed up Emerson and Thoreau and named her cat Doris Juan; she also possessed an impressive intellect. Yet her quirkiness and braininess only served to intrigue him more. No mental midget himself, Charles had never found smart women intimidating—indeed, he liked the challenge of them.

But what attracted him most to Teresa Phelps was her vulnerability, her almost maidenly modesty, the fact that she seemed to have no idea how truly lovely she was. And she was charming indeed with her thick, chestnut-brown hair, wide face with large, vibrant hazel eyes and full, lush mouth. And such a body—tall, shapely, with nicely rounded breasts, slim waist, and curvaceous hips. He went weak at the very thought of devouring her fully.

With a massive effort, he hauled his wayward senses to attention. Such lapses he could ill afford. He was a man with a mission, and he mustn't forget it. His goal was to get Teresa Phelps to trust him, and most critically, to gain from her the information he needed. After that, their association would almost certainly end, and he couldn't afford to forget this.

Besides, when she learned the truth about what he *really* wanted, she would surely end up hating him. In the meantime, he mustn't allow foolish, romantic notions to get in the way of his goals.

All at once, his thoughts scattered at the bleep of his cell phone. Fearing Teresa might hear, he rushed across the room to the chair where he'd laid his jacket, pulled the slim receiver from the pocket and pressed the receive button.

"Hello?" he asked in a low, tense voice.

The party on the other end was most unhappy, blessing Charles out for long moments. He listened, tried several times to interrupt to defend himself, but mostly ground his jaw.

At last, he got a chance to speak. "Look, why are you wringing me out on this? Damn it, you promised me a free hand with the girl. I'll find the stuff, don't worry. Now why don't you just get off my back and let me do my bloody job?"

Hearing the other party snap a blistering curse, Charles hung up in disgust. Expression grim, he replaced the receiver in his jacket pocket. Then he glanced around the room, and spotted Teresa's bag. He strode over, grabbed it, sat down on the couch, and methodically began sifting through its contents . . .

* * *

Despite the lulling effect of the alcohol, Teresa found sleep impossible. Both her brain and her body were seething. In her bed, she twisted about fitfully, while Doris Juan purred peacefully at her feet.

She couldn't get Charles Everett's stunning kiss out of her mind. Nor could her body forget the hot passion he'd stirred. Even now, a dull throbbing between her thighs reminded her that she had a need only he could assuage.

How long had it been since a man had affected her so? Had any man ever? And why *this* man? What's more, why was this debonair and gorgeous-as-James-Bond Englishman pursuing a mousy pitifully poor doctoral candidate—unless there was something very tangible he wanted from her, something that was definitely *not* her body?

Not to mention, she was allowing this modern-day rogue to sleep under her roof! He would be lying mere feet away from a woman whose body craved him. She needed her head examined.

And it wasn't just the kiss that tortured her now. She was also deeply troubled regarding their conversation about Frank. Had Charles been right? Was it possible Frank had been murdered? The very thought made her throat ache and sent a chill down her spine.

What if someone had wanted something from Frank and had killed him for it? What if that same someone was after her now for the same thing?

But what could they want? What on earth could be so valuable as to cause someone to shoot at her, ransack her home, and possibly even kill Frank?

And was finding this same elusive something the *real* reason Charles Everett had barged into her life today?

Chapter Seven

Manolo Juarez lounged on Rudy Zaragoza's gold velour couch, watching his woman, Josie, teach her six-year-old twin nieces to dance the macarena. A handsome, leanly muscular youth whose thick beard, long hair, and deep-set dark brown eyes only added to his fierce appeal, Manolo wore dusty boots, tight faded jeans, and a black T-shirt. A tattoo picturing a serpent was emblazoned on his right forearm.

The females were gathered across the small living room, scooting around next to the stereo. Manolo could barely contain his desire as twenty-year-old Josie's sleek body undulated to the Latin beat, and her arms and legs moved in perfect rhythm. She was dressed in cutoffs and a tank top, a gold necklace gleaming at her throat, gold loop earrings sparkling in her ears. She looked like a princess—auburn-tinged hair curling to her shoulders, makeup perfectly applied, lips full, red, and irresistible—especially when she smiled at him and dimpled those pretty cheeks, as she did now.

Caramba! He was suddenly glad his cap was sitting in his lap, covering a very strategic spot. Otherwise he would shock young Silvia and Sophia. The twins looked cute, too, as they glided about and moved their little brown arms. The girls wore adorable matching outfits Aunt Josie had bought them—pink tennies, lacy white socks, pink shorts, and pink and white checked tops. Josie had even cut and styled their hair—both wore thick bobs framing their sweet round faces. Damn, Josie was good with kids.

Ever since Manolo had first met her at the county hospital where she worked as an LVN, he'd been sniffing after her like a lovesick puppy. He was even glad he'd gotten in the fistfight with his parole officer that had sent him to the hospital in the first place, even though the fight had also cost him another ninety days in county lockup. Hell, if he'd never assaulted that *menudo*-head, he never would have met Josie.

It was cool being around her family too, in their modest but attractive home on Houston's east side, although all the candles and other religious artifacts placed about—including the portrait of *el Cristo*, across the room, staring him solemnly in the eye—did make him squirm a bit. But the real thorn in his side was Josie's brother, Rudy, who was always on his case, always trying to convince Josie he was a bum.

Even that Manolo didn't mind so much, as long as he could be here with her. He'd had some of the best times of his young life sitting right here on this couch. He was unaccustomed to having a respectable girlfriend, or being around a real, stable family. Manolo's father had been a construction worker who had been killed in an accident when he was five. Three years later, his widowed mother had married another man and returned to Mexico, leaving Manolo in Texas with a divorced aunt who cared a lot more about picking up men in honky-tonks than she did about raising him. By the time he was fourteen, he'd become a runaway, a toughened street kid, and he'd been involved with gangs and in trouble with the law ever since.

Until he'd met Josie, who'd lured him toward a better life.

He'd given up his gang-banging for her, but he remained focused on finding the easiest way to make a buck, mostly through burglarizing some of the poshest digs in Houston. Hell, most of those gringos were insured anyway, and there were few job opportunities available for a nineteen-year-old Hispanic parolee. Besides, he'd come a long way—he owned a car, had a cool apartment, and he wanted Josie to share his life big time. She was so different from the good-time girls he'd dated before. She made him respect her, and this made him want to win her respect, too—much as he did try to charm his way into her bed every chance he got. Heck, what else could she expect from a bad boy like him, he thought, with a perverse chuckle.

But he still couldn't get to first base with her, much less hit a home run. They'd dated for six months now, going dancing and to movies, even to her family's frequent Sunday evening fiestas. But the woman was a tease, warm as toast on the outside but cold as ice inside, and it drove Manolo crazy, making him burn to have her. . . .

The females finished their dance, Silvia and Sophia laughing and clapping their hands, Josie playfully tousling her nieces' hair. When Manolo cheered and stomped his feet, the girls giggled and bowed, and Josie smiled at him again. Oh, *Dios*, that smile! His heart melted.

"*Niñas*, go get some ice cream from the kitchen, and bring bowls for me and Manolo, too," Josie directed firmly. "And I want you both in bed before your grandmother returns from Mass."

With a chorus of "Yes, Aunt Josie!" the girls danced off to the kitchen. Josie crossed the room and sat down beside Manolo, offering him another of her coy smiles. Damn, was the woman trying to kill him? The smell of her perfume made him *loco*, made him want to grab her and jump her bones. But he knew better—Josie was a lady, and if he laid a finger on her, she'd box his ears but good. And her older brother Rudy—hell, Rudy would beat the crap out of him.

"So you liked watching us dance, eh, Manolo?" Josie teased.

He wrapped an arm around her shoulders and offered her a sexy grin. "You drive me crazy, woman. Come here and give me a kiss."

She allowed him a brief kiss, and the sweet taste of her lips emboldened him, setting his senses on fire. But she pushed him away when he tried to shove his tongue in her mouth.

"Hey, no funny business, Manolo," she scolded with a pout of her red lips. "My nieces are in the house."

"Ah, *corazón*, just one more little kiss," he coaxed.

"No. Not until the girls are in bed."

A grudging smile pulled at Manolo's mouth. "You know, you're good with those girls. And you spend so much time with them—cooking them dinner, taking them to the library, teaching them to dance."

"Well, I try to help out where I can. I can't just leave my nieces alone here. My sister-in-law works nights typing at the law firm, and Mama never misses Mass. Plus, their father comes home late from work so much of the time."

Manolo scowled. "I'm glad Rudy is late. He hates my guts."

She narrowed her gaze in reproach. "My brother doesn't hate you, Manolo, he just wants you to shape up."

"Yeah, sure." Turning mischievous, Manolo nudged her bare arm. "Hey, woman, wanna make some hay before he gets home?"

"Manolo!" she gasped. "How many times do I have to say it? *Not while my nieces are in the house!*"

He groaned, waving a hand. "Ah, woman, you always have some excuse. Six months we've been dating. It's not like I'm trying to jump you on our first date. Ain't it about time you give me some?"

With an outraged cry, Josie grabbed a throw pillow and began pummeling him with it. "I'll give you some the day we get married, you lowlife turkey!"

Laughing, Manolo was fending off her blows. "Hey, quit it!" Grabbing her wrists, he grinned, baring white teeth. "Yeah, let's get married. Then we can make some twins of our own, eh?"

But Josie broke free and stubbornly set her arms over her breasts. "Not until you get a job, Manolo. Okay, you're a cool-looking dude and we've had some good times together. You're fun to go dancing with, and I like riding in your car. But this ain't going anywhere till you take some responsibility for your life."

Manolo ground his teeth. "Josie, please—"

"And quit hanging out with those creeps you call friends!"

"Hector and Freddie ain't creeps," Manolo protested. "They quit *las Serpientes* for me."

She made a sound of disbelief. "They're a couple of lowlife, lying ex-cons."

Manolo was about to object further when the front door banged open and Josie's older brother, Rudy Zaragoza, strode inside. A tall, commanding man of thirty wearing a dark blue policeman's uniform, Rudy frowned as he opened a closet door, hung his cap on a peg, and secured his sidearm and gunbelt inside a small safe. Then he turned and took in the scene—the mussed throw pillows, and especially Josie and Manolo sitting so close together on the couch, their faces flushed. Rudy's frown deepened into a suspicious glower.

At once, Manolo gulped and sat up straight. "Hi, Rudy."

"Hi, Rudy," Josie seconded brightly.

"Hey, what's been going on here?" Rudy demanded. "You been harassing my sister, Manolo?"

His temper piqued, Manolo bolted up. "Harassing? What kind of women's lib crap is that? *Harassing*. Hell no, I ain't been harassing her. This woman just attacked me with a throw pillow."

Rudy appeared unconvinced. "If she did, I'm sure you had it coming." He jerked his gaze toward Josie. "This bum been hitting on you again?"

Josie laughed and stood. "No, Rudy, we were just cutting up with the girls, dancing the macarena, that's all."

"Uh-huh." Rudy's sullen look attested that he believed otherwise.

Luckily, further exchange was postponed as the girls danced back inside the room, each twin carrying two bowls of cookies and cream ice cream. "Papa!" they cried simultaneously, rushing across the room to embrace their father, with dripping bowls still clutched in their small hands.

Rudy was laughing, grabbing and juggling bowls of ice cream and setting them down on an end table. "Hey, watch it, *niñas*, you're gonna get gooey stuff all over me and ruin my uniform."

"We'll give you gooey kisses too, Papa," declared Silvia, grinning at her father even as ice cream dribbled down her chin.

"Yeah, me too," cried Sophia, eagerly hugging her dad.

Rudy chuckled. "Go on, girls, eat your own ice cream in the kitchen, then get ready for bed. I'll come tuck you in."

"Yes, Papa," they said in unison, grabbing their bowls and running off to the kitchen.

Rudy picked up the two remaining bowls from the end table and handed one to Josie. "Here, they brought us cookies and cream."

Josie flashed Rudy a reproachful look. "Rudy, the girls brought the other bowl for Manolo."

Rudy gave a shrug, sat down on the couch, propped his feet on the coffee table and began eating the ice cream. "So? He don't live here, or pay the bills. Let him buy his own damn ice cream. Heck, he's eating us out of house and home already."

Josie offered Manolo her bowl. "Here, you can have mine."

Manolo leered and wiggled his eyebrows. "Hey, let's share it, *corazón*. That's always more fun."

But even as Josie was about to feed Manolo a spoonful of ice cream, Rudy pounded his fist on the couch, causing the two to spring apart. "Not on your life! Josie, come park your butt on this couch, away from that snake."

Manolo tossed Rudy a belligerent look.

"Manolo's not a snake," Josie protested.

"Oh, no? Look at his damn forearm. Ain't that his gang logo?"

Although Josie glared at her brother, she handed Manolo the bowl and dutifully sat down beside Rudy.

Manolo sauntered off to park himself in an easy chair, and attempted a pleasant tone with Rudy. "So, man, how's work?"

Rudy scowled. "The pay is crap, and the hours are killing me. But that's what it's like when you have a job like mine, head of the police force at a private university. It's not like I'm on parole and can sit around all day shooting the shit."

"Yeah, I'm having loads of fun," Manolo snarled back.

"Rudy, you're not being not fair," Josie argued. "Manolo is trying. You need to lighten up on him. After all, he got his GED during his last stint at Huntsville."

"Yeah, man, cut me some slack," Manolo agreed, flashing Josie a grateful smile.

"Oh, yeah, sis, you got yourself a real winner there," Rudy mocked. "Getting his GED in prison. Ain't that great? When are you going to grow up, quit getting cheap thrills out of dating a bad boy creep, and see him for the loser he really is? Not to mention those gang-bangers he hangs out with."

Manolo ground his teeth. "Hey, man, you know I quit *las Serpientes* when I started dating Jósie. And so did Freddie and Hector."

"Yeah, give the man a medal, he's really coming up in the world," Rudy sneered. "What are those two morons doing tonight anyway? Hitting the local Stop and Rob? Or just some good old-fashioned breaking and entering?"

Manolo scowled.

Rudy wagged his spoon at Josie. "What do you want with a bum like him? Maria said she'd introduce you to one of the associates down at the law firm. A guy with a real future."

Josie smiled at Manolo. "I don't know ... Manolo may be a bad boy like you said, but in his own way, he's kind of sweet."

"Yeah," Manolo agreed, tossing Rudy a superior look.

An uneasy silence fell, with Rudy and Manolo glowering at each other like two mongrel dogs primed for a territorial battle. Rudy blinked first in the game of chicken, taking a bite of ice cream, then glancing across the room. All at once, he banged his bowl down on the coffee table. "Shit! Who the hell has been in my gun cabinet?"

"What gun cabinet?" Manolo echoed uneasily.

Rudy sprang up and vaulted over to the glass-fronted cabinet, while Manolo watched, suddenly white-faced.

Josie eyed him confusedly. "Manolo?"

Flashing her a wan smile, he sprang to his feet and ambled over to Rudy. "Something wrong, man?"

An outraged expression gripping his features,

Rudy was fishing around on top of the cabinet. Snatching down a key, he bellowed, "Girls!"

"Rudy, what's wrong?" asked Josie, who had come up to join them.

The girls dashed back into the room, faces fraught with anxiety. "Yes, Papa?" Silvia asked.

"Have you girls been playing in Papa's gun cabinet?" he demanded, shaking the key at them.

"No, sir," Silvia answered, swallowing hard.

Rudy frowned menacingly at his daughters. "Tell the truth, now. You know I said I'd wear you out if you ever came near my gun cabinet."

"No, sir, we don't even know where you hide the key," Sophia assured him, her young face pale.

"Are you sure?" Rudy pursued sternly. "Cross your hearts and hope to die if you're lying?"

Both girls solemnly crossed their hearts. "Okay, Papa?" Silvia fretted, almost in tears. "We know we aren't allowed to touch your guns, okay? We really didn't do it."

Rudy relented then, tweaking each girl on the chin. "Hey, I'm sorry, *niñas*. It just scares Papa to death to think you might hurt yourselves."

"We know the rules, Papa," Sophia assured him solemnly. "We would never touch your guns."

Appearing quite relieved, Rudy quickly hugged both girls. "I know, *corazónes*. You two go get ready for bed, and I'll come read you a story."

"Yes, Papa!" Wearing matching relieved expressions, the girls scampered away.

Josie confronted Rudy with hands on her hips. "Rudy Zaragoza, you jerk! Where do you get off going ballistic with the *niñas*?"

"They're my daughters," Rudy growled.

"They're my nieces! And you just acted like a prick with them." Josie gestured at the cabinet. "Besides, I don't see no guns missing."

"Oh, yeah?" Rudy countered. He unlocked the cabinet and slid back the glass. "Well, someone's been in here, all right. My Winchester's been moved to where my Browning was, and my Baretta . . ." With a suspicious glower, he picked up the shotgun, ran his fingers over the barrel, then sniffed it. "Shit, it's filthy! Someone's been firing this." He whirled. "Manolo!"

Manolo held up both hands and began backing away. "Hey, man, don't look at me!"

"Who else am I gonna look at?" Rudy growled, pursuing him with the shotgun still in hand. "My daughters didn't do it, and that leaves Josie, Mama, and my wife. I'd suspect the Pope before I suspected one of them. What the hell were you doing screwing around with my gun collection, you shithead?"

Glancing uneasily at the gun, Manolo pleaded, "Hey, man, would you mind putting that away?"

Instead Rudy waved the gun in Manolo's face. "Come clean, damn it!"

"All right. Cool it, will you, man?" Realizing he was caught, Manolo shifted from foot to foot. "Hell, Rudy, I only borrowed your shotguns."

"Borrowed!" Rudy bellowed, eyes gleaming with anger. "You mean stole, you piece of trash!"

"Man, we didn't mean no harm," Manolo protested almost desperately. "We—Freddie and Hector and me, we were just shooting at rats at the dump, you know, getting some kicks."

"I'd like to kick your butt back to old Mexico," Rudy ranted. "Damn it, you're a scumbag ex-con who's not even allowed to touch weapons. I should notify your parole officer."

"Hey, man, settle down, will you?" Manolo pleaded.

"Yeah, Rudy, you don't have to ream Manolo out so," scolded Josie. "You turn him in and I'm gonna quit speaking to you."

Rudy swung furiously on his sister. "What are you gonna do, Josie, team up with him now, like Bonnie and Clyde?"

Josie tossed her curls. "Oh, shove it, Rudy."

Brother and sister were looking murder at each other when the front door creaked open and an older, plump Hispanic woman lumbered in, carrying a prayer book and a rosary. "Oh, sweet *cielo*, my aching feet," she muttered. Then she spotted the others and did a double take. "Rudy, what are you doing with those guns out? Are my granddaughters in bed yet?"

"Almost, Mama," Rudy answered, hastily replacing the shotgun in the cabinet, then shutting and locking the glass doors. "I was just giving Manolo the business because he's been stealing my shotguns."

"Damn it, I only borrowed them!" Manolo repeated, waving his arms.

At Manolo's harsh words, Mama gasped and crossed herself. "Josie, why do you put up with this rat? His mouth is filthy!"

"Give me a break, Mama," Josie pleaded. "I don't need you on Manolo's case, too. Rudy has already given us enough hell. Why doesn't he ever try to help Manolo instead?"

"Hey, don't you go giving me that dirty look," Rudy scolded. "You're forgetting I got this bum a job."

Manolo hooted a laugh. "Yeah, some real glamorous job you got me, Zaragoza. Like showing up on the beach with a shovel."

"It was for one of our best professors at the school," Rudy protested.

Manolo advanced on him. "Oh yeah? Well, he ain't exactly the best now that the dude is dead."

At this pronouncement, Mama went wild-eyed and raised a hand to her heart.

A look of cynical suspicion washed over Rudy's face. "Yeah, I been meaning to ask you about that, Juarez. You know anything about the professor's death?"

"Me?" Manolo cried. "Why are you looking at me? I went to the job, damn it, and so did Hector and Freddie. We even bought the frigging shovels with our own dough. But the dude never showed up, and then he kicked the bucket."

"Yeah, a likely story," Rudy scoffed.

"Jesus, give me a break!" Manolo ranted.

At this bit of blasphemy, Mama screamed, crossed herself, and even began to wobble on her feet. Rudy rushed over to grab his mother's arm and help her seat herself, while she fanned her florid face. Hurling Manolo a blistering look, she pleaded to her son, "Rudy, do something about him, *por favor*! I can't stand it anymore. Now he's taking the name of *el Señor* in vain."

"Yeah!" Rudy agreed, hurling an ugly look at Manolo. "Get the hell out of here, you gang-banger creep."

"Rudy!" protested Josie.

Manolo swung on Rudy. "Yeah, Zaragoza, why don't you just can the crap? Like you ain't been shitting this and damning that all night long."

"Rudy!" protested Mama, eyes rolling back in her head as she clutched her prayer book. "He's doing it again!"

"That does it." Rudy crossed over and seized Manolo by the collar, hauled him out the front door, and hurled him down the steps. "Good riddance."

Manolo howled in pain as his body went spilling down the steps. He bumped and bounced over the sharp edges, until he landed in an agonized heap on the sidewalk below. Struggling to his feet with a massive groan, he could hear dogs barking, and Rudy and Josie screaming at each other inside.

He waved a fist toward the house. "Shit, man, cut me some frigging slack," he grumbled, limping off into the night, with sweet Josie and the macarena now but a painful, distant memory. . . .

Chapter Eight

Teresa jumped awake to the sound of Doris Juan hissing. She blinked at a room filled with sunshine and spotted Doris at the foot of her bed, growling and spitting at a figure hovering over her.

A figure?

Teresa jerked her gaze upward, only to go wide-eyed at a grisly vision of the Pig from Hell staring her in the eye—an evilly leering swine with horn-shaped ears, a disgusting pink snout, and huge yellow tusks protruding from its mouth. Then she realized it wasn't really a pig at all, but someone impersonating one in a hooded mask. This realization was little comfort, since the person wearing the mask was also pointing a revolver at her!

In the excruciating silence, Doris Juan hissed

for a final time, then bolted away with an irate howl. But Teresa was far too terrified to take much note of her cat, much less scream or move. Heart pounding, she regarded the intruder in appalled disbelief. She did manage to note that the trespasser was of average build and wore jeans, a dark green windbreaker, and a black T-shirt. There seemed something vaguely familiar about him.

But who was he? And what did he want from her?

"Wh-what do you want?" she managed in a squeaky, terrified whisper.

"Forty-eight hours, lady," the pig growled back in low, menacing tones, voice muffled by his mask.

"Forty-eight hours?" Teresa repeated shrilly.

"You've got forty-eight hours to turn over the papers, or I'll blow your brains out."

"Papers? What papers?" Teresa demanded.

"Don't lie to me, bitch!" he snarled, waving his gun in her face. "You know damn well what I'm talking about. The papers your beloved brother Frankie gave you for safekeeping." He pressed the barrel of the revolver against her temple, and, even as she gasped, cocked it. "Forty-eight hours. I'll be back."

He turned and ambled off toward her window, then awkwardly climbed out.

For another excruciating moment Teresa remained too frightened to react. Then a new rush of adrenaline surged in, she caught a sharp breath, and screamed her head off.

Seconds later, Charles bolted inside the room wearing only red and green plaid boxer shorts and carrying his gun, with Doris Juan tucked under his arm. "Teresa, what's wrong?"

Teresa pulled the sheet up to her neck as a half-hysterical giggle escaped her. Charles was all but naked, and with mussed hair and sleep-befuddled expression, he looked ludicrous with the gun in his hand and the cat under his arm. Doris Juan appeared more absurd still; the cat's fur stood on end, and her face was screwed up in a definitely pouty snarl.

But it was Charles himself who affected Teresa the most. Despite her state of fright, her womanly senses couldn't help noting that he had a magnificent body, lean-muscled, tan and sleek, his legs and chest covered with a sexy dusting of dark brown hair. And he was in her *bedroom*, standing there all but naked, while she lay in bed with little on herself.

"Ch-Charles, you're indecent," she stammered at last. "And what are you doing with my cat?"

Frowning, he set the animal down; Doris Juan hissed and scampered under the bed. "A moment ago she came tearing into the living room and rudely awakened me from a deep slumber by landing on my belly. Not long after that, we both heard you screaming your head off, so I raced in to rescue you, insisting Doris come along, ungrateful hoyden though she is." He drew closer and regarded her anxiously. "What's wrong? Was it a nightmare? Or did she see a mouse?"

As Charles drew even nearer, Teresa's gaze remained brazenly riveted to him. "Well, at least we've solved the 'briefs or boxers' mystery," she told him with a half-hysterical chortle. "But really, Charles, plaid? Is this the latest in secret agent attire?"

A half smile pulled at his mouth. "No one can accuse me of being without verve, my dear. Now, Tess, kindly spare me more of your preposterous humor and tell me what the bloody hell has frightened you so!"

She shuddered. "Very well. I just had a visit from . . . the Pig from Hell."

He shouted a laugh. "You're joking. No, love, it was the *Cat* from Hell."

"I tell you it was a pig and he was carrying a gun!" she declared.

Charles fought a grin. "I didn't know pigs carried guns."

"Now *you* stop joking!" she demanded. "It really happened, Charles. A man just intruded in my bedroom—"

Charles blinked. "You're serious."

"Hell, yes, I'm serious! And he was carrying a very terrifying, real gun. It was huge, a damn hand-cannon."

"You mean a .45?"

"Whatever! Damn it, he cocked it against my temple and made some threats; then he left."

"My God." Now the color drained from Charles's face as he anxiously drew close to Teresa, touching her shoulder through the sheet. "Are you all right, love?"

Warmed by his touch, giddy at the look of grave concern on his face, she managed a tremulous nod. "Still in one piece as you can see."

"Did you recognize the man?"

"Charles, he wore a hooded mask and was covered from head to foot."

"Could he have been one of the thugs who trashed your place yesterday?"

"Yes. Quite possibly."

Charles peered about anxiously. "Do you suppose he's still around?"

She waved a hand toward the window. "He went thataway, partner."

Charles dashed over to the window and peered out. Teresa couldn't help herself—she watched the fabric of his shorts pull at his hard male buttocks and all but groaned aloud. Damn, but the man had a cute rear end! Marvelous, in fact.

Charles was muttering as he leaned over. "Well, I can see how he got in—he pulled off your screen." Rattling the screen back into place, he shut and locked the window, then straightened and turned back to her. "But I don't see anyone outside."

"Thank heaven."

"Did the man say why he was here?"

"Yes, he made some demands while pointing his gun at my head."

Abruptly Charles crossed over to the bed and sat down beside her, caressing her cheek with his fingertips and eyeing her compassionately. "You poor dear. You must have been scared senseless."

Thoroughly rattled by his nearness, she panted back, "I was."

"Come here," he murmured tenderly, and pulled her into his arms.

"Charles!"

Teresa felt awash in wicked sensation as Charles enfolded her in his embrace, his actions causing the sheet to drop and reveal her skimpy, sleeveless satin nightshirt. She found herself cuddled against his warm, hard, naked chest, her face pressed to the sexy roughness of his unshaven cheek. She knew she should heartily protest his scandalous proximity, should shove him away, but it just felt too good to be comforted this way. The scent and heat of him were mesmerizing, and she could feel her nipples tightening against the warm pressure of his chest. She sorely needed his solace—and although she hated to admit it in that moment, she sorely needed *him*.

Then Doris Juan jumped onto the bed and, evidently sensing that this was a bonding moment, began to purr loudly and rub her flanks shamelessly against their bodies. Count on a cat to throw all pretense and discretion to the wind, Teresa thought, face burning.

"There, there," Charles murmured, kissing her hair.

Teresa was fighting for control, the tenderness of his gesture almost towing her under. "Er—Charles," she managed. "Has it occurred to you that neither of us has much on?"

"Oh, yes, darling," he replied with a devastating huskiness. "And frankly, I'm loving it."

He tilted her face up to his and tenderly kissed her, even as Doris Juan's purring reached an unabashed crescendo. Teresa forgot everything then—the danger, her fright, everything but Charles. She curled her arms around his neck and nuzzled herself closer. He moaned and crushed her mouth more passionately, his hand sliding down the front of her nightshirt, wickedly teasing her breast, her belly, then slipping lower to land firmly on top of her bare thigh.

That bit of brazen intimacy yanked Teresa back to reality and she jerked away, breathless, to see him grinning at her, the rascal.

"You're skittish, aren't you?" he teased.

"I have reason."

"And I have ways of soothing skittish ladies," he drawled back, confidently pulling her close again and drawing his mouth over her warm cheek in a slow, teasing caress.

Teresa melted, the brush of his lips and heat of his breath causing her to shiver deliciously. How

did he know he had this power over her? Easy—
her body told him!

"There, love, you're safe now," he soothed.
"Even the cat approves of me—just listen to her."

Indeed, Doris was now going into ecstasies,
strutting about and wantonly rubbing against
them, purring like an ever-revving sports car.
"That's because she has the morals of an alley
cat."

He chuckled, smoothing down her rumpled
hair. "Lord, you look so sexy. I love that mussed,
just-awakened look you ladies have in the mornings."

She pulled back and pinned him with a stern
look. "Ladies? Have you done a survey regarding
this?"

His fingers clutched her arm, tugging her
toward him. "Come closer and I'll do a thorough
investigation."

She managed to resist. "Charles, please. Are
you forgetting what just happened?"

He relented with a sigh. "Very well, love. Tell
me what the bad man said."

Still painfully conscious of his sexy nearness,
she cleared her throat. "Now that the immediate
danger is over, couldn't we get dressed before we
discuss the particulars?"

"Oh, of course. I'll leave you to dress then and
I'll—"

"You'll dress, too?"

"Righto. And scare us up some tea—or, er,
some coffee."

"Tea would be fine. You do that, then."

"I will."

But as he rose, Teresa couldn't help convuls-
ing with laughter as she eyed the front of his

shorts. "What's that, Charles, a salute to king and country?"

He turned, his expression unrepentant, even delighted. "Why, you wicked girl."

"Well?"

He winked. "It's a salute to *you*, love. Tell me, would you like to receive the full tribute?"

"Get out of here!"

The stud merely blew her a kiss and left.

Teresa sank back into the covers with a groan. Doris Juan crawled up to purr and lick her face. "Some watchcat you are," Teresa scolded, petting the cat. "In fact, we're both a couple of shameless hoydens, aren't we?"

Judging from Doris Juan's throaty sounds, she agreed.

Teresa smiled. She couldn't believe how calm she was. By all rights she should be terrified, unhinged. A dangerous stranger had just intruded in her bedroom and threatened to kill her.

But all she could really think about was the *other* man who had just charged into her bedroom. She savored the magic of Charles's kiss, the perverse thrill she'd gotten from knowing she'd turned *him* on. Never had any tribute seemed so sweet. She wasn't accustomed to stirring this level of desire in the male of the species. And it daunted her to know she was so intensely attracted to Charles, a man she had no business getting involved with, much less trusting.

"Better now?" Charles asked.

"Yes, thank you."

"So what did this masked stranger want?"

Twenty minutes later, Teresa and Charles were discussing the terrifying incident in her kitchen, over hot tea and banana nut muffins. Charles had put on a green polo shirt and khaki trousers. Teresa wore a blue short-sleeved-shirt, white slacks, and sandals.

Glad they were back to business following their scandalous encounter in her bedroom, she frowned over his question. "It was really bizarre. He said he wanted some papers that I was safe-keeping for my brother, Frank."

"What might those be?"

She gave a shrug. "I have no idea. The only thing like 'papers' of Frank's I know of is a manu-script from his safety deposit box that his lawyer gave me yesterday."

"May I see it?"

"Sure. After breakfast. It's in my bag."

Without a word, Charles got up, went into the living room, and came back, handing her the large bag. "You mean this?"

Teresa felt taken aback. "Aren't you accommo-dating?"

"If I'm going to help you, Teresa, I'll need to see the manuscript."

Feeling needles of suspicion, she took the bag. "Who says I want you helping me?"

Leveling a chiding glance at her, he sat back down. "Tess, really, don't be such a stick-in-the-mud. You weren't complaining when I charged in to rescue you twenty minutes ago."

She laughed. "Yes, Sir Lancelot wins the day in his designer shorts."

"The manuscript, please?" he asked with a long-suffering air.

She groaned and opened her bag, then scowled, scanning the interior, which appeared far too tidy. Her suspicious gaze shot up to his. "Hey, have you been looking through my bag?"

He paled. "What do you mean? I only picked it up two seconds ago."

She regarded him skeptically. "Yes, and it was in the living room with you all night long. Now I note that some mysterious someone has snapped my key chain back into place."

He absently stirred his tea. "You mean it wasn't in place before?"

"I'm never that neat."

His expression grew sheepish. "Very well, I'll confess. When I moved your bag off the sofa last night, the key chain and several other items fell out. So of course I snapped it back into place and restored order."

"Aren't you helpful?" she mocked.

"But it's true."

"Yes, being the kind, fastidious person you are."

Before she could proceed further, he held up a hand. "I swear I didn't look at anything else."

"Sure you didn't."

Features tightening, he sipped his tea. "The manuscript, please?"

Tossing him a grudging look, she extracted the manuscript, which was in a legal-sized file envelope, and handed it to him. Observing him opening the file and flipping through the pages with a scowl, she said, "I don't know why you're making such a big deal of this. I already examined it at the lawyer's office. It's only a photocopy of a journal purportedly written by Jean Lafitte."

He glanced up sharply. "That isn't noteworthy?"

"I do remember Frank mentioning recently that he was translating the journal. As you'll see from the stamp, the original is on file at the Sam Houston Regional Library and Research Center in Liberty, Texas."

"Hmm," he murmured, flipping pages. "So it appears."

"So the masked intruder couldn't have been after that."

"Why not?"

"Haven't we taken our ginkgo biloba today?" she taunted. "Why should the scoundrel go to all the trouble of trying to get the photocopy from me, when he can go to the library and see the original for himself?"

Charles sighed. "True. Did your brother ever tell you why he was translating the journal? Did the library ask him to?"

"No. I remember Frank mentioning that other English translations are already available. But, being a French professor, I'm sure Frank would have wanted to do his own. Lafitte was naturally of interest, since he had his headquarters here on Galveston Island during the early part of the nineteenth century."

Charles scowled. "And he left much treasure behind if my memory of U.S. history serves correctly."

"True. That's what the scholars have always thought, at any rate."

Charles's gaze narrowed. "Do you suppose Frank could have been translating the journal in order to find Lafitte's treasure?"

Teresa laughed. "No, Charles. Like I said, other translations have been available for some time." She tapped the photocopy with her fingertip. "I'm sure if there were any valid treasure instructions in the Lafitte journal, they would have been exploited long before now."

"I suppose you're right." Charles replaced the pages in the folder and set it aside. "And you have no idea about any other papers this intruder might have wanted?"

"No. None at all."

He appeared perplexed. "We must report this morning's incident to the authorities, of course. And I think we should also should go to Liberty and see what we can find out about the journal. However, first I'd suggest we go to Houston and talk with some of your brother's friends and colleagues. It could be that the papers the masked man wants are at your brother's home there."

At once Teresa felt taken aback and suspicious. "How do you know Frank had a home in Houston?"

Charles coughed. "Well, you told me he taught there, so naturally I assumed he lived there, as well."

"Uh-huh."

He shot her a superior look. "He did have a home there, didn't he? Or did he just sleep under a bridge?"

She regarded him with cool distrust.

"Teresa, we must investigate. Doesn't the encounter this morning confirm what I've already suspected, that perhaps your brother's death wasn't an accident?"

Teresa shoved her breakfast plate away. "Why are you all of a sudden an expert on my brother?"

"I'm not. I'm just trying to find an answer to our current predicament."

She regarded him angrily. "*My* predicament, Charles."

He regarded her unflinchingly. "*Ours*, love."

All at once, staring Charles in the eye, Teresa got a really creepy feeling. He did seem utterly determined to hang around, to be involved in all of her current problems, and yet his answers to her questions just weren't making sense. Why was he suddenly so curious about her life and her brother's death? Why was he so all-fired eager to help her, when he had also claimed that his sole motivation in being here was to keep her away from his father? What did she really know about Charles Everett, other than the fact that he could be dangerous, perhaps even a pathological liar? And despite his protestations to the contrary, she strongly suspected he had gone through her bag last night.

So why in hell was she putting her trust in him? He kept hinting that Frank might have been murdered. Was that because he *personally* knew the truth? Had he—horror of horrors—killed Frank himself? The possibility that she might be sheltering her brother's murderer under her roof, that she might have willingly succumbed to his kisses and allowed him to comfort her, made her half-nauseated.

It also dawned on her that Charles had been out of the room when the masked man had appeared, and there had been something hauntingly familiar about that man. . . . Could it have been Charles who came to her room in the first place? She fought a violent shudder. She was playing a cat and mouse game with a man who might well be dangerous, or even psychotic. The thought that Charles might have brazenly staged the encounter in her bedroom, then conveniently appeared all but naked to comfort her, made her blood run cold!

Good Lord, could Charles have wanted the manuscript all along?

But why? And if he did want it, why hadn't he

simply stolen it from her last night, or gone to Liberty himself to see the original?

Nothing was making sense! But one thing was certain: She needed to get away from this man, at least until she could figure out who he really was, what he wanted, and whether she could trust him. . . .

Even as Teresa's mind was churning, Charles was eyeing her with a mixture of perplexity and concern. "Teresa? Don't you think we should go to Houston?"

She hesitated for another long moment. Then it occurred to her that it might be easier to shake off Charles out in the open, especially if she retrieved her car. "Well, yes, we do need to go get my car."

"Righto." He grinned. "Excuse me a moment."

"Sure." Bemused, she watched him leave the room.

Within seconds, he strode back inside and handed her a cell phone. "Before we leave, don't you want to call the sheriff to report the intruder, as well as your landlord, to begin arranging for repairs to your windows and phone line?"

Teresa eyed the cell phone in dawning realization, then turned on Charles accusingly. "A cell phone! Now I remember. Yesterday while you were chasing me on the access road, you were talking on a cell phone!"

"Right. So?"

"So why didn't you call the cops as soon as you saw the damage here yesterday—if not then, then right after the gunfight?"

He avoided her eye. "Well, I'm not sure. Didn't Billy Bob volunteer to notify the authorities on our behalf?"

"He did. But you never even offered me the cell phone, and that's because you were afraid I'd turn you in, right?"

He flashed her a lame smile. "Can you blame me?"

"No," she responded coldly. "Not at all."

His features tightened. "Teresa, you've made your point. Do you want to use my cell phone or not?"

She snatched it from his fingers.

After Teresa grabbed his cell phone, Charles stood by grimly as she called the deputy sheriff, then her landlord. Their last conversation had not gone well. He'd allowed his guard to slip, acting a bit too curious, too eager to help her.

Now she distrusted him more than ever, and he couldn't really blame her for being leery. But he still had to stick around until he learned what she knew.

The incident earlier this morning troubled him greatly. Who was the mysterious trespasser, in a pig mask, no less, who had accosted Teresa at gunpoint in her bedroom? Was it one of the Hispanic thugs? Or someone else? Possibly even one of his own associates?

Whoever it was, Charles itched to murder the creep, which demonstrated how close he was coming to losing all sense of detachment, even control.

He was getting too personally involved with Teresa Phelps. The fact that her life had been threatened had jolted him, and comforting her in her bed had set his gut churning with desire. Worse yet, her confusion and vulnerability had again roused tender, protective feelings within him, feelings he could ill afford to have under the present circumstances.

The woman was getting under his skin in too many ways. He enjoyed her company, found her intellectually stimulating as well as physically attractive. Hell, he even liked her terror of a cat. This intense pull of romance and domesticity left him feeling hopelessly conflicted.

For the unpleasant truth was, he wasn't acting entirely in Teresa Phelps's best interests. How could he be, when he couldn't even tell her the truth?

The question then became,, which would win out in the end, his conscience or his desires? Unfortunately, Charles Everett had never possessed too burdensome a conscience. . . .

Chapter Nine

Dressed in a floral-patterned housecoat, hunched, silver-haired Maizie Ambrush was setting out breakfast on the front veranda of her Greek Revival mansion, among her beloved ferns and the striking latticework panels shielding her home from the quiet residential street. As she set out a perfect maiden's blush rose in a crystal vase, she admired her gracious table settings, the snowy linens, her Old Paris china with its delicate floral patterns and gilt edges, her ornate sterling silver and gleaming crystal. The accoutrements of an elegant life were very important to Maizie, even if, at ninety, she was getting a bit more forgetful than she cared to admit.

More and more, she just felt bone-tired and longed to rejoin her dear Walter, her husband of sixty years who had departed this life five years earlier. Walter had been a successful local shipping merchant who had bought this fine old house for his bride on their first anniversary. The house had been all but in ruins at the time, but Maizie and Walter had seen its potential; both had shared a passion for historical restoration. They'd spent a fortune lovingly restoring the home to its Victorian glory. The mansion soon came to be known as Ambrush House, and Maizie had always felt closer to dear Walter here on this porch, where they had shared so many breakfasts.

She especially savored these early-morning moments, before the Galveston heat hit like an oppressive tidal wave, when the atmosphere remained mild and she could drink her tea, listen to the chirping of her birds, and stare out at her beloved old oaks and antique roses. Indeed, she had just picked up her teapot to pour herself a cup when abruptly, her niece, Lillian Hatch, came storming out the front door in her jogging suit, rattling the old glass pane as she slammed it shut.

Setting down the teapot with a clatter, Maizie jumped slightly and clutched her racing heart. She eyed her niece in her ridiculous getup, the purple sweatshirt and matching sweatpants, the gray hair bound up on her head, the sweatband on her forehead. Face florid, Lillian was bouncing up and down, jogging in place, and the motion of it all but made Maizie dizzy.

"My heavens, Lillian, you do give a body a start," Maizie declared.

The no-nonsense Lillian took note of Maizie and grunted back, her feet pounding the floorboards. "Pour me some coffee, aunt."

"Coffee while you're banging about like that?" Maizie asked, shocked. "Why, you'll scald yourself, my dear, not to mention breaking Grandma's fine china."

Lillian sneered at her small, frail aunt. "One must keep moving to exercise properly. Keep the blood flowing."

"But won't you at least stop for breakfast?" Maizie inquired fretfully. With the sweep of a frail hand, she indicated the dainty continental repast she'd laid out. "I've put out coffee, tea, orange juice, and even baked you a raisin cake."

Lillian harrumphed. She was now performing jumping jacks, violently shaking the porch boards and setting the china to rattling even as a flustered Maizie struggled to keep all the pieces on her small table. "Ah, such are the temptations of the sedentary life, aunt. Thank heaven I'm not like you, sitting on the veranda in my housecoat all day, munching on danishes."

Now Maizie was insulted. "Why, I never! Doctor Hudson says I'm in remarkable condition for my age."

"You'd be in better condition if you jogged."

"At ninety?" Maizie inquired shrilly.

Lillian shot her aunt a superior look as she vaulted side-to-side. "It's never too late to start. And pass me that coffee, if you will."

"Why, you can't drink coffee while you're—"

"The coffee, aunt!" Lillian ordered, using a harsh tone Maizie was certain her niece must reserve for quelling delinquents.

Grimacing, Maizie dutifully poured a small cup, then gingerly handed her niece the demitasse. Lillian grabbed it and gulped down the coffee without missing a beat. "Thanks," she muttered, passing back the empty cup.

Maizie managed to corral the jiggling cup and set it down on the table. "You're welcome. But Lillian, when will you cease that infernal bouncing? You're cracking my floorboards."

"I'll stop after I've had a good run up and down Broadway. Must stay in shape these days, you know, with those maniacs who attacked Teresa yesterday still on the loose. Thank heaven I had you as my backup for lodging on this trip."

Maizie's features tightened in dismay. "Ah, yes, poor Teresa. I've been worried sick about my great-niece ever since you told me of the appalling incident at her beach house yesterday. So shocking. And you say she's taken up with some British fellow now?"

Lillian hiked an eyebrow while huffing and puffing. "And with an illiterate exterminator with stained teeth and a big bug on top of his truck."

Maizie frowned. "Oh, dear. You don't mean that nice Mr. Bob who fetched you home yesterday? He seemed a perfectly affable fellow, and even promised he'd come back to check my house for rats and termites—at no charge."

Lillian snorted. "Do whatever you wish with that cretin. It's Teresa who's gone around the bend, entertaining such riffraff. And I always thought of her as the mousy, studious type. Well, that just goes to show the little wallflowers are the ones we must worry about the most. And to think she brought this catastrophe on herself."

Irate, Maizie wagged a finger at her niece. "Now, Lillian, it's so uncharitable of you to speak of Teresa that way. Have you forgotten she's just lost Frank? Why, only weeks ago, we all made the trek to Morgan City for his funeral."

Lillian hurled her aunt a scathing look. "No, I've not forgotten. My sympathies are definitely with my older sister Gwen and my brother-in-law. However, we've *all* had our crosses to bear, haven't we, aunt?"

Knowing whereof Lillian spoke, Maizie grimaced. "Yes, dear."

"At least Frank's death was an accident," Lillian panted, back to jogging in place. "Teresa needs to maintain a stiff upper lip and get on with her life, instead of going non compos mentis."

"Do try to be a bit charitable toward her, dear," Maizie pleaded anxiously. "You know Teresa has led a commendable life and is a doctoral candidate, after all."

"A doctoral candidate with the brains of a flea."

"Lillian!"

Lillian waved a hand at her aunt. "Why don't *you* spend the next twenty years running a school for delinquent girls? Then you'll take off those rose-colored glasses and become a lot more jaded in your opinion of a wayward baggage like your great-niece."

A heavy sigh escaped Maizie. "My dear, I only wish I had the stamina, or the years left to do what you're doing."

"You would if you jogged," Lillian snapped back.

And before Maizie could reply, Lillian bounced down the steps and bounded off toward the street. Maizie shook her head. While she was unfailingly gracious to everyone in her family, she had actually come to dread her niece Lillian's annual summer pilgrimages to Galveston. Though the woman was well educated, she possessed all the tact and refinement of a barroom bouncer.

Of course Maizie had to make allowances for Lillian, since she hailed from the New Orleans branch of the family, the daughter of crazy Uncle George, who had forty years ago disgraced his family by taking a nosedive off the pediment of the Cabildo, having hallucinated he was a pigeon. If only poor George hadn't taken his flight on a Sunday morning, right as Mass was spilling out of St. Louis Cathedral. As it was, his suicide in Jackson Square had made all the national media, and Maizie knew Lillian had borne that disgraceful stigma ever since. This was why she had erected such a belligerent facade against the world. Even becoming the dean of the Fullenfelder School for Delinquent Girls had not fully restored her niece's battered self-esteem. Thus, Maizie tried to make allowances.

Nevertheless, Lillian was a pain in the neck to deal with.

Dear Teresa was another matter altogether. Maizie and Walter had been childless, and they'd always thought of Teresa and Frank as the children they'd never had. Maizie especially adored Teresa, who was one of the kindest young people she knew. Teresa came by to visit regularly, to take Maizie shopping or to church. Teresa seemed a totally upstanding young citizen.

And she had just lost her brother! Maizie hadn't known Frank quite as well, since her nephew had been a standoffish, bookish sort. Nonetheless, it had broken her heart to see such a fine, well educated young person lost, and to see Teresa and her family suffering such anguish.

Could Frank's death have been what had prompted Teresa to go around the bend as Lillian claimed? What else might have caused her niece to take up with thugs and hooligans? Of course, Maizie did suspect Lillian was exaggerating there, just as she had regarding that nice Mr.

Bob, calling the poor lad a *cretin*, when he seemed perfectly pleasant to Maizie.

Nonetheless, Maizie remained concerned about Teresa. How could she help her great-niece? Lillian was being very hard-nosed about it all, and was clearly in no mood to offer Teresa any assistance.

Maizie laid a finger alongside her cheek. What was she to do, one frail little ninety-year-old woman, whose faculties were failing? Well, perhaps she could ask that nice Mr. Bob about this when he came to inspect her home for vermin. . . .

Lillian Hatch bounded down the street, huffing for breath, sweat trickling down her face. She vaulted past striking Greek Revival mansions and cozy raised Victorian cottages in Galveston's East End Historical District.

A jaded fifty-year-old spinster, Lillian nonetheless had always found this section of Galveston fascinating. She'd been born and reared in New Orleans, and here in Galveston, the narrow-fronted mansions on their deep city lots reminded her of Rampart Street and the New Orleans Garden District. Thus it was always a pleasure to visit here—other than the fact that Aunt Maizie was becoming dotty, and Teresa had fallen in with lowlife creeps who had practically killed all of them yesterday.

Oh, well, it was all Teresa's problem now. Lillian had washed her hands of her prodigal niece. There was no telling what bad habits Teresa had picked up from that English fellow she was see-ing—drugs, gambling, you name it. Lillian had seen enough tawdry behavior as headmistress of the girl's school; she wanted no part of Teresa's trashy problems.

Returning to more pleasurable thoughts, she plodded on, inhaling the scents of dew and roses, glorying in the surge of blood through her veins as she turned a corner and continued on toward Broadway. Ah, this was the life, sweating and straining, staying in shape, so that she'd have no mercy for the little hooligans in her charge once she returned home for the fall term.

Then all at once a sensation of disquiet gripped Lillian and she felt the skin on her nape prickling, as if someone were watching her. Not missing a step, she glanced around, saw houses, trees, and parked cars, but nothing moving. She shrugged away the odd feeling, vigorously jogging on toward Broadway. . . .

What Lillian failed to note was a stranger sitting in an old, white, subcompact car parked behind her just down the street. Watching the amazon in the purple jogging suit bounce past, the man grimly smiled. He'd done his homework, and he knew this woman was Teresa Phelps's aunt. Furthermore, he knew another aunt lived just around the block.

Either or both might prove exquisite leverage in getting him what he wanted. His hands clutching the steering wheel tightened in anticipation.

Once the woman reached the next corner and turned, he started up his engine and slowly eased up to the corner, turning and tailing her onto busy, palm-lined Broadway. He chuckled at the sight of her. The woman was bounding along as if she thought she was really tough. Yes, she was big and ugly as a mud wrestler, but she was only a woman, just as Teresa Phelps was only a woman. And guns could prove very convincing.

But the British fellow Teresa Phelps was evidently now dating was another matter, a most unwelcome complication. Who was this stranger? Last night he'd spied on the two of them through the windows of Teresa Phelps's beach house. They'd been talking, drinking wine, kissing.

Why had the Brit entered Teresa Phelps's life, and what was his stake in this? Could the newcomer be after what he was after? If so, he must take steps to eliminate the threat.

He must also take action to shake Teresa Phelps up even more. One thing was for certain: She was hiding something, and lying to him. She knew much more than she was letting on.

He wouldn't be blocked from achieving his goals, not now, even if it meant kidnapping—or murdering—someone. He'd been betrayed once before, brutally double-crossed, and never again would he allow that to happen. *Never*. No matter how many people he had to kill.

Slowly he trailed the purple-clad figure as she jogged past the magnificent stone Bishop's Palace and on toward the Moody Mansion. Luckily, traffic was fairly congested, Galveston's version of the 7 A.M. rush hour, so he could coast along without raising undue suspicion.

Watching her stop at a light and bob in place, he felt his mouth going dry, his breathing quickening. Should he make his move now? He picked up his .45 from the opposite seat, clutching it in tense, quivering fingers. He could just throw open his door, jump out, grab her at gunpoint and yank her into his car. It could all be accomplished in mere seconds; then the amazon would be in his custody—and the rest of his mission might prove a piece of cake.

He hesitated, adrenaline pumping, glancing about uneasily at all the cars packing the traffic lanes around him. Damn, the woman was within his grasp, but the setting could prove disastrous. Surely to act now amid so many witnesses would be foolhardy, but . . .

A horn blared behind him, grating on his raw nerves, jerking his gaze to the light, which had now turned green. He cursed violently, watching the purple figure bound off again. Shooting the finger at the driver behind him, he accelerated, knowing that he had missed his opportunity.

For now. Gliding past his quarry, he laid his revolver back down on the seat, on top of a hooded mask of an evilly grinning pig. . . .

Chapter Ten

Teresa sat in Charles's car as he maneuvered them through the knotted traffic near the Houston Galleria. They were en route to their 11 A.M. appointment with Frank's attorney, Harold Robison. Both remained casually attired but had donned lightweight blazers for the meeting. Teresa had also put on Frank's bracelet, just as she had every morning since his death.

She glanced at Charles, who sat with one hand working the steering wheel, the other clamping his cell phone to his ear. From what he'd muttered to her a moment ago, he was supposedly checking his voicemail. Yet why did he wear such an expression of grim concentration? The sight of it gave Teresa a chill. It unnerved her that he was taking all of this so seriously.

Noting his expensive haircut, designer sunglasses, and the perfect crease of his pants, she mused that he was certainly a perfectionist, fastidious and exacting. Before they'd left her beach house, he'd insisted she contact her landlord and begin getting repairs scheduled. Then he'd prevailed on her to call Harold Robison and arrange an appointment for later this morning. When they'd arrived in Houston, he had refused to go retrieve her car before they went to the appointment, arguing that they would only end up having to follow each other all over town.

She knew the truth was that Charles didn't want to risk letting her out of his sight.

Why was this stranger so interested in her life and her brother's death, and so determined to control her every move?

She didn't know why she was still with Charles—except that he hadn't given her much choice there. She didn't know who he really was or what he wanted. She did know he had surely cast some sort of spell over her, making her all but swoon over his kisses, when she ought to have known better. Certainly, his coming to her rescue twice now was at least outwardly commendable; but there was still too much about Charles that she didn't trust.

She needed to shake him off as soon as possible.

And she remained upset and bewildered regarding the visit from the masked man this morning. Her call to the deputy sheriff had been a complete waste of time, for the bumpkin had assumed she was only pulling his leg about a visit from a man in a pig mask. But Teresa knew this was hardly a joke. Who was the masked man really? Was it Charles or someone he knew? What papers could he possibly want? Obviously he must be after something of value, but both Teresa and her brother Frank had always been as poor as church mice.

Nothing made sense!

"Is this the building?" Charles asked, breaking into her thoughts.

Teresa glanced at the gleaming pink granite skyscraper on Riverway. "Yes, that's it. And there's the entrance to the parking garage." She regarded him with a pained expression. "Although parking garages aren't exactly my favorite place these days—nor are elevators."

He shot her a wry grin. "Yes, I've heard disreputable types are known to lurk in them. But not to worry, Tess—you're with me now and you'll be perfectly safe."

"Yeah, right," she muttered.

But would she really?

"Good morning, Mr. Robison," Teresa said as his secretary admitted her and Charles into the attorney's office. "Thanks for seeing us on such short notice."

Harold Robison, a tall, well preserved man in his late fifties, wearing a dark blue pinstripe suit, slid out of his chair behind his handsome mahogany desk, then moved around it, smiling and shaking the hand Teresa offered. "No problem at all, my dear. So good to see you again, and so soon."

"Thanks," Teresa murmured. Gesturing at Charles, she added, "I'll like you to meet—"

"Charles Everett, an old friend of the family's," Charles cut in, extending his hand.

Robison shook Charles's hand. "Pleased to meet you, sir. I'm glad Teresa has a friend at this tragic time."

Charles grinned at Robison. "Yes, sir, I'm trying my best to console dear Teresa."

Teresa rolled her eyes at that.

Robison indicated two chairs facing his desk. "Please, both of you, have a seat."

"Thanks," Teresa replied.

After everyone was seated, an awkward silence fell, then Robison cleared his throat. "What can I do for you folks?"

Even as Charles was about to reply, Teresa jumped in. "Mr. Robison, since I left you yesterday, some rather alarming events have occurred—"

"Perhaps I'd best explain," Charles cut in.

She shot him a withering look. "No, *I'll* explain."

Charles gave a shrug.

Teresa turned back to Robison. "You see, when I—er—when Charles and I arrived at my beach house yesterday, we found the place ransacked."

Features paling, Robison sat upright in his leather chair. "My God, how horrible. Was anything stolen?"

"No, though someone was definitely looking for something."

"Did you notify the authorities?"

"Yes. But I'm afraid things got worse. Aunt Hatch arrived—"

Now Robison appeared avidly interested, leaning anxiously toward them across his desk. "My heavens, is Lillian all right?"

A smile pulled at Teresa's mouth. "That's right, you two got on quite well at Frank's funeral, didn't you?"

Robison grew a bit flustered, avoiding Teresa's eye. "Well, your aunt is quite a remarkable woman. I very much enjoyed hearing about her

safari to Africa, being a big game hunter myself."
He coughed. "I do hope she's unharmed?"

"Oh, yes. But she refused to stay with me, especially because of the thugs with shotguns—"

Expression aghast, Robison spoke in the merest whisper. "Shotguns? What shotguns?"

Teresa explained about the attack, then told Robison about the masked man masquerading as the Pig from Hell who had accosted her only this morning.

Robison took out a handkerchief and mopped his brow. "Good grief, what a nightmare! I'm so sorry you've been subjected to this ordeal, my dear. Why, you're lucky to be alive."

"Indeed."

"Is there something I might do to help?"

She grinned sheepishly. "Why, yes, I need to tell you where you come into this, don't I?"

"Me?" he questioned, appearing taken aback.

"You see, the masked man insisted I produce some papers Frank had supposedly given me. I was wondering if you knew anything about that."

Robison frowned. "There was the manuscript Frank was translating, the one I gave you yesterday."

"Yes, but we've looked at it and I seriously doubt that's what the man wanted. It's merely a copy of a journal written by Jean Lafitte which is already on display in Liberty, where anyone might view it."

"I see your point." Robison continued to scowl, then a look of dawning realization washed over his face. "You know, this is odd. A few weeks ago, Frank mentioned to me that he was on the verge of making a very important historical discovery."

"Did he?" Teresa asked.

"He seemed very excited about it."

"Can you tell us what this discovery involved?" Charles inquired.

Robison shook his head. "I'm afraid not. He was quite vague about it. But you might ask his roommate, Milton Peavey."

"Yes, of course, Milton," Teresa concurred.

"Since they were colleagues together at the university, perhaps Frank confided in Milton," Robison added.

"Quite possibly."

"As a matter of fact, we were on our way to Frank's former residence next," put in Charles.

Teresa cast him a pained look.

Expression preoccupied, Robison nodded. "Good idea. Teresa, please let me know if there's anything else I can do to help. And please give my regards to your folks and to Lillian, will you?"

She stood, and as the two men followed suit, she offered Robison her hand. "Of course. Thanks, Mr. Robison."

"I think Robison knows more than he's letting on," Charles muttered as he drove them away.

"What?" Teresa laughed. "You think stodgy old Harold Robison figures somewhere in this skullduggery?"

"He seemed uneasy when we spoke with him."

Teresa considered this for a long moment, then dismissed the notion with a wave of her hand. "Oh, he just has the hots for Aunt Hatch. He couldn't take his eyes off her at the funeral, and afterward, they were inseparable at the gathering at my folks' house."

Teresa's words left Charles scowling. "Robison went all the way to Louisiana to attend a client's funeral? Doesn't that strike you as odd?"

"Not really. You see, Mr. Robison used to live

in Morgan City, and was friends with my parents. That's why, after he joined a firm here in Houston, Frank went to him for legal advice."

"Ah. But I'm still not sure about him, Tess."

"Trust me, you're barking up the wrong tree."

"Perhaps. So where do we find this Milton Peavey?"

She hesitated. "Can we go get my car first?"

He raised an eyebrow. "Teresa, I've already told you I refuse to follow you all over Houston. We'll go get your car last. Now tell me where Milton lives."

"Very well. He and Frank shared a townhouse over in West University Place." She sighed. "I've been meaning to get by there anyway to see about Frank's things. . . ."

He flashed her a compassionate smile. "This is painful for you, isn't it?"

"Yes," she acknowledged in faltering tones. "And now, there's all of this mess added to it."

He reached across the console to pat her hand. "Poor dear. I'll have to comfort you later."

Despite a twinge of annoyance at his smug attitude, Teresa felt her cheeks heating at his warm touch and the sensual undercurrent in his words. Of course, if she had her way, there would be no *later*. Then, damn it, why was her body traitorously aching for just the solace Charles was offering?

She directed him to her brother's former residence off Kirby Drive. Charles parked in the street beneath the massive sweep of a water oak, exited the car, and came around to open her door. "Nice neighborhood," he remarked, motioning at the row of attractive brownstone townhouses just beyond them. "Wasn't this a bit much for your brother on a professor's salary?"

"Milton owns the townhouse," she explained as they started up the flagstone path together. "He inherited it from his mother. Since it's quite large, naturally he wanted a roommate."

They climbed the stoop, and Charles rapped the brass knocker. A moment later the door was flung open by an unshaven, bleary-eyed, and distraught-looking man in his late thirties, wearing a gray T-shirt, green khakis, and sandals.

Teresa struggled not to gasp aloud at the unsettling sight of their host. Milton Peavey was hardly a feast for the eyes under any circumstances, with his oily, pockmarked skin, blunt features, and graying ponytail. But today he looked particularly unkempt, unshaven, and rumpled—Teresa even spotted a bruise forming along his left cheek. As always, he stood awkwardly, favoring the right knee he'd ruined years ago in a car wreck.

He scowled in perplexity at Teresa. "Tess. What a surprise. I haven't seen you since Frank's funeral in Morgan City."

"M-Milton," she stammered back. "I'm sorry, we didn't mean to intrude, but . . . ." Teresa's voice faltered as she caught sight of the living room beyond, which was totally wrecked, almost a carbon copy of her own yesterday. "My God, are you all right? What happened here?"

"You tell me," Milton whined, gesturing at the debris-filled room, a hodgepodge of overturned mahogany furniture, scattered books and papers, and smashed knickknacks. "I went out this morning for a cappuccino and a danish, then came back to interrupt some burglars."

"Burglars!" Teresa gasped. "How awful! You mean you actually had a run-in with them?"

"Yes and no. The place was dark when I returned, but I sensed something was wrong as soon as I opened the door. Then someone tripped me, I felt a horrible whack on my head, and everything went black. I woke up later with a blazing headache, my bad knee banged up even worse, and with this . . ." He finished with an expansive gesture toward the living room.

"How terrible! Shouldn't you see a doctor?"

"I need to wait for the police first." Milton's gaze narrowed on Charles. "Who's he?"

"Oh, I'm sorry," Teresa muttered. "This is—"

"Charles Everett, a friend of Teresa's," he interjected, extending his hand. "May we come in a moment?"

"I suppose," Milton replied rather sullenly, ignoring Charles's hand but moving aside so they could enter. "Forgive my manners, but I've had a beast of a morning. I'd offer you both a chair, but . . . I'm afraid it would be rather like hunting for a needle in a haystack right now."

"Think nothing of it," Teresa replied. Stepping onto the marble tile in the foyer, she grimaced as she took in more of the sunken living room beyond—the cherry bookcases with smashed glass fronts, the ripped upholstery on the couches and chairs, the expensive framed art hanging askew on the walls. "What a mess."

"It's a disaster," Milton agreed, wringing his hands. "Whoever did this didn't even have the sense of a good thief. They broke all of Mother's Fabergé eggs, her rose Pompadour china, and smashed most of the Belter chairs that she paid a fortune for in Louisiana."

"Milton, I'm so sorry," Teresa said, touching his arm.

"Are you insured?" Charles added.

Teresa shot him an exasperated glance.

"Yes, thank heaven, and as I've mentioned, the police are on their way."

Charles raised an eyebrow at Teresa. "A good idea, having insurance."

"Yes, if one can afford it," she rejoined with sweet sarcasm.

"Frankie's room is trashed, too," Milton went on distraughtly. "I've been trying to keep everything together for you, Tess, but I'm afraid Frank's belongings are scattered to the four winds by now. I'm not sure Frank had insurance on his own things."

Teresa nodded. "Poor Frank."

"And you say your house was ransacked as well?" Milton inquired.

Teresa explained about her beach house, the thugs with shotguns who had attacked, as well as the man in the pig mask who had accosted her this morning, demanding "papers."

Milton whistled. "Wow, the similarities between your incidents and mine are frightening. Why do you suppose both of us have been targeted?"

"I was hoping you could tell us," Teresa replied. "Do you know anything about the Lafitte journal Frank was translating, or any other important papers he was dealing with before he died? Anything valuable enough to cause someone to trash both our homes?"

Milton frowned a moment, then snapped his fingers. "As a matter of fact, yes, I do know something about some papers. I think all that business with the Lafitte journal began when a contractor from Galveston contacted Frank regarding some papers in French he'd found under the wainscoting in an old house."

Charles and Teresa exchanged an amazed glance, then Charles demanded, "What was the contractor's name?"

Milton hesitated. "Hmm. Let's see, I believe it was Swanson . . . no, it was Swinson. Hey, I can get you Frank's appointment book—if I can find it in this mess."

"Please do," Charles said.

Milton hobbled across the debris-strewn room and checked the scattered contents of several desk drawers. "Ah, here it is." He limped back over and handed a little black book to Teresa.

"Thanks, Milton," she said, opening the book, emotion knotting her throat as she spotted her brother's familiar handwriting. "What else can you tell us about the papers this Swinson person brought Frank?"

"I'm afraid not much. I just know Swinson brought Frank the old French documents, and that's when Frank became interested in Lafitte's journal."

Charles and Teresa exchanged a meaningful look. "Do you think the two could be related?" she asked Milton.

He gave a shrug. "Who knows? It's possible."

"Can we look at Frank's stuff upstairs, too?"

"Well, we should probably wait until the cops come," Milton replied. "I'm not even sure I should have given you that book."

"I seriously doubt it will be a problem," Charles assured him.

"And we really do need to learn everything we

can about what Frank was doing before he died," Teresa added, "so we can try to solve the mystery."

Milton eyed her askance. "Are you implying you have suspicions about your brother's death?"

She gave a rueful laugh. "Considering all the shenanigans currently going on, could you blame me if I did?"

"I suppose not." Milton hesitated another long moment, then laughed. "Aha! Now I remember. How stupid of me."

"What?" she prompted, perplexed.

His gaze narrowed on her. "Don't you already know all about this, Tess?"

"All about what?" she asked.

"You see, not long before Frank died, he told me he was on the verge of making a very important discovery."

"Hey, Harold Robison mentioned this same discovery!" Teresa put in with building excitement.

"Really? Anyway, Frank claimed that this find was so valuable that there would be a number of people who might try to take it away from him. But he bragged to me that he'd fool them all. He told me you were his fail-safe device, Tess, so I assumed you knew all about it."

At this, Teresa felt intensely confused. "No, Frank told me nothing about any discovery."

"Isn't that odd," Milton muttered.

"But you think this discovery could be related to the documents Frank was translating, and the Lafitte journal?" Charles inquired.

"Could be," Milton agreed.

Teresa was about to question Milton more when a loud knock sounded at the door. "Excuse me," Milton said. "That must be the police."

Teresa watched Milton limp toward the door

135

and open it. But instead of a uniformed police-man, a Hispanic youth lounged on the stoop. Dressed in tattered jeans and a black T-shirt, he was a handsome young man; but his heavy beard and dark, intense eyes lent him a menacing air.

Milton eyed the youth with contempt. "What do you want? I don't need any chores done around here today."

The youth peered insolently into the living room, eyeing the chaos, then taking in Charles and Teresa. He sneered at Charles, then looked Teresa over in a bold manner that made her skin crawl. Teresa felt a surge of gratitude when Charles protectively stepped in front of her and glared back at the visitor.

"Well?" Milton demanded of the youth. "I said I don't need any hired help!"

The youth glowered at Milton, jerking his head toward the living room again. "That ain't exactly how it looks, man," he sneered. "You gringos must have really gone on some heavy trip last night, eh?"

"We've had a burglary here!" Milton barked back. "Now what in hell do you want?"

The youth's expression turned surly. "I wanna see Frank. Where is he?"

"Frank's dead," Milton snapped.

"Dead?" the kid scoffed. "Shit, that lying gringo owes me a hundred bucks."

"So sue us," Milton retorted, slamming the door in the kid's face. Turning around with a pained expression, he brushed off his hands. "What do you suppose that was all about?"

Teresa could only shake her head in bewilder-ment. Charles didn't answer either, instead strid-ing over to the front windows and peering out. Teresa joined him, and both watched the youth get into a flashy, metallic blue, '64 Chevy Impala low-rider. She could vaguely see two other youths inside the car.

As the low-rider drove off, Teresa glanced at Charles to see keen anxiety creasing his brow. "What is it?" she asked.

"You know, I can't be sure, Tess, but I think those may have been the same thugs who shot up your beach house yesterday."

Teresa regarded Charles in alarm. What on earth was going on here?

Chapter Eleven

Soon after the Hispanic youths departed, two uniformed policemen stopped by to take a burglary
report from Milton. They took down descriptions
of the suspicious-looking Hispanic youth, and
also listened to Charles and Teresa's account of
an alleged run-in with the same thugs yesterday
on Bolivar Peninsula, and Teresa's encounter
with the man in the pig mask this morning. The
officers appeared skeptical of Teresa's described
incident with the intruder, and seemed to dismiss
the other episodes as little more than botched
burglaries. They advised Milton to see a doctor
and call his insurance agent, then left.

Afterward Milton showed Teresa and Charles
up to Frank's room. Teresa stood just inside the
doorway, peering about the large, sunny room,

which had also been ransacked, but not as badly as downstairs. The bedding had been yanked off the mattress, books, papers, and clothing were scattered everywhere, but nothing appeared broken or ripped.

Absently she picked up a dark blue throw pillow from the floor and set it on the bed. "They don't even have respect for the dead," she muttered with a catch in her voice.

"Or the living," added Charles, regarding her compassionately.

"How true, and I've been trying so hard to keep everything straight for you, Tess," Milton remarked from the door.

She turned to smile gratefully at him. "I'm sorry I haven't come sooner, but it was hard to break away from Mom and Dad in Louisiana. They took Frank's death so hard."

"I remember how torn up they were at the funeral," Milton replied. "As we all were, of course."

"Still, I should see about Frank's things," Teresa went on, picking up one of her brother's shirts, a green and yellow plaid, and eyeing it poignantly before she folded it and laid it down.

Milton waved her off. "Not to worry, hon. After all this, believe me, I'm in no hurry to get a new roommate."

"Can't say as I blame you," drawled Charles, who was picking up scattered books from the floor and carefully replacing them in a bookcase.

Teresa crossed the room to Frank's desk, touching the high-tech computer monitor and keyboard. "Hey, it looks like Frank's computer is unharmed."

"Yeah, I must have interrupted the rats before they could trash it."

"Well, they sure annihilated mine yesterday," she confided ruefully.

"Then take Frankie's, why don't you?" Milton suggested. "My own computer also survived the demolition derby, and Frankie's certainly isn't doing him any good now."

Teresa forced down the painful lump in her throat. "Hey, thanks, that's a good idea. If you don't mind, I think I will take Frank's computer with me today. Who knows? Maybe I can find some clues to the mysterious 'papers' in Frank's files."

"Could be." Milton consulted his watch. "Well, kids, gotta run. Twelve-thirty class. It may be only American history for brain-dead freshmen, but duty calls."

"But aren't you going to see a doctor first?" Teresa protested.

"I'll take an aspirin and see how it goes. Look, make yourselves at home—such as it is—and take anything of Frankie's that you want, Tess. I'd tell you to lock the door before you leave, but the lock's broken." Stepping forward, he gave Teresa a brief hug. "Anyway, gotta go, hon."

"Take care, Milton. And thanks."

Milton turned and hobbled out of the room. Teresa looked at Charles to see him scowling. "What?"

"I don't like him," Charles replied grimly.

"Milton?" she countered, laughing. "I'll admit he's not Mr. Personality. He's a stodgy history professor, after all. But he's harmless enough."

Charles's frown deepened. "He seems very self-absorbed. And nervous. Plus, all those tantalizing details he dribbled out about Frank's so-called 'important discovery' and your being a 'fail-safe device' seemed a bit convenient." He slapped his forehead and mimicked Milton. " 'Gee, Tess, *now* I remember.' "

Teresa was exasperated. "Charles, really! He was only trying to help, and believe me, my brother was never very forthcoming about his own business. And of course Milton is nervous and a bit forgetful. He just had his home burglarized, for heaven's sake. Not to mention an encounter with some very nasty thugs who beat him up."

But Charles was shaking his head. "I'm not convinced. He could be involved in this."

"What? *Milton?* First you suspect Harold Robison, and now poor meek Milton? What do you presume he did here?" Her hand made a sweeping gesture. "Did he demolish his own mother's antiques and bash himself over the head?"

He shot her a long-suffering look. "Teresa, in any murder—"

"Murder?" she cut in, voice rising. "So now you're convinced Frank was murdered?"

He held up a hand. "Hear me out. Let's say Frank *was* murdered, strictly for the sake of argument. The authorities always claim that those closest to the victim—family, friends—are the most likely suspects."

"Great! Next you'll be suspecting me."

He groaned. "Teresa, be serious."

"I *am* serious. Tell me, Charles, are you throwing out all these red herrings to divert suspicion from yourself?"

He paled. "Just what kind of crack is that?"

"Well, don't the authorities tell us that throwing out red herrings is the typical dodge of a guilt-stricken perpetrator?"

"I beg your pardon! Now you think *I* killed your brother?"

She was blinking rapidly, her voice trembling. "Well, you must have *some* reason to be so interested in all of this."

"I told you, I—"

"And don't bother repeating your lies," she cut in. "Look at it from my perspective, Charles. Under the circumstances, my suspecting you is no more bizarre than your suspecting Harold Robison or Milton Peavey, now is it?"

A muscle twitched in his jaw. "Is that what you really think?"

"Damn it, Charles, I don't know what to think."

"Well, thanks for the vote of confidence, Tess." With quick, angry movements, he leaned over to grab a new handful of books. "Shall we look around this room, or what?"

"Sure," she muttered. "Let's get to work."

Throwing each other hot, hostile looks, Charles and Teresa went through all of Frank's belongings, straightening up as they went along, and looking for clues. Although they found nothing promising, all the hard work did seem to dissipate some of the tension hanging in the air between them.

Afterward, Teresa stood at the window, slowly leafing through Frank's appointment book. Emotion churned within her at the sight of her brother's familiar scrawl, the notes he had scribbled to himself in a rather disjointed code. She studied each entry carefully, pausing over a brief reference to a meeting with a "Clark Swinson." After she finished, she backtracked to a note that she'd found particularly gut-wrenching. That was when she felt Charles staring at her, and glanced up.

"Did you find any listings for a Swinson?" he asked.

She swallowed hard. "There's one reference to a meeting with a Clark Swinson six weeks ago, but no details at all. Not where they met, or what was discussed, or even Swinson's phone number."

"You mean there are no references to the missing papers or the Lafitte journal?"

"No."

"Did you find anything else, Tess?"

"Well, yes." She leafed through the book. "I found several references to Frank's girlfriend, Kelly Brinkman."

"Frank had a girlfriend?"

"Yes, although they weren't dating for very long before his death. She didn't even attend his funeral, although I called her family's home and left a message on the answering machine."

"It's odd you didn't hear from her."

"Well, I'm not sure just how serious she and Frank were." Teresa snapped her fingers. "Darn, I should have asked Milton about Frank and Kelly. I think Milton introduced them. Kelly was his TA or something."

Charles raised an eyebrow. "T and A?"

There Teresa had to laugh. "No, silly. TA. Teaching Assistant."

He colored. "Oh. Of course I knew that."

"Sure you did."

Awkwardly he cleared his throat. "At any rate, shouldn't we speak with Ms. Brinkman, see what light she might be able to shed on the current situation?"

"I suppose we should." Shutting the book, she recklessly added, "Then you can suspect her, as well."

"Teresa," he scolded.

"Aren't girlfriends always natural suspects?" she inquired sarcastically.

His words came in a menacing rumble. "You've made your point, Tess."

"Good for me."

He stepped closer, eyeing her quizzically. "However, the references to Swinson and Ms. Brinkman . . . That isn't what *really* upset you about the appointment book, is it?"

Taken aback, she glanced up, and struggled not to melt at his expression of tender concern. "You're very perceptive."

"What was it, then, Tess? Seeing Frank's handwriting?"

"In part."

"And the rest?"

She sighed, opening the book again, flipping to the entry. "Frank and I had a lot in common. We both used to write notes to ourselves—like he did here."

"Ah, What does this one say?"

"Nothing critical. It's dated a month ago. 'Send Mom and Dad an anniversary card. Buy Elliot Keeler's new book. Phone Teresa.'" Her voice broke on those last words.

Gently Charles stroked her cheek. "I'm so sorry, Tess. This is very hard on you, isn't it? Seeing his things. Reading his appointment book."

She nodded, while guilt and emotion warred within her. Charles was being very sweet, especially considering that she'd all but accused him of killing her brother. "It's especially hard seeing all his things ransacked this way," she confided hoarsely. "First Frank dies—or is killed. Now, this—another violation."

"The two of you must have been very close."

"Well, I'm not sure Frank was all that close to anyone," she confided ruefully. "He was an

144

intensely private person, very scholarly and involved in his studies. At times he tended to be somewhat melancholy. He was also such a tight-wad that it became a family joke—you know, wearing five-year-old suits and giving everyone white elephants for Christmas. But he was also my big brother and I loved him. It's been especially nice these last months since I've lived close to Houston. Frank would call me up and invite me to events—mostly freebies at the university— concerts, plays, lectures. I'd reciprocate by getting us tickets to the opera or ballet. We had some good times together. Looking back, I'm so grateful we had those times—although I didn't see him as often during the last few weeks of his life, while he was dating Kelly."

Charles nodded toward the appointment book. "Do you have any idea why he made that note to call you?"

"Who knows? Probably something to do with Mom and Dad. Their anniversary was almost a month ago, just days, in fact, before he died."

"How horrible. Do you remember him calling you around then?"

Distractedly she ran her fingers through her hair. "No, though it's always possible he tried."

"Indeed. You're so low-tech you likely don't even have an answering machine."

"Yes I do!" she protested.

"You do?"

She smiled sheepishly. "But it's broken."

"I rest my case." He touched her cheek again. "You okay?"

She moved away, bravely nodding. "I'll muddle through, thank you."

With a sigh, he glanced about the now tidied

room. "Well, I guess we've pretty much covered things here. Shall I disconnect and load up Frank's computer for you?"

"Yes, I'd appreciate that."

"Then we'll go calling on Ms. Brinkman?"

Teresa hesitated, remembering her decision to get free of Charles, even though the sensitivity he'd just demonstrated was making that more difficult. "Well . . . Can't we please go get my car first?"

He frowned.

Fearing he'd say no again, she rushed on. "I'm really getting worried about it, Charles. If we wait too long, I'm sure they'll tow it. Also, I know where Kelly lives—you see, Frank pointed out her parents' house to me one time—and the department store is definitely on the way. I can lead you to Kelly's place afterward, okay?"

Although his gaze narrowed slightly, he didn't protest further. "Very well."

Moments later, as they headed for the department store, their conversation turned to the things Milton had told them earlier about Frank. "I think Milton gave us some very strong leads," Charles remarked. "So your brother Frank was translating not just a photocopy of Jean Lafitte's journal, but another document, also in French, ostensibly discovered in Galveston. Do you suppose the two are connected?"

"Could be," Teresa conceded. "Logic argues that there is a connection, though of course we can't be sure until we contact Swinson and learn what this second document was."

"We must do that later today or tomorrow. You know, it does make sense that Swinson would come to Frank for a translation of an old French document, since Frank was an authority on the French language in the eighteenth and nine-teenth centuries."

Hearing Charles's words, all at once Teresa was washed with a chill. "How do you know that?"

For once her self-possessed companion appeared flustered, shifting his gaze from hers. "I—um—I believe I read it in a newspaper once."

"What newspaper?"

"The *Gulf Coast Journal*, I think."

Teresa fell silent. To be honest, she knew there had been such an article about Frank's expertise in the *Journal* a year earlier, but she was far from convinced Charles had told her the truth. What was his stake in all of this? Why was he so inter-ested, and why did he know so much?

"You know, something else is troubling me," Charles went on.

"Yes?" she asked, wrenched from her thoughts.

He eyed her curiously. "Why do you suppose Frank told Milton you were his fail-safe device, love?"

The look in Charles's eyes, half speculation, half calculating suspicion, gave Teresa pause. She was swept by new shivers, convinced more than ever that Charles Everett was not who he said he was. Yes, he could come across as sweet, sensitive, and caring, but surely he was only pre-tending in order to manipulate her. She could not afford to be lulled into believing his lies. He was clearly a man of ulterior motives . . . a man she could not trust.

"Ah, here we are," he said, pulling into the department store's parking garage. "Do you remember where your car is parked?"

Teresa directed him to the row where her small, battered red subcompact still sat. "Oh, good, they haven't towed my car as yet," she said, taking her keys from her bag.

"Your car is rather sad-looking, I must say," he commented.

She tossed him a glower. "I told you I don't have much money."

He grinned. "But you have me, love."

"Yeah, and you're such a prize," she rejoined wryly.

"There are those who definitely think so," he countered.

"Beginning with yourself?"

He glowered. "I was referring to the fairer sex—and hoping to make you insanely jealous."

"Well, you've certainly made me insane, if not jealous." She was reaching for the door handle, when abruptly he caught her wrist, and she glanced up to see a daunting expression on his face. "What?"

"You aren't contemplating trying to give me the slip again, are you?" he asked, in deceptively soft tones.

She feigned an amazed look. "What? Are you afraid I'll steal off to another tryst with your father?"

"Teresa," he chided, "frankly, I wouldn't put it past you to try to make a run for it."

"*Moi?*" She gestured toward her car. "Clearly my broken-down nag is no competition for your sleek black charger, sir."

He chuckled. "No funny business, now. I'll be on your tail every minute going to Ms. Brinkman's house."

"Aren't you always?" She nodded meaningfully toward his fingers, still tightly clamped on her wrist. "Hadn't you better release me?"

Still he hesitated, eyeing her skeptically. "Hadn't

you better give me some instructions, just in case
we get separated?"

"Don't worry," she assured him primly. "I'll
drive slowly."

Reluctantly, he released her wrist. "Straight
there, now."

She saluted him. "Aye, aye, sir."

Teresa hopped out of Charles's vehicle and
slammed the door, then unlocked her own and
slipped inside. The car was as hot as an oven, but
at least the engine turned right over, with a
throaty purr. Although Charles couldn't know it,
Teresa's car actually ran much better than it
looked. Her dad was something of a shade tree
mechanic, and he was constantly tinkering with
her engine whenever she was home in Louisiana.
Unfortunately, though, he hadn't been able to get
the air conditioning to work for some time, she
mused, rolling down her window.

Putting the car in gear, she proceeded slowly
out of the parking garage, across the lot, and into
the street, constantly glancing into her rearview
mirror to keep an eye on Charles behind her. She
eased into the heavy traffic and immediately
stopped behind a long line of cars on Westhemier
waiting for a light.

Eyeing Charles again and biting her lip, she
wondered if she really should try to make a run
for it. After all, he did have Frank's computer in
his car, and the files might hold some clues to
this current madness.

But she still didn't trust him, and for now, the
threat he posed seemed to more than outweigh
any significance those computer files might hold.
Charles had insinuated himself into her life—at
gunpoint—on an insane pretext. Everything that
had happened since then had convinced her that

he wanted something from her—just as everyone else did, it seemed. The hell of it was, she still didn't know what it was these people wanted.

But logic still warned her Charles could be dangerous. He might have even been involved in her brother's death. For all she knew, he could also be in cahoots with the Hispanic thugs who kept showing up in her life.

Her decision made, she stiffened her spine and waited. Once the light changed, she put the car in gear and drove cautiously to the loop access road, turning south on it, then revving her engine, shifting rapidly, and blending into the heavy traffic.

For a moment she seemed trapped in the clog of cars that was funneling onto the loop. Then she spotted an opening, took a deep breath, and made her move. Instead of entering the loop, she shot to her right across three lanes of traffic, amid much swerving and honking of horns from other drivers, then zigzagged onto a nearby street.

She heard the loud blaring of a horn, glanced in her rearview mirror, and saw that Charles was still on her tail! Damn him! He was also leaning on the horn and gesturing wildly for her to pull over.

Like hell she would! Downshifting and gunning her engine, she went squealing around the next corner, and continued her crazy, zigzag course, amid the blaring horns and squealing tires of the drivers in her path.

On she went, careening around blocks, flying through alleyways. She made so many twists and turns that at last she lost all sense of where she was.

Then she emerged on an unfamiliar street in a seamier part of town, filled with run-down pawn shops, ice houses, and junk stores. Glancing about at the clunkers cruising the potholed street, at day laborers gathered outside a cantina, she realized she had finally lost Charles—as well as herself. Nonetheless she felt exultant to have escaped him.

"Yes!" she cried, pulling to a halt at a light. Shifting the car into neutral, she grimaced at the sight of a strip center to her right, with a topless bar and a sex shop. Two bearded laborers emerged from a convenience store and leered at her.

Teresa gulped. She might be free of Charles at last, but she hoped she hadn't jumped out of the frying pan and into the fire. She needed to get out of this trashy area as soon as possible.

Indeed, Teresa was on the verge of raising her window, despite the heat when, abruptly, someone poked a knife inside, holding it just inches from her nose! Then her arm was grabbed by steely fingers.

Teresa screamed and jerked her gaze upward. She found herself staring into the smirking face and leering dark brown eyes of the same Hispanic youth who had visited Milton.

"Hi, chickie," he greeted her impudently. "I think it's time for you and me to have a little chat, no?"

Teresa's heart was beating so savagely, she could barely hear him. Despite the danger, her first thought was to gun her engine and take off again. But she was too late. Before her foot could even engage the clutch, her door was flung open, and she was savagely hauled out of her car.

Chapter Twelve

Teresa dared not resist or scream as the thug pressed a knife to her throat and dragged her toward his car, the same blue Chevy she'd spotted him in at Milton's. The low-rider was parked behind them across the street, about ten yards away. The youth smelled sweaty, and Teresa was sure she caught the odor of beer on his breath. He held her in a steely grip that told her he could slit her throat with little or no effort.

She was terrified, certain that at any moment, she might die. What was worse, she was forced almost to run across the street in order to keep up with her abductor's brisk stride, and she prayed she wouldn't stumble, fall . . . and manage to get her head sliced off in the process.

What a fool she had been to run away from

Charles. His abducting her in west Houston yesterday paled in comparison to this creep's vicious tactics now. She could only pray that Charles was still searching for her, and would find her soon!

"What do you want with me?" she finally managed to ask.

"Shut up," came the guttural response as the man shoved her onward.

Teresa winced as she felt the blade of the knife stinging her throat. "Hey, will you lighten up on that blade? I think you just nicked me."

"I said shut up! Or you're gonna see worse than a nick."

Teresa bit her lip, wondering who on earth this maniac really was and what he was planning to do with her. Then, within feet of his car, she watched another slovenly dressed youth pop out of the front seat, sneer a grin, and, with exaggerated courtesy, open the back door for them. Teresa's captor shoved her inside, onto a filthy seat with dirty upholstery and protruding springs. A split second later, he joined her there, seized her neck in a half nelson, and pressed the knife to her flesh again. The second youth slammed the door, climbed back into the front seat with the driver, and the car lurched off amid much exhaust smoke and squealing of tires.

"Please, can't you tell me who you are and what you want with me?" Teresa pleaded.

"Shut up, chickie," her captor replied. He waved his knife toward the driver. "Hey, Hector, put a move on it. Let's get this gringa somewhere safe where we can have a little chat."

He said *chat* in a way that chilled Teresa's blood.

"*Sí*, Manolo," called the driver, punching the accelerator.

As they went squealing around a corner, Teresa winced as again her neck was pricked. She couldn't believe this was happening! She'd been kidnapped twice in less than twenty-four hours—first at gunpoint, then at knifepoint.

But why?

"Will you please tell me what's going on here?" she begged.

"You'll find out soon enough, lady," her captor snarled back as they roared down a seamy street.

Teresa struggled to calm herself, knowing she had to keep her wits about her if she was to survive the next few moments. Still intensely conscious of the knife, she also became puzzled as she recalled the encounter yesterday with these same goons at her beach house.

"Hey, what happened to the shotguns you guys had?" she asked.

That hit a nerve, from the curse the man uttered. "What shotguns?"

"The shotguns you used to ruin my beach house!"

Even as Teresa's captor glared, the man in the passenger seat turned around and chuckled. "Hey, lady, you don't miss much, do you? Manolo got in trouble for borrowing those guns from his brother-in-law."

"Is that the old west form of 'borrowing'?" Teresa sneered. "You know, 'stealing'?"

The thug in the front seat grinned at Teresa crookedly, revealing stained, broken teeth. "Yeah, chickie. Rudy was plenty pissed about Manolo swiping his guns."

Meanwhile, the thug named Manolo was growing agitated, waving his knife at the other man. "Shut up, Freddie. You're telling this bitch more than she needs to know!"

Freddie shrugged. "Sure, man. But I don't see how it makes no difference now."

"Shut up!" Manolo yelled.

Teresa cringed at their words. Why would it make no difference what these men told her? Did they plan to kill her? Oh, heaven help her!

By now, Freddie had turned back around. Hector wheeled them into the debris-cluttered yard of what appeared to be an abandoned factory. The car screeched to a halt, then Freddie hopped out and opened the back door. Manolo exited and hauled Teresa outside with him. Just as she tottered on her feet and almost stumbled, Freddie caught her arm and hauled her upright.

"Easy, lady."

"Tell your friend Manolo," she retorted.

Manolo evidently didn't heed her warning for he seized her again, bracing the knife against her throat. He began propelling her toward the entrance, and she cried out as she stumbled over an abandoned beer bottle and the knife nicked her yet another time.

"Will you *please* slow down," she implored. "Damn it, you really cut me this time!"

"Shut up, lady, or you'll be minus a head." He hauled her toward a ramshackle shed off to one side. Kicking open the door, he pulled her through the sagging portal and shoved her inside the building.

Hearing the door grind shut behind them, Teresa lurched forward, only to trip over a board, lose her balance, and go hurtling downward. She landed hard on her hands and knees on the broken-up concrete floor. Catching her breath with a pained gasp, she glanced around, and found herself in a medium-sized work shed, where scattered spears of sunlight illuminated debris, dirt, and abandoned machinery. Frantically she searched for an escape route, a door or a window, but saw none. Hearing the sounds of birds panicking and flapping their wings, she glanced upward and grimaced at the sight of dozens of pigeons flying off through the hole-riddled ceiling.

"All right, chickie, time to talk," Manolo ordered. "Get up."

With a moan, Teresa struggled to her feet, brushed herself off, and glared at Manolo. He loomed beyond her, wielding his knife, while Hector and Freddie stood grinning nearby. "What do you want?"

"Okay, lady, where's the loot Frank was going to dig up?" Manolo demanded.

"What loot?" Teresa asked, flabbergasted.

Manolo took an aggressive step toward her, flashing the knife in her face, his dark eyes gleaming with a vehemence that told her he meant business. "You heard me, lady, the loot. The booty. Frank, he thought I was just a dumb Chicano, but I got my GED. I know when a gringo offers me and Freddie and Hector a hundred dollars apiece to buy some shovels and meet him at an ice house on the beach in Galveston, he ain't planning to dig up his grandmother, right?"

Teresa remained stunned. "My brother Frank did *what*?"

"You heard me, lady. He told us to meet him near the beach for a job."

"A job? But I have no idea what you're talking about!"

"Liar!" Manolo snarled, lunging forward and grabbing Teresa by the hair, painfully twisting her locks.

"Ouch!" she cried, doing a wild little dance trying to get away from him, and feeling as if he were yanking her scalp out. "Damn it, let me go!"

"When you tell me the truth, *puta!*"

"But I don't know anything!" she wailed. "Stop it, you're hurting me."

"Well, it's gonna hurt a lot more till you talk," her captor retorted. "Frank promised us some real *dinero*. Then he never showed up. I got me a woman who likes to have fun and dance the macarena, and I'm gonna make her happy, so we're gonna get our cut one way or another, you got it? You think I ain't smart, lady? I read the obituaries, that's how smart I am. When I read Frank's, that's where I got your name."

As he finally shoved her away, Teresa glared and rubbed her aching scalp. "But—but this morning you acted as if you didn't know Frank was dead."

He grinned. "I wanted the money, lady."

Though tempted to slap his sneering face, Teresa managed to hold on to her patience. "Then I'll give you money—two hundred dollars apiece—just to leave me the hell alone."

"Oh, no, lady. You gotta understand, when a gringo owes Manolo Juarez money, the interest is compounded daily." He waved his knife menacingly and stalked toward her. "Looks like I got me some more persuading to do."

Eyeing the wickedly sharp blade, Teresa screamed and tried to run, but the other two thugs caught her and held her as an evilly grinning Manolo steadily approached with his knife. . . .

"Women drivers!" Charles Everett cursed, pounding a fist on his steering wheel.

Ever since he'd lost sight of Teresa's car two

minutes ago, he'd been in a panic. For an academic, the woman was certainly full of surprises, and had just led him on a frantic car chase that would have put any Indy 500 driver to shame.

And it was all his own damn fault. He never should have let Teresa go off in her own car. Moreover, what insanity had prompted him to make that slip about her brother being an expert on nineteenth-century French documents? What an idiot he'd been. Now she didn't trust him at all, and he really couldn't blame her.

He raced his car through the avenues and side streets of southwest Houston, wildly scanning every car, sidewalk, and building, desperately searching for any trace of her. He zipped past street after street of ramshackle houses and tawdry strip centers, but caught no hint of her. He was damn worried about her being on the run in this seamy part of town, especially with those Hispanic thugs on the loose.

All at once he flinched as his cell phone bleeped. He yanked it out of his blazer pocket and punched it on. "Yes?"

After listening to the other party a moment, Charles interrupted. "Look, I can't talk right now. Somehow, Teresa Phelps has managed to escape me."

Predictably, the caller went ballistic, yelling and screaming at Charles for not doing his job. Charles had to hold the phone away from his ear to muffle the obscenities.

At last, losing all patience, he cut in furiously. "Damn it, quit ranting and listen to me, you prick. I promised you I could handle this, and I can. So back off and let me do my bloody job!"

A look of grim satisfaction on his face, Charles hung up the phone and shoved it back inside his jacket pocket. He wheeled his car into an industrial alleyway, but saw no sign of Teresa. Then at last he turned into a row of warehouses, cruised past an abandoned factory, and slammed on the brakes as he spotted a familiar, blue Chevy low-rider. . . .

Manolo was moving ever closer, leering and waving his knife. Just as Teresa was convinced her throat was about to be slit, suddenly the door exploded open and Charles Everett charged inside with gun drawn. Gratitude swamped Teresa in dizzying waves. She watched Charles as he quickly took in the scene, a muscle jerking in his jaw as he spotted her in the grip of two assailants, and saw Manolo advancing on her with the knife.

Charles stood his ground and pointed his gun at the creeps. His voice was deadly cold. "All right, gentlemen, let the lady go and hold it right there. I think you've got some explaining to do."

Even as Charles spoke, Manolo whirled toward him with knife in hand. Though his expression was ugly, he made no move to attack, obviously recognizing the superior strength of the automatic.

However, Freddie and Hector displayed less bravado. Exchanging a panicked glance, the two released Teresa and bolted for the door, Freddie yelling over his shoulder, "Hey, Manolo, let's split!"

For another gut-wrenching second Manolo hesitated, eyeing Charles warily. Then, with a snarl and a threatening wave of his knife, he too turned tail and ran for the door.

Charles rushed toward Teresa. "Are you all right, love?"

She nodded tremulously.

He held up a hand. "Stay there—I'll be right back."

And he spun about and ran out the door after the thugs, yelling, "Stop! Damn it, stop or I'll shoot!"

Teresa felt her body sagging with dizzying waves of relief. She clutched a support beam to keep from collapsing, and tried to calm herself with deep, steadying breaths. Thank God Charles had arrived when he had.

A moment later he raced back inside the shed, gazing at her sheepishly as he replaced his gun in its holster. "Damn. I forgot."

"No bullets?" she greeted with a crooked smile.

"Exactly." He strode quickly to her side, pulled her close, and gazed at her anxiously. "Sure you're okay, Teresa?"

She nodded again, tenderness flooding her at being in his protective arms again.

He glanced toward the door. "I'd pursue them further, but—"

"Don't be silly, you're virtually unarmed," she finished for him.

"Well, thank God they didn't know it." He moved back slightly and worriedly raked his gaze over her. "My heaven, your neck is bleeding."

She touched her flesh. "It's only a few small nicks. Manolo held his knife to my throat."

He appeared appalled. "The bloody bastard! It's a wonder you weren't killed."

"I know."

"You say the man's name is Manolo?"

She nodded. "I learned all that names—Manolo Juarez and his cronies, Hector and Freddie."

"How did they manage to abduct you?"

"Well, after I . . ."

"Escaped me," he provided, his voice hard.

She gulped. "Yes. After I—er—escaped you, they grabbed me out of my car at a light, then threw me into their car and brought me here."

"My God—but why?"

Some inner voice cautioned Teresa not to tell Charles everything she now knew, at least not before she had time to digest it all herself. "I'm not sure—something about Frank owing them some money."

Charles frowned. "Yes, Manolo mentioned something about that at Milton's place. What money?"

"I'm not sure. They didn't have long to question me before you showed up—thank heaven."

"I see." Again Charles's voice took on a harsh edge. "Now that I know you're all right . . ."

"Yes?"

Rage gleamed in his eyes as he gripped her by the shoulders and shook her till her teeth rattled. "You little idiot! I should turn you over my knee and give you an old-fashioned spanking."

"What?" Teresa cried, shoving him away. "Why, of all the nerve—"

"Nerve?" He caught her by the arms, cutting short her protest. "You want to talk about *nerve* after the nasty little stunt you just pulled on me? You wayward girl, you almost got yourself killed. I almost didn't find you. It was only through sheer luck that I spotted Manolo's car parked while cruising through this neighborhood. And don't forget that I just took on three hoodlums with no bullets in my gun. We're both damn lucky we didn't get killed."

Teresa fell silent, biting her lip. She couldn't deny Charles's words, or how supremely grateful she felt toward him for rescuing her again. God

161

only knows what might have happened to her had he not come along just now. She shuddered to think of it.

"Well, Teresa?" he prodded. "What do you have to say for yourself? Why did you run away?"

She regarded him miserably. "Why? Because I don't know who you really are or what you want from me. Because I don't trust you."

"You don't trust me? So you let yourself be abducted at knifepoint?"

"You abducted me at gunpoint!" she cut in, waving a hand.

"Touché," he conceded. "But I had your best interests at heart."

She slapped her forehead. "Oh, yes, how could I have forgotten? Gun-wielding kidnappers *always* have one's best interests at heart, don't they, Charles? How stupid of me. It's the *knife*-wielding kidnappers we have to worry about, right?"

He glared. "Spare me your sarcasm, Tess. You've still been acting like a bloody fool."

Teresa groaned. She couldn't help feeling grateful to Charles—and guilty for what she had just put him through. She realized that, while she still didn't completely trust him, she was through trying to escape him, at least for now. If it hadn't been for him, she might well be dead by now.

She met his eye and slowly nodded. "Okay, Charles, I made a mistake. And I'm very grateful to you for saving my hide." She touched his arm. "Please, don't be mad at me."

Instead of the expected soothing effect, her words seemed to reignite him. That muscle jerked in his jaw again, and his eyes darkened ominously. "Mad? Oh, you've made me mad, all right."

And he thoroughly shocked her then, by hauling her close. His lips caught hers in a punishing kiss, his tongue penetrated her mouth hungrily, and his hands roved her body freely.

Teresa was reeling, on fire. Lord, how could any man be so exasperating yet so damn sexy, she thought dizzily. The danger she'd just been subjected to only added to her feelings of reckless, unbridled desire. She had the rash, exhilarating feeling of losing control; she exulted in the erotic sensation, and knew she likely would have given Charles anything at that moment.

She felt bereft when he abruptly broke away and gave her a stern look. His voice trembled. "You scared the living hell out of me, Tess. Don't *ever* do it again. And you can't get rid of me. I'm in this with you till the end, like it or not."

Moved though she was, she could only ask in bewilderment, "But why, Charles?"

A shuttered expression gripped his face. "That will become evident in time. In the meantime, you'll just have to trust me."

"But I don't trust you!" she burst out in frustration. "Damn it, haven't you listened to anything I've said?"

"You'll have to anyway," he reiterated doggedly. "Now let's get you out of here before those thugs return—and before I lose what's left of my self-control and give you that thrashing after all."

She shot him a dirty look. Then, as he took her arm, she stumbled and let out a low cry of pain.

At once he stopped, eyeing her with alarm. "What is it?"

Teresa grimaced. "My knees hurt. I stumbled to the floor when Manolo shoved me in here."

"The monster." Charles sank to his haunches, only to whistle as he examined the front of her

163

pants. "Your trousers are ripped and..." He pulled at the fabric, stopping when she cried out in pain. "There are nasty, blood-streaked abrasions on both your knees. Are you up on your tetanus shots?"

She flashed him a sweet smile. "Yes, doctor, I never know when I may need to be immunized against someone like you."

"Cute, Teresa." He stood and hauled her up into his arms.

She gasped. "Charles, really!"

He pinned her with a look that brooked no nonsense. "Hush, silly creature, I'm carrying you." Abruptly, he grinned. "And besides, there is no immunizing against me, love."

Teresa could only eye him breathlessly. "Oh, I've noticed."

He chuckled and started off with her. "We'll get those wounds attended to as soon as possible."

Feeling giddy, as well as absurd, she protested, "Charles, really, you don't have to carry me out to your car."

"Are you kidding? I'm not letting you out of my sight again, woman."

He clutched her even closer, and Teresa's senses swam in his manly strength, his warmth, his sexy scent. It was disgraceful. She was an enlightened, intelligent woman, a doctoral candidate in recent sedimentology, for heaven's sake, and Charles Everett was behaving like a stormtrooper, taking charge of her life, dashing her resistance with bold kisses, even threatening her with thrashings.

Yet here she was, putty in his hands, her head resting comfortably against his shoulder. And through it all, like her shameless feline Doris Juan, she was tempted to purr....

Chapter Thirteen

"Are you certain you have no better idea why those men kidnapped you, Tess?" Charles asked Teresa as he drove them off.

Teresa caught a deep, steadying breath. It felt good to be safe in his car with the air-conditioning blowing. She was intensely relieved that Charles had rescued her, but still had many doubts concerning him and his true motives. Should she tell him the truth regarding what Manolo had said about suspecting that her brother was on the trail of buried treasure?

On the one hand, the idea of staid, sober Frank pursuing lost booty seemed ludicrous. From another perspective, especially considering all they'd learned today, it made a lot of sense. After all, Frank had been studying the Lafitte journal, and everyone knew Jean Lafitte was rumored to have left behind a vast fortune in gold booty in the Galveston area. Of course she doubted any untapped treasure locations were contained in the journal itself, but perhaps the old French documents Clark Swinson had brought Frank had yielded some clues. At any rate, if Frank had held the key to that sort of vast wealth, this would also explain why everyone was after her. . . .

Including Charles. Although she did trust him a little more now, he had appeared in her life all too conveniently with his absurd, fabricated tale, and she doubted he was sticking to her like glue now simply because of her boundless beauty. If there was a treasure, logic argued that Charles might well be after it for himself. That would certainly explain his barging into her life, as well as his intense curiosity regarding her present troubles.

"Tess?" he prodded, tossing her a curious glance.

She affected a shrug. "It's like I said. The leader, Manolo, just said Frank owed him some money and he wanted it."

Charles's frown hinted he was unconvinced. "You're sure that was all?"

"Pretty much. Look, shouldn't we report this incident to the police?"

His gaze flicked in the direction of her knees. "I don't know. You're pretty banged up, and I don't think we should wait long before getting medical attention."

"Oh, I'll be fine. I can clean up in the ladies' room at the police station. But those thugs kidnapped me and attempted to kill me. I think we should definitely notify the authorities."

He sighed. "I suppose you're right."

"And what about my car?"

"Teresa . . ." His look was dark.

She waved a hand. "We can't just leave it on the street. Damn it, Charles, they just dragged me out of my car and left it running with my bag still there. If we don't act quickly, I'm sure my car will be towed, if it hasn't already been stolen."

He groaned. "Do you remember where it was?"

She bit her lip. "I think so."

"Very well," he said wearily.

She directed him back toward the spot as best she could. After getting lost a couple of times, they found her car on the same corner where the thugs had kidnapped her, although someone had pushed it off to the side of the road. Indeed, a Hispanic boy in a T-shirt and jeans was slouched next to her fender.

Charles parked his car and he and Teresa approached the vehicle. The boy, who appeared to be about thirteen, grinned at her. "Hey, ma'am, I saw them guys grab you, and I've been watching your car for you." He opened the door and gestured at her bag, which still lay on the floorboards. "Some dudes came by and wanted to steal it and your purse, but I said no."

"Oh, thank you so much," Teresa told the boy. "It's good to know there are still Good Samaritans left in this world."

"Yeah." The boy turned to Charles and held out his hand. "Ain't that true, man?"

Charles nodded and pulled out his wallet. "You bet." He handed the boy a twenty-dollar bill.

"Cool! Hey, dude, thanks!" the kid said brightly, turning and tearing away with his prize.

Charles chuckled, and Teresa shot him a scolding look. "You didn't have to pay him."

"Sure I did. He deserved it. Like you said, a Good Samaritan."

"Well, thanks, I suppose he did deserve it."

"I just wish he'd stayed around a second longer. We could have given the police his name as a witness."

She snapped her fingers. "Hey, you're right."

Charles leaned over into her car, retrieved her bag, and handed it to her. "See if anything's missing."

"Good idea." She quickly scanned through the purse. "Everything looks intact. My money, credit cards, checkbook."

"Good. What about Frank's manuscript?"

"Still there."

"I'm glad nothing was stolen."

Nodding, she tossed the bag back inside, then slipped into the driver's seat, gingerly lifting her legs inside. "I suppose we should head over to the police station next and report this. If memory serves, there's one about a mile or two . . . er, thataway." She pointed to the west.

He cocked an eyebrow. "Thataway?"

"Well, I'm still not completely sure where we are, Charles, but I can head in the general direction."

"Great." He shut her door. "I'll follow you. And no funny business this time."

She groaned. "Charles, I'm all tapped out on funny business for today."

He grinned. "Then you're at my mercy."

Teresa rolled her eyes and started her engine. Honesty forced her to admit that Charles was probably right.

At the police station, Teresa cleaned herself up as best she could in the ladies' room, though she had to admit Charles had been correct to be concerned—while the little nicks on her neck seemed minor, the abrasions on her hands, elbows, and knees were very nasty. And she was already becoming sore all over from the jolting her body had taken in the fall. Nonetheless, she put on as brave a front as possible when she rejoined Charles.

After waiting for more than half an hour, they were shown to an inner office, where a young officer took their report and looked up Manolo Juarez in their department's computer files. He informed them Juarez was a local bad boy, a former gang-banger with a record, and that Hector and Freddie were his known associates. He promised that a warrant would be issued for the arrest of all three men.

By the time they left the substation, Teresa's entire body felt stiff from sitting so long. Charles helped her limp across the parking lot.

"That does it—we're taking you to a hospital," he declared.

"No way," she protested. "You're being ridiculous. I'm just a little stiff from the fall. I'll be fine tomorrow."

"You could have broken bones."

"I don't, Charles. Besides, I don't have money for a doctor."

"I'll pay for it."

"No, Charles."

"Foolish, stubborn woman," he muttered as they paused next to her car. He glanced worriedly inside. "Look, your car has a manual shift. There's no way you can drive in your condition—"

"What do you mean, no way?" she cut in. "I just drove over here, for heaven's sake, and of course I'm taking my car home."

"Damn it, Tess, then at least take my car this time. It's an automatic."

"No, Charles. I'm not an invalid."

"Foolish, stubborn woman," he repeated with growing exasperation.

She shot him a long-suffering look. "You don't have to sulk because you didn't get your way."

Surprising her, he laughed. "Oh, I'll get my way, love. I always do."

Teresa dared not respond to that, though her face burned and her toes curled.

"So, do you want to go straight home from here?" he asked.

"Weren't we going to go see Kelly Brinkman first?"

"Are you up to that?"

"Damn it, Charles!"

He waved his hands. "Very well, I give up. Let's go."

She offered him a placating look. "I know it's a long shot, but Kelly might have some insight into Frank's state of mind before he died."

"True."

"Want to follow me, then? Kelly's parents live in Meyerland, which is more or less on our way home."

"Very well. Lead on."

Teresa drove toward the Brinkman home in southwest Houston, this time being careful *not* to lose Charles, constantly checking to make sure she could see his sleek black car in her rearview mirror. Ten minutes later, she and Charles stood at the door of the cozy, tree-shaded Brinkman home, on a quiet street not far from Meyerland Plaza.

Her knock was answered by a good-looking young man in shorts and a Rice University T-Shirt. "Yes? May I help you?"

Teresa offered her hand. "Hello, I'm Teresa Phelps, Frank Phelps's sister—"

The young man solemnly shook his head. "You mean Kelly's friend who died recently? I'm really sorry, ma'am. I'm Chet, Kelly's brother."

"Pleased to meet you, Chet." She gestured toward Charles. "This is my friend, Charles Everett."

The young man shook Charles's hand. "How can I help you folks?"

"Could we speak with Kelly?" Teresa asked.

Chet eyed them apologetically. "Sorry, but Kelly's in the south of France doing graduate study for the summer. She left a month ago."

"Oh, I'm sorry to hear I've missed her," Teresa said. "I did wonder why she wasn't at the funeral, and of course that explains it."

Chet nodded sadly. "Yes, ma'am. My folks got your message on the answering machine, and I know Mom wrote Kelly about Frank's accident. I'm sure you'll be hearing from her."

"Oh, no problem at all," Teresa assured him.

"Look, won't you folks come in and have some iced tea or something?"

"Thanks, but we can't stay."

He nodded. "Again, I'm real sorry about your brother."

"Thanks."

Teresa and Charles said goodbye and soberly walked back to their cars. Noting her downtrodden expression, he regarded her with keen sympathy. "Sorry, Tess."

"Another dead end," she muttered.

171

Chapter Fourteen

An hour later, Teresa and Charles arrived back at her beach house to a thrum of activity. As Teresa eased up the driveway with Charles following, she spotted a workman's truck and a phone company van parked outside.

Seconds later, as she and Charles climbed up to the front porch, she noted that a new brass dead bolt lock gleamed on the front door, and a workman stood nearby, puttying in the last of several new windowpanes.

The young Hispanic man greeted them with a grin and a wave of his putty knife. "Hi, ma'am. You the tenant?"

"Yes."

"Your landlord sent me over to fix these."

"Yes, I knew he was planning to do so."

"By the way, ma'am, the locksmith told me to tell you your new key is inside on the coffee table."

"Thanks," Teresa murmured.

Charles opened the door for her and they stepped inside. She spotted a shiny key on the coffee table; nearby, a man from the telephone company knelt on the floor with his equipment, testing her line.

The man set down his receiver and nodded to them. "Are you Ms. Phelps?"

"Yes."

"Forgive me for just letting myself in, but the front door was wide open when I got here."

"That's fine. Does my phone work now?"

He nodded, and began disconnecting his equipment. "Someone cut your outside lines, but I've restored service."

"Good. What do I owe you?"

He grinned. "Oh, you'll receive the charges in your next phone bill."

"No doubt."

"I'm afraid your cat kind of freaked out with all the noise." Standing up, he nodded in the direction of the sofa. "I think she's hiding under the couch."

"Thanks."

Watching the man stride out, Charles smiled and shook his head. "I'm amazed at the efficiency of your landlord, Tess."

She laughed. "Oh, he's plenty efficient as long as I'm paying the bills."

"Sorry."

Teresa went over to the sofa and gingerly knelt down, lifting the upholstery flap. "Doris Juan? Are you under there, kitty?"

A low growl was her only answer.

"Oh, come on, Doris, don't be such a pill," Teresa scolded, reaching under the couch and grabbing the cat by the scruff of her neck, then dragging her out. Although Doris's ears were tucked back and her fur was on end, she didn't protest further when her owner scooped her up.

Charles rushed over. "Teresa, you've no business being on the floor with those injured knees. Hand me that cat."

She eyed him skeptically. "You sure? Doris is in a pretty pissy mood—"

"I'm accustomed to females in a pissy mood," he rejoined dryly.

"Cute."

He held out his arms. Teresa handed him the cat. At once, Doris hissed, spit, and snarled, swinging at Charles with her paw; flinching, he dropped the cat on the sofa like a hot potato.

Teresa laughed.

Charles regarded her sternly and extended his hand. "Now let me help you up."

"Thanks." Grimacing, she allowed him to pull her to her feet. They sat down together on the couch; Teresa picked up the cat again.

"Is she all right?" Charles asked, skeptically eyeing the tense animal in her arms.

"Sure. Cats just don't like change."

He reached out to pet Doris, and she spit again, baring her fangs at him. He snatched back his fingers. "So I've surmised."

Teresa chuckled.

"Well, since the fickle Ms. Juan has rejected me, shall I bring in your brother's computer?"

"Yes, why don't you?"

While Teresa took Doris Juan out to the kitchen and fed her, Charles brought in the computer, and the two of them set it up in the spare bedroom that served as Teresa's office. As he looked on, she booted up, launched Frank's word processing software, and began examining her brother's files. Now obviously in a much friskier mood, Doris Juan bounded up on the desk and strutted about, sniffing the unfamiliar equipment, even hissing at the CD-ROM drive when it engaged. Chuckling and shaking his head, Charles wandered off to check on the workmen.

After a few moments he returned, grinning at her from inside the doorway.

She glanced up. "Why are you looking so smug?"

"All the workmen are gone now." He wiggled his eyebrows lecherously. "Alone at last, my love."

She wrinkled her nose at him. "I've Doris Juan to protect me. Watch out."

"I'm terrified," he assured her wryly, then gestured toward the PC. "Any clues to our mystery in your brother's computer files?"

Teresa shook her head. "I'll examine them in greater depth later, but so far it just looks like the typical professor stuff—research papers, lesson plans, exams."

He nodded. "Come on out to the kitchen, why don't you? I've made us a pitcher of margaritas."

"My, aren't you industrious."

Teresa followed Charles out to the kitchen, where he poured them both drinks. "What shall we toast to?" she asked, raising her glass.

"To better luck tomorrow?" he suggested.

"Indeed. To better luck."

They clinked their glasses together and both took a sip. "Nectar from the gods," he murmured, licking his lips.

"You make a mean margarita," she agreed, grimacing slightly at the tartness.

Eugenia Riley

"I do, indeed." He looked her over slowly. "And now, dear lady, I want your pants off."

"Wh-what?" Teresa stammered, very taken aback.

He advanced on her with a determined gleam in his eyes. "You think I've forgotten about those nasty abrasions on your hands, elbows, and knees? Or your muleheaded refusal to seek medical attention?"

She slammed her drink down on the counter. "Now I'm muleheaded?"

"As well as obstinate, unruly, and ungovernable."

"Oh!"

"I've also searched your bathroom for medical supplies, and you're sorely lacking, Tess." He pointed to a bottle of vanilla extract and several clean washcloths stacked nearby. "Anyway, my mum used to use vanilla on my scrapes, so we'll try that."

She balled her hands on her hips. "Are you nuts? I can take care of the abrasions myself."

"You haven't done a very good job so far." He gestured toward her trousers. "Off with them, Tess."

"You're trying to get my pants off!"

He grinned wickedly. "Precisely."

"Oh!" She waved a hand. "This is ridiculous."

His look was menacing. "Don't make me force you, Tess."

"*Force* me? You wouldn't dare."

He raised an eyebrow ominously. Then, before she could react, he pinned her against the counter, froze her resistance with a formidable look, and slowly unbuttoned her waist.

Face burning, she drew a seething breath. "Charles!"

Just as deliberately, he unzipped her trousers. "Must I do the rest?"

"You're terrible."

"Quite." He wiggled his eyebrows menacingly. "Call me 'Charles the Terrible.' Then take off your pants."

Conceding defeat with a sound of impotent anger, Teresa lowered her trousers and stepped out of them, feeling grateful that her shirttail was long and she'd worn sensible cotton panties today. "There—are you satisfied?"

His baldly curious gaze raked over her long, bare legs. "Ecstatic."

"Oh, hush."

With a chuckle, he set down his drink, caught her beneath the arms, and lifted her onto the countertop. His fingers slid over a soft thigh, and his eyes glowed with an unnerving, passionate light. "Has anyone ever told you you have gorgeous legs, Tess?"

Teresa's heart was beating savagely. She eyed him cynically. "Oh, yes, all my lovers do. Let's see, there's Caruso, Valentino—"

"And me," he murmured, leaning toward her.

Teresa was drowning in his nearness, his wonderful scent. "You're not my lover."

"*Yet,*" he murmured meaningfully.

Breathless, she pushed him back as he would have kissed her. "I thought this little exercise was strictly clinical."

Though the smile pulling at his mouth gave him away, he stared at her legs and feigned a scowl. "Well, to be strictly clinical, those are very nasty abrasions on your knees."

"So they are."

He caught one of her hands. "And your elbows and palms don't look much better. The little nicks on your neck appear okay, but we'll have to get all of it very clean to avoid infection."

"Very well," she conceded. "Get it over with."

"My pleasure."

Charles ran some warm water, wet a clean cloth, and began washing her neck, palms, and elbows. His touch was quite delicate, until he took a new cloth, poured vanilla on it, and began dabbing the areas he'd cleansed. That burned like hell!

"Ouch!" she yelled, pulling away.

"Sorry—and be still," he ordered, continuing to dab the inflamed areas. "There, we're done with those, but the worst is yet to come. Your knees are a real mess."

"Oh, Lord."

He shoved her drink back into her hand. "Fortify yourself."

"Thanks," she muttered, giving him a surly look, then taking a gulp.

Teresa alternately grimaced, winced, and complained loudly as Charles thoroughly rinsed both her knees and dabbed them with vanilla.

"Satisfied, Doctor?" she asked at last.

"Well, that looks somewhat better." He took a deep breath. "And you certainly smell marvelous. You didn't have any bandages in your medicine cabinet, but it's probably best just to keep the areas clean and let them air dry."

"Sure. Whatever." She slurped her drink.

"But there could be other problems," he went on ominously.

"Oh?"

He reached out, stroking her flesh teasingly just above one knee. "We really should have taken you to a doctor, Tess. There could be some damage underneath, to bones or cartilage."

"I feel fine now," she told him recklessly.

"That's the tequila, love."

"Yeah," she muttered, waving a hand to cool her hot face. "You know, this drink does seem *awfully* strong, Charles."

His fingers were circling beneath her knee now, teasing the sensitive flesh, even as he moved closer. "Yes, it is strong—strictly for medicinal purposes."

"Yeah." She felt his fingers slipping between her knees, and automatically her eyes grew enormous and her breathing quickened. "What are you doing now?"

"Checking your reflexes," he murmured.

"Sure you are."

He was so close to her now, his scent and heat inundating her, his passionate gaze piercing her. His fingers edging relentlessly upward between her thighs.

Her thighs clenched, trapping his fingers mere inches away from a most vulnerable spot.

He smiled. "Very strong instincts, I'd say."

Teresa's breathing was ragged now. "Stop it, Charles."

His fingers didn't budge, and it occurred to Teresa fleetingly that this was like an armed truce—his fingers trapped between her thighs, while his thumb circled sensuously, raising gooseflesh, like a hawk lazily moving in for the kill. All the while his expression was maddening, so sexy and confident.

"You know, Tess, you really led me on a merry chase today," he murmured. "You took charge of everything, sent my whole life spinning out of control."

"Oh, come on, Charles," she scoffed, though in quavering tones. "You're the one who has

179

unleashed havoc on me. Now you claim *I* have the power to send your life out of control?"

"Indeed, you do."

"So this is my punishment?" she asked.

"Perhaps it is. Why don't I take charge of you now?"

His fingers tried to push upward, and she gasped with mingled frustration and arousal. "You already have, Charles—and I don't like it."

"You don't? Put yourself in my shoes, Tess. What if I had run away from you today and ended up in harm's way? Would you have cared?"

It was sheer hell having this conversation with him, when he literally had her cornered, when she was half-naked, so vulnerable. When it was so damn difficult to think!

"Would I . . . ?" she managed. "Well, yes, I suppose."

"And you think I don't care now?"

"Well . . ."

"If not, then why did I run after you?"

She regarded him in helpless confusion. "Because there's something you want from me, something you want more than you want *me*."

He flinched in apparent confusion. "That makes a helluva lot of sense."

"It's true."

"You're saying there's something I want more than I want you?"

"Y-Yes. Exactly."

His fingers teased her relentlessly. "You know, love, you're begging me to prove you wrong."

She shuddered. "Damn it, Charles, remove your fingers."

He leaned very close, his hot breath tickling her lips. "I can't, love. You're holding on too tight."

Teresa's next protest was crushed by Charles's

kiss, by the breathtaking plunge of his tongue into her mouth. Disarmed, reeling with heady desire, she moaned and relaxed just the tiniest bit. At once his fingers slid brazenly between her thighs, all the way up, until he touched her through her panties.

His boldness was sense-shattering. Teresa went insane, her own logical instincts at war with her out-of-control libido. Charles's touch was like molten fire, penetrating through the cloth of her panties and sending pleasure thrusting, throbbing, deep inside her. She realized she was utterly on the edge, her emotions raw from the life-and-death encounter today, and the urge to give in to him, to lose herself in mindless passion, was almost overwhelming. The urge to throw her arms around him and haul him close was even more potent.

Nonetheless, she managed to resist, squirming against him, unwittingly aiding his own efforts and arousing herself almost beyond redemption. Charles handled her panic deftly, slowly, deepening his kiss until she ceased fighting. He pressed even closer, until she could feel his hard arousal nudging her knee.

At last he pulled away and studied her dazed face.

Mingled fury and desire had rendered Teresa breathless. "Will you kindly remove your fingers?" she demanded.

"Will you let go?" he countered.

"Oh." Realizing at last that her thighs still clutched his fingers in a death grip, she relaxed and spread them slightly. He looked down and smiled. Her face flamed.

"Damn you! What was that all about?" she demanded.

Eugenia Riley

He touched the tip of her nose. "Teresa, don't ever pull a stunt like that on me again, or next time, you may really turn me into a caveman."

Teresa was stunned. "A caveman? You're joking. I was expecting to see you waving a bone and scratching your butt any second now."

"Touché, then." Grinning ruefully, he caught her beneath the arms and stood her up. "Better now?"

Teresa could only stand there and tremble.

He looked her over greedily. "Hey, I've got an idea."

She caught a sharp breath. "I don't know if I can stand another of your ideas."

"Oh, you'll like this one. Let me take you out to dinner."

A startled laugh burst from her. "Really?"

"I think we both need a break."

She regarded him suspiciously. "Well, I suppose . . ."

"So you'll let me take you out?"

She gave a shrug. "It definitely beats staying here."

He feigned a wounded look. "Ouch! You're hell on a man's ego." He tousled her hair. "But you're forgiven."

"*I'm* forgiven?" she repeated, irate.

"Go get dressed, then. I'm famished."

"No doubt," she mocked. "But you'll have to wait. I'd like a bath first."

He lifted an eyebrow lecherously.

She wagged a finger at him. "And I don't need any further assistance—with *anything*—thank you very much."

He pressed a hand to his chest. "Miss Phelps, you break my heart."

"As if you even have one."

"Didn't you just feel it?" he teased.

"If what I *felt* is any indication, then your heart is as hard as a rock!"

Teresa was so furious, she blurted out the words without thought. She suffered the consequences as Charles roared with laughter.

"Oh, shut up!" she ordered, her face beet-red.

His laughter echoed after her as she left the room. She hoped he could not see the wobbling of her knees.

Charles watched Teresa leave the room, the swing of her sexy behind and flash of her long bare legs tempting him, tormenting him with memories of how delicious she'd felt in his arms just now. When he'd felt her warm, wet mouth trembling so sweetly beneath his own, when he'd touched her and felt her dampness through her panties, he'd almost lost all control. He'd longed to strip her naked and feel every inch of her hot, incredible body quivering beneath his own as he consumed her fully. Even now his body still ached with frustrated desire, and he knew from her own response that she wanted him too. He sensed that neither of them would be able to resist this potent attraction much longer.

The woman was making him abandon his better judgment. She'd scared the hell out of him today when she'd managed to escape him. And damn those creeps in Houston who had abducted her! Who were they really, and what did they want from him and Teresa? How dare they threaten her life!

Was seeing her in death's grip what had sent him over the edge?

He tore his fingers through his hair. He'd only known her for a day, and yet he wanted all of her . . . and more. So much, in fact, that before this was over, she'd surely lose all of her illusions and end up hating him. But he couldn't help himself. She fascinated him. He wanted to protect her *and* to possess her.

He was unaccustomed to feeling this way about a woman. Yes, he'd known passion before, but he'd always managed to keep his emotions in check. Now this woman possessed the power to penetrate his facade and touch his deepest feelings, and this he found both threatening and ill-advised. How could he share his heart with her when he couldn't even tell her who he was?

Clearly, his fascination with Teresa Phelps was getting in the way of his doing the job he'd been assigned. He was breaking all the rules with her. But then, Charles Everett never had been a man to play by the rules. . . .

Chapter Fifteen

Manolo Juarez sat in a corner booth at Mama Osa's on the east side of Houston. As a Selena ballad spilled out of the old jukebox, he nursed his beer and furtively eyed the scene. Mama Osa's was a clean but modest *taqueria* with plain furnishings spiced up by red-checked tablecloths, piñatas hanging from the ceiling, and on the walls, mirrors with colorful papier-mâché frames.

Manolo had his meals here several times a week. The food was cheap and good, the beer cold, and Mama never asked for his ID. The joint was popular with hungry day laborers and old men from the neighborhood with time on their hands to shoot the breeze or play dominoes. Since Mama ran a very tight ship, no fighting was allowed, and the cafe was only rarely visited by the police. Avoiding the authorities was Manolo's biggest priority at the moment—that, and whether or not Josie would meet him here like she'd promised on the phone.

Damn, but he had really screwed things up today. Why couldn't Teresa Phelps just tell him where the treasure was? Manolo was certain her brother Frank had been onto something really big. Why else would Professor Phelps hire him and his friends to dig something up at the beach? Then the creep had stood them up and croaked, leaving him and the others holding the bag. If he could just get his hands on that loot, then his problems would be solved. He could take off with Josie for Mexico, and to heck with everyone else, especially her jerk of a brother.

But Teresa Phelps hadn't cooperated at all. Even with her life in his hands, the woman had played dumb. He'd had to be rough with her, something he hated doing with females. Then that pain-in-the-ass boyfriend of hers had showed up waving his gun, and had ruined everything, chasing him and his amigos away. Things couldn't have turned out worse.

Caramba! Now the woman was on the loose and she knew his name—shit, all of their names! Damn, what an *idiota* he'd been to just spit it out. She'd probably filed a police report by now, and since he and Freddie and Hector all had records, there were surely warrants issued for them all. This was why Manolo had not dared return to his apartment, or even show up at Rudy's house. He was hiding at a cheap motel on the south loop, and he'd been forced to borrow his cousin's motorcycle, hiding his low-rider in an abandoned gas station so it wouldn't be spotted.

As for Freddie and Hector, they were holed up with Freddie's uncle, who owned a pool hall somewhere off Almeda Road. There was no telling how long the three of them would have to lay low—another reason he was pissed at Teresa Phelps. Somehow, he had to find a way to get his hands on that loot. His future with Josie depended on it. . . .

All at once, Manolo's ears perked up as the door to the *taqueria* swung open. With relief, he watched Josie bounce in. His heart thumped at the shapely sight of her in tight jeans and a pretty white blouse, curls bobbing on her shoulders, gold necklace, earrings, and bracelets gleaming.

She didn't spot him right away, though every laborer at the joint spotted *her*, turned, and was drooling. Manolo popped up, glaring at the men, then waving a hand at Josie. "Yo, Josie! Over here."

Her gaze swung to his, and her chin came up. Damn, she was pissed. Was every female in the world steamed at him today?

She arrived at the booth and flounced down on the seat opposite him. The scent of her perfume wafted over him, inflaming his hungry senses. But Josie's perfect red lips were still pouting.

She waved a beautifully manicured hand. "So, Manolo, why did you ask me to meet you in this dump?"

"Dump?" he repeated with a nervous laugh. "Don't let Mama Osa hear you say that."

"I have nothing against Mama Osa," Josie replied defensively. "I'm just tired of you dragging me off to sleazy places."

"Sleazy?" Manolo repeated, voice rising. "Look, woman, I don't need this crap right now. I brought you here 'cause I want to have a serious talk."

She crossed her arms over her bosom and glared. "Me too."

"Oh yeah?" he asked, pride bristling. "What do you want to talk about?"

Her dark eyes flashed with anger. "You're dragging me down, Manolo."

"What?"

"You heard me. You're trashing up my life, right when my family is coming up in the world."

He waved a hand. "What are you talking about, woman?"

"I'm saying our family is going places, Manolo. We come from a proud tradition which you can't begin to understand."

Manolo groaned. "Not that family tree crap again? Give me a break, Josie."

Her eyes flashed angrily. "It isn't crap, Manolo. I've been trying to tell you what we're really about for a long time, but you got no respect."

"Here it comes," he grumbled.

"My grandfather started out in this country as a migrant laborer in the Valley, then he moved here to Houston, got a job at the Ship Channel, married my grandmother, and bought her a home. The next generation is doing even better. Rudy is the head of a private police force, my sister-in-law Maria works at a law firm, and I'm an LVN. We're working hard to contribute to the third generation, to build an even better life for Silvia and Sophia."

"Yeah, right," Manolo muttered, nursing his beer. "It's like friggin' *I Love Lucy*, ain't it?"

Josie waved a fist. "Then there's you, Manolo. I've tried to make allowances for you because of your past. I know it's gotta be rough, your mom abandoning you, and living with that crazy aunt.

But you're just not changing, and I'm losing my patience. I don't think this is gonna work."

Now Manolo was feeling threatened. "Josie, give me a break. Look, what do you want from me?"

She gestured again at their surroundings. "Well, look at this joint. Why don't you ever take me someplace really cool? Why do we always have to meet at some dive?"

"We've had lots of fun at those dives, woman," he retorted. "I'm just trying to get on my feet."

"Well, you been trying for as long as I can remember, and you're still stuck on the starting line. Rudy calls you a bum, and I'm starting to believe him. Plus, Maria has been pushing me to date her friend at work. He's a good Hispanic man with a great job, and he attends Mass every Sunday."

Manolo rolled his eyes. "Sounds like a real loser to me."

"Who are you to call someone else a loser?" she snapped back. "Maria's friend wants to take me out for lobster and champagne, not for greasy enchiladas at some *taqueria*."

Manolo waved a hand. "Will you stop about the *taqueria*? I'll take you out for friggin' steaks next time."

"You're missing my point."

"Oh yeah? What is your point?"

She crossed her arms over her bosom. "I could have a decent life with a guy like that."

Feeling desperation creeping into his gut, Manolo flashed Josie his sexiest smile. "Come on, *corazon*, you don't want to turn your back on our love. Remember how much fun we had at the beach last month, drinking beer and dancing in the moonlight? Remember how we kissed when the moon was full?"

Obviously moved, Josie swallowed hard. "Yeah, we've had our good times, but sometimes a man has to think of his responsibilities."

Leaning toward her, Manolo clutched her hand and spoke earnestly. "That's what I'm doing. Look, Josie, I brought you here to tell you something very important. I'm on to something really big. Just be patient a little while longer, baby. Then I'll be loaded and we can run off to Mexico together."

"Run off to Mexico?" she cried, snatching her fingers away. "Are you loco?"

"No. Baby, we could have a great life there."

"You mean living like *bandidos*."

"No, we'll go in style," he argued. "I just have this deal to wrap up first."

She eyed him suspiciously. "Manolo, are you in trouble with the law again?"

"No," he denied, too vehemently.

"Then why did you ask me to meet you at this hole-in-the-wall? And why do you want to run off to Mexico?"

"It will be real cool, baby, you'll see."

Indignantly she waved her hands. "Cool, my butt! This is just what I'm talking about, Manolo. You have no sense of responsibility or respectability. You think I'm just going to leave my mother, my brother, my sister-in-law, my nieces, and run off with a bum like you to Mexico?"

"Josie, please!" he pleaded. "You've been listening to Rudy too much."

She shot him a surly look. "Well, maybe I have. Too bad you haven't listened at all."

The two were glaring at each other when plump Mama Osa, in her colorful Mexican-style dress and apron, swept up with order pad and pencil in hand. "You folks ready to order?"

190

Josie tossed her curls. "Maybe he is, but I'm not hungry." She stood. "*Adiós*, Manolo."

"Baby, please," he pleaded.

But she turned and flounced out of the restaurant without a backward glance. Manolo pounded his fist on the table and cursed under his breath.

Mama Osa grinned and gestured toward the departing woman. "What got stuck in her craw?"

Manolo groaned and gulped his beer. "Respectability," he muttered.

Chapter Sixteen

"Well, you know what they say about oysters, love," Charles remarked.

In the gilded light of the fading day, the two sat on the patio of a seafood restaurant on the boardwalk in Kemah. Teresa eyed Charles in mock reproach, noting the devilish expression on his face as he picked up a shell and neatly downed a raw oyster.

Teresa had been pleasantly surprised when he had suggested they drive up the coast to eat at the popular entertainment district, which consisted of a long, winding boardwalk lined by trendy restaurants, upscale shops, carnival rides, and an amusement arcade. The area was very popular with both locals and tourists, and was well frequented tonight. Around Charles and Teresa other diners ate seafood, drank beer, and talked gaily, while a few couples danced to the music of a jukebox spilling out through the open doors of the restaurant. On the boardwalk, couples and families strolled past, admiring the spectacular view of Kemah harbor and the rolling waves of Galveston Bay beyond. A striking, fifty-foot sailing yacht glided past, heading into port, while shorebirds dived about its billowing sails. Out in the bay, several shrimp boats were chugging back toward harbor, and on the distant horizon, a huge merchant ship added an exotic touch.

The setting was treacherously romantic, Teresa mused ruefully, as was her companion. Charles had been giving her lecherous grins and covetous glances ever since they'd left her beach house. She doubtless hadn't helped matters much by wearing a green gauze sundress with a fairly risqué neckline and spaghetti straps, but it was the only garment she owned with a short enough shirt to allow the abrasions on her knees to air properly. She'd worn a light sweater for modesty's sake, but had been forced to remove it when Charles had suggested they eat outside. Although it was windy here, the ebbing day was still quite warm. Perhaps getting her out of her sweater had been his true motive in suggesting they dine on the wharf—to which his devilish manner now seemed to attest.

He was a charmer indeed, and she was hardly immune to his appeal. Following their sexy encounter in her kitchen, she felt more excited by him than ever. And he looked so dashing in his crisp blue-and-white-striped sport shirt and white trousers, the wind whipping through his dark, thick hair. He seemed in an almost celebratory mood tonight, and this too she found contagious.

Yet doubt continued to nag her regarding who he really was and what he wanted.

"Tess?" he prodded, cutting into her thoughts. "Didn't you hear my comment about the oysters?"

She wrinkled her nose at him. "I heard, you scoundrel. And I think we both know you hardly need any help in the virility department."

He howled with laughter. "You wicked girl. Why, you've literally been stroking my ego all day."

Trying to hide a hot blush at his double entendre, she sipped her beer. "I haven't meant to."

"Haven't you?" He winked solemnly and lifted a shell. "Here, have an oyster, love."

"Charles—"

She shouldn't have opened her mouth, for he used the opportunity to slip the oyster in, chuckling all the time. Teresa could barely swallow as his sexy fingers lingered on her lips and his beautiful blue eyes made clear precisely the metaphor he intended.

"An easy matter, oysters," he went on teasingly. "Just let them slide in . . . then swallow."

She gulped down the oyster with a pained grimace. He all but split his sides laughing.

"Charles! You are perverted!"

His gaze slid over her with lazy ardor. "We're together, Tess. We may as well enjoy it."

Her cheeks bloomed again. "You mean have sex for convenience's sake?"

His expression darkened. "That's not what I meant."

She crossed her arms over her bosom. "Well, it seemed precisely what you wanted this afternoon when you kissed me."

Storm clouds darkened his eyes. "How do you know what I wanted then?"

"It seemed pretty obvious at the time."

"Indeed?" His voice was charged with anger. "Perhaps my passions were running rampant today, but you're the woman who sent me out of control with that wild goose chase you led me on in Houston. As for what happened afterward at your beach house, believe it or not, Tess, for me, a moment of tenderness turned into something deeper and more intense. Now you seem to want to turn it all into something cheap and tawdry. Is that because you find sex cheap and tawdry?"

She was outraged. "Oh! Talk about twisting things around!"

"Well, I refuse to feel ashamed for anything that happened between us today," he went on passionately. "But perhaps you're one of those uptight, sexually repressed females—"

"Uptight, sexually repressed?" she cut in, furious. "At least I don't come on like a sex-crazed adolescent!"

Totally unabashed, he leaned toward her. "And you didn't encourage me? Your body didn't encourage me?"

Much as his words tormented her, she faced him bravely, a victorious smile hovering on her lips. "Uptight, sexually repressed females don't encourage, Charles."

"Ah, yes, they do," he countered with maddening confidence. "They're the ones who know precisely how to drive a man craziest of all."

He had her there, and Teresa could only stare at him, face hot. She had no idea how to deal with his blunt, provocative statements. So she drove him crazy, did she? He was driving her pretty damn nuts at the moment!

Luckily, the waiter came by, depositing their

seafood platters and breaking up the tension. They ate quietly for a few moments.

Then Charles flashed her a conciliatory smile as he savored a bite of fried snapper. "Ah, this is excellent. You know, Tess, I haven't had a meal this good since I last visited London. My family used to spend an occasional holiday there in the summers. We'd dine on oyster stew and cod at our favorite restaurant on Maiden Lane, then we'd attend the opera at Covent Garden, or the Sunday band concerts at Hyde Park."

"Sounds marvelous. I've always wanted to see London."

He winked. "Perhaps I'll take you there."

Unwilling to touch that topic with a ten-foot pole, she murmured, "You've made me curious, Charles. Tell me a little more about your upbringing in England. Were you an only child?"

"Trying to change the subject, are we?" he teased.

"What subject?" she echoed innocently.

He chuckled, sipping his beer thoughtfully. "Yes, I'm an only child, and my upbringing was, I'm afraid, dreadfully ordinary. I grew up in a small village in Surrey. Famous area for weaving and iron foundries. The cottage I grew up in was like so many others there—a seventeenth-century Tudor covered with vines."

"Sounds divine."

"I was away at school for much of my childhood. Through some excellent family connections, I was able to attend Eton College."

"Impressive. Did you play polo like Prince Charles?"

"Oh, of course," he rejoined modestly.

She cleared her throat and carefully asked, "What did your parents do?"

He appeared uncomfortable then, shifting in his chair, turning to watch some laughing children run past. "Oh, they're landowners in the area."

She raised an eyebrow delicately. "Your father is landed gentry? Sounds a bit stodgy for a man I allegedly had an affair with."

Charles glowered.

"You did say your parents are in America now?" she continued smoothly.

"Yes," he answered carefully.

"Here in Galveston?"

"Yes."

"Are they staying with you?"

"No, they have their own accommodations on the island."

"Ah. When may I meet them?" She feigned a melodramatic sigh and slapped her forehead. "Oh, damn, what am I saying, Charles? You'll have to forgive me, but the fact that I've already met your father and had a sleazy affair with him seems to have totally slipped my mind. Tell me, does your mother despise me now?"

"Teresa," he scolded, jaw tight, "you're pushing."

She stared him in the eye. "Indeed I am, Charles. I'm about ready to push you to the damn wall. So what do you have to say for yourself?"

He paused as the strains of a Phil Collins love song, "You'll Be in My Heart," spilled out from the jukebox. "I say let's dance."

"Charles! Now *you're* changing the subject."

"Indeed. And not a moment too soon."

Devilment gleaming in his eyes, he popped up and caught her hand, pulling her up into his arms and leading her away. Though exasperated, Teresa found it hard to resist as Charles maneuvered her expertly around the small dance floor.

The sea breeze felt so warm and sweet on her face, and Charles's arms around her felt so reassuring and strong. He smelled wonderful, too, his spicy cologne mingling with the natural scent of him. . . .

Charles, too, felt exhilarated as he danced with Teresa. She looked so beautiful in her sexy green dress, her chestnut brown curls blowing about her exquisitely lovely face. She felt divine, warm, curvy, and luscious in his arms. The scent of her hair, her perfume, tormented his senses.

But guilt also gnawed ferociously at his gut, especially following her questions just now. Guilt for deceiving her, for not revealing the truth. Guilt because she'd almost gotten killed today, and perhaps he could have done more to prevent it. Guilt because desire for her was all but eating him alive. He wanted her so badly, was so tempted to get in deeper, though surely he would only hurt her in the end. Nonetheless he clutched her closer and kissed her fragrant hair. . . .

When Charles pressed his lips to Teresa's hair, she couldn't help moaning aloud. She felt so safe, so secure, so warm and wanted in his arms. The song lyrics only increased the poignancy of her mood as the artist crooned a soulful promise to protect and cherish his loved one. Despite all her doubts, wasn't Charles doing precisely that with her now?

"What are you thinking, Tess?" he asked huskily.

Gazing up at him and seeing the tenderness etched on his handsome face, she dared to be honest. "I'm thinking it's wonderful to be here, dancing with you, when only hours ago Manolo's knife was at my throat and I saw my life flash in front of my eyes."

Clutching her close, he replied, "I know, Tess. It scared me badly, too. And you were so brave, darling."

His tender words were purest torture. "I tried to be."

"You've had to bear so much lately, haven't you?"

She nodded.

He raised her hand and gently kissed it. "Your brother's death, now this mess."

"And you," she added, in obvious turmoil.

"Yes, me," he solemnly agreed. "You're wrong about me, you know, Tess."

Puzzled, she glanced up at him.

"Today you accused me of wanting something more than I want you."

Her expression was torn. "Well? Do you deny it?"

"Let's say, strictly for the sake of argument, that it was true at first."

Her features paled.

"But it's not true any longer," he quickly added.

Miserably, she shook her head. "I wish I could believe that."

His features tightened in hurt. "Why is it so difficult for you to believe I could be genuinely interested in you, could really care?"

"Call it sad experience," she confided ruefully.

"Then stop listening to your experience and listen to me," he went on intensely. "You must know how much you intrigue me, Tess. I've never met anyone quite like you. You've fascinated me ever since the moment you mixed up Emerson and Thoreau."

"What?" she laughed. "Now there's an original line."

"Tess, it's not a line. That comment about quiet

desperation really intrigued me. That . . . and your cat."

"My cat?"

"You and Doris Juan are quite alike, aren't you?" he went on thoughtfully. "Both loners, both living lives of quiet desperation out there on the Bolivar mud flats." He pulled her closer as the music swelled. "Why is your life so quiet, Tess? Why so desperate? Why are you so reluctant to believe I could really care? Is it because you're locked up in yourself, afraid to trust, or perhaps scared I'll get through and discover the real woman inside you?"

Teresa was sent reeling by his insightful words. "Charles, please, don't do this to me," she pleaded. "Don't make me need you."

He lifted her chin, forcing her to gaze up into his probing blue eyes. "But I want you to need me, love. Seems to me you've been carrying too much of a burden for far too long. Why not depend on me for a change?"

Frustration burst in her with a sigh. "Because you scare me, Charles. Don't get me wrong—I realize now that you have no plans to deep-six me. In a number of ways, you seem a nice, regular guy. But there's still so much about your life, your motives, that mystifies me. And that scares me because I feel drawn to you. Who are you really? What is your stake in this? Surely you don't think I believe all that crap about your investments—any more than you believe I'm really your father's mistress."

He hesitated a long moment. Then they moved apart as the music stopped, their locked gazes as bereft as the empty air hanging between them.

"Tess, take a walk with me," he suggested.

"Okay," she replied.

He paid the bill. Then they strolled off together to a deserted section of the boardwalk, just beyond the carnival rides. They paused at the railing, and for a long moment Charles stared out at the gold-tipped rolling waves of the bay, his expression turbulent.

At last he turned, stroked her cheek, and smiled at her, a troubled smile. "Tess, there's much I want to tell you, but I'm just not free to do it as yet."

"Why?"

He held up his hand. "Will you be satisfied with a beginning?" When she would have protested, he quickly added, "It's all I can offer for now."

"Very well," she agreed heavily.

"What if I told you I was a friend of your brother's from college?"

"My God!" she cried. "Were you?"

He nodded. "What if I told you that I heard from Frank shortly before he died—and afterward suspected his death wasn't an accident? What if I told you I had to get close to you in a hurry to protect you?"

Amazed by these revelations, Teresa burst out, "But if all that is true, why didn't you just tell me the truth in the first place instead of inventing such a wacky story?"

He sadly shook his head. "That I can't reveal, I'm afraid."

Teresa felt as if she might die of frustration. "Damn it, Charles! Do you have any idea of the hell I've been through since you barged into my life? Do you know I actually suspected that you . . ."

"Might have had a hand in your brother's death?" he finished in keen disappointment.

"Yes," she acknowledged, lifting her chin. "Can you blame me for being suspicious?"

"No," he admitted with regret.

"You just seemed to know so much about Frank."

He caught her by the shoulders. "Teresa, listen to me. That's precisely why I'm telling you what I am now. Frank was my friend, and you must know I had no involvement in his death. None at all. Do you believe me?"

She regarded him in exquisite torment for a moment, studying his sincere, tense face. Then, slowly, she nodded.

A sigh burst from him. "Thank heaven."

"But why can't you tell me more?"

Charles dragged his fingers through his hair. "I just can't, Tess. It's complicated. There are confidential matters I'm just not free to divulge."

"Charles—"

"I'm sorry. I just can't." He turned away to stare moodily at the bay.

Teresa seethed in silent frustration. How could Charles have told her all those things about knowing Frank—amazing revelations, really— then just slam the door shut in her face, refusing to say more? All because it was "complicated"?

But Teresa feared it wasn't "complicated" at all. If Frank and Charles had been friends, if the two men had spoken shortly before Frank's death, then logic argued that surely Frank would have told his friend that he was on the trail of buried treasure.

Then had Charles kept silent about knowing Frank because he didn't want her to know he was after this same treasure? Had he wanted to hide his own greed? Under the circumstances, logic argued that he might well be in this for himself, and trying to disguise his true motives.

But on the other hand, at least Charles was trying to share with her and had made a beginning at being honest. She didn't doubt that what he had just told her was true; there were just so many more blanks he needed to fill in.

She studied his face in profile, noting his tightly set jaw and deeply troubled frown. Yet she saw no clue in his expression that could answer any of her questions.

She turned to stare at the colorful Ferris wheel soaring and spinning behind them. The carnival ride seemed an appropriate metaphor for her entire relationship with Charles so far. Wild. Exhilarating. Romantic. And dangerous.

Of course, on the ride itself, danger was merely an illusion. Yet with Charles, Teresa still feared the danger might prove all too real. . . .

Chapter Seventeen

At home Charles suggested they have a brandy on Teresa's back deck overlooking the Gulf. She had already seated herself on a patio chair when he stepped outside with two half-filled snifters.

"Thanks," she said, taking her glass. "And thanks for a lovely evening."

"You're welcome." Slipping into his chair, he held up his snifter. "To the end of a memorable occasion."

"Cheers." She clicked her glass against his.

"And perhaps the beginning of an even more spectacular one?" he suggested.

The mischievous though ardent look in Charles's eyes took Teresa's breath away. She set down her snifter, stood on her wobbly legs, and walked over to the railing. He soon joined her, standing close, stroking her bare arm with his warm, strong fingers, raising shivers.

"Teresa, what is wrong?"

"Oh, I just wanted to look out at the night—the breeze has cooled, and the moonlight on the water is so pretty."

"You're avoiding me," he accused.

"Charles . . ." Turning her troubled face toward his, she said, "I've got a lot on my plate right now."

"I'd like to have *you* on my plate, love."

She gave a low laugh. "In a manner of speaking, perhaps you already do."

"I'm pleased to hear it." He toyed with a curl at her earlobe.

Shuddering, she pulled away. "Charles, please. I don't think we should just dive into something rash like this when things are still so . . . confused, and dangerous."

That comment raised a frown. "You still think I'm dangerous, Tess?"

She turned toward the Gulf with a sigh. "I didn't say that. But you're certainly confusing. Let's just look at the ocean for a moment, okay?"

"Okay." For several moments, they both stared out at the smooth shoreline, at the silver-capped waves, the moonlight sparkling on the water. Then he nudged her arm and said, "Tell me why you like it here so much."

She turned to him with a puzzled smile. "You mean here, on this deck?"

"Yes."

"Well, it's where I watch my birds."

"Fun in the morning, eh?"

"And I come out here a lot to think, to write notes for my dissertation."

"All that sexy stuff about backwaters and tidal surges, eh?"

"Right."

"Exactly how long have you lived here, Tess?"

"Nine months. It's good to be close to my subject matter, exploring the shoreline, studying tide pools. And living near the ocean this way—there's just something so primal and soothing about it. There's life everywhere—fish, plants, and turtles in the ocean, birds and crabs along the shoreline."

He gestured about them. "But you're like a hermit crab yourself, Tess. You're isolated here. No close neighbors."

She gave a shrug. "I like it that way."

"I've noticed."

She regarded him wryly. "Are we back to the 'quiet desperation' bit again?"

"It's true, Tess. Your companions are books, rocks, the tide, and an ill-tempered cat."

"She's not ill-tempered."

"Nor is she a person. And like her, you prefer to remain aloof."

Teresa eyed him askance. "You're one to talk, the original Mystery Man."

He chuckled and curled an arm around her waist, pulling her close. She stiffened slightly.

He pressed his mouth to her ear, and she shivered. "You don't like me getting too close, do you, Tess? That's why you're feeling threatened and off-balance right now."

"Don't presume to tell me my feelings."

"Am I wrong?"

She pulled away. "If I feel threatened and off-balance, it's because I don't know you, Charles."

Studying her face outlined in moonlight, he asked huskily, "Do you know how much I want you?"

Teresa fell silent, her expression torn.

He leaned over, whispering at her ear. "How much I want to be close to you?"

"I know." Shuddering, Teresa slipped away from him again. Charles's nearness was too tempting, and the night was so sensuous, with the scent of the sea, the roar of the wind, the glorious sight of moonlight dancing on the water.

"Tess?"

She turned to him; he looked so gorgeous with the silvery light etching his fine features. "I'm hardly immune to you, either, Charles. I just think it's so—unwise"—

"Then let's be unwise," he murmured, pulling her close. "Let's be foolish, love."

He kissed her, just as behind them, a wave roared, and again his potent sensuality proved all but irresistible. Teresa found her control slipping away like the ebbing tide. She clung to him giddily, their lips hungrily mating, their tongues devouring. His hands roved all over her body, caressing, molding her to him, igniting a need that was frightening in its intensity. Teresa could not catch her breath or control her spinning thoughts. She wanted Charles so badly she throbbed inside.

As their lips parted on a deep sigh, he slipped down her spaghetti strap and caressed her bare shoulder, wrenching a moan from her. Teresa couldn't help herself, it all just felt so right. Then his mouth followed, his lips burning down her soft neck, settling at the base of her throat. His fingers slipped inside her dress, touching her breast, stroking her nipple.

Helplessly Teresa cried out. The little peak puckered at his touch, tightening almost painfully, even as fiery threads of desire penetrated downward, permeating every part of her with rampant need.

When his hand grew bolder, cupping her bare breast, his lips streaking down the same treacherous path, sanity at last crashed in on her. She knew she was about to do something she had no business doing, with a man she barely knew. Frantically she pulled away, reeling, gasping for breath. Tears stung her eyes.

"Teresa, what is wrong?" he asked.

"I can't, Charles. I just can't. This is too soon for me, and way too intense."

He crushed her close again, kissing her cheek, the corner of her mouth. "I want this so intense that we're both dying for it."

Somehow she managed to break away. "No, it's not right. Not yet. Maybe not ever."

Before she could lose all of her resolve, she ran back to the shelter of the house. . . .

Charles watched Teresa fleeing with a groan. Why was she so skittish? He wanted her—really wanted her—and he very much sensed the attraction was mutual. But she seemed inhibited about sex, even frightened. And this was strange for a woman of her age and sophistication. Her almost maidenly reluctance was also as provocative as hell, only intensifying his own desire. The more he learned about this woman, the more he wanted to find out what really made her tick.

He went inside to the living room and found Doris Juan asleep on the couch, but no Tess. He went to her bedroom and gently knocked on the door.

"Tess?"

"Go away."

He opened the door and stepped inside. The

lights were off, moonlight spilling in from the window, illuminating the bed where she lay. She was sprawled across the mattress, her face turned away from him. She appeared lovely, fragile and vulnerable in the flimsy sundress, her arms bare, her long beautiful legs revealed to him. Tenderness tore at his gut.

"Teresa, what is wrong? Why were you on the verge of tears just now when I kissed you?"

"Will you please go away?" she pleaded.

"No." He crossed over and sat down beside her. When he touched her arm, she flinched. "Hey, relax. I don't bite."

Her voice came muffled. "You do everything else."

He chuckled. "No more verbal sparring, love. We're going to discuss this now."

She sat up, regarding him mutinously. "Not on my bed we're not."

He watched her get up, cross the room, turn, and press her back against the wall, her lovely hair falling across one cheek, half shuttering her face.

He stood and smiled quizzically. "You're afraid of me."

She glanced away and he watched her throat work.

"Well, Tess?"

Her voice was low, vibrating with emotion. "What you said outside was true. I don't want you to get to know me. Not really."

"So the truth is out at last."

She lifted her chin defiantly. "Can you blame me? You barge into my life yesterday at gunpoint, an act which, may I point out, did not exactly inspire my trust. Since then you've stuck to me like glue. Now I've known you for little more than twenty-four hours, and you're coming on like some oversexed—"

He took a step toward her. "Now wait just a minute. You were hardly clawing my eyes out just now. What's the problem, Teresa? We're two adults who are attracted to each other—"

"It may be that simple for you, but it isn't for everyone else, Charles."

He scowled. "Very well. I'm listening."

Clenching her fists at her sides, she appeared miserable in the darkness. "Men don't want me."

Charles couldn't help laughing. "What?"

Now her voice trembled with anger. "You heard me. I said, men don't want me."

"Then how do you explain me, love?"

"You just . . ." Anguish all but cut off her next words. ". . . find me convenient, especially under the circumstances. You don't really want me. And—and if this went further, you wouldn't stay."

Now he shook his head in perplexity. "I don't understand at all. Why would you say such things about yourself?"

She faced him bravely, eyes glowing. "Because I'm not the type who inspires earth-shattering passion in men. I'm not beautiful."

Instantly filled with compassion for her, he stepped close and touched her arm. "Oh, Tess. You're beautiful to me."

She pulled away. "Charles, don't do this. Don't try to charm me."

"I'm not. You're so lovely to me, Tess, really you are. Your pretty face and shiny hair, your fine eyes, your feminine, slender body."

Much as his words were swaying her, she pressed on. "You must understand that the men I've been with—well, let's just say it's not every day that I'm romanced by a gorgeous hunk like you."

"Gorgeous hunk, eh?" Appearing delighted, he quipped, "Well, love, I suppose there's a first time for everything."

Teresa couldn't help but laugh. "So modestly put, as always. But you're still missing my point."

"Which is?"

"Must I say it?"

"Please do. I'm dense."

She flung a hand outward. "My sex life has been an unqualified disaster."

He grinned and pulled her into his arms. "Is that all? Well, we can remedy that—and quickly."

Irate, she wiggled away. "Damn it, Charles, will you take me seriously?"

He appeared mystified. "But I thought I was doing precisely that."

She began to pace, waving a hand. "You have no idea what it's been like for me."

"Then tell me, Tess. Tell me."

She groaned. "I—er—had my first experience when I was in high school, with the school nerd, Kirby Skelton—he was the president of the science club."

"Sounds charming."

"To tell you the truth, I mainly wanted to get it over with, so my girlfriends would quit teasing me about being the last living virgin on the planet and all that."

"I see."

"Anyway, Kirby and I were in the park, in the backseat of his dad's Chevy, just, well, going at it. It was humiliating for me, not to mention intensely uncomfortable. But the worst part was, right in the middle of it, a park ranger caught us, shining his spotlight on, well, our you-know-whats."

He laughed. "Ah, yes, the sight of bare pink bums thrashing away on the backseat of a Chevy."

"Charles!"

His voice was sympathetic. "Darling, many young people have had humiliating experiences similar to yours. Haven't you learned to laugh about it yet?"

She regarded him proudly. "No. I still don't find it amusing."

"Don't tell me the ranger arrested you?"

"No, he just chased us off with a stern warning, didn't even tell our folks, thank God."

He kissed her cheek. "So you had an unfortunate initiation into sex, darling." Huskily he murmured, "Just trust me. We'll change that."

Reeling, she pulled away. "You don't understand."

"Go on."

"In college—well, it was no different. I dated mainly science and math majors, and it just seemed like any time things got heavy, I would freeze up. Finally I just gave up on it all."

Pulling her close, he traced a finger over her lips. "Then you're almost like a virgin, darling, aren't you?"

"Charles, I assure you I'm not."

He caressed her cheek and regarded her tenderly. "But you've never really known the true pleasure of making love with a man, giving yourself to him."

She tried to twist away, face hot, but he held her tight, arms clenched about her waist.

"Tess?"

She could feel the hardness of his desire rising between them, and it was devastating to her senses. "I—I think we've discussed this quite enough."

"And I think we've just begun. Don't you have any idea, darling Tess, how irresistible your dilemma is to me?"

"Charles—"

She couldn't speak after that, for Charles's lips were tenderly taking hers, his tongue stealing inside her mouth to thrust and possess in a most brazen and erotic way. She winced helplessly and clung to him. She wondered what was wrong with her; she wanted to resist him, but his kiss was overwhelmingly sexy, like a bolt of hot lightning shooting straight through her, leaving her weak and hungry for more.

He roved his lips over her face. "Teresa, I want you to give yourself to me. Lose yourself in me. Believe that I really want you for *you*. You got hurt before because you were so tied up in yourself, in your fear, that you couldn't let go and let yourself feel the pleasure. Do you have any idea how good it can be between a man and a woman when both abandon all inhibition and succumb only to each other—to pleasure?"

Teresa was gasping. "I—I think I'm beginning to get an idea."

He backed away then, going to sit down on the edge of the bed. His eyes burned at her in the night.

"Tess, come here and give yourself to me."

His words staggered her. She stared at him, heart pounding in the silence. "Charles, please don't do this to me. You're tearing me apart."

"And you'll tear me apart if you don't come here." His voice was stern yet raspy. "I'm waiting, Tess."

At last she managed to breathe. "I'm too scared."

"Of what, darling?"

"I don't know!" she burst out helplessly.

"Then tell me to go."

"I—I can't."

"Then come here."

He said nothing more, just stared at her with such desire that she went weak. She felt her heart would explode in the silence of the room. At last, like one hypnotized, she kicked off her sandals, then crossed the room and went to stand between his spread legs.

His strong arms caught her about the hips. "Good girl, Tess. Good girl." He reached up and undid both ties on her sundress, then slowly slid it off her.

Teresa shivered in ecstasy, standing before him in only her strapless bra and panties.

"My God, you're so lovely," he murmured, tracing a finger over the smooth flesh of her belly. "How can you think of yourself otherwise? I've never seen such skin." Pressing his mouth to her midriff, he slid his hands upward, clutching her breasts through her bra. "Your breasts are exquisite."

She moaned, dizzy with desire.

He opened her bra then, and his hand boldly squeezed a bare breast. She reeled.

"Look at me, Tess."

She dared to gaze down at him and felt herself going wet at the look in his eyes.

"Does that feel good?"

"Oh, yes."

"I want you so badly I could devour you." He stretched upward and gently bit her nipple.

She cried out, his wet, hot mouth and skilled tongue making her insane with desire. She began ripping at the buttons on his shirt. She roved her fingers over his smooth muscles, his dark curls. She knew she was being damn foolish, but she just didn't care, she wanted him so much.

He pulled her down forcefully on his thigh, kissing her ardently, roving his hand over both her breasts, down her belly, over her thighs. "How does that feel, darling?"

She was moaning. "Wonderful. I'm hurting inside, Charles, hurting for you."

"Are you hurting here?" He stroked her through her panties.

"Oh, yes. I'm burning."

"Enough not to be afraid anymore?"

"Oh, yes."

He nudged her to her feet, nestled her between his spread thighs. "You look so damn beautiful standing there."

She pulled at his shirt, tugging it off him. "No fair—you're wearing all the clothes."

"Not for long." He pushed himself back on the bed, and removed his shoes. She took an eager step, but he held up a hand. "Take off your panties, then come make love with me."

The hoarse words staggered Teresa with such desire, she was trembling all over. Charles looked so gorgeous waiting for her on the bed, eyes aglow with desire, chest bare, trousers bulging.

He was touching himself and smiling at her. "Do it, love. Show me how much you want me."

With trembling hands, Teresa removed her panties and stepped out of them.

His gaze burned over her, searing her with its heat. "So beautiful. Now come closer."

She eagerly did, crawling onto the bed with him. "Unzip me."

She complied, feeling his hardness pressing against her fingers. Her eyes widened as he finished the task, pulling his trousers and boxers down over his hips.

She gulped. "My God."

"Look at me. And touch me."

Though she felt brazen, Teresa couldn't take her eyes off the beautiful, hard, smooth shaft. She reached out tentatively, touching the satiny, warm flesh.

He hauled her body on top of his and fiercely kissed her, grinding his teeth against hers. The feel of their naked flesh touching and melding sent shock waves all through her.

Charles pushed her onto her back and pressed his mouth to her breast, caressing with his tongue, nipping with his teeth, then sucking deeply. The sweetness of it all brought tears to her eyes. She cried out, quivering violently, but he held her still. Even as he continued devouring her breasts, his hand slid down her belly, and lower. Instinctively her legs tensed, but his fingers slipped inside anyway, touching her curls, stroking lower. Then both hands were there, pulling her thighs apart. She half panicked and bucked against him.

"Easy, love. Relax."

But relaxing became impossible for Teresa, as her body felt as though it were connected to the most delicious hot current. Charles's merciless fingers found just the right place, caressing the center of her passion, stroking the incredibly sensitive spot, and inexorably building her ardor. She wiggled, moaned, even fought him, but there was no escape, and to be honest, she wanted none. When his finger boldly penetrated her womanflesh, she felt as if she were coming out of herself, she was so out of control. She kissed him with desperate need and her hands roamed all over his body, stroking his back, grasping his buttocks, touching his passion, tearing groans from him.

He rolled and brought her on top of him again. His words came roughly. "Straddle me."

For a moment she froze, breathless, staring into his eyes. The passion she saw there told her he intended to consume her utterly.

"Now, darling," he urged.

Catching an agonizing breath, Teresa instinctively guided herself into position, her knees straddling his hips. She felt feverish, deliciously vulnerable to him. Then she felt the hot, hard tip of him piercing her flesh so pleasurably, and she raked her nails over his chest and whimpered his name.

A violent shudder shook him, then he possessed her in a powerful upward thrust. She cried out and squirmed, so full of him she was throbbing, frantic, unsure she could bear the torrid sensations tearing her apart.

"Oh, God, Charles, you feel incredible. You're like a rock inside me."

His voice was tortured. "You feel wonderful, too, love. So soft and hot and snug."

His arms clutched her close as he began pumping vibrantly. Their mating was hot, intense, the pressure exquisite. Soft sobs shook Teresa as she began climaxing immediately, uncontrollably, her body racked by passions so overpowering that she feared she might faint. Charles crushed her to his chest and kissed her desperately as he drove them both to even greater summits of rapture. And she knew in that moment just what he'd meant about a man and a woman giving themselves to each other entirely as they became completely one.

Chapter Eighteen

"Sure you don't want to come along, Aunt Maizie?" Lillian Hatch called. "You know, it's never too late to start an exercise regimen!"

At 7 A.M., Maizie Ambrush again sat on her shady porch, sipping tea and watching her niece Lillian jog in place out on the sidewalk, once again preparing to take off for her morning constitutional. Steam hung in the torpid air, an early-morning thunderstorm having just passed.

"Oh, no, dear, you go on ahead," Maizie replied. "I'll be just fine here with my tea. You know, I don't see how you can do it, dear. I swear I'm dizzy just from watching you bounce about. And the heat! Seven A.M., and it's already hot enough to melt the iron fencepost."

"Practice, aunt, practice!" Lillian heaved back,

bobbing in place. "Just think, you could be out here sprinting away if you chose to—and no more dizzy spells. All a matter of self-discipline, you know."

"Yes, dear."

"Well, toodle-oo, then!"

Maizie shook her head as Lillian spun into a turn, then went vaulting off. She felt exhausted from the encounter with her niece. And she was growing weary of Lillian's snide comments regarding her own lack of exercise and self-discipline. She thought she was doing famously for a ninety-year-old. So she didn't trim her roses in the heat of the day. Everyone knew roses should be cut early in the morning, anyway.

Lillian's carping was not particularly beneficial to Maizie's blood pressure, which was quite unpredictable at her age. Doctor Hudson always warned her to try to remain calm. "Just relax and smell your roses, Maizie," he always said.

Maizie picked up her crystal bud vase and sniffed the delicate Peace bloom she'd placed there earlier. Yes, this was all she really needed in her life now—some peace and quiet.

But it wasn't easy. Aside from Lillian's relentless harangues, Maizie remained quite worried about Teresa. She had tried to call her great-niece yesterday, but had received no answer. She must try again today. . . .

Lillian jogged down the sidewalk, taking deep breaths of hot, moist, nectar-soaked air. Again she relished the sweat trickling down her face, the pounding of blood through her veins.

For a fifty-year-old, she was in prime shape. Her aunt was another matter. Lillian was quite concerned about Maizie's sedentary lifestyle. At ninety, Lillian's aunt was slowing down and becoming forgetful. She seemed capable of doing little more than keeping her house, attending to her own business, helping out at church and at several other charitable organizations, and serving as president of a local historical society. Lillian was convinced Maizie was capable of a much more vigorous existence. Why, the woman had lost all interest in world travel, and now preferred going on banal domestic bus tours to Charleston or Nashville with other members of her seniors club.

Lillian sorely hoped her own life would never sink to such a depressing level of inactivity. Why, Maizie had refused Lillian's invitation last summer to go on the African safari she'd organized for her own faculty members. Clearly her aunt was failing. She needed a brisk exercise regimen and a daily dose of ginkgo biloba.

Lillian resolved that she must discuss her aunt's frailty with Teresa—that is, *if* her wayward niece ever mended her own intemperate behavior. Of course, Lillian knew she had best not hold her breath there.

She turned onto Broadway, where again cars jammed the wide avenue. She passed an old gentleman walking his Pekinese and a young mother in sweats pushing a baby jogger. The baby boy in blue gurgled at Lillian as the two bounded past.

That was the idea, Lillian thought stoutly. Exercise from the cradle. The prospect brought a smile to her face, but as she continued along, the smile faded, as a funny feeling again crept over her, as if someone were watching her. Strange, but she'd had the exact same odd sensation yesterday during her jog. She glanced at the street, but spotted nothing unusual, only people driving to work wearing the usual, half-comatose expressions.

Shaking off the disquieting twinge, she forged on past the beautiful Italianate brick facade of Ashton Villa, then turned onto a shady side street. As she rounded the corner, a battered subcompact car wheeled around ahead of her, cutting dangerously close to her body and spattering her legs with mud.

"You imbecile!" Lillian shouted after the car, waving a fist.

The vehicle chugged on, turning at the next corner. Muttering something unladylike, Lillian continued on her jaunt. She had just reached the corner and was about to cross that same intersection, when all at once, a figure clad in black jumped out at her from behind a tree.

Lillian screamed and skidded to a stop.

Heavens! It was a swine! A man wearing a hideously grinning pig mask stood before her. He sported yellow tusks and grotesque pointed ears sickening enough to make Lillian want to vomit. And the beast was carrying a gun—and pointing it at her! Lillian could only stare in consternation and fright.

"What on earth—"

The rest of Lillian's comment was drowned out as the pig raised his weapon, then pounded Lillian over the head with the butt of his revolver. An explosion of light and pain forced her to her knees. Consciousness blurred in and out as, with a low moan, she collapsed in a heap at the pig's feet. . . .

Lord, this broad was heavy, the man thought. Grunting and groaning, he dragged Lillian

Hatch's deadweight to the passenger side of his car. Somehow, he managed to pull, heave, and shove the woman facedown over the seat. Panting for breath, he lifted her legs and feet and hauled them inside, then slammed the door. He hurried around to the driver's side of the car, climbed in, and drove off in a squeal of tires.

His trembling, moist hands struggled with the steering wheel. His heart pounded with explosive beats. Damn, the mask was strangling him and he could barely see with all the sweat trickling into his eyes! Glancing at his captive through the corner of his eye, he spotted no movement. Good, the amazon was out cold. He ripped off his hooded mask and sucked a huge breath into his parched lungs. Lord, he was sweating like a pig, he thought, wiping his dripping face with his sleeve.

Then at last a smile of grim satisfaction settled over him. Hot damn, he'd done it. He actually had the amazon in custody, which meant he had the leverage he needed to force Teresa Phelps to cooperate.

He had much to do. He had to get the amazon over to the flophouse, sneak her in, handcuff and gag her. And then it might be time to pay Teresa Phelps another nice little visit. . . .

Chapter Nineteen

Teresa was dreaming a beautiful dream about Charles making love to her when she jerked awake at the feel of something cold and hard probing against her temple. Blinking open her eyes, she was horrified to see the Pig from Hell again leering down at her. It was the barrel of his deadly revolver that was pressed to her scalp.

Too terrified to scream, she used her elbow to jab Charles, who was lying next to her. At once he flinched, opened his eyes, and scowled at her. She shot him a beseeching glance and rolled her eyes toward the gun. Spotting both the weapon and the intruder, Charles went wide-eyed, sat up, and glared at the man, though he wisely resisted trying to grab the revolver.

"Who the bloody hell are you and why are

you pointing that gun at Ms. Phelps?" Charles demanded.

Ignoring Charles, the man growled to Teresa, "I've got your aunt, lady."

"You've what?" she cried.

"You heard me! I've kidnapped the broad in the purple jogging suit. I'm prepared to blast her brains out, and it'll be goodbye, golden years. So, get me the papers in twenty-four hours or you're next!"

"What papers?" Charles demanded.

The man removed the gun from Teresa's temple and began haltingly backing away. "Twenty-four hours," he repeated ominously, hooking a leg over her windowsill, then ducking outside.

After he left, it took Teresa a moment to remember to breathe. Then Charles was shaking her, demanding, "Teresa. My God, darling, are you all right?"

With a low cry, she fell into his arms.

He clutched her trembling body close. "There, there, love. I can't believe that maniac just pointed a gun at you. I felt so helpless."

"Me too."

"I wanted to defend you, but—"

She pulled back and shook her head. "Charles, no, there was nothing you could do. He would have blown my head off, and yours. Besides, I think you acted pretty belligerent under the circumstances."

Jaw tight, he made a move to get out of bed. "I'll go after the bloody bastard now."

She grabbed his arm. "No, Charles, don't. He might still shoot you and—damn, you don't have any bullets in your gun."

"You're right," he muttered, snapping his fingers. "Then you must go fetch my clip, and I'll—"

"Oh, my God!" she cut in.

"What is it, Tess?" he asked urgently.

As the reality of the masked man's words at last sank in, she went wide-eyed. "Did he say he has Aunt Hatch?"

Charles nodded grimly. "Now, Tess, you must try to remain calm—"

"Remain calm? When a maniac with a gun has my aunt?"

"He might be bluffing."

"I don't think so, Charles. Did he strike you as the type to bluff?"

"Well . . ." Charles avoided her eye.

Teresa wrung her hands. "Oh, God, he must really have her! This is awful!"

Charles was scowling massively. "Tess, try to calm down, we have to think."

"Think about *what*? If you're referring to the papers he wanted, I still have no idea what in the hell they are!"

"I realize that, dear. But, er, let's see. . . . Did you recognize the man? I mean, did he seem at all familiar to you?"

Incredulous, Teresa waved a hand. "Charles, he was wearing a pig mask, for heaven's sake! Did he seem familiar to *you*?"

"What I mean is, might he have been one of the Hispanic thugs who kidnapped you yesterday?"

"Possibly." She buried her face in her hands. "Oh, damn it, Charles, why are we debating this when Aunt Hatch's life is in danger?"

Charles's brows rushed together. "You're right. We'd best get a move on." Kissing her quickly, he hopped out of bed.

Teresa's head popped up and she stared. Shameful though it was, in that moment her attention was riveted to the sight of Charles's gor-

geous naked body. And she got a full view as he
jumped out of bed and turned. He was tanned,
leanly muscled, had a gorgeous backside, and an
even more impressive front. His chest was beautifully contoured and covered with crisp hair, his
belly was flat and lean . . . and that glorious shaft
that had made her climb the walls last night lay
peacefully against his thigh, tempting her to
stroke it back to life again.

Heavens, how could she be thinking about sex
at a time like this? Her aunt might well be in the
clutches of a maniac. She was utterly wanton.
Face going hot with embarrassment, she pulled
the sheet up to her throat. Then Charles moved
off to the window and peered outside, leaving
Teresa wincing with unbridled lust. She could see
everything—and she wanted it all!

"Well, the bastard is gone already, so no point
trying to pursue him now," he muttered, pulling
the screen into place, then shutting and locking
the window. "Damn it, I could have sworn I locked
this window yesterday. Looks like he must have
jimmied it again. I'll shove a piece of dowelling in
the track tonight."

That last comment seemed unbearably erotic
to Teresa under the circumstances—she shamelessly wanted Charles shoving himself into *her*.
"Yeah. You do that."

He turned to regard her in bemusement. "Tess,
love, why is your face so hot? Have you been
ogling me, you bad girl? Look, there's no time to
dawdle. Hop out of bed right this minute."

"But . . . I don't have any clothes on."

He grinned. "That's the idea, love, you need to
get out of bed and *put* them on."

"But . . . you'll see me."

Charles tore over to the bed and ripped back the

sheet, grinning as she blushed from head to toe. "Tess, you think I didn't see you naked last night? Why, I spent a delicious hour, while you were sleeping, examining you from head to toe in the moonlight."

Though her cheeks burned, she chortled in glee. "Why, you reprobate!"

"Reprobate? You have wild, passionate sex with me, and now you're complaining because I've seen you naked?"

"A girl has her standards," she said primly.

He leaned over and kissed her breasts, sensually abrading them with his unshaven cheeks and prompting more ecstatic moans. "Get up, silly girl, before I give you a good wallop to get you moving. You're forgetting Aunt Hatch—and her kidnapper."

"Oh, right, I'm just horrible." Teresa hopped up, rushed over to the dresser, and opened her lingerie drawer. Pulling on clean undergarments, she watched Charles don his boxers and felt a sense of belated relief. At least she knew now that he could not possibly have been the mysterious masked man who had accosted her yesterday morning—the man who now claimed to be holding Aunt Hatch captive.

Her emotions must have shown in her eyes, for he turned to regard her quizzically. "What is it, Tess? Why are you staring at me again?"

Teresa rushed over to the closet and pulled out a clean shirt and a pair of slacks. Embarrassed, she muttered, "Oh, it's nothing. Actually, I was just thinking about Aunt Hatch being in the clutches of that man."

"Of course you were."

Stepping quickly into her clothes, Teresa returned to the dresser and put on Frank's bracelet. Pulling a hairbrush through her hair, she added sheepishly to Charles, "You know, this is a terrible thing to say, but if he really did kidnap her, I almost feel sorry for him."

Charles laughed and reached for his trousers.

They quickly finished dressing and rushed out to the kitchen. Teresa grabbed her personal phone book from the counter and began leafing through it. "Guess the first thing I'd better do is call Great-aunt Maizie in Galveston to make sure Aunt Hatch is really missing."

"Good thinking. I'll pour us both some orange juice and grab some muffins."

Teresa dialed Great-aunt Maizie's number in Galveston. After several rings, she felt relieved when an elderly voice trilled out, "Hello?"

"Great-aunt Maizie, hi, it's Teresa."

"Oh, hello, Teresa darling, how are you?" Maizie replied solicitously. "You know, I tried to call you yesterday, but you weren't home."

"Oh, that's right, we were out. Sorry. Um—is everything all right there?"

"Well, as far as I know," Maizie replied guardedly.

"May I speak to Aunt Hatch?"

Maizie sighed. "Well, that's a problem, dear. Lillian went out jogging two hours ago and still hasn't returned home."

Teresa's stomach sank. "Oh, dear. Is that like her?"

"Not at all. Usually she's back promptly within forty-five minutes. I'm beginning to get a bit worried."

Though Teresa bit her lip, she forced a cheerful tone. "Great-aunt Maizie, please don't fret. She probably just stopped off somewhere for breakfast."

"You think so? Well, I suppose that's possible." Teresa hesitated. "Can you tell me what she was wearing?"

"Is that important, dear?"

"Oh, I'm just curious."

"Why, let me see. I believe she was wearing her purple jogging suit."

"Damn," Teresa muttered.

"Is something wrong, dear?"

"No, sorry," Teresa went on in a rush. "You see, I just singed the toast. Look, a friend and I are on our way to Galveston right now, and we'll hunt for her, okay?"

"Of course, dear. And stop by for tea, will you?"

"Certainly. We'll come by and give you a report. Bye now." She hung up the phone and turned to Charles, who was eyeing her expectantly. "Aunt Hatch went jogging two hours ago . . . wearing a purple jogging suit, just as Pig Face claimed."

"Pig Face?" queried Charles. "An apt name for our intruder."

"Indeed. And our friendly neighborhood swine may very well have Aunt Hatch, because she still hasn't returned."

"Bloody hell," Charles muttered, stepping forward to touch her arm. "I'm sorry, dear. Guess we'd best get over there ASAP and notify the authorities."

"Unless we want to deal with Bobby Mack, the county mountie, again," she put in drolly. "All he did was to guffaw loudly when I reported Pig Face's visit yesterday."

"Yes, bad idea," he agreed.

Grabbing fruit and muffins, they dashed out the door. Driving toward the ferry, Charles spoke up reassuringly. "Try not to panic about your aunt, love. She's only been gone two hours, and I

229

still suspect that the maniac who accosted us may have only been bluffing."

"I wish I shared your confidence," Teresa replied. "Perhaps if he hadn't known what she was wearing . . ."

"I know, that doesn't sound too good," he grimly concurred.

"We can always pray Aunt Hatch will show up, but in the meantime we must report this."

"Oh, I agree." He frowned pensively. "And while we're in Galveston, we need to check out Clark Swinson, too."

"That's right."

Charles handed her his cell phone. "Why don't you try to call him now?"

"Good idea." Taking out her notepad and pen, Teresa called information and got Swinson's address as well as his number, then punched it in. After four rings, a voice answered. She listened for a moment, then said to Charles, "It's Clark Swinson, all right, but we got his answering machine."

Charles rolled his eyes. "It's more likely he has voicemail."

"Whatever. *I* have an answering machine—"

"That doesn't work," Charles finished for her drolly. He extended his hand. "Being as technologically challenged as you are, why don't you just give me the phone?"

With a shrug, she handed over the receiver.

Charles listened a moment, then said crisply, "Mr. Swinson, my name is Charles Everett and I must speak with you immediately about a very important business matter. Please call me on my cell phone at . . ." He rattled off his number and hung up.

"We're not having much luck playing detective, are we?" Teresa asked.

Stopping his car to wait for the ferry, Charles turned to her. "I'm not so sure that's true, love. It *is* odd that Swinson is out right now, don't you think?"

Teresa gasped. "Are you suggesting he could be Pig Face—and that he may have kidnapped Aunt Hatch?"

"It's possible," Charles acknowledged. "Although I'm still inclined to suspect Manolo Juarez or Harold Robison."

She rolled her eyes. "Right. You suspect everyone. And don't forget good old Milton Peavey."

He chuckled. "Right. Milton, too."

After they boarded the ferry, they climbed to the upper deck and stood at the lookout railing, watching the gray churning waters of the channel as the boat glided toward the mainland ahead. The day was already quite warm, but the sea breeze felt good as it blew across Teresa's face and hair. Now that things had settled down a bit, she had time to think about what had transpired this morning—and to feel bittersweet regret over what had happened last night.

Whatever had caused her to throw caution to the wind?

Obviously, the man standing next to her now.

Charles seemed to sense her troubled thoughts. Wrapping an arm around her waist, he asked, "You okay, love?"

She flashed him a brave smile. "Yes."

He pulled her closer. "You know, it killed me seeing you in so much danger this morning—knowing there was nothing I could do."

"It scared me, too," she admitted with a sigh,

then lifted her troubled gaze to his. "But we played a pretty dangerous game last night, as well."

Disappointment washed over his features. "Are you regretting last night already?"

"Charles, it was beautiful—"

"Indeed it was, love."

"But I do think we rushed into things when we still don't know each other very well. And I'm afraid it could be the danger that's really bonding us, pulling us together, rather than—well, genuine emotion and affection."

His expression grew vehement. "Speak for yourself."

"We even forgot about . . ." Feeling her cheeks going hot, she finished, ". . . you know, safe sex, taking precautions."

He reached out to tenderly stroke her cheek. "Do you think you might be pregnant, Tess?" he asked solemnly.

Her throat clenching with the emotion his touch and gentle words stirred, she considered the calendar. "Perhaps not at this moment, though of course we shouldn't tempt the fates."

He nodded. "Don't worry, my dear, no matter what, we're a team now."

"Yeah, right," she rejoined dryly.

"I mean it, Tess. You really think I wouldn't take responsibility for what happened between us?"

"Well, I didn't say that."

He pulled her close and tenderly kissed her. "What will it take to convince you I care?"

As always his nearness was magic. She curled her arms around his neck and kissed him back. Forcing a more optimistic tone, she murmured, "Well, I think you're making a pretty impressive beginning."

Chapter Twenty

Once they reached Galveston, Teresa phoned
Great-aunt Maizie again, only to discover Aunt
Hatch still hadn't returned. "This is beginning to
look really bad," she told Charles afterward.

"I know. We'll stop at the police station first."

At the station house, they were directed to a
Sergeant Varga, a polite, well-groomed man in
his thirties, who listened with patience as well as
obvious misgivings as Teresa gave her account of
the intruder this morning, and yesterday.

"Let me get this straight, ma'am," Varga said
afterward, stroking his jaw. "You're saying for
two mornings now, a pig has climbed through
your bedroom window and held a gun to your
head? And this morning he also claimed he has
kidnapped your aunt?" He fought a smile. "I'm

not crazy about swine myself, but I've never heard of one stooping to breaking and entering, not to mention kidnapping and assault."

"No, it wasn't a pig per se," Teresa explained. "It was a man in a pig mask."

"Ah. And this—er, this pig intruder—really said he has your aunt?"

"Yes."

"Are you sure she's missing?"

"Yes, I've already checked twice with Great-aunt Maizie. You see, Aunt Hatch is staying with her. Anyway, Aunt Hatch went out jogging at 7 A.M. this morning and still hasn't returned. And she was wearing a purple jogging suit, which the pig—that is, the intruder—knew about."

Varga consulted his watch and frowned. "Maybe your aunt just isn't finished jogging yet."

"Three hours later?" Teresa demanded. "That's a lot of jogging in this heat!"

"Good point," Varga acknowledged. "But we'll check with this Maizie person, anyway."

"Oh, please don't," Teresa pleaded, panicking at the thought. "Great-aunt Maizie is ninety years old and she couldn't take the shock of knowing Aunt Hatch is really missing. Besides, she doesn't know anything."

Varga appeared skeptical. "Well, if you say so, ma'am. You know, we should also check with the local hospitals. Maybe your aunt is just suffering from heat exhaustion."

"Oh, I hadn't thought of that!" exclaimed Teresa. "Yes, we should check the hospitals."

"My point is, we need to make sure this lady is really missing," he continued. "I mean, the pig mask and all . . . Are you folks sure this whole thing isn't just some kind of practical joke?"

At this comment, Charles stiffened his spine.

"Sergeant Varga, I assure you that the gun I saw pointed at this lady's head was hardly a joke."

Varga fought a smile. "Were you there, sir?"

Even as Teresa blushed, Charles proudly replied, "Indeed I was."

The detective swung his gaze to Teresa. "Okay, then. Did this man ask for anything—money, valuables?"

"Well, yes, I suppose. He asked for some papers that my bro—that is, my deceased brother—was supposed to have given me for safekeeping."

"Do you have these papers?"

"No, and I actually have no idea what the man could have been referring to. Except—"

"Yes?" Varga encouraged.

Teresa hesitated a moment, noting Charles's questioning look. Then she forged on. "Well, yesterday Mr. Everett and I heard that a contractor in Galveston had brought my brother some old French documents to translate."

Now Varga appeared puzzled. "Old French documents? Excuse me, ma'am, but this is sounding stranger by the moment. What was this contractor's name?"

"Clark Swinson."

"Swinson . . ." Frowning, Varga snapped his fingers. "You know, that is odd. I think we had a missing person's report filed on him a few weeks ago."

Charles and Teresa exchanged an amazed glance. "Clark Swinson is missing?" she asked.

"According to what I last heard."

"Do you know who filed the report?"

"I believe it was his mother."

"Do you have her phone number?"

"Well, not on me. I believe Detective Fredericks handled that report. . . ." Varga paused to glance around the office. "And she's not in right now." He cleared his throat. "Anyway, is there anything else you can tell me about the attack this morning?"

"Well, not really," Teresa replied.

Varga opened a desk drawer, pulled out a phone book, handed it to Charles, then pushed a telephone his way. "Okay, folks. Mr. Everett, why don't you call the local hospital emergency rooms and inquire about Ms. Hatch, while I take down a detailed report from Ms. Phelps?"

"Good idea," Charles said, flipping open the phone book.

Varga reached for a clipboard and pen, then turned to Teresa. "Okay, ma'am. Give me your aunt's full name and description, and let's get started. . . ."

Half an hour later, when Teresa emerged with Charles from the police station, she knew they both felt dispirited. Although a report had been filed, Varga had not been particularly encouraging, and Charles had had no luck at all in calling the hospitals.

Teresa glanced ruefully at him. "Sergeant Varga was nice, but I don't think he really believed us."

Charles gave a wry laugh and opened her car door. "Love, truth to tell, I don't think anyone has believed us about anything so far." He rounded the car, opened his own door, and swung himself into the driver's seat. "But it is odd about Swinson being missing, isn't it?"

"You bet it is," she replied. "We'll have to stay on his trail, see if we can't locate his mother."

Charles shut his car door and started the engine. "Well, I checked the Galveston phone book for another Swinson while we were in

Varga's office. But I'm afraid Clark is the only one listed."

Teresa waved a hand. "Great. Do you suppose they might live together?"

"It's possible."

"Well, we'll track down the mother later on. Right now, I'm much more worried about Aunt Hatch."

"What would you like to do?"

"We could cruise around Great-aunt Maizie's neighborhood, look for Aunt Hatch, then stop by the house and see if Great-aunt Maizie has heard from her."

Charles backed the car. "Sounds like a plan, love."

"But we'll need to be careful regarding just what we tell Great-aunt Maizie about Aunt Hatch," Teresa added. "Like I told Sergeant Varga, if we mention the visit from Pig Face, she'll panic. She is ninety, you know."

"Don't worry, love, we'll be discreet."

They cruised up and down Broadway, with its spectacular old palm trees and striking nineteenth-century homes, while Teresa scanned every inch of the landscape for any sign of Aunt Hatch—all to no avail.

As they were approaching Seventeenth Street, Teresa pointed. "Turn here. Great-aunt Maizie's house is in the East End Historical District."

"Ah—my favorite part of town," he replied, easing his car around the corner.

They cruised down block after block lined by magnificent old trees and handsome antique homes, a charming hodgepodge of raised colonial cottages, two-storied frame shotguns with gingerbread across the front, and full, pillared mansions. Again Teresa searched fruitlessly for her aunt, although Charles seemed more focused on the architecture.

"Damn it, Aunt Hatch, where are you?" she cried at lat, clenching a fist.

"No doubt with Pig Face," Charles rejoined wearily.

Teresa sighed. "We may as well go on to Great-aunt Maizie's house. First go two blocks down, then right."

"Aye, aye, captain," Charles replied, while staring at a stately stone mansion. "Damn, but these houses are spectacular, aren't they, Tess? I love how everything is maintained in this neighborhood."

Teresa eyed him askance. "How can you think of houses at a time like this? Where do you live, anyway? In a tenement?"

"Hardly," he laughed. "I have a condo on the west end, across from the beach. But if I remain here in Galveston, I'd like eventually to buy one of these old mansions. It'll take a pot of money, though."

"Yes, we'll have to hope those investments of yours really pay off." She eyed his expensive car, his sharp clothes. "You strike me as the kind of man who likes the good life."

"Oh, I do."

She harrumphed. "Then at least we know you're not after me for my money."

He shot her a downright devilish look then. "Are you so certain, love?"

His words gave Teresa pause, especially as she remembered yesterday's encounter with Manolo and his mentioning the treasure, then Charles's admitting he knew Frank. Was she right in suspecting Charles might know about the treasure—and might be after it for himself? And now she was involved with him! Her life seemed like some runaway train.

Teresa was so absorbed in her thoughts that she almost missed the next turn. "Hey, left there!" she shouted, pointing.

Charles careened the car around a corner and shot her a dirty look. "I'm not a mind reader, love."

"Sorry. There's Aunt Maizie's house just ahead on the right—the white frame Italianate one with all the Carpenter Gothic gingerbread across the front."

Within feet of the house, Charles eased the car to a halt and gaped at the magnificent edifice with its beautiful lattice archways, its delicate pillars and railings shielding deep verandas on both stories. "I'm in love," he declared.

"Really?" she teased. "Dare I hope it's with me?"

He turned to regard her in awe. "I've never seen a more magnificent house, Tess."

Though miffed that he appeared to be choosing the house over her, Teresa couldn't help but be filled with some pride. "Well, some do think Ambrush House rivals Sonnentheil House. But before we stop, I need to warn you again about Great-aunt Maizie. She is quite old and getting a bit forgetful."

"Ah. Any chance she'll leave you the house in her will? If so, we'll get married tomorrow."

"Charles! I hadn't realized you were so mercenary." She grew quiet. "Though I suppose I could have guessed."

He leaned over and pecked her cheek. "Just pulling your leg, love."

Though Teresa smiled back, his words hardly convinced her.

Then, as Charles eased the car up to park at the

curb, she frowned, spotting the battered rear end of a familiar pickup truck protruding from the driveway on the other side of the house. "Well, would you look at that," she muttered. "Is that who I think it is?"

Charles craned his neck. "Looks like Billy Bob's truck, all right. Wonder what he's doing here?"

"Well, he brought Aunt Hatch home the day before yesterday—perhaps he's trying to stir up some business with Great-aunt Maizie."

Charles's scowl deepened. "We must warn her, then—old people can be so easily exploited."

"Yeah. Right," Teresa cynically agreed. "You'd be the one to know, wouldn't you?"

He shot her a dirty look, then got out and came around to open her door, helping her out. He escorted her across the sidewalk, opened the iron gate, and ushered her into a yard lush with crepe myrtle and blooming roses.

"Ah, the smells of summer," he murmured, taking a deep breath.

As they proceeded through the yard, a harsh, squeaking sound and a flash of motion drew Teresa's eye upward to a charming, small dormer window, just in time to spot Billy Bob's carroty head popping out.

"Why, hello there, ma'am!" he called, grinning down at them.

Teresa paused, laughing. "Billy Bob, what on earth are you doing up there in the attic?"

"Why, checking your aunt's attic for riots and termites."

"Find any?" she called.

"Nope. So far, all's I found is a heap of dust and cobwebs, but I'm still hunting."

"Good for you."

Charles wagged a finger at Billy Bob. "See that

you give Teresa's great-aunt a fair shake. We won't allow you to rip her off."

His expression one of pious disbelief, Billy pressed a hand to his heart. "Me?"

Teresa shot Charles a scolding glance. "Charles, really. That's against Billy Bob's code of conduct with the Bug Brigade."

Charles rolled his eyes.

"Ma'am, I'll come check your place again soon as I get a chance," Billy Bob added.

"Fine. You do that. Bye."

Laughing, Teresa went up the steps with Charles. He glanced about, drinking everything in, the hanging baskets and cozy wicker porch furnishings. "The place is in beautiful shape, Tess. No peeling paint here—and certainly no termites for that con artist Billy Bob to find."

She uttered a cry of outrage. "Con artist? Really, Charles!"

"And just look how those lead glass panels gleam on the front door."

Teresa stifled a groan and rang the doorbell.

A moment later, the door was opened by a hunched, silver-haired woman wearing thick glasses, a housedress, and an apron. She squinted up at them, then smiled at Teresa. "Why, Teresa, dear. I'm so glad you've come. For a moment there, I thought you might be Mr. Bob wanting some lemonade."

"Oh, no, he's staying quite busy up in your attic," Teresa assured her aunt, leaning over to give her a hug. "Hi, Great-aunt Maizie."

"Hello to you, dear. So nice to have you here." Maizie turned to squint at Charles. "And you've brought a nice young man with you."

"Yes. Great-aunt Maizie, I'd like you to meet my new friend, Mr. Charles Everett."

"Why, hello, Mr. Everett," Maizie said, shaking his hand with her small, frail one. She frowned. "You know, that name sounds familiar. Everett. Wherever did I hear it?"

"Perhaps Teresa mentioned me earlier when she called?" Charles suggested.

"Well, that could be it, I suppose. So many new names to remember. You, that nice Mr. Bob, and . . ." Maizie's wrinkled face lit with a grin. "Oh well. Despite my years, I do try my best."

"Of course you do, Great-aunt Maizie." Teresa turned to Charles. "Charles, meet my great-aunt, Mrs. Maizie Ambrush."

Charles gallantly took Maizie's hand and kissed it. "My pleasure, Mrs. Ambrush."

Maizie laughed and blushed. "Oh my, aren't you a charming fellow? And British, to boot. Please, both of you, come on in before you melt. I've been so worried about Lillian."

"You still haven't heard from her?" Teresa asked, stepping inside.

"No, and this just isn't like her. Not at all."

Inside the hallway, Charles shut the door behind them, then glanced around at the handsome antiques and oriental runner lining the corridor, and the striking oak staircase beyond. He stepped to his right and peered into the vintage parlor. "My word, Mrs. Ambrush, it appears your parlor is furnished in genuine Duncan Phyfe."

"It is, indeed," said Maizie, warming to the subject. "Are you a connoisseur of antiques, Mr.—er—"

"Everett," Teresa reminded.

"Everett." Maizie was scowling again. "Forevermore, where *did* I hear that name? Oh well. Anyway, Mr. Everett, you'll appreciate the lamp on the writing desk over there—a rare Tiffany wisteria pattern."

Charles stepped over to admire the lamp. "Great Scot, you're right. And look at those green velvet portieres, the silk brocade wallpaper. And Egyptian marble on your fireplace." He grinned. "I love this place, madam. It even smells marvelous." He took a deep breath. "What are those heavenly essences in the air? Perhaps orange pekoe tea . . . and banana bread?"

Maizie clapped her hands. "Why, yes, that is exactly right, Mr.—er—oh, I give up. Anyway, I just baked the bread this morning, and I was about to offer you some with tea."

"We accept," said Charles graciously.

"Should we invite Mr. Bob, as well?" Maizie added.

"I'd wait awhile on that," Charles advised. "Mr. Bob is pretty heavily involved in his vermin hunt right now." He offered each woman an arm. "May I escort you ladies to the kitchen?"

Maizie giggled, then placed her frail hand on Charles's arm. "Oh, dear, you're such a charmer. Teresa, darling, you're in trouble."

"I know," she muttered, linking her own arm through Charles's.

"Very well, everyone," Maizie continued happily. "This way."

In Maizie's cozy kitchen, they all sat around her antique oak table, eating hot, moist banana bread and drinking tea.

"I like your young man," Maizie told Teresa.

Teresa shot Charles a conspiratorial smile, and he winked back. "Thanks. I rather favor him myself."

"Any chance wedding bells may be in the offing?" Maizie asked.

"Great-aunt Maizie," Teresa scolded.

"They may be," Charles put in wryly, sipping his tea. "Especially if you're thinking of remembering Tess in your will."

While Teresa's mouth dropped opened in horror, Maizie only laughed until her sides shook. "Oh, I do love your young man, Teresa. Bit of a rascal in him. Always did love a man with a devilish streak, you know. Makes me wish I was sixty years younger."

Teresa shot Charles a glower. "But he's being positively brazen."

"But I like a young man who speaks his mind. Reminds me of my dear, departed Walter. Silver-tongued devil, that one. Lord, how I miss him."

"We know you do, Great-aunt Maizie."

Charles took an elegant sip of tea, then flashed Maizie his most charming smile. "My sympathies as well, madam. And you know, it is quite critical that you entrust your magnificent home to someone who can properly care for and appreciate it."

Maizie nodded.

"Charles!" Teresa scolded.

Unrepentant, he continued to Maizie, "If I may be so bold, I must add that a woman of your impressive years should also be leery of unscrupulous contractors such as exterminators who are inclined to rip off the elderly."

"Oh, dear," muttered Maizie.

Teresa waved a hand. "Charles, really! How do you know Billy Bob is unscrupulous?"

"Yes, Mr. Bob seems perfectly nice," Maizie put in, frowning.

"Just a word to the wise," Charles told Maizie.

"Oh, you're so nice to show such concern," Maizie replied, patting his hand. "But we're all forgetting poor Lillian, aren't we?"

Teresa was still staring murder at Charles. "Yes, we are."

"Have you contacted the police, dear?" Maizie asked. "You know, in case of an accident?"

Flustered, Teresa replied, "Well, yes, we did stop by, strictly as a formality. They've heard of nothing, of course, and know of no accidents involving Aunt Hatch." Teresa touched Maizie's arm. "Please try not to fret. I'm sure she'll show up."

"But why would Lillian just disappear like this?" Maizie asked.

"Maybe she got lost while jogging," Charles suggested.

"Could be, I suppose," Maizie conceded. "But I do feel so badly. You see, this morning, Lillian was again taking me to task for not going exercising myself—"

"Exercising? At ninety?" Charles cried, aghast. "Sounds like a recipe for cardiac arrest to me."

Maizie chuckled. "Well, yes, but Lillian's a child of the sixties, you see, and took most seriously Mr. Kennedy's campaign for physical fitness. But I do feel guilty since, after Lillian again criticized me, I found myself wishing she would just leave me in peace for a while. Oh, you don't suppose that I—"

"Of course not, Great-aunt Maizie," Teresa cut in, patting Maizie's hand. "We all find Aunt Hatch to be a pain in the neck, and believe me, if wishing alone were enough to make her disappear, she would have been history decades ago."

"Well, yes, I suppose you're right," Maizie concurred rather confusedly.

"Anyway, Tess and I shall continue searching for her," Charles assured Maizie. "I'm sure she'll turn up in due course."

Maizie fondly touched Charles's arm. "Oh, with

you in charge, Mr. Everett, I'm sure she will. Such a masterful young man you are. Almost remind me of that James Bond fellow." She shook a finger at her great-niece. "Teresa, dear, you must hang on to this one."

Her lips twitched. "Perhaps I will."

Maizie frowned and laid a finger alongside her cheek. "Now if I could just remember where I've heard your name, young man."

Abruptly, Charles coughed. "Not to change the subject, madam, but—er, Tess, shouldn't we be going? Be about our mission and all that?"

"Well, I suppose . . ."

Charles stood and pulled out Teresa's chair. "Well, it's been lovely, Mrs. Ambush—"

"*Ambrush,*" Teresa corrected.

"Righto. Mrs. Ambrush."

Maizie was laughing, shaking a finger at Charles. "Now *you're* having trouble with names, young man."

"Indeed." He gently assisted Maizie to her feet. "Do you suppose your malady is catching?"

The two were still laughing when some banging noises sounded out, causing them all to turn toward the back staircase at the side of the kitchen. A moment later, a sweaty Billy Bob trudged down the steps and entered the room. He was breathing hard, his face beet-red and streaked with dirt; cobwebs hung in his hair and on his clothes, and he reeked of grime and sweat.

"Howdy, folks," he greeted them with a crooked grin, then turned to Maizie. "No riots or termites, ma'am. You got a clean bill of health."

"Oh, splendid," Maizie declared, clapping her hands. "Would you care for some tea, Mr. Bob?"

Billy Bob glanced askance at the steaming teapot on the table, and fanned his hot face with a hand. "Shore, ma'am, if you'll plunk some ice in it."

"I'd be delighted to." Maizie made a clucking sound to Charles. "See, now? Mr. Bob is perfectly honest."

But Charles regarded Billy Bob skeptically, nonetheless.

Teresa slanted Charles a long-suffering look. Now he suspected poor Billy Bob? Would Great-aunt Maizie be next?

Chapter Twenty-one

"Charles, you are just incorrigible!" Teresa declared as he drove them away.

"What did I do?" he asked, feigning innocence.

"How about giving poor Billy Bob such a hard time? Why next you'll be suspecting *me* of terrorizing myself."

He eyed her in feigned suspicion. "Hmmmmm. There's a thought."

"Oh, hush." She hurled him an exasperated glance. "Not to mention trying to con Great-aunt Maizie into leaving me her house."

A lazy grin spread across his face. "Actually, the old girl rather liked my brash qualities."

"Brash? Try mercenary."

"Well, I offered to marry you, didn't I? What could be more noble?"

"You offered to marry me *if* I inherit the house," she pointed out crossly.

"Temper, temper," he teased.

"Charles, I don't find any of this very funny!"

"Oh, Tess, quit being such a stick-in-the-mud," he cajoled. "Besides, we need to proceed with more practical matters. What's next on the agenda?"

For a moment she gritted her teeth in supreme frustration, then she sighed. "Very well. Could we drive around the neighborhood a bit more, see if we can't locate Aunt Hatch?"

"Certainly, love."

Again they cruised all over the East End Historical District, only to catch no glimpse of Aunt Hatch anywhere. This time, they questioned a few citizens who were out in their yards or taking walks, but no one had seen anything.

"What now?" Teresa asked Charles afterward. "I suppose we should call Harold Robison, just in case he's heard from her."

"Or abducted her himself," Charles suggested.

"Really, Charles, I think you're overestimating the stodgy Mr. Robison."

"It's the stodgy types one must worry about," he replied. "We need to try to reach Mr. Swinson again, too. Look, I've an idea. Why don't we stop by my apartment on West Beach? I need to check my mail anyway, and we left in such a hurry this morning, I didn't even get a chance to shower or shave. While I attend to all that, you can make some more phone calls. Then I'll take you out for a nice lunch."

"Sounds like a plan," she admitted. "But don't forget that at some point we need to go over to Liberty, too, and see the Lafitte journal."

"Perhaps we can do that this afternoon. Do you still have the photocopy in your bag?"

She lifted the heavy bag. "Still here. I hate the thought of leaving the island with Aunt Hatch's fate up in the air, but the truth is, the more we learn about the mystery, the better chance we have of finding her."

"I agree completely."

Charles drove them out onto the sunny, breezy seawall, with rows of posh hotels and condos flanking them on the north, and the billowing Gulf stretching beneath them to the south. Teresa studied the people below—families, couples, and teenagers in colorful swimsuits, throwing beach balls, sunbathing beneath umbrellas, swimming, or paddling into the Gulf on surfboards. How nice it must be to be so carefree, she mused.

"Ah, here we are," Charles was saying. He drove them up to the gate of a luxurious condominium project—attractive yellow stucco buildings with green tile roofs.

"This is nice."

Charles had stopped his car at an unmanned guard building, and was punching in a code on a keypad. "It'll do until something better comes along."

"Looks like it'll more than just do."

An iron gate eased open, and he coasted the car inside. Wheeling around the first building, he parked under an awning, then escorted Teresa to a unit on the bottom floor.

"Wow," Teresa said as he swung open the door and bid her enter. From a quarry tile entryway, she stepped down into a huge, sunken living room with beige berber carpeting, handsome brown suede contemporary couches, colorful abstract paintings with seagoing themes, and a cathedral ceiling accented by a center beam and a soaring stucco fireplace. Beyond was a raised dining room with a striking glass table and expensive contemporary chairs.

She raised an eyebrow at Charles. "You like the good life, eh?"

"I like sophistication in my surroundings."

She wrinkled her nose at him. "Then forget about me."

He stepped close and hugged her. "My dear, you do yourself a disservice. I find you most sophisticated—and intriguing."

"Right."

He pulled his keys from his pocket. "Well, I'm off to check my mailbox." He gestured toward a door on the far side of the room. "If you'd like to try Swinson's number again, and call Harold Robison, there's a phone on the nightstand in the bedroom—"

"Trying to get me into your bedroom, eh?" she cut in.

His expression was devilish. "I'm hardly averse to the idea." When she would have protested, he held up a hand. "However, as I was about to say, the Houston phone book is in the drawer of the nightstand."

"Excuses, excuses," she scolded.

Charles leaned over and quickly, possessively kissed her lips. "Darling, where you're concerned, I don't need any."

As he started away, she snapped her fingers. "By the way, where are the pictures?"

He turned, frowning. "What pictures?"

"Of me and your father," she taunted.

He blanched. "Oh, those pictures. Wonder where I put them?"

"Yeah, wonder where," she chided.

"I'm sure it will come to me." Blowing her another kiss and whistling a jaunty tune, he left.

Teresa could only shake her head, though a grudging smile pulled at her mouth. She wandered over to the bedroom door, opened it, and slipped inside. Turning on the light, she stared at the king-sized bed with its forest-green coverlet. She stepped over, folding back the quilt, and smiled at the sight of cream-colored, satin sheets.

"Why, you rascal," she murmured.

She smoothed down the quilt and turned away. Then she noticed the dresser flanking the bed, and gasped.

Quickly she crossed over, making a sound of outrage as she stared at the top of the dresser, which was lined with pictures of beautiful women! Blondes, brunettes, a redhead, all displayed in impeccable contemporary frames. There were at least eight of them, arranged in a neat row.

Teresa was shocked at the hot jealousy that flooded her. The man was shameless! She would kill him.

Furious, she flounced down on the bed, got out the phone book, and made her calls, glowering at the pictures all the while.

"Any luck, love?"

She turned to see Charles lounging in the doorway, looking every bit as sexy and debonair as the scoundrel he was. Resisting the urge to spring up and strangle him, she said testily, "I got Swinson's answering—er, *voicemail*—again. Harold Robison is on vacation all week."

"Aha!" Charles said, shaking a finger. "Robison on vacation? That sounds suspicious to me."

Teresa had had enough, and popped up angrily. "Yeah, that really makes him an ax murderer, doesn't it? As for being suspicious—how about this?" She gestured angrily at the row of portraits.

"Oh, that." He had the grace to appear chagrined.

"Yes, that. What is it, Charles? Your trophy collection?"

He came to her side, shrugging sheepishly. "What can I say, Tess? I've always been fond of the ladies."

"A ladies' man?" she asked shrilly.

"Now, Tess. You of all people should know that the female of the species tends to find me irresistible."

She shoved him away. "Oh! Your ego is staggering!"

"Tess. Come on, love. All that is in the past."

Again she gestured at the row of portraits. "Then what in the hell are they all doing on your dresser?"

He laughed. "You're jealous."

"I'm leaving." She tore away toward the door.

He caught her arm. "Oh, no, you're not." Though she struggled, he easily pulled her to the dresser, released her, and then with a broad sweep of his hand, he sent all the pictures flying.

Teresa was flabbergasted, cringing at the sounds of the frames crashing to the floor, picture glass breaking. "My God, Charles."

He appeared quite proud of himself. "I've always liked the sound of glass splintering."

"No kidding."

He clutched her close. "And I want you to know that the *only* woman I want on this dresser is you." He gripped her waist and easily lifted her up onto it. His hands began tugging at the tails of her blouse.

"Charles, damn it—"

His lips were nibbling at her throat. "I think we need to do something about those second thoughts of yours, love."

The rest of her protest was quenched by his kiss, while his hands roved her body freely, lifting her blouse, caressing her bare flesh. "Come on, Tess, don't go away in a temper. We need each other right now."

She was struggling to get free. "Go play with one of your bimbos."

He only chuckled and kissed her cheek, her ear. "Darling, simmer down. Give me a chance to get cleaned up, then I promise I'll make it up to you. In fact, why don't you come help me?"

"Help you what?"

"Shower and shave."

"You've got to be kidding."

But he had already pulled her down off the dresser and was tugging her resisting body toward the bathroom door. "Come on, let me show you the real reason I leased this place."

"No."

"Yes."

"Will you promise to give me custody of the razor?"

He laughed. "Tess, you're incorrigible."

"I'm incorrigible?"

Inside the bathroom door, she stopped. And gaped. It was huge, with marble and glass everywhere. Beyond her stretched an enormous sunken tube, surrounded by luxuriant green plants and sheer glass windows looking out on a small patio, fenced for privacy. To the right of the tub, French doors offered direct access to this lush, cozy area with its ferns, philodendrons, blooming hibiscus, and freshly mown grass.

Then she dared to glance upward, and felt heat suffuse her cheeks. "Good Lord, Charles, you're depraved. A *mirror* over your tub?"

He had already turned on the water and was pouring in some aqua-colored bath gel. "Care for a bit of the bubbly, love?"

"You can't expect me to—"

He winked solemnly. "You know, love, you didn't get a chance for a bath this morning either, did you?"

Now she was irate. "Are you hinting that I need a bath?"

He crossed over and took her by the shoulders. "No, I'm saying I want you with me in that bathtub." Leaning over, he just brushed his lips over hers. "Correction, I want you *on* me in that bathtub."

Teresa couldn't help herself. She wasn't even in the tub with him, and already she was drowning in the wicked images his words elicited. She shuddered with helpless desire. "Charles, this is hardly prudent—"

He was unbuttoning her blouse. "Come on, be a good girl."

"You mean be a *bad* girl."

"Precisely." Casting aside her blouse, he confidently unhooked her bra, removed it, then caught the waistband of her slacks, tugging down her slacks and panties in one smooth stroke.

All the while, Teresa couldn't seem to resist. Breathing itself was a trial, and when Charles rubbed his palms sensuously against her taut, aching nipples, she knew she had passed the point of no return.

Soon she stood naked, burning beneath his bold scrutiny. "In the tub, woman," he ordered.

Teresa eagerly hopped into the tub, sinking down into the warm, sudsy water.

He ripped at his own clothes, grinning all the while. "See how hot you've made me?"

She stared at his erection and gulped. "Yeah."

He stepped into the tub at the opposite end, sat down, and flipped a switch. She moaned in pleasure as the hot jets of the whirlpool pulsated against her body. She could feel Charles's muscular legs wedged against her own.

"Yes, I can see why you leased this apartment," she murmured, stretching ecstatically.

He was shutting off the faucets. "You know, I'm thinking it might be safer for us to stay here for now, what with Pig Face on the loose and all."

"Well, it's a thought," she agreed.

"Now quit making idle conversation and come here, woman," he added huskily.

She raised an eyebrow. "Now *I'm* making idle conversation?"

He winked. "Come hither."

She grinned and crawled forward. He pulled her the rest of the way, settling her in a straddle on top of him, then shocked her as he entered her quickly, fully.

Teresa gasped, reeling in shattering, decadent sensation, her nails sinking into Charles's shoulders. "Charles—oh, damn!—we're forgetting this isn't safe."

He merely chuckled sensually and nipped at her tight nipple with his teeth. "Neither sex—nor anything else—is safe with me, love."

"Lord, you've got that right," she managed, panting for breath.

"Hush, and get to work, love," he ordered. "I want to watch."

"Watch?"

He gestured at the mirror above them.

"Oh." Her cheeks flushed scarlet.

But Charles was not embarrassed at all, his expression one of avid fascination as he leaned back slightly, heightening the delicious pressure inside Teresa. Already out of her mind with sensation, she began to move. The sheer eroticism of it all was overwhelming. The hot jets massaging her body, the depth and intensity of Charles's thrusts, the beautiful look of awe in his eyes as he watched them mate.

Charles, too, could barely endure the ecstasy of loving Teresa so brazenly. She looked so gorgeous bobbing there on his lap, her body slick and glossy, her nipples puckered and red, her womanhood squeezing him so pleasurably. Most beautiful of all was the look of mingled pleasure and desperation on her face, the languor in her lovely eyes, making him want to drive her to even greater heights of mindless need. He clutched her closer and plunged deeper, exulting in her whimpers and the sensual way she tossed back her head. He knew he was driving her crazy and loved the feeling. When she tried to squirm away, he held her fast, the wetness of her body granting him the deep, penetrating strokes he most craved.

The pressure built, until she was sobbing with the sheer frustration of total sensual bombardment. It was then that he took mercy on her. He sat upright, captured her mouth in a shattering kiss, and concluded their coupling in a rush of breathtaking thrusts. His own powerful climax left him groaning; and when he felt her melting sweetly against him, his eyes burned with emotion.

Afterward, she lay gasping, limp in his arms. "Charles, my God, that was incredible."

"Are you okay?" he murmured, voice trembling, hand stroking her smooth spine.

She laughed. "I'm exhausted."

"Really? I was thinking it was your turn to watch."

"Charles!"

He grinned unabashedly. "See what you do to me, love?"

Teresa went wild-eyed as she felt Charles growing hard inside her again. She was absolutely drained from the fierce passion they'd just shared; and yet as she felt him push and throb within her again, the urge to mate became overpowering once more.

She stared at him breathlessly—only to go wide-eyed when she heard the sound of some sort of yard tool. She glanced out the patio window and spotted a man in dungarees outside in the courtyard, a grass blower in hand, setting clippings and leaves swirling about.

"Charles!" she cried, scandalized, pointing at the window. She tried to struggle off his lap but he held her, solidly and pleasurably impaled. "Charles, please!"

"Stop wiggling, Tess, or you're going to get much more than you bargained for." He glanced out at the courtyard and frowned. "Not to worry, it's only my Japanese gardener with his grass blower."

"But he'll see us!" she whispered frantically.

"He's far too discreet to look, and besides the two of us are down too low, and the plants on the windowsill are shielding us. Don't worry, he'll have the grass blown out in just a minute, you'll see."

"Charles, damn it, if there's going to be any

blowing going on here, I don't want a ménage à trois!"

He chuckled and playfully tugged at a strand of her wet hair. "Very well, love, you just sit tight and I'll hop out and go get you a robe." He arched his hips experimentally, then winked at her. "That is, if we can manage to get unwedged."

"Oh, it'll be tight, but we'll manage," she assured him dryly.

But even as he began to pull himself out of her body, both of them jerked slightly as the man spun, turned, dropped his blower, and reached for something in his pocket, then whipped it out.

Panic seized Teresa as she spotted the too-familiar, frightening visage. "Charles, it isn't your Japanese gardener at all! It's P-Pig Face, and he's got a—!"

A split second later, Charles shoved Teresa beneath the water. Hot, freesia-flavored liquid choked her just as a bullet screamed in, shattering the glass. . . .

Chapter Twenty-two

A second later, Teresa was yanked from beneath the suds, and Charles's white face loomed over her. "Are you all right?" he whispered frantically.

Spitting out water, she nodded.

"Are you hit?" he added, quickly running his hands over her body, then glancing anxiously at the windows.

"No," she managed. "Is Pig Face still there?"

"No, the coward fired one shot and took off." Bolting out of the tub, he grabbed her hand and yanked her out as well. "Now get in the bedroom, Tess, and stay put!"

And before Teresa's astonished eyes, Charles went running, stark naked, out the French doors into the courtyard. Grabbing a towel, she tore after him. "My God, Charles, don't you think you should put on a . . . ?"

Too late, since he had already streaked through the open gate, which Pig Face had left ajar. Quickly wrapping the towel around her own body, Teresa felt consumed with worry for Charles. What on earth did the man think he was doing, pursuing Pig Face stark naked, armed with only a . . . ? She giggled hysterically.

"Good heavens, the man has lost his mind," she muttered.

Then she heard the sounds of female shrieking and the shrill barking of a dog. A split second later, Charles vaulted back inside the courtyard, slammed shut the gate, and bounded back into the bathroom.

Teresa stared at him in amazement. He appeared hot, flushed, breathless, and his legs were covered with grass clippings. Then her gaze settled in the most delicious spot.

He was gazing at her, appalled. "Damn it, Tess, I told you to get your derriere into the bedroom!"

"My God, Charles, I can't believe you just did that!"

He waved a hand. "Well, I did it. Call it the heat of passion. Besides, I was a bit too slow on the draw this morning when Pig Face appeared."

Teresa couldn't resist a laugh. "No kidding! But I would think you'd have better judgment than to go off half-cocked like that."

"Cute, Tess." Breathing hard, he took an aggressive step toward her. "My dear, I assure you I am *fully* cocked."

Gazing at him brazenly, she licked her lips. "You are indeed."

Muttering a curse, he grabbed a towel and

wrapped it around his own middle. "Well, for a woman who just almost got killed, you are certainly full of clever repartee."

"Charles, what you just did obliterated all memory of dodging bullets."

He uttered a sound of exasperation. "Then why the hell didn't you try to stop me before I ran out and . . . ?"

"I ran after you with a towel and yelled at you, but you were already gone. And by the way, who screamed?"

"Two elderly ladies out walking their poodle. The Barnstaple sisters, I believe, and I'm praying to God they didn't recognize me, or I'll be joining the ranks of sex offenders here in Galveston County."

She chortled. "I doubt they were looking at your face."

He shot her a glower. "At any rate, when they started shrieking, I finally realized that I'd . . . Well, I'd lost my head."

Glancing deliberately downward again, she grinned wickedly. "That's debatable."

"Oh, hush."

Teresa was still fighting laughter. "How well do you know those women?"

He tore his fingers through his hair. "Only in passing. And I think I managed to get back around the corner and inside the courtyard before they could determine which apartment I'd come from."

"Good. Any further sightings of Pig Face?"

"No. The incident with the women pretty much mixed further investigation." He strode over to the broken window, examining the bullet hole, the flecks of glass on the ledge. "Damn, what a mess."

"I know. So what do we do now, call the police?"

"Bloody hell, are you daft?" he asked. "The last thing I want to do is to bring this charming little episode to the attention of the authorities. The Barnstaple sisters are no doubt reporting me for flashing at this moment."

She winked at him. "No, they're probably just counting their blessings . . . and kicking themselves for not bringing along their camera."

He shook a finger at her. "Now you're asking for it, woman."

Teresa giggled. "I still think you should report this to the police. I'm sure their interrogation would prove quite interesting. 'Precisely what were you doing, Mr. Everett, when the man fired?'"

He scowled menacingly. "Smart-mouthed wench. Get out of here before I wallop you."

"But you need to rinse the grass off your legs."

He sat down on the edge of the tub, rinsed off his legs, then stood and caught her arm. "Come on, Tess. This room isn't safe."

Teresa managed to grab her clothes and a hand towel as he tugged her out the door with him. In the bedroom, she began briskly drying her hair. Now that she'd had a chance to think about what had transpired, all sorts of questions were troubling her.

"Why do you suppose Pig Face attacked us again?" she asked. "Wasn't this morning's intrusion enough for him? And what about Aunt Hatch? Where was she when he . . . ?" She gasped. "You don't suppose he's already—"

"No, love," Charles quickly reassured her. "The man wants something from us—so I'm sure he'll keep it in his pants until he gets what he wants."

"It?" she inquired uneasily.

"His gun. I'm saying he won't be so foolish as to shoot your aunt."

"You really think so?" she inquired with frail hope.

"Yes." Huskily, he added, "I want something, too."

Still drying her hair, Teresa turned to see him sitting on the bed, still wearing only the towel, and staring at her. "Charles, aren't you going to get dressed?"

The intent look in his eyes told her it wasn't likely. "Come here."

She crossed over, flashing him a tremulous smile. He pulled off her towel and gazed steadily at her damp, naked body. She burned at his intent perusal.

"Charles what are you doing now?"

He kissed her bare midriff, raising gooseflesh, then pulled back, running a bold hand down her flesh. "Are you sure you're not hurt anywhere, Tess?" he asked tenderly. "There could have been glass fragments, you know."

"I'm fine, really," she answered, shuddering.

His fingers slid over her thigh, her knee. "Your abrasions are healing nicely."

"Thank you, Doctor."

Slowly he traced his fingertips back up over her belly, her breasts, her arms, while she moaned and felt the heat of passion throbbing within her once more. "Now turn around."

She felt herself blushing all over. "Charles."

"I want to be sure you're not hurt anywhere. Do it."

With a moan of mingled frustration and arousal, she complied. His hands swept tenderly over her back, her arms, then his fingertips teased her bottom.

She whirled, and he hauled her down onto his lap and kissed her ravenously. She could feel his hard erection pushing against her hip, even as his strong hands caressed her. Even after the wild passion they'd just shared, she found herself reeling with desire once more—the memory of the intrusion by Pig Face, the bullet which could have killed either or both of them, only intensified her feelings.

Shuddering, she asked, "Charles—er, don't we have work to do?"

He was kissing her shoulder. "We have unfinished business to attend to first, that's for certain, love. You know this last episode really troubles me, Tess. That was a real bullet and you could have been killed."

So he'd felt as shaken as she had! "Really, Charles, I'm okay," she whispered back, shivering with delight. "I wasn't hurt."

"But you could have been." His voice was very intense.

"So could you," she replied, a catch in her voice.

Abruptly he pulled her back on the bed with him, rolled her body beneath his, and spread her thighs. Ardor gleamed in his eyes as he whispered, "It all made me realize how much you've come to mean to me, Tess. And it makes me want to get so deeply inside you that you'll never get rid of me."

She clutched him close. "I don't want to get rid of you."

He groaned, his mouth against her cheek. "Oh, Tess, you've no idea what your words make me want to do to you."

She rubbed her tight nipples sensuously against his slick chest. "Sounds unbearably sweet. Tell me—then do it, please."

He whispered an erotic suggestion that scorched her ears. And then he thrust into her, deeply and confidently, and it was sweeter still. . . .

Chapter Twenty-three

Lillian Hatch struggled against her bonds, wiggling in impotent fury as helpless, smothered sounds arose in her throat. Gagged and handcuffed to an old iron bedstead, she lay on a sagging mattress in some cheap flophouse not far from the Gulf. Although she didn't know exactly where she was, she could hear cars going past outside and vague sounds of surf, so she assumed she couldn't be too far from the seawall. The room itself was utterly wretched, smelling of mold and urine, with disgusting cockroaches streaking up and down the peeling wallpaper. The appalling horror chamber didn't even have a phone—not that Lillian could have reached one if it were there.

She still could not believe this had happened to

her! Her existence during the last hours had been a nightmare! One minute, she'd been happily jogging along, not far from Aunt Maizie's house. Then the man in the revolting pig mask had loomed over her, raising his gun. She'd been so horrified by his grotesque appearance that she hadn't reacted in time, instead freezing in her tracks.

Pain had exploded in her head and everything had gone black. She'd awakened in this horrible place, gagged, bound, dizzy, head throbbing . . . and alone. For agonizing hours she'd waited, until her cruel captor had at last reappeared in his revolting mask. He'd removed her gag but had refused to answer any of her, questions regarding who he really was, why he had kidnapped her, or where he had brought her. He had released her briefly to go to the bathroom, and had allowed her to eat a cold hamburger he'd brought back with him, all the while wielding his gun and threatening her with death if she made the slightest untoward move. Ignoring all her protestations, he'd then gagged and shackled her again, and left.

He'd returned once since then, and Lillian had tried everything in her power to get through to him—pleas, threats, hysterics, you name it. But this monster whom she now privately called "Pig Face" had proven immovable.

She wondered if anyone was worried about her, looking for her. Surely by now Aunt Maizie would have called the police, or at least called Teresa. Teresa—now there was a laugh. Her niece was currently in such a disgraceful state that Lillian knew she could hardly count on the shiftless girl to be of much help.

Remembering her harrowing experience at her

niece's beach house two days earlier, Lillian wondered if there might be some connection between the violence there and her abduction. Good Lord, what had her miserable niece sunk to now?

From her experience at the helm of the reform school, Lillian knew that most young women got in trouble due to various addictions, such as drugs or alcohol. Had her previous suspicions regarding her niece been correct? Had Teresa been targeted because she was involved with drug dealers, or perhaps owed gambling debts? The sleazy creature! There was simply no excuse for a doctoral candidate to behave in such a shameful, shocking manner. Now Lillian might well be a pawn in a dangerous game being played between Teresa and drug dealers, or even mafiosos.

Which meant she might well be sleeping with the fishes tonight.

The very thought flooded Lillian's mind with panic and made her head throb even worse. She cautioned herself to calm down. All her life she'd possessed an iron will and steely self-discipline, and she couldn't afford to slacken off now. She knew she must keep her wits about her if she were to escape her current predicament alive. It was not as if she could count on her profligate niece to come storming through the door and rescue her.

And unfortunately, Lillian's captor had thus far been very cagey around her. Even when he let her get up briefly, he kept his distance and constantly held his gun trained on her. Lillian had gained a black belt in karate as part of her physical fitness training, but even she was not foolish enough to charge a man with a loaded gun.

However, surely at some point her captor would drop his guard. He must sooner or later, and she would have to be ready. . . . When it happened, he would never even know what hit him. That was all she needed, just that one slip on his part. In the meantime, she could only pray he wouldn't kill her before she got her chance.

All at once Lillian flinched as the door to the disgusting room creaked open and her captor, in his gruesome pig mask, stepped inside. Lillian yanked at her bonds and entreated the man with strangled pleas.

Pig Face waved his gun, and spoke in a voice muffled by his mask. "Stuff it, lady, I don't want to hear it. I know, you have to go to the john, right? Well, quit that squirming and moaning or I'm not going to give you the damn key."

At once Lillian quieted, though her eyes gleamed with spite.

"That's better." He tossed her the handcuffs key and trained his gun on her.

By now Lillian knew the drill with this monster. He was cunning, and wisely recognized her superior physical strength. Rather than risk uncuffing her himself, thereby putting himself in possible physical peril, the monster would toss her the key, stand guard at gunpoint while she unlocked the cuffs, then demand she throw back the key.

Hurling him a glare, Lillian twisted about on the mattress until she managed to get the key between her fingers, then through various painful contortions, she slipped it into the lock and the handcuffs sprang open. She removed them, sat up, and tore off the gag, worked her sore mouth in a grimace, and rubbed her aching wrists.

"When in God's name are you going to release me?" she demanded of her captor.

"Throw me the key, lady," he growled.

She tossed it back. "Are you going to answer my question?"

"No."

"I'll have you know I am not a well woman."

"Ha! You look healthier than an ox."

"I'm—I'm on blood pressure medication," Lillian tried desperately. "Very strong drugs. Without them, I could have a stroke, any minute, I'll have you know."

"Be my guest."

"Oh!"

He waved his gun. "Are you going to go to the can, or just flap your stupid mouth all day? You'd best get a move on, lady, because I can't stay long."

"Will you please tell me who you are and why you have kidnapped me?" Lillian pleaded.

"Not a chance."

"I have some money," she implored. "Quite a nice nestegg put away. I'll give it all to you if you'll only release me."

"Forget it, lady. I'm on to bigger fish."

Lillian pounded a fist on the mattress. "*What* bigger fish? Will you please tell me what's going on?"

"Will you *please* go to the can?" he snapped back.

Grinding her jaw, Lillian got up, went into the bathroom, and slammed the door. Inside the tiny, incredibly filthy room, she was tempted to scream her frustration, but knew if she did, Pig Face would likely shoot her. And the bathroom did not even have a window, so there was no possible escape. Eyeing her face in the crazed and cracked mirror—the features distraught with fright, the deep purple lines under her eyes, she gasped aloud. She was looking almost as vile as her captor. She turned on the rusty faucet and splashed water on her face. . . .

Outside, Pig Face stood silently brooding. The aunt was a damn pain in the ass, and he was tempted to shoot her just to shut her up. But that wouldn't get him what he wanted, so he'd have to put up with the loudmouthed harridan a while longer.

Frustration seethed inside him as he thought of how he was still no closer to achieving his goal. He remembered his last encounter with Teresa Phelps and her pretty boy lover, and cursed under his breath. How dare the two of them just be boinking away in the tub when they were supposed to be finding him his precious papers! Well, maybe that shot he'd fired would put the fear of God in them.

If not, he still had the aunt. What did mafiosos do in such a situation, he wondered. Hell, a good mobster would likely send Teresa Phelps one of the aunt's fingers. A shame he was too squeamish for that.

The toilet flushed loudly, and the woman emerged from the bathroom, eyes churning with spite, features twitching with anger. He almost shuddered at the revolting sight of her.

He waved his gun toward the bed. "All right, back on the bed, and in the cuffs."

"You are a fiend," she declared.

"Don't forget it."

He watched her lie down, hook the handcuffs on the bedframe, and snap them on her wrists. He walked over, checked the cuffs to make sure they were securely locked, and reached for the gag on the mattress.

"Wait!" she cried. "I'm hungry."

"Too bad. I already fed you lunch, and that'll have to do you for a few more hours."

"A few more hours? Where do you go when you're not here?"

"None of your damn business!"

She eyed him with growing suspicion. "Tell me, do you like Italian food, or have an Uncle Vinnie?"

Pig Face snorted a laugh and waved his gun in her face. "Oh, yeah. I also love snuffing people out and tossing their bodies in dumpsters, especially pain-in-the-ass bitches like you!"

She sucked in a great breath and went gray in the face. "Oh—you pig!"

About ready to strangle her, he shoved his gun in his waist, then picked up the cloth gag, yanked it between the woman's teeth, and tied it securely around her head. A sense of vindictive pleasure washed over him to see her rendered helpless again. Nonetheless, he shuddered at the sight of the huge, gray-haired woman, lying in her jogging suit manacled to the bed, nostrils flared in fury as she murdered him with her eyes.

And to think *some* people got their jollies this way. He ought to shoot the old biddy and be done with it. But he couldn't afford to. Not yet.

"Later, lady," he snarled.

The sounds of her choked, furious protests followed him all the way out the door.

Chapter Twenty-four

When Teresa and Charles drove back up to her beach house, they spotted a familiar truck with a big bug perched on top of it. "Billy Bob is here," she remarked.

Charles ground his jaw. "So he pops up conveniently again."

Seconds later, as he was opening her car door, the straw-haired young man in his khaki uniform stepped out from beneath her house, carrying a brown sack labeled RODENT BAITS. "Well, howdy again, folks. I was beginning to think I'd missed you."

"Billy Bob, what brings you back out here?" Teresa asked.

He pointed beneath the house. "Oh, just puttin' out a few baits for the riots."

"Really, you're too kind."

"My pleasure, ma'am. 'Sides, ever since your house got shot up the other day, I been worried about you. And that nice Mrs. Hambrush asked me to stop by and check on you."

"*Ambrush*," Teresa corrected, laughing.

"Yes, ma'am. Anyhow, might say I'm like one of them guardian angels they got on the tube."

"How sweet."

He gestured at the cottage above. "Looks like you're getting this here shack fixed up right good, ma'am."

"Yes, it's a much nicer shack now," she agreed. "But we're still having some problems."

"Oh, yeah?" he asked.

Teresa was about to explain, then hesitated briefly when she caught Charles's cautioning look. Nonetheless, she forged on. "You see, we've been visited twice now by a gun-waving maniac in a pig mask."

Billy Bob's jaw dropped. "No shit, ma'am!"

"And he claims to have kidnapped my aunt."

"Huh?" Billy Bob scratched his head. "You mean that nice Miss Hatch that was dodging buckshot with us the other day? The one that I toted over to Mrs. Hambrush's house?"

"*Ambrush*, Billy. And yes, that very one."

"Well, damn. When I come by Mrs. Ham—uh, Mrs. Ambrush's place this morning, she didn't mention that other lady being shanghaied."

"We haven't told Great-aunt Maizie about the kidnapping as yet," Teresa confided.

Billy Bob pondered that a moment. "Can't take it at her age, huh, ma'am?"

"Precisely. She thinks Aunt Hatch still hasn't returned from jogging."

He slowly shook his head. "Well, if that don't

beat all. So, poor Miss Hatch sure enough got dry-gulched."

Charles regarded Billy Bob suspiciously. "You wouldn't happen to know anything about Ms. Hatch's whereabouts, now would you?"

He pressed a hand to his breast. "Me?"

Teresa turned to him scoldingly. "Really, Charles. This is our good friend, Billy Bob."

"Well, we can't be too careful," he told her sternly. "Anyone could be suspect."

She flashed him a poisonously sweet smile. "Oh, I completely agree."

He made a sound of frustration. "It *is* rather odd that Billy Bob keeps dogging our tracks, don't you think?"

"No, it's not odd at all," Teresa shot back. "Billy Bob is with the Bug Brigade, and the Bug Brigade never gives up." She grinned at Billy. "Isn't that right?"

This conversation evidently went over Billy Bob's head, for he merely grinned back. "Sure, ma'am. Well, folks, I can't be staying long—but I did bring you something."

He motioned them over to the rear end of his truck. Tossing his sack of baits into the truck bed, he opened the gate, pulled out a small cooler, and flipped it open to reveal several large, greenish gray fish on ice.

"Sea bass," declared Charles.

Billy Bob grinned from ear to ear. "Yep, it's been a right slow afternoon, so I did me a bit of fishing off the flats, and caught some real beauts. You folks are welcome to take a few."

"Why, thanks," said Charles. "As it happens, I'm quite a good fish chef. Of course, I've found the best sea bass come from Portugal, but these will make an excellent dinner."

"You should stay and eat with us," Teresa offered.

Charles shot her another scowl.

Billy Bob brightened. "Hey, can't say I mind if I do, ma'am. Ain't nothin' like a home-cooked meal. That is, if you're sure it's no trouble—"

"None at all," Teresa assured him.

His grin broadened. "Well, thanks, ma'am, I'm right obliged. But first, think I'd best go scrub up at your hydrant yonder."

"Be my guest."

Watching Billy Bob grab a filthy bar of soap from his truck bed, then stride off toward a faucet at the side of the house, Charles raised an eyebrow at Teresa. "You invited him to *dinner*, Tess?"

"Seems only fair, when he has provided the main course. Besides, this will give you the perfect opportunity to grill him—if you'll pardon the pun."

"Right," Charles rejoined sardonically.

Wearing a long-suffering expression, Charles gripped Teresa's arm and escorted her up the steps.

Charles did cook an excellent dinner, and over food and white wine, Billy Bob regaled them with tales of his various leisure activities—rat killing, boat racing, horse betting, and possum hunting. Charles also asked Billy Bob questions regarding his background, and threw Teresa a victorious glance when the young man admitted having had one misdemeanor conviction for being drunk and disorderly—this also being the reason he couldn't get a better job than with the Bug Brigade, or so he claimed.

The fish Charles had steamed was excellent, but

after two glasses of wine, Teresa found herself feeling drowsy and even nodding off. Soon, she excused herself. In her bedroom, she curled up with Doris Juan and was asleep within seconds. . . .

Much later, a harsh sound at her window made her jerk awake with a gasp. Her heart raced as she spotted the shadowy figure of a man. "Who is it?" she demanded.

"Just me, darling," Charles answered. "You can relax, love. We won't be getting any more unexpected visitors tonight. I just shoved a dowel rod in your window track."

Teresa couldn't resist commenting on that. In a low, suggestive voice, she asked, "Why don't you come over here, handsome, and try that again?"

A wicked chuckle escaped him. "Why, you wanton girl." He came to sit beside her on the bed, smoothing her hair away from her brow. "I'd be delighted to accommodate you. But how much wine did you drink tonight, anyway?"

She yawned. "Enough to make me sleepy, I guess. Is Billy Bob gone?"

He leaned over to kiss her cheek. "Yes, an hour ago. I just finished tidying up the kitchen—and feeding the leftover fish to Doris Juan. The shameless creature is going into ecstasies on the kitchen floor right now. And now the fickle feline has decided she likes me, after all."

Teresa chuckled. "Thanks for taking care of everything." She ran her fingertips over his muscled forearm. "That was a great dinner. Sorry for bugging out like I did."

He smiled tenderly. "You've been under a great deal of strain, darling."

"We both have. But you know, you were wrong to suspect Billy Bob."

Charles frowned in the darkness. "I'm not so sure. He's been dogging our steps like a puppy. First he appears at your great-aunt's house, and now here. Like I said before, we can't be too careful."

She laughed, then drew her index finger along his jaw. "Charles, the truth is, we're not being careful at all are we?"

He grinned wryly. "Ah, I suppose you've got a point."

"And I feel so guilty because, while we've been making hay, we still haven't found Aunt Hatch. Not to mention the fact that that maniac threatened to kill her tomorrow."

Charles took her hand, raised it, and kissed it. "Easy, love. Try not to worry. I'm sure Pig Face won't do anything rash until he gets what he wants."

"You think so? But what does he want?"

"I wish I knew. At any rate, Ms. Hatch is his only bargaining chip. If he harms her, he's out of the game."

"I do hope you're right." She shuddered. "Oh, I just feel so helpless."

Charles caught her close. "Try to relax, darling. Tomorrow, we'll investigate more. We'll go see the Lafitte journal, and try again to track down Swinson or his mother."

"Yes, let's do that."

He nuzzled her hair. "No more worrying now, Tess. Let me help you out of your clothes."

"Again?" she teased.

He was already unbuttoning her shirt. "Didn't you just make a most lascivious request—which I intend to oblige fully?"

"Ah, yes," she murmured, curling her arms around his neck. "Feel free to start obliging."

279

He had discarded her shirt and was removing her bra. "No more worries, tonight, Tess," he murmured, leaning over to kiss her breast.

She moaned ecstatically and sank her fingers into his hair. "No more worries . . ."

Chapter Twenty-five

Teresa was grateful when the following morning brought no repeat performance from Pig Face, though she remained quite worried about Aunt Hatch. Before she and Charles left the beach house, she called Great-aunt Maizie and the Galveston police, only to learn that neither had any news of her aunt's whereabouts.

Was Charles right that they might find some clues to the mystery in Liberty?

As Charles drove them there, Teresa took out her brother's photocopy of the Lafitte journal and examined it in greater detail. Although she possessed only a rudimentary knowledge of French, she was able to make out various passages here and there. She discerned that the journal had been written after Lafitte ceased being a privateer, and detailed both his prior years at sea and his life afterward as a private citizen and family man. She had to admire Lafitte's elegant nine-teenth-century penmanship, the dramatic flour-ishes around his capital letters, and his signature. She noted that he had interspersed his journal entries with newspaper clippings, even bits of poetry. And she noticed something else. . . .

"This is odd," she murmured to Charles, flip-ping back and forth between two pages.

"What is odd?" he asked, glancing at her before returning his attention to the road.

"Well, the pages of the journal have been very carefully numbered," she told him. "But there's a gap. The numbers jump from 164 to 167. Pages 165 and 166 are missing."

"Hmm," Charles murmured. "Do you suppose Frank lost those two pages?"

"Could be. It's something to ask about at the library."

"Definitely," he agreed.

Forty-five minutes later, they entered the grounds of the Sam Houston Regional Library and Research Center. The complex, which included a stately pillared library and several antebellum houses, was ensconced on a lovely wooded property.

As they stepped inside the lobby of the library, a smiling young woman at the front desk asked, "May I help you?"

"Yes, we'd like to see the Lafitte journal," Teresa replied. "I understand it's on file here?"

The woman gestured to their left. "The original is in our exhibit room, in the display case in the far corner."

"Thanks. Is it possible to examine it?"

"I'm afraid not, ma'am, since it's very fragile. It

even went through a fire, I understand. But we have copies you can look at."

Teresa held up her bag. "As a matter of fact, I already have a copy which belonged to my brother, a professor in Houston. And we have some questions we'd like to ask about it."

The woman nodded. "One of our volunteers knows a lot about the journal, and she's here this morning. If you want to go look at the exhibit, I'll find her and send her on in to answer your questions."

Teresa thanked the woman, and she and Charles entered the large exhibit room. They strolled past the display cases with Indian arrowheads and ranching paraphernalia, then paused at the case in the far corner. There the journal lay open, its binding charred, its parchment old and yellowed. Teresa recognized Lafitte's distinctive script from the photocopy she'd examined.

"Goodness, it certainly does look fragile," Charles remarked.

"Indeed," she agreed.

"Are you the folks needing help?" a voice asked from behind them.

Teresa turned to watch a slender, silver-haired woman approach. "Yes. I'm Teresa Phelps and this is Charles Everett. We were hoping to see the Lafitte journal—to examine the original, if possible."

The woman stepped closer. "I'm sorry to say that isn't allowed. I'm sure you can see how delicate the original is. I understand you already have a copy?"

"Yes."

"May I see it?"

Teresa took the copy from her bag and handed it to the woman. "It belonged to my brother, who was a French professor in Houston."

The woman leafed through the pages. "Ah, yes, this is definitely a copy we made. You see, the center provides copies as a courtesy to various interested scholars and teaching facilities. Can you tell me why your brother wanted the copy?"

"Yes. As a French professor, he wanted to do his own translation."

"I see. We have several such scholars working on their own translations." The woman frowned. "You say your brother 'was' . . . ?"

"He died several weeks ago in an accident."

"Oh, I'm so sorry. So you've come here to—"

"To see what else we can learn about the journal," Charles put in.

"Such as?" the woman prompted.

Teresa smiled. "Well, for starters, did Lafitte really write it?"

The woman laughed. "There's quite an ongoing debate about that, but I'm inclined to think he probably did. The paper the journal is written on has been authenticated as nineteenth-century parchment, and several handwriting experts have compared the writing in the journal with known samples of Lafitte's handwriting, and have concluded that all were written by the same man."

"That is impressive," Teresa commented.

"Will the journal tell us where Lafitte's treasure is buried along the Gulf coast?" Charles asked with a glint of mischief in his eyes.

"Afraid not, sir. In fact, in the journal, Lafitte claims at one point to have forgotten where he left much of his treasure—especially booty he dumped while being chased by warships."

"Too bad," lamented Charles. "By the way, Ms. Phelps has noticed that there are two pages missing from our copy of the journal. May we see them?"

The woman shook her head. "They're not missing, sir. There is a two-page gap in the pagination."

"A gap?" Teresa inquired, perplexed. "Does that mean those two pages are missing from the original as well?"

"Well, the pages aren't in the original either, but we're more inclined to think it's just a numbering mistake, since the narrative continues without interruption, and there's no evidence pages have been ripped from the journal itself." The woman laughed again. "Although there has been much speculation about what those two phantom pages might have contained."

"Like Lafitte's treasure locations?" Charles suggested eagerly.

"You said it, sir, not I."

Charles and Teresa exchanged a look of dawning realization.

"At any rate," the woman continued. "I'd be happy to let you compare your copy with one of our own. We also have English translations, if you'd like to see one."

"Oh, we'd love to," Teresa declared.

She gestured toward the door. "If you'll follow me, then."

The volunteer led them to a research room, and helped them get signed in and settled at a table. She then brought them another copy of the journal for comparison with their own, as well as one of the published English translations. Teresa and Charles then spent several hours embroiled in the materials, comparing the two copies—which turned out to be identical—and reading one of the published English versions.

Driving away, they compared notes. Charles shook his head at Teresa. "Well, if that journal was truly written by Jean Lafitte as the experts seem to feel, he certainly lived a very different and laid-back life after leaving Galveston, marrying and raising a family in Missouri, and quietly spending his profits."

Teresa nodded. "And just as the volunteer told us, he claimed he had forgotten where he'd left much of his treasure in the Galveston region."

"All retired pirates claim that," Charles teased.

"Lafitte was a privateer," she reminded him.

"I stand corrected." Charles frowned thoughtfully. "It was interesting that there was no difference between your brother's copy of the journal and the ones they have on file. The only thing that still perplexes me is those missing pages."

"I know. Me too."

Charles snapped his fingers. "Here's an idea. As we've both noted, Lafitte inserted stuff throughout his journal."

"Right. Clippings and memorabilia."

"What if those two missing pages were another insert that was later removed. . . ."

Teresa grinned. "You mean like a treasure map?"

Charles nodded. "Precisely. And it all makes sense, Tess. From reading the journal, it's obvious Lafitte didn't forget *every* location where he'd hidden his booty."

She regarded him in amazement. "Are you thinking what I'm thinking?"

"That perhaps Clark Swinson found the missing pages hidden in an old house in Galveston, then brought them to Frank to be translated?" he pursued eagerly.

"Yes!" Teresa cried. "And that could also be the reason Frank wanted to study the entire journal. Oh, Charles, it's all finally making sense to me!"

"I agree. But the question remains, where are the pages?"

"I have no idea," she replied. "And here is another question: Are the missing pages from Lafitte's journal the same pages Pig Face wants?"

"I'm betting yes," Charles said grimly.

"I agree," Teresa rejoined. "Then is Clark Swinson really Pig Face, trying to get his papers back?"

"Possibly," Charles concurred with a scowl, "though we still can't afford to rule out anyone."

"Yes, I suppose that would be foolish."

"At any rate, we need to talk to Swinson or his mother at once. Clark could hold the key to all of this."

"So it's back to Galveston, then?"

"With all due dispatch."

As Charles began driving furiously for the island city, Teresa's mind was humming at an even faster clip. Everything *was* finally making sense to her. So Frank might have really been on to Lafitte's treasure, thanks to Clark Swinson. And someone might have killed Frank for it. But who? Was it Swinson? Or Pig Face? Perhaps Manolo and company? Or even someone else?

Even Charles? She glanced at him, his visage so determined as he drove. She was coming to care for him, *really* care. But the hell of it was, she still suspected his motives were less than pure. That made her the worst kind of fool, even if she couldn't seem to help herself. All she could know for certain was that she and Charles were playing a very dangerous game.

Indeed, Charles had just turned south onto the Gulf Freeway when Teresa jumped at a loud popping sound behind them. She glanced about wildly. "What was that? A car backfiring?"

Charles glance anxiously in his rearview mirror. "No, my dear, I'm afraid *that* was a gun."

"A what?" Teresa twisted about to see a familiar low-rider just inches away from their bumper, a man's head and arm thrust out the driver's window. "Oh no, it's Manolo and company. And he's firing a pistol out his window!"

As another shot rang out, Charles glanced about frantically at the thick traffic. "Damn it, Tess, get down! I'll see if I can't shake off those maniacs."

Teresa unfastened her seat belt and scampered to the floorboards just as Charles accelerated and swerved his car to the left. From the sound of a horn's angry blare, she guessed he had changed lanes. "Did you get away from them?"

"No—the idiots are still on my tail."

All at once a third shot rang out, followed by a metallic pinging sound. "My God, Charles, have we been hit?" she cried.

"Bloody hell!" he cursed. "That is enough!"

Teresa cringed as the car careened to the right, then screeched to a halt. "Charles, what are you doing now?"

He slammed the car into park and shut off the engine. "I'm going to have a word with those imbeciles."

"*Those* imbeciles?" Frantic, she glanced up at him. "Charles, no, don't confront them! They'll shoot you."

But Charles was already leaving the car, while shaking a finger at Teresa. "You stay down!"

"Charles!"

The door slammed and he was off. Defying his order, Teresa climbed up to the seat and peered over it, wide-eyed. Charles now stood on the shoulder at the back of his car, angrily waving his arms and shouting at Manolo, who stood perhaps five yards behind them, beside his own car—with pistol still in hand.

She heard Charles yell, "You bloody fool! Look what you've done! You've blown a hole in my gas tank."

"We want our cut, man," Manolo shouted back, waving his gun at Charles.

Charles yelled back, "You won't be getting a dime if you shoot our heads off. Back off, you idiot!"

Teresa watched, flabbergasted, as Charles stalked back to the car, threw open the door, got inside, and slammed it shut. "Are you satisfied now?" she asked sarcastically.

He jerked on the ignition. "Stow it, Tess, I've had enough torment for one afternoon."

Then she flinched as she felt a tap at her door, and twisted about to see Manolo grinning at her, his pistol now stowed at his waist. She rolled down her window and inquired nastily, "What do you want?"

Manolo chuckled. "Sorry about the hole in your rear, ma'am."

Teresa's face burned, and she jerked a thumb toward Charles. "It's *his* rear."

Manolo slowly shook his head. "Your boyfriend really has *cojones*, ma'am."

"And you're a prick," she spat back.

Now he appeared insulted. "Hey, watch who you're calling names, gringa!"

Heedless of his warning, she demanded, "Tell me, you snake, do you have my aunt?"

"What aunt?" he yelled.

Teresa was about to educate him when Charles's car lurched forward, spewing dirt and gravel all over Manolo. She looked behind them to see Manolo waving his fist, his mouth working furiously, then turned back to Charles, who was grimly maneuvering them into traffic. "Are you crazy? I was trying to ask Manolo about Aunt Hatch!"

Charles laughed scornfully. "Do you think if he had her, he'd tell us? Besides, I didn't like your talking to that bastard. It isn't safe."

"Isn't safe!" she mocked. "Spoken by a deranged thrill junkie! What about you, having a shouting match with Manolo at the side of the freeway, and inviting him to kill us both!"

Charles gave a bitter laugh. "Manolo wouldn't have the guts. He and his friends are strictly garden variety thugs who get their jollies blowing holes in people's gas tanks or shooting up their beach houses. Besides, I don't really think he has your Aunt Hatch."

Teresa angrily crossed her arms over her bosom. "Gee, I'm so reassured. That means Clark Swinson must have her. Or perhaps Billy Bob or Harold Robison."

He shot her a dirty look. "Well, it's certain we're dealing with at least two sets of antagonists here—Manolo and cronies, and whoever has your aunt."

Observing his tense expression, she sighed. "Is the damage to your car bad?"

"What do you think? There's a hole in my bloody gas tank. We'll have to take the car to the dealer . . . and hope no one throws a lit cigarette in our path before we get there."

"I'm sorry."

"Are you?" he mocked.

"Of course."

He shot her a hard look. "Then what was that

290

business Manolo was spouting about wanting his cut?"

She glanced away guiltily. "Oh, that. He just meant Frank owed him some money—you know, like he claimed before."

But Charles doggedly pursued the subject. "Being owed money is one thing. Like somebody washes the windows, and doesn't get paid. A cut is something else. Well, Tess?"

Feeling bad for withholding information from Charles—especially after the danger they'd just been exposed to—Teresa flashed him a sheepish look. "All right. I may as well tell you. Manolo thinks my brother Frank was onto buried booty."

His brows shot up. "What? Explain that."

She wrung her hands. "When Manolo kidnapped me, he told me Frank had hired him and his cronies to dig something up on the beach in Galveston. But Frank never showed up at the convenience store where they were all supposed to meet."

Charles shot her a fuming look. "So all of this *has* been about Lafitte's treasure, and Frank really did discover the location, perhaps even from Swinson. Thanks for trusting me, Tess."

"Can you blame me?" she countered. "Besides, you claim to have known my brother. Didn't Frank tell *you* about the treasure?"

Grinding his jaw, Charles replied, "Teresa, you must understand—"

"I know," she cut in bitterly. "It's complicated."

She turned and stared moodily out the window.

Across from Teresa, Charles seethed in silent frustration. It maddened him that Teresa had withheld information from him, but could he really blame her? She still didn't trust him.

If only he could tell her the truth. His feelings for her were deepening every day, with frightening intensity, and he longed to come clean with her about everything. The frustration and guilt of withholding what he knew were tearing him apart.

But the sad reality was, at this juncture, coming clean with her might only make her distrust him more . . . or even hate him.

Chapter Twenty-six

Once they were within a few miles of Galveston, Charles handed Teresa his cell phone and suggested she again try calling Clark Swinson's number. She got his voicemail yet another time and left a new message, this time giving her own name and telephone number.

Hanging up, she caught Charles's troubled look. "Something wrong?" she asked.

"Should you have left Swinson your name and number, considering the suspicions we have about him?"

She laughed. "If he is Pig Face, Charles, then he already knows where I live, right?"

Charles smiled wryly. "Good point."

"Besides, I've been thinking about this, and we

have no real proof that Clark Swinson is involved in this, do we?"

"No, only what Milton told us about Swinson's bringing your brother documents to translate."

"Most likely he's a general contractor, not Jack the Ripper—and the man is missing, for heaven's sake."

"That he is."

Teresa glanced at her notepad. "I have Swinson's address written down. Why don't we swing by there and see if we can speak with a neighbor—or perhaps even his mother, if she does live with him?"

"Good idea," Charles agreed. "We'll do that as soon as we drop off my car."

She nodded, laying down his phone on the center console.

A few minutes later, they arrived at the dealer where Charles had bought his car, and dropped it off for repair in the body shop. Afterward, they were given a loaner—a small, older subcompact that wasn't in much better shape than Teresa's car, although at least the air-conditioning worked.

As they pulled away from the dealership, Teresa chuckled, watching Charles grind the car into gear. "Not quite up to your standards, eh?"

He tossed her a surly look. "Not at all—and unfortunately, the body shop manager told me it will be three to five days before my car will be ready. They have to order a new gas tank, then install it and make the body repairs."

"Oh, brother."

"Shall we swing by Swinson's house now?"

"Yes. Then we must go check on Great-aunt Maizie, and perhaps go check in with Sergeant Varga again, as well."

"Will do," he agreed, grimacing as the car lurched forward.

They drove over to Clark Swinson's house in a neighborhood just south of Broadway. The ramshackle two-story Victorian sat on a weedy, neglected-looking lot.

"Doesn't look too promising," Charles muttered, parking the car.

On the Swinson front porch, Teresa noted that the shades were drawn, and the house, like the yard, bore a deserted air. As Charles knocked, her eye was caught by a small note posted next to the door; she squinted at the scratchy writing.

"Listen to this, Charles: 'Dear Mr. Tibbles, I am at the doctor's this afternoon, but go ahead and mow the lawn. I will pay you tomorrow. Cora Swinson.'"

"Ah, so there is someone around." Charles glanced at the note, then rapped on the door again. "Wonder if she isn't the mother."

"Probably so." Teresa waited a moment, then added, "And since no one is answering now, I guess we'd best come back tomorrow."

"Right."

They left and drove to Maizie Ambrush's house. As they pulled up to the property, Teresa spotted her great-aunt outside, standing by the mailbox in her housecoat. The little old woman appeared ashen-faced and shaken, and was clutching in her hand a letter and what appeared to be a scrap of green cloth.

Deeply concerned, Teresa popped out of the car the instant it stopped. Rushing over, she touched Maizie's arm and felt it trembling. Maizie's button mouth was quivering; her green eyes were filled with turmoil and gleamed with unshed tears.

"Great-aunt Maizie, what is it?" Teresa asked. "You look as if you've seen a ghost."

By now Charles had joined them. "Yes, Mrs. Ambrush, you appear to have had a bad shock."

"I have indeed." With shaking fingers, she handed Teresa a woman's green sweatband. "It's Lillian's."

Teresa stared at the green fabric band. "You're sure?"

"Yes. She was wearing it when she disappeared yesterday."

"But how—"

Maizie shoved the envelope into Teresa's hand. "It came in this hideous letter. Read it."

Worriedly Teresa scanned the outside of the envelope, which was blank and unsealed—meaning it must have been hand-delivered to the mailbox. She opened it and pulled out a note. Scrawled in crayon in deliberately juvenile script were the words, *Tell Teresa Phelps to cooperate, or next time I'll send you the head that wore this.*

Reading the words, Teresa gasped. "Oh, my God."

"It's just awful," agreed Maizie, wringing her hands. "How could anyone be so cruel as to say something like that about poor Lillian?"

"Let me see that," demanded Charles. He grabbed the letter from Teresa's hand, scanned it quickly, and whistled. "Why, the bloody bastard. I'm so sorry this happened, Mrs. Ambrush."

Maizie shuddered, a tear trickling down her wrinkled cheek. "But what does this mean, Teresa? Has someone kidnapped Lillian? I've been so dreadfully worried about her, and now. . . . Is someone planning to—to kill her?"

"Of course not, Great-aunt Maizie," Teresa reassured her.

"Then where is she? And why did someone send me this note?"

At a loss, Teresa glanced at Charles.

He protectively wrapped an arm around Maizie's frail shoulders. "Mrs. Ambrush, dear, it's hot as blazes out here, and you appear quite wan and weak. Let's get you inside before you have a heatstroke."

"But, Lillian—"

"You can't help her if you're in the hospital," Teresa interjected, throwing Charles a grateful look. "Charles is right—let's get you into the house."

Inside, they tried their best to calm the agitated Maizie, even though they had no real answers. They attempted to whitewash the dire situation, telling her they had no proof that Lillian had actually come to any harm, and pleading with her not to worry. Though they had little luck allaying the old woman's fears, Teresa did manage to persuade her great-aunt that, given the strange, threatening letter, she should spend the night with a neighbor. After helping Maizie pack a bag and get settled in at Mrs. Jacoby's down the block, they left, promising to take the letter and sweatband straight to the police.

At the police station, they again spoke to Sergeant Varga at his desk. Teresa handed him the note and the sweatband and explained what had happened.

A frowning Varga carefully examined both. "Well, ma'am, I must say this is starting to look pretty serious."

"Indeed," Teresa agreed.

"Unfortunately, we still have no leads on your aunt, though of course we'll be investigating this new twist thoroughly," he added.

"We're pleased to hear it," Charles put in.

"Also, since this is looking more and more like a kidnapping, we'll likely contact the FBI field office in Houston for assistance with profiling information and so forth."

"Yes, I'm sure they have reams of information on pig-faced kidnappers," Charles put in dryly.

Varga gave a shrug. "What can I say, sir? We'll try our best."

Teresa and Charles thanked the sergeant and left.

"I just feel so helpless," she told Charles as he drove them home to her beach house. "It infuriates me to know that monster terrorized poor Great-aunt Maizie. And damn, how I wish there were something we could do to find Aunt Hatch. Should we go looking again?"

Charles sighed heavily. "I know you want to, love. But there's little we can do other than just drive through the streets, which we've already done several times. It's all rather like hunting for a needle in a haystack, isn't it?"

Miserably, she bit her lip. "Are we missing something, Charles?"

He slowly shook his head. "Seems to me we've pretty much covered the map in trying to find your aunt."

"But it still hasn't been enough."

When they entered the beach house, it was to the sound of a ringing phone. Teresa rushed over and picked up the receiver. "Hello?"

"Did you get my message, bitch?" growled a low male voice.

Teresa went wide-eyed as she recognized her tormenter. "You monster! How dare you terrorize my poor great-aunt that way!" Watching

Charles advance toward her as if to grab the phone, she waved a hand and vehemently shook her head. He kept his distance, though his frustration was apparent.

Meanwhile, Teresa was listening intently. "I'm through playing games, bitch," the voice went on. "Meet me under the San Luis Pass bridge tomorrow at sunset, with the papers. No cops, or your aunt goes out with the tide."

"But I don't have any papers!" Teresa exclaimed, exasperated.

"Yes, you do, so quit lying to me, bitch. Bring them tomorrow, or the amazon is history."

"Damn it, you have to give me more time," Teresa pleaded. "Tell me who you are, and why you are—"

Teresa didn't get to finish her sentence, as the line went dead in her ear. "Oh, hell!" she muttered, slamming down the receiver.

"Pig Face?" Charles grimly inquired.

She nodded. "He wants me to meet him under the San Luis Pass bridge tomorrow at sunset with the papers, or he says he'll kill Aunt Hatch."

"He wants *you* to meet him under a bridge?" Charles asked, voice rising. "No way, Teresa!"

"Charles! Aunt Hatch's life is at stake here!"

"And yours will be at stake if you go."

"So what the hell am I supposed to do?" she demanded.

He raked his fingers through his hair. "We'll figure something out. At least we have some time. We must notify the authorities, so they can be there and catch Pig Face."

She laughed bitterly. "That's just what Pig Face warned me not to do. And it seems to me it would be damn difficult to ambush anyone out at San Luis Pass. It's open, flat marshlands at the westernmost tip of the island. No real places for the cops to hide, not even around the bridge."

"So you're saying we shouldn't notify the authorities?"

She bit her lip. "No, I'm not saying that. I think we should call Sergeant Varga and report this— and see if the police can't find a way to help us."

"I agree." He shook a finger at her. "But no matter what, you're not going to meet that monster."

"Let's see what the police have to say."

He handed her the receiver. "Yes, let's. I'm betting they'll agree with me."

Teresa called Sergeant Varga and reported the incident. He seemed extremely concerned this time and listened intently. They discussed various options, and then she hung up.

"Well?" Charles asked.

"He wants us to come into the station first thing in the morning to discuss this further. He said they'll find a way to be at San Luis Pass tomorrow to apprehend Pig Face. And he mentioned getting a policewoman to go out there and impersonate me."

A relieved expression washed over Charles. "Good."

She sighed, offering him a tremulous smile. "At least we know there's a good chance Aunt Hatch is still alive, and we may still be able to save her."

Charles caught her close. "Yes, love. At least we know that."

She flashed him a brave smile. "I'm starved. How about you?"

They made chicken sandwiches, and ate them on the living room couch while sipping beer. Doris Juan bounded up and begged for leftovers. After they finished, as Teresa sat petting her cat, she noted that Charles was staring at her thoughtfully, a brooding quality in his eyes.

"Something on your mind?" she asked.

"Yes, something has been troubling me for several hours now."

"Then spit it out."

He regarded her sternly. "I was thinking about the incident with Manolo today. Do you have any idea how badly it scared me?"

"You think it didn't freak me out, too?"

"You easily could have been killed, Teresa," he went on, eyeing her worriedly. "And to think it might all have been avoided had you simply told me about Manolo's demands when he kidnapped you. When are you going to start trusting me, Tess?"

She was silent for a long moment, then raised her chin and met his gaze soberly. "When are you going to tell me the truth about who you really are and what you want?"

His expression was deeply torn. "Teresa, there are things I'm simply unable to tell you just yet."

Teresa gave a groan. "Yeah, right. And you think stonewalling makes me trust you?"

"Teresa, damn it, the only way we're going to figure this thing out is to work together."

"So when do *you* want to begin?" she asked.

Jaw tight, Charles didn't answer her.

The atmosphere remained strained between them for the rest of the evening, and even though they did make love that night, their coupling was intense and urgent rather than sweet and tender, and much tension still lingered between them.

Then, just before dawn, Teresa awakened to feel Charles gently shaking her. "Hey, sleepyhead, let's go for a swim," he suggested.

"Now?" she asked groggily. "What about Aunt Hatch?"

He kissed the tip of her nose. "There's nothing we can do for her at the moment." He tugged on her hand. "Come on, let's have a last respite before we tackle what promises to be a very daunting day."

She nodded. "Okay."

They donned their swimsuits, grabbed towels, and ran out to the surf in the coolness of morning. As dawn painted the horizon a stunning flamingo pink, as the morning light gilded the edges of the brisk whitecaps, Teresa gloried in their moments alone in the surf, Charles swimming next to her, his body frequently rubbing against her own. He looked so splendid in his black swim briefs, his hair wet and gleaming, his sleek body dripping and aglow, his smile dazzling. While her own navy swimsuit was modestly styled, she knew from the many appreciative looks he cast her way that he liked what he saw. When he caught her close for a slow, lingering kiss even as a cool, exhilarating wave slid over them, she was in heaven.

Afterward, they cuddled together on beach towels, letting the warm sea breeze caress their bodies and listening to the soothing roar of the surf. Nibbling on Teresa's arm, Charles murmured, "Still mad at me?"

She ruffled his wet hair. "Are you referring to our little spat yesterday?"

He solemnly nodded.

With a saucy wrinkle of her nose, she replied, "Well, you make it rather difficult for a gal to stay mad at you, I must admit."

He squeezed her hand. "Teresa, please know that I'm sharing with you everything . . ."

"That you can?" she finished ironically.

He nodded again. "Will that be enough?"

"I guess it will have to be," she murmured sadly.

He kissed her cheek and spoke with uncharacteristic emotion. "When this is over, darling, I'll reveal all."

He appeared so earnest when he said the words that Teresa didn't have the heart to scold him further. "Promise?"

"Yes, promise."

"All right, then."

He smiled, appearing relieved. "These moments alone have been sublime, Tess. But now I suppose we must get back to work."

"I know," she agreed, kissing his strong jaw. "The mystery to solve . . . and Aunt Hatch's fate."

Charles sat up and pulled Teresa up beside him. He braced his forearms on his knees, his expression abstracted. "If only we could figure everything out, then surely we could get a handle on it and save her."

"I know."

His fingers sifted through the sand. "But I just can't piece it all together, Tess. Did your brother drown that night at the lake? Or was he murdered for what he might have uncovered? Was Manolo Juarez his murderer? Or was it Pig Face? And who is Pig Face really—Clark Swinson, Harold Robison, one of Manolo's cohorts—"

"Or someone else," Teresa finished. "It's enough to make one's head spin. And with all we've done, we still seem no closer to solving the mystery, or finding Aunt Hatch."

"So much just doesn't make sense," Charles continued. "For instance, assuming your brother was murdered, why would anyone kill Frank before finding out where Lafitte's treasure was buried, if that was, indeed, what Frank discovered?"

"I know. And why does the masked man think I somehow hold the key to this—and what in hell has he done with Aunt Hatch?"

"And where does Clark Swinson fit in to the puzzle?" Charles added.

She eyed him tenderly. "You're really taking all of this very seriously."

"Of course I am. Damn it, Tess, your life is in danger."

"So is yours," she pointed out.

"I'm much more concerned about you, love."

She traced her fingertips over the stubble on his jaw, and her voice caught as she spoke. "Then you care."

He laughed bitterly. "Damn right, I care. What did you think? That I wanted to seduce you just for the hell of it?"

She stared out at the surf. "Charles, it's been hard to know what to think."

"Doesn't my kiss tell you more than that?" He leaned over and tenderly touched her mouth with his lips.

"Umm. That's a hero's kiss, all right."

His blue eyes, so deeply sincere, held her own troubled gaze. "Remember, Tess, there are just the two of us now. Only each other to depend on."

"I'll remember." She circled an arm around his neck and eagerly kissed him back.

Teresa savored the shelter of Charles's strong arms, all the while wondering what this day would bring. There was no doubt in her mind now that Charles did care for her, and that he was determined to protect and help her. Yet his motives still remained under a cloud. As close as she felt to him now, there was still a layer of mistrust separating them. . . .

As Charles held Teresa, he found himself burning with frustration, afraid of what new dangers this day might hold for her. If only he could keep her here with him forever, and shield her from all harm. He knew he couldn't, that they had to brave the dangerous world again, they had to save her aunt and solve the mystery. Nonetheless, he would find a way to keep her safe. He had to, because he was coming to love her. . . .

Chapter Twenty-seven

At 7 A.M., Manolo Juarez sat at the kitchen table of Rudy Zaragoza's home. A crayon in hand, he was scrawling silly faces to entertain Josie's nieces, Silvia and Sophia. As the twins, dressed in matching blue T-shirts, shorts, and sneakers, looked on with expressions of fascination, he drew an absurdly grinning face with wild eyes, huge ears and teeth, and psychotic hair. The girls clapped their hands and laughed in glee.

"You're so good, Manolo," declared Silvia. "Show me how to draw a face like that."

"No, show me first!" protested Sophia.

"No problem, *niñas*, I'll show you both," Manolo promised. Handing each girl a crayon, he then tore off three clean sheets of paper from the tablet he was using and slapped one down in front of each of them. "Now, you girls just watch Uncle Manolo, and copy what he does."

"Okay!" cried Sophie.

"*Sí, Tío Manolo,*" added Silvia proudly.

Manolo grinned and mussed Silvia's hair. Then his hand froze at the sound of an irate female voice.

"Manolo Juarez, what in the hell are you doing here, and why is my niece calling you 'uncle'?"

All three jerked around to see Josie standing in the kitchen doorway, wearing pink, baby-doll pajamas. Manolo's heart pumped with excitement at the sight of her—her gorgeous thick hair disheveled from sleep, her womanly curves and beautiful sleek legs beckoning to him. And her fluffy pink cuffs filled him with a desire to grab her, haul off those slippers, and nibble on one of her shapely toes.

Were the girls not present, he might have jumped her bones. "Josie, *mi corazon,*" he greeted huskily. "Good morning."

"Good morning, Aunt Josie," the girls called in unison.

Josie flounced into the room, glaring at Manolo. "Don't you 'good morning' me, you rat. How did you get in here, anyway?"

"I let him in," answered Silvia fretfully.

"Oh, you did?" Josie scolded her niece. "You know better, *niña.*"

"Sorry, Aunt Josie," Silvia replied, head downcast.

"And where is your grandmother?"

"She took Papa to work," explained Sophia.

Josie gritted her teeth. "Girls, go upstairs and get ready for day camp."

"But we're already dressed," protested Silvia.

"Really? Are your beds made?"

Both girls guiltily avoided their aunt's eyes.

"*Vamos*," Josie ordered, clapping her hands. "You girls go get your rooms shipshape, and I'll call you when breakfast is ready, okay?"

"Yes, aunt," said Sophia, dour-faced.

"Thanks, Manolo," said Silvia, grinning shyly at him.

"You're welcome, *niña*," he replied. He picked up two drawings. "Here, each of you take one of these."

With a chorus of "Thanks, Manolo!" the girls grabbed the drawings and danced out of the room.

Manolo flashed Josie a cajoling smile. "Woman, why are you being so mean to Sophia and Silvia? They're only little girls."

She tossed her curls and cast him a superior look. "I don't want them around you. You're a bad influence, Manolo."

With a melodramatic air, Manolo stood and pressed a hand to his chest. "Ah, woman, you're breaking my heart, and I was about to offer to cook breakfast for all three of you."

"If Mama catches you here, she'll fry you up with her *huevos rancheros*," Josie retorted irritably. "Get out of here."

He took a step toward her. "But I just arrived."

"You better split now, or I swear I'm calling the cops."

Manolo shook his head in disbelief. "Woman, why is your tail in such a snarl?"

"Why? Because you're a wanted man, Manolo."

He blanched. "Who told you that?"

"Rudy did. He has friends in the Houston Police department. He said some lady filed a complaint on you, Freddie, and Hector, that you're all wanted for kidnapping and assaulting her."

"I didn't assault her," Manolo snapped back.

Josie's eyes went wide. "So you did kidnap her?"

He glanced at his boots. "It's complicated."

"Complicated, my butt! Tell the truth, Manolo."

He glanced up angrily. "Yeah, I kidnapped her."

"My God!" Josie cried, incredulous. "And you assaulted her?"

He waved a hand. "The bitch tripped."

Josie emitted a cry of outrage and slapped Manolo's face. He glared back at her and clutched his stinging cheek.

"How can you say that about the poor woman?" she demanded.

"She was a pain in the neck."

"Of course she was a pain in the neck! You *kidnapped* her, Manolo! I can't believe you did that! You have no respect for women. You have no respect for me."

"Yes, I do."

"If you respected me, if you respected yourself, you would go beg that poor woman's forgiveness, then turn yourself in to the law."

Jaw tight, he took a step toward her. "You don't understand. The woman's brother owed me *dinero*—a lot of *dinero*."

"Then why didn't you go to him?"

"He's dead."

Josie gasped and began backing away.

He followed, hands extended beseechingly. "Hey, I didn't kill him, okay?"

"I don't believe you! I've tried to be patient with you, Manolo, but I've had it." Josie stalked over to the back door and threw it open. "Get out."

His dark eyes beseeched her. "Josie, please, give me one more chance."

But her own eyes seethed with fury. "I've already given you too many chances. Rudy's right. You're a bum. I want nothing to do with you unless you clean up your act. Then . . . well, I don't even know about then."

Grinding his jaw, Manolo stepped out onto the stoop. "Josie, you gotta listen to me. I'm onto something big. Really big. I'm gonna be rich. Then you'll change your mind, you'll see."

Sadly she shook her head. "Manolo, you still don't get it. It ain't about money, it's about *respectability*."

She slammed the door in his face.

Manolo slunk away, brooding to himself. Josie was being a real pain, still ranting about respectability, when, to Manolo, the way to *get* respect in this world was to buy it.

Well, he would buy it—that, and whatever else it took to win Josie back. Somehow he'd get the *dinero*. Then he'd change her stubborn mind. . . .

At 9 A.M., Teresa and Charles sat in front of the desk of Sergeant Varga at the Galveston police station. Since the battery in Charles's loaner car had died this morning, leaving only her own unairconditioned car, they'd both changed into lightweight clothing before leaving for the island. Teresa had donned a low-necked, sleeveless hot pink dress emblazoned with old-fashioned sailing ships and nautical symbols, a rather garish number that at least looked good with her brother's bracelet; Charles had chosen a green tropical shirt and tan shorts—causing Teresa's gaze to stray more than once in the direction of his cute knees and lean, muscular thighs.

Across from them, Sergeant Varga was rapping his pencil and frowning thoughtfully. "So, Ms. Phelps, this man who claims to have your aunt wants you to meet him under the San Luis Pass bridge at sunset."

"Right. He wants me to turn over some papers—even though I still don't have anything to bring him."

Varga nodded. "Well, we're certainly planning to be there to apprehend this creep. We're planning a task force of at least four officers."

"But won't he recognize you out there on the marshlands?" Teresa fretted.

Varga shook his head. "We're planning to go disguised as fishermen."

"Good thinking," put in Charles. "And what about Ms. Phelps's safety? She mentioned you might use a decoy."

"That's the plan," Varga replied.

"But won't Pig Face know it isn't me?" Teresa asked.

The sergeant shook his head. "One of our policewomen is about your height and build. Her hair color is different, but we can have her wear sunglasses and a scarf, and drive your car. Of course we'll have her take along some sort of large envelope, so the perp will think she's brought the papers—whatever they are. Anyway, by the time this man gets close enough to realize it's not you, we'll nab him."

"Sounds like a plan," Charles agreed.

The sergeant consulted his watch. "Why don't you two come back here around three-thirty, and drop off Ms. Phelps's car? We'll coordinate everything from here, and if you like, you can wait at the station while we apprehend this lowlife."

"You know you have to catch him alive if we're

to have any hope of rescuing Aunt Hatch," Teresa put in anxiously.

"You just leave that to us," Varga replied.

"Thanks, sergeant," Charles said.

As Teresa and Charles left the police station, she still felt full of doubts. "Do you think Varga's plan will work?"

He put his arm around her waist and ushered her down the sidewalk. "There's a good chance—if the police don't spook the man."

"Perhaps I should go instead of the police-woman."

He swung around to regard her harshly. "Not on your life. You actually think I'd allow you to meet Pig Face under a bridge? Teresa, the police are trained to deal with these situations. You're not."

"I suppose you're right," she admitted dully.

He forced a smile. "What now?"

"Let's go check on Great-aunt Maizie, then swing by Swinson's house again."

"Okay." He caught her hand. "You look so anxious, love."

She shuddered. "I'm very worried about Aunt Hatch. Time must be running out for her."

"I know. But it'll work out." His gaze flicked over her, lingering on her long legs. "Have I told you yet how much I love your dress? Especially that short skirt?"

Staring down at the bright, gaudy print with its skimpy hem, she laughed. "One of my girlfriends gave this to me as a bon voyage gift when I left for Bolivar—I think mainly as a joke. It's not at all like the usual, conservative me—but it sure is cool in this heat."

"Well, I must say I rather like your more capricious side. You could do with a few more risqué garments." Lowering his voice, he murmured suggestively, "Not that I don't like you best without any clothes at all."

She blushed. "Charles, really."

He chucked her beneath the chin. "And I'm happy to see I've raised a smile from you."

Her expression turned bittersweet. "Thanks, Charles. It may be my last one for a while, I'm afraid."

Charles hugged her close. "Courage, love. Courage."

In her room at the flophouse, Lillian Hatch sat on a flimsy chair pulled up to a miserable scarred table. She chewed on a stale doughnut and glared at her captor, who stood across from her with gun drawn. As always, he wore his revolting pig mask.

"These doughnuts are atrocious," she declared, "and the coffee is cold. Where did you pick up this garbage, anyway? I bet you stole it from a home for the indigent."

"Shut up lady, and be grateful you have food at all," Pig Face growled back.

"Whether or not this garbage can be called food is debatable," she snapped.

"Eat up, I don't have all day."

"When are you going to release me?" she demanded.

That question raised an evil chuckle from her captor. "As a matter of fact, soon. This is all going to end today . . . one way or another."

Lillian swallowed hard; she did not at all like the way Pig Face had sneered his last comment. She stared at the cheap paper plate placed in front of her. Only a few bites of the disgusting doughnut left. Which meant the maniac would soon insist she handcuff herself back to the bed. Then when he came back it would be settled . . . one way or another.

Lillian was street-smart enough to know precisely what *that* meant. Kidnappers didn't leave witnesses, so she would definitely land in the dumpster, or in the drink, tonight. She must make her move now or never.

"I said, eat up, lady!" her captor ordered.

"As you wish," she coldly replied.

Now or never, Lillian told herself again. *Now or never*. Taking a deep breath, she grabbed a hunk of doughnut, opened her mouth, and hurled it inside. She promptly began choking violently. She clutched her throat and jerked about so furiously that she broke her rickety chair and went crashing down onto the floor, her body rolling about frantically. . . .

Across from Lillian, Pig Face was at first startled by the amazon's wild demonstration, then he grew cynically amused. He was wise enough to recognize an act when he saw one. And this broad was definitely out to win an Oscar. By now she was down on the floor, jerking, pitching, helplessly pointing at her throat, features bright red and her eyes bulging out.

"Don't give me that crap," he sneered. "Pretending to choke on a doughnut when you really want to escape. That's the oldest con in the business."

Her response was more frenzied gyrations on the floor. She was good at this, he thought, watching her flip, flail, convulse, undulate, and heave. She even twitched, writhed, and rattled.

Then suddenly it was all over and she went deathly still, stiff as a corpse.

Pig Face eyed the woman askance. She lay facing him on her side, features contorted, arms extended, fingers splayed and fixed frozenly in the air. Now he wasn't so sure this was a trick. Stealing over, he glanced down and noted her face was purple, her eyes bulging and bloodshot, vacantly staring.

Damn, had the witch kicked the bucket after all? Maybe it was for the best.

But he had to know. Keeping the gun in his hand, he knelt down on one knee and cautiously bent toward her. She was totally still, no signs of breathing or movement. Cautiously he shook her shoulder.

It was then that the corpse spun, its arm shooting up, its voice bubbling up in fury.

For Pig Face, the blow seemed to come out of nowhere, lightning swift, impacting his wrist and knocking the gun out of his hand. He howled in pain and clutched his wrist, certain it must be broken. But his ordeal had hardly ended. In a split second, the she-devil sprang to her feet. He caught a horrifying glimpse of her face—nostrils flared, eyes wild with rage—heard a bloodcurdling karate yell, then the side of her hand descended with the swiftness of a guillotine blade. Pain seemed to split his neck apart, then everything went blank and he crumpled to the floor in a heap. . . .

Lillian Hatch grinned at the sight of Pig Face, lying powerless, in a disgusting mound on the floor. She spat out the chunk of doughnut, brushed off her hands, then calmly crossed over to the door and reached for the latch.

Then the sound of a moan made her blood run cold. Damn, the blow hadn't been stunning enough! She should have finished off the creep!

"You bitch!" exclaimed a low, gritty voice.

In horror, Lillian whirled about to see that Pig

Face had staggered to his feet and was weaving about, gun in hand, mask garishly hanging half-on, half-off his face. He appeared as if he might pass out again at any second, but she couldn't be sure.

Lunging toward her, he yanked off his mask. "You're dead, lady!"

Backing away, Lillian gasped as she recognized a familiar face, the features now contorted in fury, and twitching spasmodically. "My God! Why, you're—"

"That's right lady, we've met before," he roared back, "at your beloved nephew Frankie's funeral. And now I'm going to frigging kill you!"

Lillian stared appalled at her advancing nemesis. She knew she had to act now, or die. But could she act in time? Even as her attacker cocked his revolver and lunged closer, she gave a second, bloodcurdling karate yell, and her enormous body vaulted into action. . . .

Chapter Twenty-eight

"You know, Tess, this house must have really been grand at one time," Charles remarked, "though it needs a lot of work now."

Late that morning, he and Teresa again stood on the porch of the dilapidated Swinson home. Glancing about, Teresa had to agree with Charles's assessment; the original majesty of the Greek Revival mansion was apparent in its classical lines, carved pillars and pediment, and lavish wraparound verandas, but with cracking paint and rotting porch boards, it appeared sad and neglected now.

"At least someone mows the lawn," she replied to Charles, jerking her thumb toward the clipped though dried-out grass in the yard behind them.

He glanced briefly at the yard, then knocked

on the front door. "Yes, though it's not much of an improvement."

She tossed Charles a rueful look. "You mean you're not going to suggest the Swinsons leave the house to you in their will?"

"Cute, Tess," he replied, rapping again on the door.

They waited, but the only response was silence and the chirping of birds out in the yard. Strolling about the creaky porch, Teresa peeked in the windows, only to find that the shades were drawn. She peered around the corners of the old veranda, seeing only dirt and piles of summer leaves.

With an expression of disappointment, she returned to Charles's side. "Not a soul in sight. Guess Cora Swinson must be out again."

"Guess so."

"Should we try the neighbors?"

"Yes, let's do."

They had climbed back down the steps and were crossing the yard when both paused at the sight of a Galveston police cruiser pulling up to the curb out in the street. Teresa glanced at Charles in perplexity, and he gave a shrug. Both watched a young uniformed officer get out, stride around to the other side of the car, and help out an elderly woman wearing a pink dress and carrying a cane. After the officer opened the gate for her, he returned to his car and drove off.

As Charles and Teresa walked toward the woman, she called out in a frail yet irritable voice, "May I help you?"

"Are you Clark Swinson's mother?" Charles asked.

The woman, hunched and squinty-eyed, with frown lines well worn into her aged face, nodded warily and continued haltingly toward them. "Yes, I'm Cora Swinson. I live in the downstairs apartment."

"Pleased to meet you, Mrs. Swinson," Charles greeted. "I'm Charles Everett and this is my friend, Teresa Phelps."

The woman nodded to Teresa, but didn't offer her hand to either of them.

Teresa flashed Cora an ingratiating smile. "Mrs. Swinson, we were wondering if you could tell us how to get in touch with your son."

Cora appeared taken aback. "You mean you don't know?"

"Know?" Teresa repeated, bemused. "You mean about your son being missing? Why, yes, the police mentioned that to us the other day, and we're so sorry."

Cora harrumphed. "Well, they sure didn't mention enough. What do you want from me?"

Although put off by Cora's harsh tone, Teresa answered politely. "It's possible Mr. Swinson may have some information we need. You see, Clark was in touch with my brother right before Frank . . . well, my brother died in a accident about a month ago."

Cora gasped and went pale. "How peculiar. As a matter of fact, I've just come from the morgue myself."

"My God!" Teresa cried. "You don't mean Clark is—"

"Dead," Cora finished for them, eyes gleaming with emotion.

Teresa and Charles exchanged an astonished glance.

The old woman stared at them intently for a long moment, then slowly nodded. "Perhaps you two had best come inside."

* * *

Mrs. Swinson's decorating could only be described as "Victorian Macabre." Sitting on a black horsehair settee next to Charles, and drinking some suspicious-tasting, bitter tea in a cracked and stained china cup, Teresa reflected that never in her life had she seen so much black. Black silk brocade wallpaper covered the walls. Large cast-iron dogs with teeth viciously bared guarded the old onyx fireplace, while a sooty black parlor stove squatted in the filthy grate. A black silk wreath adorned the mantelpiece.

All around the room, black urns and vases reposed on Chinese lacquered tables next to crusty brass lamps with black shades. A huge arrangement of black silk roses cluttered the center tea table. A black Persian rug with faded floral adornments was spread upon the floor. An odor of dirt, mold, and mustiness hung in the air.

Mrs. Swinson was ensconced in a black bentwood rocker. She looked a ludicrous sight with her pale-as-death, wrinkled skin and her pasty-pink silk dress. At her feet stood two stuffed poodles—one white, one black, the black one with a paw aloft. With a shudder, Teresa realized the poodles must be the woman's former pets, preserved for posterity thanks to the skills of the taxidermist.

She hadn't the heart to ask if there was a current one.

She forced a smile. "Mrs. Swinson, Mr. Everett and I are so sorry for your loss."

"Thank you," Cora muttered distractedly.

"You must have had quite a shock this morning," Charles put in.

"Well, yes—although this wasn't entirely unexpected," Cora told them almost matter-of-factly.

320

"You see, Clark has been missing for over a month, and it was totally unlike him to disappear. He wouldn't have wanted me to worry. He didn't make much money as a contractor, you know, but he still took care of me in my declining years, allowing me to live here in his home. Since my arthritis is so bad, Clark let me have the downstairs. He resided upstairs, that is, until . . ."

Charles took a sip of his tea and grimaced. "If you don't mind my asking, just how did your son die, Mrs. Swinson?"

Cora sniffed. "According to the coroner, it was something of a freak accident, I'm afraid. They think Clark got trapped in a secret room beneath a staircase in one of the homes he was renovating."

"How awful!" Teresa exclaimed.

"Indeed. A couple interested in purchasing the house noticed a rather appalling odor as they strolled down the hallway early this morning. The authorities were called. . . . and Clark's badly decomposed body was soon discovered."

"Madam, my deepest sympathies," Charles said, shuddering.

Cora sniffed in seeming indifference. "They found Clark's wallet with his driver's license, and that's how they knew to contact me. I just got back from identifying the body. . . . Most unpleasant."

Teresa exchanged a puzzled look with Charles. Cora Swinson was giving her the creeps. The woman seemed more annoyed than grief-stricken over her son's death.

However, to Cora, she flashed her most compassionate smile. "Again, I'm so sorry. Do the authorities have any idea how this terrible tragedy occurred?"

Cora shook her head. "Only that Clark must

have been working in the secret room when the trap door somehow got jammed shut and locked him inside."

"How ghastly," declared Charles. "Do the police suspect foul play?"

Cora tweaked her nose disdainfully. "Why, no. Poor judgment on Clark's part, perhaps, but not foul play. Of course they'll know more after an autopsy is performed, but considering the decomposition of the body . . . well, they're not promising much."

Teresa fought down a tickle of nausea at Cora's almost glibly gruesome remarks. "Still, under the circumstances, it does seem odd. With my brother knowing your son, and both of them dying in unusual accidents."

"I must agree, it is strange," Cora concurred. "What happened to your brother?"

"He drowned in a boating accident at Clear Lake."

"Ah," Cora murmured. "And you say Clark had been in contact with him?"

"Yes. You see, my brother was a French professor, and evidently Clark took Frank some old French documents he'd found, hoping my brother could translate them."

Screwing up her face, Cora waved Teresa off. "Oh, phooey. Clark was always gathering up old papers and junk he found in the houses he renovated. You can bet whatever he brought your brother was worthless."

"Well, actually . . ." Teresa was about to comment when she spied Charles shaking his head in warning. "What I mean is, with both of them gone, we may never know."

Cora, grimacing, didn't seem to have noticed the look that had passed between Teresa and

Charles. "Well, I do hope your brother left you in better financial shape than Clark left me," she declared with a wave of a frail hand.

"I beg your pardon?" Teresa asked.

The old woman's eyes gleamed with indignation. "Can you imagine, Clark had no life insurance! I kept begging him to get some, but he never listened, of course. You know how irresponsible these young people are. What a horrid way to treat his poor, invalid mother. And just look at this place, falling down around my ears. Why, the ceiling is leaking"— she pointed at some stains overhead—"and Clark promised me years ago that he'd paint this house, then he never so much as lifted a brush. I feel like a shoemaker's child—never any decent shoes of my own."

"Well, yes, I'm sorry," Teresa managed, squelching a look of horror at Cora's mercenary tirade.

Charles cleared his throat. "Madam, is there anything else about Clark that you might be able to tell us?"

"No," Cora answered peevishly. "But perhaps, young man, you might be able to tell me how in the world I'm going to settle all Clark's debts, much less pay his funeral expenses, me with only my Social Security check. I'm sure I'll have to fight his creditors for this house, and I'll be lucky if I'm not thrown out on the street. But I suppose I can always get a paper route—me, eighty-three years old, with advanced arthritis."

"We're very sorry, madam," Charles told her, while nudging Teresa as if to say, *Let's get out of here.*

They wound up the conversation, thanked Mrs. Swinson for her hospitality and help, and left. As Teresa walked with Charles to her car, he pulled a face. "My God, what *was* that tea?"

She grimaced back. "I was afraid to ask. I sincerely hope it wasn't hemlock."

"Well, at least neither of us drank much."

"Yes, thank goodness for that. And what a horrible woman! Her son dies in the most hideous way, she's just come home from the morgue, for heaven's sake . . . and all she cares about is whether he left her any life insurance!"

"Well, you know, Tess, Clark did leave his mum in something of a financial bind," Charles pointed out.

Teresa couldn't resist a cynical smile. "Yes. And good old mercenary you would be quick to realize that. Tell me, are you and Cora related?"

He leveled a chiding glance on her. "Shouldn't we report this latest turn to Sergeant Varga?"

"Yes, although surely he's been notified about Clark's being found. At least we know now that Clark couldn't have been the one who kidnapped Aunt Hatch, although this shouldn't change our plans for later today."

"I agree," said Charles. "Let's give Varga a ring. Do you still have my cell phone in your bag?"

She fished through her bag, then snapped her fingers. "Oh, damn, I'm sorry, Charles. I left it in your car at the dealer."

"Great. Guess we'll call him from a pay phone." He opened her car door for her.

As he drove them away, she murmured, "You know I still can't get over the fact that both Clark and Frank died in accidents."

Charles nodded soberly. "Teresa, I'm beginning to suspect neither death was an accident."

"Really?"

"I suspect Clark Swinson may have discovered something valuable enough to endanger his life—and Frank's."

Teresa whistled. "Good heavens. Do you think Cora knows something she didn't tell us?"

He shook his head. "No. If she'd suspected Clark was on to anything of value, she would have gone into a feeding frenzy that would have put any shark to shame."

"Yes, I must agree she was obnoxious in the extreme. You know, she and Aunt Hatch would get along great." Then, realizing what she'd just said, Teresa gasped. "Oh, damn—poor Aunt Hatch. We're still no closer to finding her. I feel awful."

Charles patted her hand. "Don't worry, love, we won't give up."

She eyed him in genuine concern. "Charles, too many people have died."

His jaw tightened. "I know, love. It's time for us to put a stop to this."

Charles and Teresa stopped on the seawall for sandwiches, and tried to call Sergeant Varga, who was also out at lunch. Afterward they decided to return to her beach house to kill time until they were due at the police station.

Inside the house, Teresa flung herself down on the couch. "What now?"

Expression determined, Charles glanced about the room. "You know, Tess, we'd have a much better chance of nabbing Aunt Hatch's kidnapper today if we had the real papers he wants."

"I agree. But we don't have the papers—or know anywhere they might be."

"But you must have them, Tess," Charles argued. "Remember how Milton told us Frank called you his fail-safe device?"

"Yes."

"That means they must be here."

She waved a hand. "Charles, if the goons who trashed this place couldn't find them, then they're not here."

But he shook his head. "We must be overlooking something. Our next step will be to go through everything in this house."

"Charles, you're being ridiculous," she declared. "Besides, we already went through everything in this house when we put it all back together the other day."

"We must try again, anyway."

He proved adamant, and ultimately Teresa gave in. They set to work—Charles examining every shelf, drawer, cabinet, nook and cranny of the living room and kitchen, Teresa combing over her bedroom, bathroom, and office. Doris Juan followed along, eyeing their efforts with interest. But neither found anything useful. Two hours later, both were exhausted and sweaty, and sat on the couch together drinking lemonade, while Doris Juan sat between them grooming herself.

"Think, Teresa, think," Charles directed. "Frank must have sent the papers to you."

"No, he sent me nothing."

"Are you sure? Think of any time he communicated with you during these past few months."

Teresa concentrated fiercely for a long moment. "There's nothing, Charles." Then she frowned and slowly raised her wrist, ruefully adding, "Only this tourist trash bracelet Frank sent me for my birthday. Frank was a real cheap-skate, bless his heart."

Charles's gaze became riveted to the bracelet. "Let me see that!"

"Charles, it's only worthless junk. Cheap, obnoxious little tokens smeared with black and gold paint. You can buy them at any tourist shop on the seawall."

He held out his hand. "The bracelet, Teresa."

"Very well." She unclasped it and shoved it into his hand.

Examining the bracelet carefully, Charles exclaimed, "Do you realize, Tess, that this piece of junk has real Spanish doubloons dangling from it?"

"You're kidding!" she replied, astonished. "Everything on it looks so cheap and cruddy."

"Look, Teresa."

She glanced at two coins he had pointed out—both small, odd-sized, with strange gothic crosses and crude holes notched in them to hold the links. Eyes widening in awe, she touched the coins, feeling their irregular surfaces. "Well, I'll be damned, you know they do appear authentic. I never really looked at those coins before."

"That's because someone smeared them with black paint to obscure them."

"You're right."

"Please concentrate, Teresa. What did Frank say to you when he gave you the bracelet?"

She pondered the question. "You know, that was odd. He sent me the bracelet with a birthday card, and a message saying that if anything ever happened to him, he wanted me to have this to remember him by."

"Teresa!"

"Damn it, Charles, I just didn't connect the two. Frank was something of a depressive, plus a notorious skinflint. I just thought he decided if a truck mowed him down the next day, he was relieved to have spent his two dollars and fifty cents on me."

"Tess, do you realize there's a key on this bracelet?" Charles asked.

She glanced down, frowning. "Sure. There's also a treasure chest . . ." She paused, electrified as realization dawned. "Oh, my God—"

"Some of the charms are junk," Charles went on excitedly, "but the doubloons and the key are real and have obviously been added on. Damn, there's a number on the key. I wonder what it means?"

Teresa stared at the key—it was old-fashioned, with a wide, round head and a thin blade notched on both sides. The streaks of black paint made it look even older. "Could we try the obvious first?"

"You mean, this could be a key to a post office box in Galveston?"

"Could be."

"Or to a safety deposit box in Galveston, or in Houston," Charles added ruefully. "Or anywhere."

Teresa shook her head. "If the treasure is in Galveston, I think the solution would be there, too. Frank was very structured and dogmatic."

"Okay, Tess, we'll try the obvious first. But if the key is to a post office box, then the number on it is no doubt in code."

She eyed him suspiciously. "Why do you think that?"

He avoided her eye. "Never mind. But I do think I know someone who can pull some strings for us in the postal department. Hand me the phone?"

Teresa was on the verge of complying when there was a sharp rap at the front door. Tensing slightly, she got to her feet. "Guess I'd better see who that is."

Charles also stood, taking out his gun. "I'll come with you."

The two walked to the door together. Teresa peered through the peephole, gasped, then flung it open. "Aunt Hatch!" she exclaimed.

Chapter Twenty-nine

Teresa stared flabbergasted at the haggard woman in her tattered, filthy purple jogging suit. "Aunt Hatch, is it really you? Are you all right?"

Sporting mussed hair and a purple-tinged eye, Lillian Hatch marched into Teresa's living room. "Of course it is I, Teresa. I promised Sergeant Varga I'd stop by and inform you that, since I am now a free woman, the ransom trade at sunset is off. He did want to call you himself, but I felt a personal visit was in order."

Teresa was astonished. "Wait a minute. How do you know Sergeant Varga?"

"Because I have just come from the police department, of course," Lillian replied irritably. "I managed quite nicely to escape the hoodlum who abducted me. And I'm quite all right—no thanks to you, I might add. Sergeant Varga informed me that my captor was after some papers you claim you don't even have."

"That's true, I don't have them."

"A likely story. I tend to believe you've fallen in with ruffians, drug dealers—and God knows what else." Casting a baleful look at Charles, Lillian stormed over to the couch and sat down, landing on the cat's tail and causing Doris Juan to go sailing off with an indignant yowl.

"Aunt Hatch, really!" Moving closer, Teresa winced at the sight of her aunt's nasty-looking black eye. "You've been injured, haven't you?"

A crooked grin pulled at Lillian's mouth. "As the popular saying goes, you should see the other fellow. Well, Teresa, what do you have to say for yourself? I think you've neglected me quite shamefully."

"Aunt Hatch, we have been frantically trying to find you," Teresa protested.

"Yes, Ms. Hatch," added Charles. "We notified the authorities as soon as we learned of your disappearance, and we've been doing everything in our power to uncover your whereabouts since then."

"Everything in your power, eh?" mocked Lillian. "Obviously, Teresa, you never considered not getting involved with such a scuzzy crowd to begin with. That was certainly within your power."

Teresa sat down next to her aunt, flashing her a lame smile. "We're sorry, Aunt Hatch. But where have you been and who kidnapped you?"

"I'm afraid it's a rather involved story—"

"Please, we're all ears," Charles put in, sitting down in an armchair nearby.

"Well, I was just minding my own business,

jogging down Broadway, when suddenly some hoodlum in a pig mask appeared—"

"He visited us as well!" Teresa cut in excitedly.

"Well, at any rate, the monster bashed me over the head, and the next thing I knew, I came to in a sleazy rooming house off the seawall. I was gagged and handcuffed to the bed, with Pig Face again looming over me."

"Teresa and I also encountered your kidnapper," Charles interjected. "And we too dubbed him Pig Face. He kept popping in and threatening, well, dire consequences to your person if we didn't cooperate. He invariably carried a gun, and even fired at us once."

"Yes, the miscreant was armed, all right," Aunt Hatch concurred with a brisk nod toward Charles. "At any rate, most of the time I was held hostage, the scoundrel kept me bound and gagged. He left me alone a lot, coming by only a few times to let me eat or visit the lavatory . . . while he stood guard with his gun. Then this morning, he mentioned that things would end today, one way or the other . . . and I realized I had to act."

"Go on," urged Charles.

"Well, that's when he and I mixed it up," Lillian related proudly. "I managed to catch the creep off-guard, and felled him with a karate chop to the neck."

"You're kidding!" exclaimed an astounded Charles.

"Aunt Hatch has a black belt in karate," Teresa explained.

"Ah."

"I thought he was done in," Aunt Hatch continued grimly. "But even as I was reaching for the doorknob, the monster came to, pulled off his mask and . . ." She heaved a great gasp. "That's when I recognized him."

"Who was he?" Teresa demanded breathlessly.

Ignoring her's niece's question, Lillian forged on. "I managed to knock the gun out of his hand with a well-placed karate kick. But he did get in one good punch before I subdued him." She grimaced and rubbed her bruised eye.

"But who did you subdue?" asked Teresa in growing frustration.

"Yes, who?" echoed Charles.

Casting both of them an irritable look, Lillian resumed her account. "Then I handcuffed him, called the police—and we waited. Oh, the things he said then made my blood run cold. To think that monster turned on my poor nephew Frank. He even bragged to me of killing him."

"Oh, my God!" gasped Teresa.

"But who?" queried Charles.

Aunt Hatch pounded a fist in frustration. "I shall get to that, children. In the meantime, will you both kindly quit interrupting my story?"

Both meekly nodded.

"Anyway, I was about to say—before you both so *rudely* interrupted—that I recognized the blackguard due to having met him at Frank's funeral. But don't worry, the scuzzball is safely behind bars now." She crossed her arms over her bosom and vehemently nodded.

Charles cleared his throat. "A most fascinating account, madam. Now—would you mind telling us who is behind bars?"

"Why, Milton Peavey, of course," Aunt Hatch declared. "Haven't you two figured it out by now?"

"Milton!" Teresa shrieked. Then she snapped her fingers. "That's it! I knew there was something vaguely familiar about Pig Face. Now I realize what it was—he walked with a slight limp, just like Milton. But . . . did he tell you why he killed Frank?"

Aunt Hatch flung a hand outward. "How do you expect me to know? I've been a hostage, for heaven's sake!"

"Yes, Aunt Hatch," Teresa concurred with a grimace.

"It may have to do with those papers he wanted," Lillian continued peevishly. "However, the villain really was babbling after I decked him for the second time—so why don't you ask him yourself? He's in the Galveston jail, of course."

Teresa gulped and nodded. "We will."

Lillian stood and consulted her watch. "Well, I must run, children, as I've got a cab waiting outside. I still haven't seen Aunt Maizie, although of course I phoned from the jail to let her know I'm all right. At any rate, I've promised her I'd help her fix tea for the pastor and his wife, who are due at her home in just over an hour. But I did want to let you kids know you didn't have to meet that rat."

Teresa stood and hugged her aunt. "We're so glad you're safe."

Lillian awkwardly backed away. "Well, yes. And I'm glad to see you've fixed up the place a bit, Teresa. Toodle-oo, kids."

"Goodbye, Ms. Hatch," said Charles.

After she left, Teresa gazed at Charles helplessly, then fell into his arms. "Oh, Charles."

He rubbed her back. His words came worriedly. "You're trembling, love."

"I'm just so relieved that Aunt Hatch is all right."

"Indeed. Despite the fact that she's a royal pain in the neck."

She moved away, casting him a chiding glance. "Really, Charles. She's been through the wringer."

"You're right. Sorry."

"But what she told us is so mind-boggling. To think that Milton killed Frank and kidnapped Aunt Hatch! And he acted so cool, so innocent, that day we went to his townhouse."

"I know. What a fiend."

"I suppose I never really suspected him before because he was a target, too, because Manolo and his cronies evidently trashed his place, too, just like they did mine."

"Yes, all of that did deflect suspicion away from him."

"But *why* would he kill Frank?"

Charles slowly shook his head. "I wish I knew." He nodded toward her bracelet. "But clearly it has something to do with the missing papers—and perhaps with the key you hold. Come on, darling, let's go over to the island and see if we can find the post office box—or whatever."

"Okay. But would you mind if we stop at the police department and the jail first, Charles? We need to wrap up some loose ends with Sergeant Varga, and I also want to talk to Milton."

"Of course we'll go see the sergeant, but Tess, there's no guarantee you'll be allowed to see Milton."

"Please, Charles, we have to try," she pleaded. "I have to ask him why he murdered Frank."

"Okay, dear. First let me call my friend regarding the key; then we'll leave."

"All right."

He cleared his throat. "Tess, I'll need your bracelet—or at least the key, so I may describe it to my friend."

She hesitated, then took off the bracelet and handed it to him.

Studying her rather suspicious mien, he appeared troubled. "You still don't trust me, do you, Tess?"

She regarded him sadly. "Perhaps I could, if I knew what you really wanted."

Charles stared back at her a moment, then sighed in resignation and went off to the bedroom. Teresa seethed silently, fully aware that he didn't trust her enough to make the call in her presence.

After a moment, he returned. "My friend is in a meeting, but I left a message with all the particulars. I'll try him again from Galveston—and perhaps by then he'll have something for us."

She nodded toward his hand. "My bracelet?"

He paused a moment, then handed it back. "Of course, Tess."

Chapter Thirty

An hour later, after wrapping up some loose ends with Sergeant Varga, Charles and Teresa sat side by side in a visiting room at the jail, a wire mesh wall separating them from the plain desk and wooden chair on the opposite side. Teresa stiffened as she watched Milton Peavey limp into the cubicle in an orange jumpsuit, and sit down, glowering at them. She glanced uneasily at Charles and felt him squeezing her hand.

Shifting her gaze back to Milton, Teresa mused that Aunt Hatch had been right to claim Milton had gotten the worst of it—straggles of hair were torn loose from his ponytail, lending him an unkempt air. He sported two black eyes and a bloody nose, plus an ugly purple bruise across his neck. He also wore a wrist brace and bandage, and Teresa assumed his wrist must have been either sprained or broken during his encounter with Aunt Hatch.

"Well, hello, Tess," Milton greeted her with a nasty smirk. "What a nice surprise."

Teresa heaved an angry breath. "How dare you sit there grinning at me, Milton Peavey, when you admitted to my aunt that you murdered poor Frank."

Milton sneered back. "I should have murdered your aunt, too. That battle-ax practically killed me. Be grateful I didn't send her back to you in pieces."

"Oh!" Staring at the man across from her, his features contorted in anger, his green eyes gleaming like a snake's, Teresa could scarcely believe it was actually Milton Peavey she was looking at. He'd been a self-centered jerk before; now he seemed a sinister friend. She realized that all he really needed was his macabre pig mask to complete the picture of unmitigated evil.

Meanwhile, Charles was leaning toward the glass, his expression menacing. "Mr. Peavey, I'd caution you to mind what you say to Ms. Phelps."

Milton cast Charles a haughty look. "Oh, I'm terrified. If you're planning to have me arrested for murder, pretty boy, sorry, that's already been done."

"Just watch it," Charles snapped back.

Ignoring him, Milton turned disdainfully to Teresa. "As for Frank, that bastard got just what he deserved."

Horrified, Teresa retorted, "You . . . you pig! How can you say that?"

Milton cynically shook his head. "Tess, you're such a naive fool. Don't you know the truth yet?"

"What truth?" she countered furiously. "Other

than the fact that you're a kidnapper, an extortionist, and a murderer?"

He leaned toward her, grinning sadistically. "But Tess, your dear sainted brother Frankie murdered poor Clark Swinson."

"What? You're lying!" she declared.

His countenance gleamed with vindictive triumph. "No. Think about it, Tess. You know how greedy Frank was. When Swinson brought him the missing pages from the Lafitte journal with the location of the treasure, Frank couldn't resist."

Teresa fell miserably silent. Frank, a murderer? Surely it was impossible.

And yet, she couldn't deny that, if her brother had had a fatal flaw, it was indeed avarice. Oh, God, what if Milton were telling the truth?

She pulled herself together and coldly addressed him. "So, you're telling us Swinson *did* find the missing journal pages?"

"Yes. And quite a bonanza it was. Frank was beside himself with excitement after he saw Lafitte's sketch and translated the instructions. But of course he didn't want to share his find with anyone. That's why he killed Swinson."

Struggling to speak past the revulsion she was feeling toward Milton, Teresa asked, "Are you actually saying Frank locked Swinson beneath the staircase to—to shut him out?"

"Literally," Milton replied with cruel relish. "Swinson only wanted a translation from Frank, but Frank wanted a great deal more from Swinson. Everything, in fact."

"I still say you're lying!" she exclaimed.

He gave a shrug. "Your choice."

She leaned intently toward him. "Now, you scoundrel, you tell me why you killed my brother!"

"That bastard!" Milton jeered with an angry wave of his hand. "You see, I'm the one Clark Swinson came to in the first place. I referred Swinson to Frank. Then Frank turned on us both, the ingrate. He stole the journal pages, got rid of Swinson, and decided to cut me off without a dime. He even stole my girlfriend, and bragged to me that he planned to run off with Kelly to the south of France."

"Kelly was *your* girlfriend?" Teresa gasped.

A muscle began to twitch in Milton's cheek, and he spoke in a hiss. "Yes, Kelly and I had been dating for several months before Frank met her and stole her away from me. When I found out how he had sneaked her out of the country and was planning to meet her in France, that's when I snapped. I hit Frank over the head with a bronze statue, then I took him out to the lake and dumped him. Good riddance is what I say!"

"Oh, my God!" Teresa cried. "You are a monster."

Milton only grinned.

"But why did you kill Frank when you still didn't have the translation?"

"Because you have it, Tess," Milton replied with a scornful chuckle. "Frank told me you were his fail-safe device, remember? That's how I knew he gave it to you."

Teresa slowly shook her head. "You're wrong. I don't have it."

"Oh, but you must have it, Tess. If it had been with Frank's things, or in his computer files, I would have found it long ago."

She snapped her fingers. "So that's why you didn't hesitate to let me have Frank's computer."

He gave a cruel laugh. "I even kidnapped your harpy of an aunt, just to make you cough it up.

But you were too selfish, weren't you, Tess? You didn't give a damn if the old shrew bought the farm. You wanted to save it all for yourself, didn't you, bitch?"

Now Charles lunged forward furiously, shaking a fist at Milton. "Watch what you say, you lowlife bastard, before I come over there and yank out your filthy tongue!"

Charles and Milton were glaring at each other when a guard stepped up. "Sorry, folks. Time's up."

Teresa regarded Milton with all the revulsion she was feeling. "I hope you burn in hell."

Unabashed, Milton stood, smirking at Teresa. "Then your brother will surely be there with me. So long, folks."

He turned and hobbled out of the room.

Teresa was trembling badly as Charles escorted her from the building. As soon as he assisted her into her car, she burst into tears. His expression was one of deep concern as he got in beside her and pulled her close. "Darling, please don't cry."

"That bastard!" she sobbed. "He killed Frank, and . . . and now he insists Frank killed Clark Swinson! Oh, what are we going to do?"

Charles tenderly kissed Teresa's brow and brushed tears from her cheeks. "If it makes you feel any better, love, I don't think your brother murdered Clark Swinson. You see, Milton may be able to get off with a life sentence for a crime of passion, but first-degree murder carries the death penalty in this state. Milton's only trying to cover his own behind."

She gasped, staring up at him with frail hope. "You really think so?"

He nodded solemnly. "Yes, I do."

Teresa felt encouraged by Charles's words,

which did make sense to her. "But—what if Milton won't confess? My brother's memory would always bear a horrible stigma."

"He'll confess," Charles assured her. "The man is clearly an egomaniac. He wouldn't be facing a murder indictment now if he hadn't shot off his mouth to Aunt Hatch. In time, I don't think he'll be able to resist revealing his cleverness in the Swinson murder. Besides, you're forgetting that in this box we're looking for Frank may have left a letter or something that could establish his innocence."

"Right," Teresa agreed bravely. "We need a phone."

Charles groaned. "And my cell phone is still in my car at the dealer's." He flipped on the engine. "Why don't we just run by my condo, grab something cold to drink, and make the calls?"

He was backing out of the parking space when Teresa touched his arm. "No, don't be silly. Great-aunt Maizie's house is much closer than your condo. And I'd like to check on both her and Aunt Hatch again anyway."

"Great-aunt Maizie?" Charles inquired with an eager smile. "But of course I'd be delighted to see the lovely Mrs. Ambrush again."

At last Teresa smiled too, if ruefully. "You would be."

Chapter Thirty-one

Teresa and Charles's knock on the door of the Victorian mansion was at once answered by a beaming Maizie Ambrush, daintily dressed in a silk floral-patterned dress and white patent leather pumps, her cheeks rouged and hair styled in wispy silver curls framing her wrinkled face. Maizie bought with her the sweet scent of lavender perfume, as well as the tantalizing aromas of baking breads and spicy hot tea.

"Well, hello, loves. What a wonderful surprise," she greeted. "You're just in time for tea."

Teresa hugged her great-aunt and smiled apologetically. "Great-aunt Maizie, we're sorry just to drop in on you like this. But we wanted to check on you and Aunt Hatch, and to use your phone if that's okay."

"But of course, darling, though I wouldn't dream of not offering you refreshments." She turned to Charles, extending a frail hand. "So good to see you again, dear."

He squeezed her hand and leaned over to kiss her cheek. "And you, Mrs. Ambrush."

Beaming, Maizie gestured toward the hallway. "Come along into the living room, now. Lillian is there, along with the pastor and his wife. And I've got all the makings of an authentic English tea almost ready out in the kitchen. Why, I've baked scones, crumpets, plum cake, even strawberry tarts. Plenty for us all."

At the mention of the pastor and his wife, Teresa inwardly groaned; it had totally slipped her mind that Maizie was entertaining them. "It all smells marvelous, Great-aunt Maizie, but we can only stay a moment." Glancing ruefully at her dress, she added, "As you can see, Charles and I are hardly attired for a social occasion."

"Oh, nonsense, you both look fine," declared Maizie, leading them on. "Besides, this is Galveston—practically the tropics."

"We're charmed, Mrs. Ambrush, but we really are in a bit of a rush," added Charles.

Maizie laughed and turned to shake a finger at him. "In a rush to be alone with my great-niece, aren't you, you devil?"

Charles flashed both women a lame smile but didn't reply.

"Ah, here we are," Maizie said, leading them through a carved archway into a drawing room filled with beautiful Duncan Phyfe mahogany chairs and settees upholstered in blue and white striped silk organza. "Everyone, Charles and Teresa are here."

Amid the clatter of teacups, the three occupants of the drawing room turned to look their way. Regally ensconced in a wing chair next to the fireplace was Aunt Hatch, looking remarkably well groomed for a woman who had just escaped a kidnapper, her hair modestly styled and bruises covered by makeup, her lime-green cotton dress well starched. Across from her on the sofa sat the minister and his wife, a slender, graying, fine-looking pair, the man in traditional clergyman's garb, the woman in a nicely tailored navy silk dress. On the coffee table in front of the couple reposed a beautiful sterling silver tea service, surrounded by elegant Paris china plates and cups.

The setting could not have been more genteel, Teresa mused. But why was the couple seated on the couch staring at Charles with such amazement? The man wore an astounded grin; the woman had gone wide-eyed.

Then she glanced at Charles to see he appeared equally flabbergasted as he regarded the couple.

"Charles!" exclaimed the man in a clipped, British-accented voice.

"Chuckie," declared the woman.

Teresa's gaze jerked to the couple, then back to Charles. *"Chuckie?"* she whispered. "Do you *know* these people?"

Avoiding her question, Charles cleared his throat and awkwardly replied, "Hello Mother, Father."

Teresa's jaw dropped. "Mother? Father?"

"Well, isn't this an interesting turn," put in Aunt Hatch drolly, staring from the startled couple to the stone-faced Charles.

"Charles, what is going on?" Teresa demanded.

He grimaced and avoided her eye.

All at once the terrible tension was broken as Maizie chortled and clapped her hands. "Aha!"

she declared, wagging a finger at Charles. "I knew there was something familiar about your name, young man. Of course! You're Vicar Everett's son!"

"The vicar's son?" cried Teresa.

Looking miserably put on the spot, Charles continued to stare at his feet.

Meanwhile, the woman got up and rushed over to Charles's side, smiling and hugging him. "Chuckie, darling, what a nice surprise."

Charles flushed furiously. "Mother, please don't call me 'Chuckie.' Makes me sound like a creature from a horror film."

She laughed giddily and waved him off. "Oh, Chuck—er, Charles, you're such a cutup. Always making the wry quips." Her composure recovered, she smiled brightly at Teresa. "And who is this delightful young lady?"

"Teresa Phelps, grand-niece of your hostess," Charles announced with obvious reluctance.

The woman extended her lovely, slim hand to Teresa. "How do you do, dear?"

Teresa shook the woman's hand, noting her fine features and the bright blue eyes that she'd definitely bestowed on her son. "Good to meet you, Mrs. Everett."

"And you too, dear."

Now the vicar stood and crossed over to them, grinning at Teresa. "You're Maizie's grand-niece, young lady? And you know our son? Why, what a small world it is!"

Teresa glared at Charles. "I'll say." Forcing a more pleasant expression, she offered her hand to Charles's father. "Pleased to meet you, Vicar Everett."

He pumped her hand. "The pleasure is all

mine, young lady. I must commend my son's excellent taste."

"Thank you," murmured Teresa.

Mrs. Everett cast her son a scolding look. "But Charles really should have introduced you to us before now. He's so secretive about his young ladies."

Teresa flashed Charles a poisonous smile. "I'm sure he has his reasons."

Charles's responding glower attested that he was a man in pain. Once again the tension was thick enough to cut, until Lillian spoke up peevishly. "Everyone, may we please have a bite to eat? Maizie, those breads of yours must be done by now. Not to be rude, but I am quite famished, and my captor didn't exactly feed me properly over these past days."

At once the vicar crossed over to Lillian. Expression eloquent with sympathy, he patted her hand. "Of course, my dear Miss Hatch. We are so sorry. From what few details you've given us regarding your ordeal, you have surely endured a terrible trauma, and some nourishment is definitely in order." He straightened, nodding toward Charles. "It's just such a nice surprise for Audrey and me to see our son, and to meet his young lady."

Lillian gazed with barely disguised resentment at Teresa. "Actually, your son's 'young lady' had a bit to do with my abduction."

"You don't say!" exclaimed the vicar, appearing perplexed.

"Why, that is odd," added an equally puzzled Mrs. Everett.

"Aunt Hatch, I think you've said quite enough," warned Teresa, mortified by Lillian's tactlessness.

"Why, I've only just begun," asserted Lillian and with a self-righteous lift of her chin. "Teresa has clearly fallen in with thugs and—"

"Now, Lillian, you've been babbling nonsense about my grand-niece ever since you arrived back home," Maizie cut in, also obviously embarrassed. "I'll not hear such unpleasant subjects broached while we have guests. Besides, I can't imagine my darling grand-niece having any involvement in such dastardly doings."

"Indeed not," agreed the vicar, smiling at Teresa. "She's clearly a fine young lady."

Although Lillian made a sound of contempt, she wisely resisted further comment and continued sipping her tea.

Maizie clapped her hands and addressed Teresa and Charles. "Now, you two just sit down. I'll go fetch the breads, and Lillian will pour you some tea."

"Teresa would love some tea," answered Charles, practically shoving her into a vacant chair and prompting an indignant look. "But I really must use your phone, Mrs. Ambrush."

"Oh. Would you like to use the one upstairs in the bedroom, dear?"

"Sounds lovely." He raised an eyebrow at Teresa. "The bracelet."

While the others appeared puzzled, Teresa glowered.

Charles reached down, unclasped the bracelet, and snatched it off Teresa's wrist. The others gasped.

"Charles, really!" cried his horrified mother.

"Son, that was a rather ungallant display," added his frowning father.

Charles flashed his parents a contrite smile.

"Sorry Mum, Dad, but I promised Teresa I'd get her bracelet fixed."

He dashed out of the room, leaving bewildered silence in his wake.

Teresa stood, flashing the others a stiff smile. "Excuse me just a minute."

She rushed into the hallway, catching up with Charles by the stairs. "So *that's* the reprobate I was supposedly sleeping with?" she hissed furiously, jerking a thumb back toward the parlor.

Pausing on the bottom step and turning to her, he appeared wretchedly embarrassed. "Tess, please don't tell the others about that."

She gave an incredulous laugh. "You actually think I would tell your dear parents the slanderous things you said about your own father? Well, I'm hardly without scruples like you, Charles. Has it never occurred to you that you have horribly insulted all three of us?"

He groaned. "I'm sorry, Tess. I'll explain everything later. Everything. Now, please go back and wait with the others."

He vaulted off up the stairs. Exasperated, Teresa returned to the living room. Maizie had left for the kitchen; the others were regarding her in bewilderment.

Lillian coughed. "A rather odd young man, bolting off that way."

Teresa resumed her seat. For some reason, she felt obligated to defend Charles. "Well, it's just that he promised me he'd get my bracelet fixed, and he's determined to do so. It's a sentimental piece, you see, left me by my brother, who—er—died recently."

Both Everetts sighed. "Our deepest sympathies, dear," said the vicar.

Eugenia Riley

"Indeed," seconded his wife. "Maizie has mentioned to us the terrible tragedy your family has suffered."

"Well, yes, thanks," Teresa muttered, tugging down her short skirt. "Anyway, the clasp on my bracelet isn't working properly, so of course Charles wanted, well, you know. . . ." Voice trailing off, she felt ridiculous.

Beaming at her niece's discomfort, Aunt Hatch picked up the teapot. "Tea, Teresa?"

"Yes, thanks." Grateful for the distraction, she crossed over and took the filled cup and saucer, shot Lillian a surly look, then returned to her chair.

"So, dear, how did you and my son meet?" Mrs. Everett asked.

Teresa almost choked on her tea. "Er—how we met?"

"Yes, dear."

For a moment, Teresa went blank. Luckily, Maizie reentered the room bearing a doily-lined silver tray heaped with breads and tarts. The next few moments were taken up with the rituals of serving and passing around plates filled with the various culinary delights.

"So, have all of you gotten acquainted now?" Maizie asked, delicately munching on a tart.

Savoring a crumpet, the vicar replied, "I think Teresa was about to tell us how she and our son met."

"Oh, sorry," muttered Teresa, setting down the scone she'd been eating. "Charles and I—er—we ran across each other at a department store in Houston a few days ago, and we've been—er—dating a bit since then."

"And I'll have you know Teresa is not just anyone," put in Maizie with pride. "My grand-niece is quite well educated—a doctoral candidate in recent sedimentology."

"My, how impressive," declared Vicar Everett.

"Indeed, we're thrilled to see Chuckie with such a cultured young lady," added Mrs. Everett. "We just don't see enough of Charles, and the rascal never tells us anything about the women in his life."

"From some things I've observed over the past days, I'd be inclined to agree that your son *is* a rascal," Lillian put in snidely.

While the Everetts exchanged a look of chagrin, Teresa scolded, "Really, Aunt Hatch!" She smiled apologetically at the Everetts. "You'll have to excuse my aunt. We suspect she may have suffered brain damage during her abduction. She was gagged for days on end, you see." Watching ire rise in Lillian's eyes, Teresa raised a hand and quickly pressed on. "So, what brings you two here to the States?"

The vicar flashed Teresa a grateful look. "We're here in the U.S. on a summer exchange program sponsored by the Methodist Church," he explained. "I've taken over the assignment of Maizie's pastor here in Galveston, while he is at the helm of our parish back in England."

"How fascinating," Teresa remarked.

Audrey added, "We love being here. Of course life here is quite different from our pristine little village in England, where the biggest event of the year is still the fair on the green or boat races on the Thames. Quite a lot more hustle and bustle here in the States. But Galveston is a fine old town, the people of our parish have been lovely to us, and we're especially thrilled that we can visit with our kith and kin here—Kingsley's brother and his family in Austin, and of course our darling only child, Charles."

"Speak of the devil," Teresa muttered, watching him stride back into the room.

Expression tense, Charles came to Teresa's side and handed her back the bracelet, this time, she noted, minus the key. Contritely he turned to Maizie. "Mrs. Ambrush, I apologize profusely, but Teresa and I must leave at once."

"B-but you haven't had your tea!" protested Maizie.

"Chuckie, really," scolded his mother. "I thought we reared you with better manners than this. You've only just arrived."

"Sorry, Mum, but this is a matter of utmost urgency, perhaps even life and death," Charles replied grimly.

"Getting a bracelet repaired?" gasped his father.

"What?" Charles muttered.

Realizing he was determined for them to go, Teresa set down her dishes and popped up. "I'm sorry, everyone, but we really do have to leave."

Charles grabbed her hand. "Cheerio, all."

Further discussion was postponed as he all but yanked her out of the room, amid the shocked mutterings of the others.

"Well?" she demanded as they rushed out the front door. "What did you discover that will excuse your rudeness back there?"

He cast her an irritable look. "My friend was able to find the post office box, Tess, and we've hit the jackpot. The box is here in Galveston—and it's registered in Frank's name."

"Good heaven," Teresa muttered. "I had no

idea Frank even had a post office box here. He never once mentioned it."

"Well, the box definitely is his."

"And he gave *me* the key," she went on in awe. "So the logical conclusion is, there's something in the box for me."

By now they had arrived at her car. He swung open her door. "Yes, that's how it appears."

Teresa was stonily silent as they drove to the small post office substation. Inside she was seething with anger, still reeling from the encounter at Maizie's house, and the proof she'd gained that Charles had lied to her from the outset. Saying she'd been having an affair with his father, a proper English vicar! Clearly Charles was without shame. She was tempted to light into him, to rail out at him for his deception and trickery, but she sensed it would get her nowhere. All along, he'd steadfastly refused to come clean with her. Why would he change his stripes now?

She did catch him looking her way several times, his expression anxious, questioning, uncertain. She avoided his eye and stared moodily out the window.

Charles noted Teresa's distance, and it was killing him. She'd been on such an emotional roller-coaster ride today—discovering her aunt was safe, learning the devastating truth about her brother's murder, confronting Frank's murderer, then meeting his own parents and learning what a damnable liar *he* was! He couldn't blame her for being furious with him now, and he ached to take her in his arms and heal this painful rift between them. But how could he, when he still wasn't free to tell her the truth? The look of disillusion on her lovely face told him that only complete honesty could save their troubled relationship. Yet he still couldn't admit what he knew. What he wouldn't give to be able to come clean with her.

When they reached the post office substation, an older building on a shady side street, they parked and hurried into the building. Charles quickly found the box, unlocked it, and pulled out a large manila envelope.

"My God," muttered Teresa.

Charles studied it intently. "This appears to be addressed to you, my dear, care of Frank."

"The mysterious 'papers' Milton wanted?" she asked ironically.

"Quite possibly."

Teresa took the envelope and stared at it in awe. "It's from Frank, all right—that's definitely his handwriting, and return address." She glanced at the postmark. "It was mailed a month ago, just days before . . ." She shuddered.

Charles touched her arm and flashed her a compassionate smile. "This may well be the missing pages from the Lafitte journal, with the treasure locations."

"Yes, I would assume it might be," she replied ironically.

He expelled an impatient breath. "Well, Tess? Aren't you going to open it?"

She raised her angry gaze to his. "No."

"No?" he cried.

She regarded him through hot, furious tears. "This is where you get off, Charles."

"*What?*" he demanded.

She choked back a sob. "I've had it with you and your lies, Charles Everett. I'm unloading you and going home."

He caught her arm and eyed her beseechingly. "Tess, please don't. I know you're furious with me, and you have every right to be. All right, I'll admit it. I invented the story about you and my father. It was a stupid ruse. But I had to think of some way to get close to you, to protect you—"

"So you could steal this for yourself," she finished bitterly, waving the envelope in his face.

Teresa felt devastated when Charles didn't deny her charge. Indeed, a muscle working in his jaw seemed to give him away. "What are you going to do with the envelope, Tess?"

"Oh, you'd love to know, wouldn't you, Charles?" she went on in choked tones. "You pointed out to me once that there were two sets of antagonists in this. You lied then, too. There were always three, weren't there? Manolo and company, Milton Peavey, and you. You're the third, aren't you, Charles?"

Dodging her accusation, he reiterated, "What are you going to do with the envelope?"

"Burn it," she declared.

"What?"

"I'm burning the damn envelope. It's caused everyone nothing but grief."

"But Tess," he reasoned, "there could be information in that envelope that clears Frank of Clark Swinson's murder."

Again, she waved the envelope in his face. "As if you care! There could also be information that implicates him. In any event, I don't want to know anymore."

Feeling heartsick, Teresa turned and walked out on him.

Chapter Thirty-two

At home, Teresa sat on the couch and stared at the large envelope in her lap for a long time, her throat tight, and unshed tears burning her eyes. She didn't want to open it. . . . She was afraid to face the truth.

But ultimately, she couldn't resist. At last, with trembling fingers, she undid the brad and opened the flap.

Teresa pulled out the materials: a handwritten letter from Frank to her; a large, aged, double page of parchment encased in a plastic sheath, with a faded map on one side and equally faded paragraphs handwritten in French on the other; and some notes in Frank's handwriting that appeared to be translations of the text.

She eagerly read Frank's letter first:

Dear Teresa,

If you receive this letter, dear sister, I very much fear it may be under tragic circumstances. If so I must apologize for involving you in the melodrama that has become my life.

You will find enclosed a double page from an historical document, a journal purportedly written by the privateer Jean Lafitte. As I'm sure you know, Lafitte was headquartered in Galveston in the early part of the nineteenth century, and allegedly buried much of his booty in the Galveston coastal region. The original journal is on file at the Sam Houston Regional Library and Research Center in Liberty, Texas. However, that document contains a two-page gap . . . and it is my absolute belief that you now hold those two pages in your hands.

Teresa has to pause then. Her heart skipped a beat as she reread Frank's last sentence. With trembling fingers, she picked up the yellowed double journal page and more closely examined it, studying the faded map which depicted the Galveston coastline, with an X neatly inscribed next to a sketched-in cove. Then she studied the notes on the opposite side, written in a neat, bold hand that looked exactly like Jean Lafitte's distinctive script, by now quite familiar to her. The possibility that she held such an historic document in her hands was awe-inspiring. To think that Jean Lafitte himself might have actually drawn the map and written the instructions!

Managing to calm herself a bit, she continued reading:

Eugenia Riley

To explain how these pages came to be in my possession: After a referral from my roommate, Milton Peavey, a contractor from Galveston named Clark Swinson brought me a double page from an old French journal to translate, pages Swinson found in a Greek Revival cottage he was renovating in Galveston, pages he suspected might have been written by Jean Lafitte. Swinson begged me to keep his find confidential, and even offered to share with me any proceeds gained from his discovery.

Of course I cooperated and began an exhaustive investigation of the pages. I started by having a lab test a small fragment of the parchment, and they were able to authenticate the age of the paper and ink. I then went to Liberty, secured a copy of the memoir, and discreetly compared Swinson's pages with the original journal in its case. I soon concluded that the pages were the actual missing pages from Lafitte's journal. I was able to translate the instructions included with the pages, and I am sure I have discovered the location of a large cache of Lafitte's treasure, directions to which are enclosed.

Teresa, I do hope I haven't placed your life in peril through my efforts—I'm very concerned because Clark Swinson has mysteriously disappeared. I feel some guilt in pursuing the treasure without him. But if anything should happen to me, Tess, I want you to have my share. There's more, but I've little time to tell you. I may have to leave the country for a while until things settle down. Milton's very angry with me right now; he figured out what Clark and I were doing, and he's furious because we aren't willing to share the treasure with him. He also hates me because I took Kelly away from him. But after I found out how he used to go into jealous rages, and even beat her, I knew I must get her away from that monster and out of the country. As for that rat Milton, he doesn't deserve one bit of the treasure. . . .

Teresa, if you should be reading this after my death, please try to find the treasure and please try to get Clark Swinson's share to him or his mother. And take good care of Mom and Dad for me.

Love always,
Frank

Wiping away tears of mingled sadness and relief, Teresa folded the letter. She again studied the old journal pages, then read Frank's translation, which turned out to be step-by-step instructions for locating a large cache of treasure in Galveston, on West Beach! Afterward, she carefully replaced everything in the envelope and refastened the brad.

At least she knew now for certain that Frank had not murdered Clark Swinson, and she knew that no matter what else she did, she must be sure to show his letter to the police. That would mean making the treasure public, and she assumed the government would likely seize it, but the treasure had never really mattered to her anyway. All she really cared about was Frank—and Charles, the man who had violated her trust.

All at once, Teresa's thoughts scattered as the front door burst open. She screamed, then watched in horror as Manolo and his cronies barged inside. All three men wore ugly, belligerent expressions; Manolo held an open switchblade in his hand and Freddie had a pistol tucked at his waist.

Seized by panic, Teresa bolted up and tried to make a run for the back doors. But Manolo was quicker than she. He vaulted across the room and grabbed her by the hair, brutally twisting her locks. Even as she screamed in pain and terror, he leered at her, waving his knife in her face. "Hi, chickie."

Teresa struggled to break free. "What in the hell do you think you're doing? Let me go and get out of my house!"

Ignoring her protests, he hauled her back toward the center of the room. "No, lady, we got some unfinished business to attend to." He jerked his knife toward Freddie. "Shut the frigging door."

Grinning, Freddie slammed the door shut then braced a straight chair beneath the knob.

At the same time, Manolo spotted the envelope on the coffee table; he shoved Teresa away and snatched it up. "So, Frankie sent you some goodies, eh?" he asked Teresa in triumph, waving the envelope in her face.

"Give me that!" she demanded, rubbing her scalp.

Shoving her down on the couch, Manolo snarled, "Shut up, lady. You should have known we were onto you. We watched you and your gringo lover come out of the post office together. You're getting sloppy."

Even as Teresa cringed on the couch, Manolo ripped open the envelope and rifled through the contents. He waved one of Frank's translated pages at Freddie. "Well, lookie here! Looks like good old Frankie left us a little treasure map."

"Cool!" declared Freddie.

"Yeah, man, let's ditch this joint and go get the treasure," added Hector, rubbing his hands together.

"Not so fast." Setting down the pages, Manolo hauled Teresa to her feet and again wielded his knife in her face. "First, it's payback time for me and the lady. I'll teach her to call me names." Leering at her, he added, "Unless she can suggest a better way to even the score."

As Manolo's cronies laughed ribaldly, Teresa spat back, "I'd rather drown."

"Your wish may be granted," Manolo sneered.

At this juncture, all four of them turned at the sound of someone kicking at the front door; the chair was jerking about as the person outside attempted to dislodge it. Manolo motioned to Freddie, who ducked into the corner behind the door and pulled the pistol from his waist. A split second later, the door crashed open, and Charles stormed inside with his own gun drawn. As Teresa frantically tried to catch his eye while jerking her head toward Freddie standing behind him, he quipped, "These dramatic rescues are getting tiresome, love."

Unfortunately, Teresa didn't catch Charles's eye in time. Even as he spoke, Freddie surged forward and poked his pistol into Charles's spine. "Drop it, mister!" he ordered.

Charles hesitated, features fraught with terrible indecision. Manolo hauled Teresa to her feet and brought his knife up to her throat. "Drop that gun right now, man, or I'm slicing this bitch's throat," he yelled at Charles.

Still Charles wavered, his anguished gaze fixed on Teresa.

"I mean it, man!" barked Manolo.

Teresa winced as Manolo nicked her.

Charles stepped forward aggressively, features white with fury. "You leave her alone!" he roared at Manolo.

"You drop your frigging gun!" Manolo shouted back.

"Damn!" Charles muttered, dropping his weapon.

Freddie grabbed Charles's gun, and all three thugs howled with victory.

"Come on, man, let's go get the treasure," said Hector.

Manolo still held his knife at Teresa's throat. "First, we've got to deal with these two or they'll squeal on us."

"So deal," said Freddie with an air of boredom.

Glancing from Teresa to Charles, Manolo seemed to be ruminating. "I don't know if I want to risk a murder rap."

The other two jeered. "You're a woman," said Freddie.

"Yeah, man, you got no *cojones*," sneered Hector.

"I got big *cojones*," Manolo protested. "But shooting or knifing these two would be messy."

"So?" asked Freddie.

"I know," put in Hector with a gleeful expression. "Why don't we take 'em outside and drown 'em like the lady wants?"

Charles and Teresa exchanged a horrified glance.

"Yeah," said Freddie, rubbing his hands together. "I got some strong twine in the trunk of the car—we can tie 'em up and throw 'em in."

"Yeah. There's a plan." Manolo shoved Teresa

away, then growled, "All right, you two. Outside."

"You're joking," declared Charles.

Manolo waved his knife. "Does it look like I'm joking?"

"You'll all go to prison for the rest of your lives," Charles argued.

"Not with no witnesses," Manolo retorted. "Outside, both of you!"

Prodded by the villains' weapons, Teresa and Charles lurched toward the door. . . .

"Hey, man, what's the best way to drown these gringos?" Freddie asked Manolo.

"Hell, I don't know," Manolo answered. "Just tie some chunks of driftwood to 'em and pitch 'em in the drink, I guess."

Teresa glanced with dread at Charles. He tried to smile back bravely, but she could tell from the emotion in his eyes that he was just as scared for their safety as she was. They stood about ten feet from the billowing Gulf, Hector busily tying their hands and feet, while Freddie and Manolo stood beyond them arguing about the best way to drown them. She glanced frantically up and down the beach, but unfortunately there was not a soul in sight to come to their rescue, only shore-birds dipping into the surf.

She winced as Hector cinched the twine about her wrists at her back. "Hey, ouch! That hurts!"

"Don't worry, ma'am, it won't be for long," Hector replied with an evil chuckle.

Meanwhile, Freddie had noticed a derelict rowboat sitting a few yards from the water. He strode over to examine it, then grinned at Manolo. "Hey, man, this boat has a big hole in it. Why don't we put 'em in it at the edge of the water and let the tide do the dirty work?"

"Oh, damn," Teresa muttered to Charles. "I knew I should have gotten that rowboat fixed."

"You?" queried Charles, rolling his eyes.

Manolo sauntered over to the rowboat, looked at it, and grinned. "Yeah. Cool. Now they really get to sweat it. Let's do it."

The three hauled the rowboat to the water's edge, then converged on the helpless Teresa and Charles. "Gentlemen, if you proceed with this, I assure you you're going to regret it," Charles warned Manolo.

"Oh, shut up, man, or we're gonna gag you both," he growled back.

He grabbed Teresa and began pulling her toward the rowboat, while Freddie and Hector grabbed and dragged a struggling, cursing Charles. Both were unceremoniously shoved into the rowboat, first Teresa, facing skyward with her middle propped over the seat, then Charles, face-down and half on top of her. She felt miserable with his weight pinning her down, the seat poking the small of her back. Her discomfort only increased as Freddie looped lengths of twine around both their waists and lashed their bodies tightly to the metal seat.

"Hey, ain't those two a sexy sight," jeered Hector afterward.

"Yeah, maybe they can make it before they meet their Maker," quipped Freddie.

"Please, you can't just leave us like this," pleaded Teresa.

"Ah, shut up," snarled Hector. "You're lucky we didn't shoot you both."

"This is lucky?" protested Charles, twisting his neck to glower at the thugs.

"*Adiós*, folks," said Manolo with a mock salute.

The goons ambled off, guffawing the entire time. Teresa cringed as a wave washed over her and Charles, drenching them both with tepid water even as the boat lurched frighteningly toward the Gulf. She gave Charles a pained look. "Garden variety thugs, eh?"

"Very funny," he replied humorlessly.

His weight was killing her back. "Please, can't you get off of me?"

"I'm trying," he replied, wiggling away a bit. "Better?"

A new wave sluiced over them, making Teresa choke on gritty water. She grimaced and spit out grit. "Oh, just peachy keen. We'll be dead any moment now. What's there to worry about?"

Charles groaned. "Well, love, just in case we don't make it out of this situation with all our hair in place, I guess I can break the rules for once and tell you who I really am."

As a new wave billowed over them, then ebbed, tugging them closer to the Gulf, she replied, "I'd say it's a bit late."

His anguished blue eyes met hers. "Please, Teresa, listen. We haven't much time."

"All right. Spill your guts."

"The truth is, I'm a Treasury Agent—"

"Treasury Agent!" she cried.

"And I was also a casual friend of your brother's from college, just as I claimed. Six weeks ago, Frank came to me, quite excited, and asked me, strictly off the record, what the government regulations would be regarding the discovery of gold booty inside U.S. territory. I informed Frank that even unearthing such buried treasure is a criminal offense in Texas, and that any such cache would instantly be snatched up by the state, if not federal, government. Frank clammed up then and said nothing further regarding the treasure, although we did chat a bit, catching up on old times. He spoke quite fondly of you. In fact, he told me you were the one person in this world he trusted the most."

"He said that about me?" she inquired in an emotional voice.

"Indeed, he did, darling. Soon afterward, he thanked me and left, and I heard nothing further from him. But when he turned up dead, I of course reported the incident to my superiors. We felt Frank's death was highly suspect, and surmised that the treasure he'd described to me was most likely real. We decided that I should go undercover to seek Frank's murderer, find the treasure—and protect you. Given what Frank had told me, we figured you would have been the one person he might have entrusted with details regarding it."

Teresa was stunned by these revelations. "Well, I'll be damned. You might have told me, Charles!"

He regarded her contritely. "Teresa, my boss gave me a free hand, but forbade me to reveal my true identity to you or to anyone, because frankly, love, we thought you knew the location of the treasure, and we couldn't count on your motives being totally altruistic. I wasn't even supposed to tell you I knew Frank."

Teresa gave a bitter laugh. "How ironic. I never cared about the treasure, not that it matters now. So you're a government agent, are you, Charles Everett? I wondered how you managed to pull strings so quickly in the postal department today."

"I knew you must be wondering about that—and much else."

Anguish assailed her as she considered the full implications of what he'd just told her. "And what about us?" she asked, voice choked with emotion. "What about making love with me? Was that just part of your mission, getting close to me so you could use me, manipulate me, and get to the treasure?"

Pain flared in his eyes. "Teresa, no, darling. How could you think—"

Yet his words ended in her scream, as a much heavier wave rolled over them, drenching them, then sucking them back toward the ocean. They exchanged looks of sheer misery.

"Teresa, I'm so sorry for getting you in this muddle," he said feelingly.

"Charles, you aren't the one who started this."

"But I feel so responsible. I should have done a better job of protecting you."

He appeared so torn that her conscience compelled an honest response. "I—I think you tried your best there."

He flashed her a tremulous smile. "Darling . . . about what you just said. I want you to know that, as far as you and I are concerned, that wasn't part of the job, or part of the bargain. Ever. I pursued you romantically because I wanted you, not to get information. Indeed, I could have been fired for fraternizing with the target in an investigation."

"I'm a target?" she demanded, voice rising.

"Hear me out," he pleaded. "Of course we had our suspicions. Of everyone."

"Yeah, I remember," she concurred bitterly.

"My point is, the last thing I could afford to do

was to fall in love with you. But I did anyway."

"You—you love me, Charles?" she asked haltingly.

He regarded her with great tenderness. "With all my heart. You've fascinated me since the day I met you."

Tears burned her eyes. "Oh, Charles. I think I love you too."

Joy lit his eyes. "You do? Now give me a kiss."

"A kiss to die for?" she asked poignantly.

"Every kiss with you is a kiss to die for," he responded gallantly.

They exchanged an emotional, lingering kiss. As another wave shook them, she shuddered and asked in an emotional voice, "Is it goodbye then?"

He gazed at her in anguish for a moment, and then suddenly he smiled. "Hey, wait, I've got an idea, love. Try to roll over."

"*What?* Charles, really."

"Don't worry, I'm not going to try to ravish you in a rowboat. Roll over and perhaps I can twist about enough to gnaw at your ties with my teeth."

"My, what an irresistible invitation."

"Teresa, do it. I'm not sure how many more waves we can withstand."

"No kidding."

Though the rope tied around her waist was tight and it was excruciatingly awkward, Teresa managed to squirm over. She felt damn ridiculous with her belly draped over the seat and her butt in the air. With her short skirt twisted up high over her hips, she knew all her charms were lavishly revealed to Charles. "There, are you satisfied?"

His low whistle confirmed this. "My, what a fetching position."

"Hush and start gnawing."

He chuckled; then she felt him wriggling his body half over hers—and felt his teeth chewing at her wrists. "Ouch!"

"Sorry, love, I'm doing the best I can, but this twine is damn tough."

"Hurry up, will you?"

"I'm trying."

All at once, Teresa heard the flapping of wings, followed by a loud cawing sound. Then Charles muttered, "Damn it, what next? Now there's a bird on my butt."

She twisted about to see the creature. "Well, there's a *man* on mine. Besides, it's not a bird, it's a laughing gull."

"I'm sure he's laughing at us. Hold still, will you?"

Charles continue to bite at her bindings for several more, painful moments, while she moaned and yelped. Then a powerful wave dislodged the craft, tugging them into the surf at shore's edge.

"Charles!" Teresa implored frantically. "Hurry up, damn it! I—I think we've just been launched—and *without* a champagne toast."

"Don't panic, Tess, just a little bit longer," he replied, biting her again.

"Ouch! Charles—" Then abruptly she stopped speaking, as she heard a familiar voice shouting in the distance. At first she feared she was imagining things, but yes, the voice was definitely there. "Charles, do you hear that?"

"Hear what?"

"Listen, damn it!"

Both listened intently, as the voice called out, "Hey, ma'am, that you yonder?"

"Over here!" Teresa yelled back hoarsely.

She heard the thud of approaching footsteps,

the huffing and puffing of a winded runner, then a familiar, if bewildered, visage loomed over them. "Hot damn, ma'am!"

Both of them twisted about to stare at the newcomer.

"Billy Bob!" Teresa cried.

Chapter Thirty-three

"Hey, folks, this ain't no way to get your jollies," Billy Bob scolded. "What the Sam Hill do you think you're doing?"

Expression horrified, he loomed above them, clipboard in hand and bill cap tipped back. Charles twisted about and shot him a glare.

"We're drowning," he snapped back. "Now will you kindly quit making inane quips and give us a hand here?"

"Oh, yeah. Sure, folks." Laying down his clipboard, Billy Bob leaned over, heaved a massive grunt, then hauled the boat out of the surf and dragged it up onto the beach. He pulled out a pocket knife, flipped it open, leaned over, and began cutting their bonds. "There. That better?"

"Thank heaven." Shrugging off a tangle of

twine, Charles struggled out of the boat and offered Teresa his hand. "Are you all right, love?"

She accepted his assistance, grimacing as he pulled her to her feet. "Just peachy—other than being drenched and covered with mud."

"How did you know to come help us?" Charles asked Billy Bob.

He grinned crookedly. "Some dude named Manolo stopped me down the beach and told me there was a couple down here 'bout to drown doing kinky things in the mud. You know, it's kinder funny, ma'am, but he looked like one of them fellars that shot up your house. Good thing he stopped me, cause I wasn't planning to do no job down here today."

"Well, thank heaven you came along!" declared Teresa. Gazing tremulously at Charles, she felt emotion knot in her throat as she realized how close they had come to losing their lives. "We made it, Charles."

With a shudder, he pulled her close. "Yes, darling, we made it." Quickly, passionately, he kissed her. Then he turned and offered his hand to Billy Bob. "Thanks, friend."

Shaking Charles's hand, Billy Bob grinned and shifted from foot to foot. "Shucks. No problem, folks."

Teresa quickly hugged Billy Bob. "Thank you. We both owe you our lives."

He blushed deeply. "Ah, don't thank me, ma'am. All in the line of duty for the Bug Brigade." Retrieving his clipboard from the beach, he glanced back toward the house. "Hey, you folks want I should look for them riots again while I'm here?"

Teresa chuckled. "I think the riots are gone

now . . . *and* the rats. But you be sure to send us a hefty bill, anyway."

"No problem. Well, guess I'd best mosey on down to my next job. Take care, folks."

As he sauntered off, Teresa fell into Charles's arms again. "Thank God we made it. It seems old Manolo had a heart after all."

Charles nodded. "Manolo wanted the treasure, but he wasn't willing to just cold-bloodedly kill someone, like Milton Peavey did."

"Damn Milton," Teresa said feelingly. "I hope they lock him up and throw away the key."

"I'm sure they'll do just that, love."

She eyed him quizzically. "Well, Mr. Treasury Agent, aren't you going after Manolo and his pals?"

"Actually, I think Manolo deserves a head start for his mercy," Charles replied, brushing wisps of damp hair away from her brow. "Besides, he took the envelope, so we don't even know where to look."

"Oh, but we do." She grinned. "I peeked inside the envelope, right before he barged in."

Charles appeared delighted. "Teresa, you didn't! I thought you weren't going to."

"Well, I did it." With a shudder, she admitted, "I saw everything—the old French journal pages, including a treasure map—"

"My heaven!" Charles interjected excitedly.

"—Frank's translation, and his letter to me. Just as we assumed, he had no part in Swinson's death and was even very worried about Clark's disappearance." She sighed. "I only regret that we don't have his letter now to show to the police and help clear his name."

He kissed her forehead. "I know, love. But

we're both alive—that's all that really matters. Let's head inside."

But inside her house, a wonderful surprise awaited them. Teresa gave a yelp of joy as she spotted the manila envelope on the coffee table, and the pages of Frank's letter scattered on the floor beneath. "Look, Charles!"

He quickly crossed the room, gathered up the envelope and letter pages, then handed it all to Teresa.

Teresa looked inside the envelope, which predictably was empty; setting it aside, she clutched her brother's letter to her heart. "Thank God! Manolo only took the instructions and the journal pages. Now we can show this to the police."

"That's wonderful, Tess," Charles agreed.

"So, what do we do next? Aren't you going to call your superiors and tell them about the treasure?"

Charles grinned sheepishly. "Well . . ."

"Or do you want to try to keep the treasure for yourself—assuming Manolo doesn't already have it?" she asked, smirking.

Appearing scandalized, he pressed a hand to his chest. "Me? Try to keep the treasure?"

"Don't lie to me, Charles. I know how mercenary you really are." Setting down Frank's letter, she playfully curled her arms around his neck. "Besides, you already admitted that you broke some rules by being intimate with me. How else are you willing to bend the law?"

He chuckled, nestling her closer. "Well, I must confess that over these last days, I've found much I'd like to keep for myself, darling Tess."

"Then make your move," she teased.

"Very well." He leaned over, sliding his hand up her bare leg in a sultry caress that raised gooseflesh. Catching the hem of her damp dress, he pulled the garment up and over her head. She gladly raised her arms to assist him, feeling a flush of excitement as he tossed the dress aside and his eyes devoured her in her wet, transparent underwear. His low whistle raised a delighted chuckle from her.

"Well, aren't you bold," she teased.

Gaze hot, Charles was busy kissing her while unsnapping her bra and pulling it off. Leaning over to flick his tongue over her tight nipple, he murmured, "Oh, don't you taste deliciously salty, love. Next, darling Tess, we're going to strip all this icky mud—and everything else—off our bodies. Come along, you incredibly sexy woman."

Teresa squealed as Charles chased her into the bathroom. He turned on the shower tap in the bathtub, then grabbed her and ripped off her panties. She laughed, pulled off his shirt, and caressed the strong muscles of his chest. He quickly doffed his shorts and boxers, then pulled her into the tub with him, tugging the curtain shut and kissing her wildly.

Teresa felt totally enraptured as they kissed, stroked, and lathered each other's bodies, while the hot, sensual water poured over them. Charles's hands felt divine on her breasts, her belly, her bottom. When she ran the soap over his erection, he uttered a moan and his eyes burned into hers. He crushed her close and kissed her ravenously, his tongue stroking deeply, erotically in her mouth, their hot wet bodies tightly locked. When she hiked her knee between his thighs to stroke him again, he shoved her back against the cool tile wall. His fingers reached down to part and enter her; she trembled in pleasure, her mouth hungrily seeking his, her hand curling about his arousal again.

Eugenia Riley

Abruptly he hauled her out of the tub, tossing her a towel as he turned off the water. His eyes greedily raked her naked body. "Come here, you wanton wench, I'm going to devour you alive."

Teresa shrieked and raced off for the bedroom. Charles pursued her, catching up with her just as she went sailing for the bed, his body falling half on top of hers. She screamed with pleasure as his teeth playfully sank into her bottom. She squirmed and flipped over, then nearly died of the pleasure when he slid his slick body slowly, sensuously, up her own. She clutched him close and moved her pelvis suggestively against him. Her reward was a staggering kiss as his hands roughly kneaded her aroused breasts.

After a moment, he groaned and looked down at her, expression half-dazed with desire. "You know, love, I rather enjoyed the new position we tried outside. What say you turn over?"

"Charles! Wasn't it enough to bite me?"

His chuckle was devilish. "Let's say I want to sink my teeth in fully."

"Greedy, aren't you?"

"Now don't be coy." He rolled off her, pushing her over on her belly. "God, how delicious you look." He roved his hand over her backside, then slid his fingers underneath, parting and stroking her again.

"Oh, Charles." She felt him positioning himself behind her, and arched upward to meet him. "You know we're forgetting something."

"What could we possibly be forgetting?" he queried, stroking her boldly.

She groaned. "The . . . Oh, God, the bird?"

He howled with laughter. "Teresa, really. How kinky you are." He whispered at her ear. "We don't need ménage à trois my love. I want you all to myself."

He proved it by pulling her to her knees and driving himself fully inside her tight womanflesh.

"Charles!" Her protest was more a sob of ecstasy. So full of him she ached at the exquisite tension, she nonetheless wantonly tipped her hips to take more.

His agonized grunt rewarded her. "Oh, good girl." Charles thrust vigorously and nibbled at her shoulder. "How I love this. You feel splendid, so snug and hot."

"Charles . . . Oh, you do, too. But, damn. We're forgetting safe sex again."

He chuckled. "And you're forgetting what I already told you—neither sex, nor anything else, is safe with me."

"Uh-huh," Teresa managed.

"Besides, it's no longer a concern, love."

"Oh?" she asked, writhing against him.

Again she pulled a moan from him. "Now stop wiggling and listen to me," he ordered roughly.

"But I like to wiggle." She demonstrated.

"Here's something you'll like more." He clenched his arms about her middle and held her tightly while pumping quickly, fully, making her cry out again and again. And then he paused. "I love you and I want you to marry me, Tess."

His lusty power—his tender words—sent rapture shuddering through her in devastating waves. "You . . . want an answer—now?" she panted.

"What better time, love?"

"Yes! Oh, yes! I love you, too!"

Teresa was rewarded by her lover's feverish kisses on her cheek, his renewed, frenzied dance inside her. Eagerly she succumbed to a shared rapture that tore the breath from her lungs. Blissfully exhausted, she fell on the bed. As Charles collapsed on top of her, his breath hot and sweet on her face, for once she was glad—so glad—that nothing was safe with Charles.

Chapter Thirty-four

Afterward, they lay cuddled together, Doris Juan curled up at their feet, as Charles spoke on the phone with his boss at the Treasury Department.

"Yes, George. Manolo took the treasure instructions, but Teresa saw them first. She has told me everything she remembers. As best she can recall, the instructions placed the treasure on West Beach, thirty paces northeast of Old Pirate's Point. You and the boys might run over there now and try to head off Manolo and his cronies. Ms. Phelps and I will be along soon, all right?"

After a brief pause, he set down the receiver; she smiled at him.

"There, are you satisfied?" he asked.

"You bet." She kissed his chin. "In *every* way. I'm really glad you did the right thing in the end, Charles."

He grimaced. "I was a good boy—painful though it was."

"Oh, hush," she scolded, feigning a pout. "I had to know it was me you wanted, and not just the treasure."

He ran his hand over her bare thigh. "You doubted that?"

She tweaked her nose at him. "Hadn't we better get dressed and head over to meet your boss and the others?"

"You bet." Popping out of bed, he went to his bag and pulled out a pair of boxers, some jeans, and a polo shirt.

Teresa sat up in bed and shamelessly watched him. "You know, I think the biggest treasure may be here."

"Wanton wench." Zipping up his jeans, Charles confided with a laugh, "You know, this is going to be really hilarious, Tess."

"What's going to be hilarious?"

"Figuring out the custody of the treasure, assuming there even is one when we arrive."

"Ah."

"If my memory of the applicable statute is correct, the state of Texas should have jurisdiction over it. But, given the fact that it's buried along the shoreline, and knowing our federal government, we may well try to claim it as shipwreck treasure. Of course, I had to alert our boys first, out of departmental loyalty."

"Oh, of course," she wryly agreed, going to her dresser to grab clean undergarments, and then to her closet, where she pulled out a sundress and sandals.

Charles plopped himself on the bed and ogled her greedily. "My turn to watch."

"Voyeur," she teased, pulling on her panties.

"Yes, and you'd best step lively, love, or we won't be leaving here any time soon," he warned, clearing a suddenly raspy throat.

Thirty minutes later, they pulled up to the appointed site along the shoreline on West Beach, where a dark blue Ford with government licence plates was parked. As Charles opened Teresa's car door, she spotted four men in dark suits standing on the beach beyond. All four carried shovels and were gathered in a tight circle around a deep hole, with huge piles of sand ringing it. As Charles escorted Teresa toward the others, she noted that all wore glum expressions and were sweating in the heat.

"Hello, gents," Charles greeted the others cheerily. He turned to Teresa. "Teresa Phelps, meet my boss from the Department of the Treasury, George Fidal, along with Agents Fleming, Munoz, and Wardon."

"Pleased to meet all of you," Teresa said. She noted that Fidal appeared older than the others, balding and a bit paunchy, while Fleming, Munoz, and Wardon were all average-looking men in their thirties.

"Gentlemen, meet the lovely Teresa Phelps," Charles added.

All four men offered Teresa polite greetings.

Charles edged closer to the excavation, peering downward with a frown. "So, what do we have here?"

"An empty hole," reported Munoz.

"It was already dug when we arrived," put in Fleming.

"No kidding," remarked Charles.

"I suspect we got skunked," added Fidal.

Charles whistled. "You don't mean Manolo and his cronies actually beat us to the treasure?"

"That's how it appears," stated Wardon, wiping his sweaty brow.

Fidal glanced at Teresa. "Ms. Phelps, are you certain this is the spot your brother described in his translation?"

"Oh, yes," she replied eagerly. "Absolutely certain."

Fidal scowled.

"Well, boys, guess we're just snakebit," Charles quipped.

That comment brought a frown rushing to Fidal's face. "We're snake what?"

"Snakebit. Jinxed. Down on our luck," Charles explained.

Fidal gave a shrug. "We'll get a crew down here to explore further, but we're really not expecting much." He turned to Teresa. "Ms. Phelps, I want to thank you for your cooperation."

She smiled sweetly. "Should I thank you for making me a target of your investigation?"

Fidal groaned. "I'm sorry, Ms. Phelps, but as I'm sure Charles has explained to you, we just weren't free to tell you about our investigation. Private citizens such as yourself really have no place in the reclamation of shipwreck treasure such as this."

"Is that because you suspected I wanted the treasure for myself?" she asked sarcastically. "Or did you merely assume I'd killed my own brother for it?"

"Tess!" put in Charles, throwing her a cautioning glance.

Fidal flashed her an apologetic smile. "Never did we suspect that, Ms. Phelps, and as you're aware, your brother's murderer has now been arrested. Furthermore, let me assure you that there will be nothing negative about you mentioned in our files. On the contrary, my report concerning this incident will indicate you cooperated in every way."

Watching Charles fight a snicker, Teresa muttered, "Well, I'm certainly grateful to hear that."

Fidal gestured to the others. "All right, men, let's pack up. Nice to meet you, Ms. Phelps."

"Likewise," she said, lips twitching.

Charles watched the agents trudge off toward their car, then turned to frown at Teresa. "Why do I suspect there's something going on here that you still haven't told me about?"

Her countenance gleamed with secret mischief. "Why, Charles, whatever do you mean?"

Scowling suspiciously, Charles pointed at the hole. "Is this *really* the spot Frank detailed in his translation?"

She smirked. "Indeed, it is."

He raised an eyebrow. "The *actual* spot, Tess?"

"Yep," she replied glibly. "Hey, Manolo and his cronies took the instructions and they dug *this* hole, right? What other 'actual spot' could there be?"

Yet he appeared unconvinced, frowning sternly. "All right, Tess, out with it!"

"Out with what?" she asked innocently.

"What do you know that the rest of us don't know? Why have you been smirking like the cat who swallowed the canary? Why have you been in no hurry whatsoever to get to the treasure? And, most importantly, why did Frank call you his fail-safe device?"

She regarded him in mystification. "Why, Charles Everett, whatever are you babbling about?"

"Don't play games, Tess! Come clean."

Teresa convulsed into laughter. "Manolo and his friends just dug an empty hole."

"What?"

"You see, I was Frank's fail-safe device because he knew I was an expert in sedimentology."

Charles flung a hand outward. "What does that have to do with the price of gold?"

Still laughing, she shook her head. "Listen carefully, Charles. Frank translated the document in strict historical terms, placing the treasure thirty paces northeast of Old Pirate's Point at this location on West Beach. But he realized only I would know that the tide has eaten away a healthy chunk of the coastline in the intervening years since Lafitte was here, and the Point itself has shifted inland from where it used to be."

"Tess, you mean—"

"I'll have to consult some charts and maps, make some calculations, but yes, I'm confident I can determine the actual location of the treasure."

"You don't mean it."

"Think, Charles," she continued intensely. "The treasure's here, or Frank wouldn't have been able to send me the doubloons. As a matter of fact, he always was poking around in my textbooks, asking me questions about geographical changes in this area. He must have determined the site himself, and poked around enough to find a few loose doubloons that had worked their way close to the surface. Then he hired Manolo and company to do the heavy digging for the bulk of the treasure. But unfortunately, that's when Milton Peavey came into the picture and killed poor Frank." She sighed. "Anyway, when Frank sent me the translation, he knew I'd realize the instant I read it that the coordinates have changed, because that's what I do. So that's it: Fail-safe, right?"

"Fail-safe," Charles agreed in awe.

She nodded toward his associates, who had placed their shovels in the trunk of their car and were getting inside. "Shall we tell them?"

He grinned wickedly. "You know, Tess, it seems rather a shame to put the poor boys to any more trouble."

"Oh, yes, all that strenuous digging. Built-in hernias for the lot of them."

"Indeed."

Teresa hugged him. "Then what shall we do, my love? Shall we dig it up, share it with poor Clark Swinson's mother, or just leave it here?"

He fell quiet, brooding.

She kissed him. "I guess we'll have all night to discuss it, won't we?"

Holding her close, Charles fervently replied, "You're wrong, my love. We'll have the rest of our lives."

His lips took hers in a fervent kiss as the tide roared behind them, the wind rippled their clothing, and the sunset cast their bodies in a golden glow. . . .

Epilogue

Six weeks later

Music set to a calypso beat drifted over from the beach pavilion as Teresa swung to and fro on the hammock on the private patio of their cabaña. She wore a brightly patterned bikini and a colorful sarong; her hair was still wet from the swim she and Charles had just taken.

The patio was shielded by bougainvillea-hung trellises on two sides, giving them a private view of the flawless white beach and the blue, gleaming Caribbean. The day was warm, clear, and beautiful, gulls dipping about in the white surf.

"Another drink, Mrs. Everett?"

Teresa grinned up at her husband, who had just emerged from the cabaña dressed in swim trunks, with a mai tai in one hand and the other hand behind his back. She roved her gaze over his sleek, tanned body, noting particularly how his swim briefs molded to his delicious maleness, and felt a surge of joy that he was hers.

"Mrs. Everett," she murmured, glancing down at her wedding set—a stunning, huge diamond, set in a platinum- and gold-edged band, with a matching wedding ring. "That takes some getting used to."

"We'll have a lifetime, darling."

"We only got married yesterday."

"My, how time flies when you're having fun." Kneeling beside her, he handed her the drink. "Were you happy with our wedding back in Galveston? I hope it wasn't too small."

Remembering, Teresa felt a joyous tear stinging her eye. "Charles, what could have been more perfect than having your father officiate at the ceremony at the chapel?"

He winked. "From all the tears my mother shed, it must have been sublime."

"Oh, I do love Audrey," she replied, "as well as your dad, and your aunt and uncle from Austin. And it was so sweet of your folks to invite us to visit them in England for Christmas. Plus, your family got on so well with mine. After losing Frank—well, I think the festivities really cheered up my parents."

He nodded. "Speaking of cheer, I thought I was going to have to pry Billy Bob away from the punch bowl, or gag him when he started telling that off-color story about sheep and the full moon. But I'm glad you invited him to our wedding, anyway, love."

"But of course we had to invite him—he saved our lives!" she declared indignantly. "And your

Eugenia Riley

folks did insist on driving him home afterward, much as your father seemed to disapprove of his—er, colorful behavior."

"I'm not sure my folks will ever become fully accustomed to these brash Americans," Charles confessed wryly. "I also observed Dad raising an eyebrow when he spied your Aunt Hatch and Harold Robison kissing in the shadows."

"No!" Teresa cried, delighted. "I never saw that! Although I did wonder why they both disappeared so early."

"By now, the two are no doubt off hunting big game in Tanzania." He wagged a finger at her. "I must say, my dear, your sleuthing skills are growing rusty."

She lovingly drew her gaze over him. "That's because I have eyes only for my new husband."

"I'll drink to that." Instead Charles leaned over to kiss her.

Afterward, she studied him curiously. "Now, tell me what you have hidden behind your back."

He winked wickedly. "A surprise, my love. Any moment now, I'm going to whip it out."

She laughed heartily. "*What* are you hiding, Charles? A sex toy?"

"Moi?" he replied innocently. He took the glass from her hand and brought it up to her lips. "Here, love, have a sip."

She grimaced and shook her head. "I'm still spinning from just two sips of the first one. You make a mean drink, mister."

"I aim to please."

"You want to compromise me."

Setting down the drink, he lifted her hand and kissed her fingers. "Haven't I already done that—in every way?"

"Yes, you have. Delightfully so." She turned

388

serious, gazing at him tenderly. "You've also helped me get my life straightened out, and for that I'll be eternally grateful."

"Only doing my job, love," he rejoined gallantly. "But I must agree that things ended rather well back in Galveston. We could leave knowing all the loose ends were tied up."

She nodded solemnly. "Yes, I was pleased when Milton copped a plea for two counts of second-degree murder for killing Frank and poor Clark Swinson, saving us all the trauma of a trial."

"Didn't I tell you he'd do everything in his power to avoid the death penalty? Once he was confronted with all the evidence, including your brother's letter, he totally caved in."

"Quite true."

Charles frowned. "But you were far too generous toward Manolo Juarez, agreeing to his plea-bargain arrangement with the D.A."

"Well, he turned himself in, didn't he? Besides, he's so young. I hadn't realized he was only nineteen. Six months in a boot camp should shape him up."

"Still, he did kidnap you, and rough you up."

"I know. His apology at the sentencing hearing helped. But what really persuaded me to accept the plea bargain was the call from his girlfriend. You know, Josie is the one who persuaded him to turn himself in, and she told me he did so because he loves her. Very romantic."

"Yes, grandly romantic." Charles kissed her hand. "There's no end to what the love of a good woman can do."

"I agree."

Charles gazed ardently into her eyes. "Now our honeymoon is perfect, with all the unpleasantness behind us. Just think—seven days and seven nights, having you all to myself, totally at my mercy. I have such decadent plans—like coating you with honey and licking it off your toes."

"Charles!" With a smirk, she added, "Well, I've had a few fantasies about you . . . and whipped cream."

He snapped his fingers. "Drat, love. None in the bar fridge. Would you settle for maraschino cherries?"

"Now there's a thought." Her gaze flicked over him wickedly. "Where do you suppose I should put them?"

"Let your imagination run wild, love."

"Oh, I will."

He chuckled. "Time for your present, darling." He pulled out a velvet jeweler's box and handed it to her. "With all my love."

"Oh, Charles." She opened the case, only to gasp at the glittering masterpiece that lay inside. "Charles! It's the bracelet Frank gave me—only it's different."

"A replica—made of twenty-four-carat gold." He lifted out the gleaming charm bracelet with its dazzling copies of the doubloons, the skull and crossbones, the treasure chest, and the key, and carefully fastened it about her wrist. "I had a jeweler make an exact copy."

"Oh, Charles, you're so dear!" She hugged him, wiping away happy tears. Again she stared at the gleaming piece. But after a moment, she smirked. "Only, wherever did you get the gold, Mr. Everett?"

He pinned her with a scolding glance. "Mrs. Everett, you're not a woman to be asking that—not after we had so much fun on the beach at midnight . . . with our shovels."

She shook with laughter.

"Suffice it to say, I found the gold the same place Cora Swinson has gained her own new-found wealth—the means to renovate her house and live in style for the rest of her life."

"Yes, Cora is now one happy camper," Teresa agreed. "I'll never forget the look on her face that morning when we stopped by to tell her the good news—"

"And swear her to secrecy," Charles added wryly.

"It was the least we could do after what happened to her son." Glancing again at the bracelet, Teresa turned solemn. "Charles, this is so beautiful, but you know, the gold never mattered to me that much. All along, I just wanted to know . . ."

"Yes, love, what did you want to know?" he whispered.

Gazing up into his beautiful eyes, Teresa could barely contain the love and tenderness surging inside her. "Well, it was just always so important to me . . . You're so gorgeous, charming, and glib, Charles, and I never did quite know what you saw in me—"

"Now, Teresa, I won't be hearing this," he cut in sternly. "You're damn gorgeous, charming, and glib yourself."

In a halting voice she finished, "And I just wanted to know that you loved me for me—and not just the treasure."

"Teresa, darling, of course I love you for yourself," he replied passionately. He moved aside her sarong and slid his fingers down her belly and thigh.

She gasped in pleasure. "You're a mighty convincing fellow."

He offered her the drink again. "Now drink up, woman. Then I'm going to ravish you."

"Charles . . . I have something to tell you."

"Yes, darling?"

She smiled straight from her heart. "I—I think I'm pregnant."

His hand froze, and joy lit his eyes. "You are?"

"Are you happy?"

"Of course. Ecstatic. But when . . . ?"

"I think it happened the day Manolo almost drowned us—you know, afterward, when we made love so wildly."

He grinned. "Yes. So lovely. And minus the bird."

She eyed him soberly. "And if I am pregnant, then I really shouldn't be drinking anything anytime soon."

"Indeed, yes." He set down the drink, then climbed up onto the hammock with her, setting it erotically swinging. "Come here, you glorious creature—my bride, and the mother of my children. Lord, I love you so much."

He clutched her close and kissed her hungrily. She stared up at him breathlessly. "I love you, too. And I have something else to tell you."

One of Charles's hands was unclasping Teresa's bikini top, while the other tugged down the bottom. "Mrs. Everett, I'm not certain how many more of these revelations my poor heart can bear."

She giggled. "Well, Charles, since I know now that you didn't want me just for the gold—"

"Yes, my love?"

"I can tell you."

"Yes?"

She grinned. "Great-aunt Maizie is leaving us her house."

He howled with laughter.

She glowered. "Did I say something funny?"

"No. It's just—well, I already know that, love."

"You what?" she demanded.

"Maizie told me three days before the wedding," he revealed with a shameless grin. "The bequest of her house is in fact her wedding gift to us. Why else do you think I went through with the marriage?"

"Oh! You gigolo!" She pummeled him with her fists. "Charles Everett! Of all the dirty, rotten—"

He grabbed her wrists. "Hush, my darling."

His lips thoroughly silenced her even as his manhood thrust gently, fully inside her, setting the hammock into delicious motion, her glittering bracelet jangling to the accompaniment of their coupling. Teresa melted with pleasure and smiled up into her husband's eyes. He looked down with so much love that at last Teresa was convinced that Charles Everett wanted *only* her.

AUTHOR'S NOTE

Dear Reader:

I hope you've enjoyed my first big contemporary romance from Dorchester Publishing, *Lovers and Other Lunatics*.

I'd like to tell you about a couple of other books I have written, available from Dorchester under the Love Spell imprint: *Bushwhacked Bride*, a fun, sexy time-travel romance set in the Old West and *New Year's Babies*, an anthology that includes my Victorian time-travel novella, "The Confused Stork."

I have two other projects forthcoming from Dorchester this year: my novella "Night and Day" will be included in the Leisure Books anthology, *Strangers in the Night*, to be released in September of 2000 and *Embers of Time*, a haunting, emotional time-travel romance set in Charleston, South Carolina, due out from Love Spell in November of 2000.

I welcome your feedback on all my projects. You can reach me via e-mail at eugenia@eugeniariley.com, visit my website at http://www.eugeniariley.com, or you can write to me at the address listed below (SASE appreciated for reply; free bookmark and newsletter available):

Eugenia Riley
P.O. Box 840526
Houston, TX 77284-0526

BUSHWHACKED BRIDE
EUGENIA RILEY

"JUMPING JEHOSHAPHAT! YOU'VE SHANGHAIED THE NEW SCHOOLMARM!"

Ma Reklaw bellows at her sons and wields her broom with a fierceness that has all five outlaw brothers running for cover; it doesn't take a Ph.D. to realize that in the Reklaw household, Ma is the law. Professor Jessica Garret watches dumbstruck as the members of the feared Reklaw Gang turn tail—one up a tree, another under the hay wagon, and one in a barrel. Having been unceremoniously kidnapped by the rowdy brothers, the green-eyed beauty takes great pleasure in their discomfort until Ma Reklaw finds a new way to sweep clean her sons' disreputable behavior—by offering Jessica's hand in marriage to the best behaved. Jessie has heard of shotgun weddings, but a broomstick betrothal is ridiculous! As the dashing but dangerous desperadoes start the wooing there is no telling what will happen with one bride for five brothers.

___52320-5 $5.99 US/$6.99 CAN

BELOVED WARRIOR
JUDY DICANIO

Jennifer Giordano isn't looking for a hero, just a boarder to help make ends meet. But Dar is larger-than-life in every respect, and as her gaze travels from his broad chest to his muscular arms, time stops, literally. Jennifer knows this hulking hunk with a magic mantle, crystal dagger, and pet dragon will never be the ideal housemate. But as the Norseman with the disarming smile turns her house into a battlefield, Jennifer feels a more fiery struggle begin. Gazing into his twinkling blue eyes, she knows she can surrender to whatever the powerful warrior wishes, for she's already won the greatest prize of all: his love.

___52325-6 $5.50 US/$6.50 CAN

Dorchester Publishing Co., Inc.
P.O. Box 6640
Wayne, PA 19087-8640

Please add $1.75 for shipping and handling for the first book and $.50 for each book thereafter. NY, NYC, and PA residents, please add appropriate sales tax. No cash, stamps, or C.O.D.s. All orders shipped within 6 weeks via postal service book rate. Canadian orders require $2.00 extra postage and must be paid in U.S. dollars through a U.S. banking facility.

Name_____
Address_____
City_____ State_____ Zip_____
I have enclosed $_____ in payment for the checked book(s).
Payment <u>must</u> accompany all orders. ❑ Please send a free catalog.
      CHECK OUT OUR WEBSITE! www.dorchesterpub.com

Paradise

MADELINE BAKER, NINA BANGS, ANN LAWRENCE, KATHLEEN NANCE

The lush, tropical beauty of Hawaii has inspired plenty of romance. But then, so have the croonings of a certain hip-shaking rock 'n' roll legend. In these tales of love by some of romance's brightest stars, four couples put on their blue suede shoes and learn they don't need a Hawaiian vacation to find paradise. Whether they're in Las Vegas, Nevada, or Paradise, Pennsylvania, passion will blossom where they least expect it —especially with a little helping hand from the King himself.

___4552-4 $5.50 US/$6.50 CAN

DARK PRINCE
CHRISTINE FEEHAN

He comes to her in the night, a predator—strength and power chisel his features. The seduction is deep and elemental; he affects her soul. Her senses aroused, she craves the dangerous force of his body. And he has only touched her with his mind. She comes to him at dawn, his bleakest hour. As the beast rages inside him, threatening to consume him, he vents his centuries-old despair in an anguished cry that fills the waning night. And she answers, her compassion, courage, and innocence awakens in him an exquisite longing and tenderness. Apart, they are desolate, bereft. Intertwined physically and spiritually, they can heal one another and experience an eternity of nights filled with love.

___52330-2 $4.99 US/$5.99 CAN

THE Last Viking

SANDRA HILL

He is six feet, four inches of pure unadulterated male. He wears nothing but a leather tunic, speaks in an ancient tongue, and he is standing in Professor Meredith Foster's living room. The medieval historian tells herself he is part of a practical joke, but with his wide gold belt, callused hands, and the rabbit roasting in her fireplace, the brawny stranger seems so... authentic. Meredith is mesmerized by his muscular form, and her body surrenders to the fantasy that Geirolf Ericsson really is a Viking from a thousand years ago. As he helps her fulfill her grandfather's dream of re-creating a Viking ship, he awakens her to dreams of her own until she wonders if the hand of fate has thrust her into the arms of the last Viking.

___52255-1 $5.99 US/$6.99 CAN